OBSERVATION HILL

A NOVEL OF CLASS AND MURDER

Also by Tim Jollymore

Listener in the Snow
a novel

Pendulum
a play in five acts

Lake Stories
short stories

This book is for

Carol once again

and for

Amy Eden

ACKNOWLEDGMENTS

Thanks to Carol Squicci, my graphic designer who creates all but the words; to original readers Fred Devinny, James Richter, Marylene Cloitre, Mary Walfoort, and to readers Dennis Hamlet and Carol Squicci who also proofread; to David Landau, my editor; to Jim Farrell, Marvin Rintala, and Stuart Lord, my magnificent proofers.

Cover background and maps used with permission from the collections of Richard Kivela.

The books: *By the Ore Docks* by Richard Hudelson and Carl Ross; *Will to Murder* by Gail Feichtinger with John DeSanto and Gary Waller; *The Geology of the Duluth Metropolitan Area* by George M. Schwartz; *Lost Duluth* by Tony Dierckins and Maryanne C. Norton, *A Postcard Perspective of Historic Duluth* by Tony Dierckins, and *Boomtown Landmarks*, Laurie Hertzel, ed. and Kathryn Marsaa, illustrator, all of which tickled my memory with images I had known.

St. Louis County Historical Society where from 1967 to 1970 I worked surrounded by Duluth's memorabilia, extensive newspaper files, and many resident-supporters of the Society.

University of Minnesota, Duluth - Glensheen staff both protective and helpful.

The people of Duluth: Union workers, unorganized laborers, the bosses and employers, and the folk of Duluth's patrician tradition all of whom made the city what it has been and is.

PRONUNCIATION NOTE: THE SURNAME TUOMI IN FINNISH IS PRONOUNCED (TOO - O - ME) AND OFTEN SPOKEN IN DULUTH (TWA - ME). THE READER MAY CHOOSE EITHER.

JULY, 2015

OBSERVATION HILL

A NOVEL OF CLASS AND MURDER

TIM JOLLYMORE

**FINNS WAY
B O O K S**

ISBN 978-0-9914763-2-9

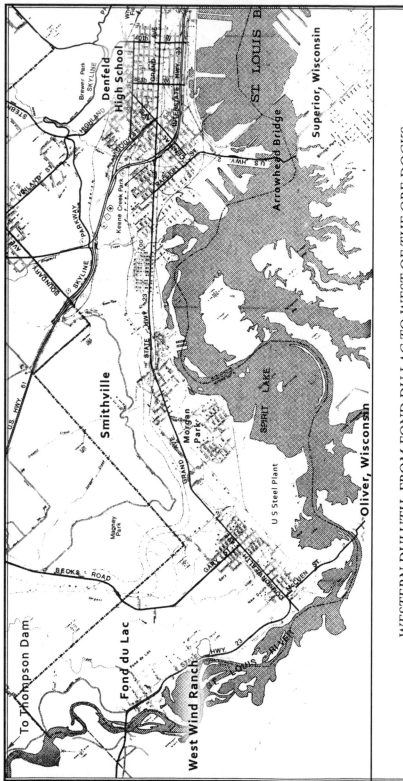

WESTERN DULUTH: FROM FOND DU LAC TO WEST OF THE ORE DOCKS

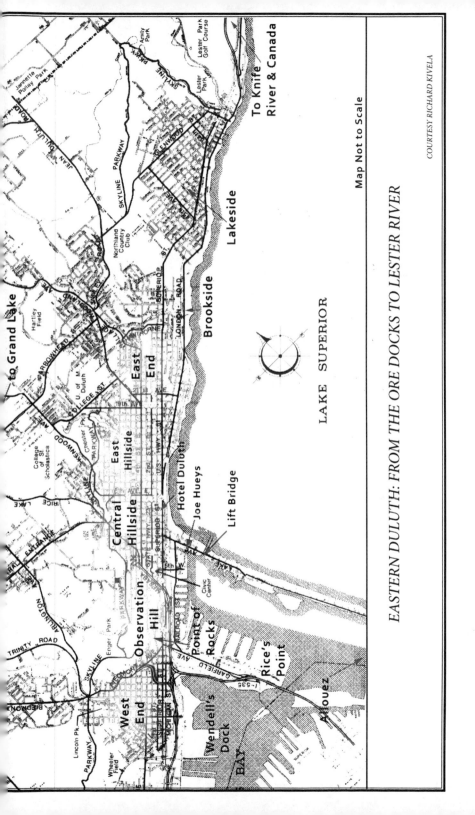

EASTERN DULUTH: FROM THE ORE DOCKS TO LESTER RIVER

Map Not to Scale

COURTESY RICHARD KIVELA

OBSERVATION HILL

A NOVEL OF CLASS AND MURDER

Overture

THE CITY DOESN'T SPRAWL, IT STRETCHES. From the Lester River on the North Shore of Lake Superior to the crossing of the St. Louis River at Fond du Lac, Duluth reaches out in a thirty-mile arc, northeast to southwest. It resembles a splayed hand—thumb to the north, pinky to the south, the extended index finger being Park Point, the middle and ring curl together as Rice's Point. The bulky part of the hand rises to a hump from downtown to the West End's steep hillsides. The knuckles of middle and ring fingers form the Point of Rocks.

The town is thin. The narrow, old communities platted from the lake to the hilltops now form slices of this long, splayed-handed community. The city's shape and the historic settlement layout have made it possible to live near water or have a view from any point along its thirty miles. This layout also makes it easy to live in any of the communities sandwiched along its longitude and to have commerce only with those enclaves right next door.

The town is stratified horizontally along parts of the hand. In East Duluth—the northernmost tracts—lie the brain and money trusts, the medical school, the university, the high schools of the college-bound, leafy streets, wide lush lawns, and oversized stone houses. Downtown, contiguous to the east, rise thirteen-story bank buildings, old-fashioned skyscrapers, as symbols of control and opprobrium. Lofting above these edifices, Central Hillside—a neighborhood in the shape of an upside-down heart—spreads over the hill above downtown; for a century, it let spill from its terraces the labor to keep and clean the downtown monoliths. To the south, toward what is called the West End, Observation Hill, a bulge of gnarly knuckle atop the Point of Rocks, separates east-hand from west-hand; skilled workers house themselves as cheaply as they can on the steep rise above factories, assembly plants, shipping lanes, and wide swaths of railroad tracks. Farther to the west, larger, newer factories puff smoke over St. Louis Bay; wide lots of parked buses and idle trains spread on the river's plain, waiting for day; while still farther along, where the harbor narrows to the Saint Louis River proper, the steel, cement, and wire plants hum through the night in the least-populated stretch of the hand, as far away from the eastern thumb as can be.

As in any working city or any healthy hand—as far flung as the neighborhoods or digits may be—below the surface run ties that bind: nerves, tendons, muscles, bones, arteries, veins and capillaries, cells of a hundred descriptions all controlled from a central point, all in concert and common with each other.

In this town, that certain point lay in the east. Twenty-five miles down the pike a man said, "Slow," and the factories ground slowly. He said, "Fast," and the populace scurried to pump it up. He said, "Fired," and men lost their jobs. He said, "Close," and plants faded into ghostly shambles. So, when he said, "Enough," whether enough or not the workers had to make do—or say with their collective voice, "Stop it."

Even when pickets went up on cold mornings, still that evening sumptuous meals were served along London Road in the eastern part of town.

1

Observation Hill

THERE IT WAS AGAIN. When had she last heard it? Had she slept? No, that was impossible. But her ears had been somewhere else, as if she had unhooked them, mislaid them on a shelf in the kitchen. Yes, detached. Off in another realm.

She had been listening down below, for her grandson. For any movement, for music, for the strike of a match, even for low breathing. There was nothing. Then it was there again. Something outside that she seemed to think of but did not hear. She strained, listening.

The foghorn startled her. Even a mile away, down the steep and across the water, its double blast bellowed, staccato and then long. The horn rattled Berta's open sashes with the final flap of its metallic vocal chords. Its second, lower register warned of the silence to come. Then it quit. No, that wasn't it; she'd heard the horn. It had been sounding all along. She couldn't miss it.

Then, in the silence, a note circled her ear like a moth, papery and soft from out of the dark, skittering over the fog.

Oh, that was it. Berta caught the final chime of Central High School's clock, away down Third Street. Yes, the tower clock had brought her back. She had been hearing the foghorn since nearly two. It was the clock that moved her from hearing to heeding.

Four? She checked. Yes, four. Nearly three hours without a sound from downstairs. No toilet flushing. No stirring in bed or dropped shoes. Did Roger lie in dreadful silence? Did he lie?

"I don't know," Berta answered nobody. "He could be in his chair." She could not go down there. She was afraid. But she had promised, hadn't she?

"I've an hour to go." She had no notion how she had waited. None of how she could abide.

The fog lay heavy out on the lake and across the bay. It smothered all streetlight below her house. It crept across the Central Hillside as far up as Cascade Park; it swirled and layered against the Duluth gabbro that shouldered Observation Hill and Berta's house. The diaphone sounded again. Its deep voice called out, "WARN – ning – HUHH," just once, and then retreated beneath the fog.

Berta moved from the front windows through the dining room. She crossed herself. "Lord," she said to the picture beside the crucifix, "come to my assistance in this great need, that I may receive the consolation and help of heaven." As she circled the table she held the backs of the chairs.

Her stations were there, her people, her saints, her losses. Her cross, Jesus, and Andrew Carnegie above the sideboard. She dusted the gilt frame with a finger. Her husband, Wendell, and Eugene V. Debs stared out from their frames between the dining room windows above a snapshot of the two of them with Elizabeth Gurley Flynn and Helen Keller. One above the other, Wendell Jr. and his best friend, Paul, hung next to the kitchen. Flanking the doorway to the living room were a younger Wendell Jr. and her daughter Betty—their graduation pictures. Berta brought both hands to her cheeks. Oh, I have nothing of Roger.

She turned to the kitchen. She felt better there. No conflict, no loss. She stood at the bread table, listening. Out beyond her screens, the fog stretched solidly to far-off Wisconsin.

Wisps of fog floated below the kitchen windows in the back yard and along the drive that curved around the house. That's where she had heard them.

They'd killed their engine and lights. They rolled down the drive, crunching the gravel she'd had Paul spread in the low spots. The stealth fully woke her. The drive sloped just below her bedroom.

By the time she'd adjusted her robe and tip-toed back to the kitchen porch, they were heaving a carpet, sodden with bulk. Roger wasn't with them, though there was someone sitting in the car. She didn't know the boys, but then she didn't know many of the friends Roger had taken up with lately. One struck her as a sailor. No, he was too young. Too thin and boyish, but he was the one who directed the two taller ones. They looked older, just by build. The sailor-boy pointed, held up his hand in a halt sign, and then swept his arms to say, "come on."

She heard him open the screen and door. The screen-door spring strained and yowled. They bumped something. One swore. "Shush." Their whispering made Berta freeze. If the phone had been there, she'd have called. Why didn't I listen to Paul?

"You're always in the kitchen, Memma," he'd said. "Why not put it here?"

"No," she'd told him, "it'll just be in the way and get all floury and sticky."

"Okay, every time you have to run to the front hall to answer it, think of me."

"Oh, Paul, I don't like to talk on the phone."

"Only over coffee and cake, yes, I know," he'd laughed.

So she hadn't gone to the phone, had not called. Instead she listened to them fumble in the dark. She heard the screen spring stretch again. Out they came, this time without the carpet. Right then she wanted Paul. She went to the phone. He'd be deep asleep, she knew. She touched the receiver. Then, as she heard the car start and slip past the front of the house, still without lights, she thought she heard water running. Still on tiptoe (Why? She wondered) Berta went to the kitchen to listen at the pipes. Nothing.

I'm getting old. Old and afraid. Yes, she'd have called out, would have gone down if it had been Wendell Jr. But fifteen years makes a difference, and she felt more alone now. More afraid. Paul would come right away, she knew.

No, I just have to wait.

The foghorn had started about two. Who flipped the switch? She couldn't guess. Probably someone's husband who's up all night for little pay. Like Wendell. Poor Wendell. He was buried in some smelter in Pittsburgh or Gary. Crushed and grated into the ore he loaded down that ship's belly. Had they found him? Did they lie? She hated to think so but yes, they must have.

"He was right there," Marty had jabbered wildly at the service, "and then he was gone." How long? Marty couldn't tell anyone. "It might have been a while. I'm sorry." Four more gondolas had unloaded, and the chute had opened, before he noticed Wendell's absence.

Four gondolas. Four. It was four now. I'll start a coffee cake, Berta thought. Paul will want some when he gets here.

Berta lit the oven. The whoosh filled the silent room. The gas hissed joyfully. Berta was famous for her coffeecakes. She brought them to all the party gatherings, to the neighbors, to church functions.

The coffee parties she held on Wednesday afternoons were the best, all the women said. The cakes came hot from the oven with perfumes of apples and cinnamon. Coffee aroma swelled through the sweet, warm steam of the streusels to silence the chatter and laughter in the dining room.

"Oh, what's that I smell?" everyone said. "Berta's coffee cakes are ready!" The women jiggled and twisted in their chairs.

In the quiet hours after those boys left, she had brought out the milk and eggs. The butter was soft. Now, Berta worked the streusel. Holding the apple in her hand she coiled the peel to the table. Two are enough. She had soured some cream yesterday. The weather had been fine. The butter creamed easily with the sugar. Berta was happy. Her quick hands moved surely. She worked backwards up the recipe that she knew by heart. When the batter lay in the pan, Central High's clock tolled the half-hour. Berta stopped. She listened. Nothing. The foghorn rasped again. I'll call when it comes from the oven. The apples and streusel were ready. She topped the batter. It all went to the oven.

Berta loaded the percolator basket and ran the water cold for a long time. "Start it after you call," she said. Her voice sounded small and wavery in the stillness. She cleaned the work board and brought cups and plates to the little table that sat at the rear kitchen window. She set two places and peered out at the empty drive.

Returning to the dining room, Berta caught the door jamb with her shoulder. She reeled and, grabbing a chair-back, flopped onto its seat. I'm tired. Old and tired. .

Time dragged. She looked at Wendell Jr.'s portrait. He had been right to leave. There was nothing left here for him. The jobs had been drying up long before. His father may have seen clear to push him into school, but she couldn't do it. Yes, leaving was the right thing. He had a good job with Caterpillar. Or was it John Deere? Anyway, it was union.

Strong. Good wages.

Wendell Jr. had said it. "Duluth is dying, Mom."

"Oh, it's not dying," she'd said, "not yet anyway."

"For me, it is." Wendell Jr. shook his head. "Look, I have to go. There's a good job for me down there, and it's union too. I have to do what I know."

Even losing both Wendell's in the same year, Berta had felt secure. She had the women, the party, and the church. She was not alone. Things then were better for Betty. She was pregnant with her Roger. Even with Glen carousing, Betty had been happy. She knitted. There seemed to be a future.

Junior was right. Even after Betty died, he didn't move back. By then he was shop steward. He was respected; he had a home. Later on she might have used his help, but at the time Roger was only in fourth grade and not yet wild. The boy went to school right down the street. She had Paul, too. And the insurance money was a help. Well, she thought, Wendell Jr. had it right. He had to go. It wouldn't have been good to come back.

And now? Now what?

Berta listened. She knew the tower clock would strike quarter-to at any moment. The fog was lifting. An ore carrier signaled the bridge. The bridge replied. Who is the operator? Barney? She wasn't sure. She heard the bridge begin to rise. Quarter-to. She clutched the chair-back, rose slowly, and went to the oven.

The coffeecake was fine. Fifteen minutes more. She sat at the little table and watched the carrier enter the canal and the harbor. She watched the bridge descend. She wondered, where does the fog go?

The sky was lightening over Wisconsin. The coming sun piqued the air to movement. The lake carrier headed to the ore docks. The docks roused her memory. Your docks,

Wendell. The company had modernized. Wendell Jr. couldn't hold a shift there. Laid off one too many times. He was right.

Her buzzer sounded. She took the streusel from the oven to the rack on the breadboard. The room, already swelling with sweetness, now blossomed like apple trees. She plugged in the coffee pot and waited until it gurgled. Berta went to the phone and dialed.

It rang only twice. "Paul," she spoke low to the receiver.

"Memma, it's five a.m."

"Paul, something is terribly wrong."

He didn't have to say he'd be right there.

2

East End

Paul

PAUL TUOMI HAD BEEN LYING AWAKE FOR A WHILE. The light bothered him. The *Andrew Carnegie* had passed and signaled off in the distance. He waited for bridge to sound. The blast carried over the lake, and he thought he heard the alarm bells sounding as the bridge rose. Unmistakably, the long – short – short greeting from the ship and the echoed reply from the bridge reached him.

In his mind's eye, he saw the laker slide toward the Duluth, Mesabi and Iron Range Dock Number Six. He had sailed one season between sophomore and junior year. Paul had come for ore nine times that summer. Wendell West's dock, he thought. He could never separate the two.

He turned to Pam snoring next to him. She appeared to be an astronaut. Her bulbous curler cover, reflective sleep mask and tightly buttoned pajama collar framed her lower face. So grim. She looked ready for blastoff. Maybe I should wear a mask in summer, he mused. The light had wakened him. No, leave it. Summers are like that.

"Shit."

Paul thrust his hand for the phone, but it cast out two rings before he could get it. Pam stirred.

He heard his own name and heard her voice. "Memma," he said, "it's five a.m." He knew it was trouble before she said anything else. His heart raced.

He vaulted out of bed, drawing on his pants in a motion. Pamela was awake. "Why do you have to call her that?"

"Go back to sleep, Sweetheart."

"That old lady is more important to you than your own wife," she countered. She had slipped the mask to her forehead overlapping the yellow curler cap.

Patience.

Paul sat back on the bed, buttoning yesterday's shirt. He touched her knee through the sheet. "You're the most important person in my life, Babe. Mem . . . Berta is an old and dear friend, but you are my darling wife."

She grimaced. "God, how you lie."

"She's got trouble."

"She is trouble," Pam answered. "Everyone out there is."

Paul was lacing his shoes. Patience.

"At least take a shower and put on clean clothes. Someone will see you."

"I'll be back in an hour. I'll do it then," Paul told her. He was heading toward the kitchen to the garage. He stopped in the hallway. Kiss her, fool. He came back into the room, but Pam had replaced the mask and faced away. "Okay, bye, then." He went for the car.

In the garage he slowed. "Take the time," he told himself. He unlocked the tool chest and picked up the service revolver inside. He checked it and placed it in the glove compartment of his Buick. He locked the chest again. He rolled up the garage door and said to no one, "Let's go."

In the bright morning weather his dread at Berta's call faded. He worked hard to keep his worlds apart, and mixing those two, Pam and Memma, was always bad.

"I suppose you'd be pleased," he'd said in one fight, instantly regretting it, "if she died!"

Pam was hot. "You damned right. Then you could get

down to business, mister."

"You're the most cold-hearted woman I've ever met."

"Why'd you marry me, then?"

"Honestly, I don't know," he'd admitted.

Paul nosed the Buick down London Road.

The light breeze rustled summer leaves; early light spangled through the tall estate trees and splashed on the Buick's windshield and hood. He unsnapped the visor and flipped it to the open window.

He wasn't alone on the road. Now who's this?

The kid's hair flew back along his denim vest. Andrew might have looked like that, Paul thought. Too skinny to play for a sport's team. He slowed going past. On the sidewalk, the young man kept a rhythmic pace. Well, nice morning walk. Paul saluted out the window. The kid kept walking.

Paul had to admit it. The East End was a beautiful place. Yes, he missed the hubbub and closeness of the old neighborhood; it was beautiful, too, in its own way, if less manicured. Yet the quiet and freshness of the east side charmed him. He wished that Pamela would go easy and just enjoy it. She had wanted something bigger, grander. The bungalow hadn't thrilled her, but it was the most he could afford when Andrew was born.

"Forget 'Daddy's' money," he'd said. "I'll provide."

Pam had been pushing ever since to "get off the numbers," as she put it, and move around the corner to Greysolon Road; but Paul was too busy in the Department to think of even looking.

"Let's let it rest now," he liked to say.

"I can't even hold an event in this house," Pam complained. "It's a cracker box."

"You and your mother do quite well for all that," he said.

"But that's her house, not mine. I'm not my mother."

Paul wasn't so sure.

Then they'd lost Andrew. Time passed. Pam scarred over with new prominence. Paul fought against Daddy's money. But sometime soon, he knew, he'd have to get off the dime, especially if he were promoted again. That would be the time.

Above the Tischer Creek basin and rail overpass a few trucks idled, waiting on deliveries; cars turned downtown toward the business district. Paul straightened in his seat.

He could see Observation Hill from there. Memma's worried, he thought. Yes, Berta would have hesitated to call the house. And at that hour! She knew Paul would have stopped by in the afternoon in any case. So it was urgent. Must be trouble with Roger again.

Memma was the name Paul gave to Berta when Wendell Jr. first took him home. Third grade, he thought. Thirty years ago. He guessed he combined "momma" and "Berta" to get Memma. Wendell Jr. called her Mom. She seemed so much like a mother. Always, she had fresh oven goods ready after school. Cookies, pies, her famous coffee cakes. Soft butter and cool milk. Not even during the longest of strikes did she stint on her baking. The kitchen had warmed him and Wendell Jr. with food and soft talk after the hard seats and instruction of school.

Ice cream. Paul drove past Bridgeman's up the hill along 14th Avenue East and turned west on Third. West, he thought. Toward home. It was a straight shot from there. Her voice had been apologetic, breathless, tired. He passed a block uphill of the Department. No siren needed. "We'll keep it in the family," he said. Whatever it is.

He had been stopping in at Berta's daily for nearly thirty years, take away the four he had spent at college in Minneapolis. Pam said, "You're in love with that woman." It was true. She was like a mother to him, much more than the one he had at home. He heard that voice:

"Paul Jr., is that you?" Violet's slender question reached him downstairs.

"Yes, Mother."

"Come up. I need some water."

He trudged up the stairs. Every day, he thought.

"Please. Pick up your feet. My head throbs."

When he entered the dark room, the odor of medicine sickened him. "Where's the glass?"

"Here on the nightstand," the thin voice trickled down her bony arm to the table.

No wonder his father worked such odd and long hours. "Soon you'll be on your own at college," he'd told Paul. He didn't have to say the rest: "And out of this loony bin." Paul felt he was like a ghost, passing through without being noticed.

Violet focused on her health. Paul was to serve and comfort her. It was Memma who asked Paul about school, about the teams, even about the girls.

"How are you and Cindy getting on?" Berta was interested.

Paul turned away, shy. Wendell Jr. answered for him, "Oh, they're going to get married as soon as school's out."

"What about that college idea?"

Paul had to answer, "We might wait."

Memma liked the idea. "You can get married anytime. Your dad wants you to go to Minneapolis."

"It's a long way away, but I'm afraid he won't let up," Paul answered. "He thinks I need to get away."

Get away, yes. From Violet, who had only one interest. "Add a little warm water to it this time."

Paul took the glass to her bathroom sink. Medicine bottles lined up across the shelf. He brought the water back to the nightstand. "Can you heat the casserole for yourself?" she asked.

33

"Sure, Mother."

When the true mother calls, Paul knew, you go. It didn't occur to him yet that Memma's call was professional. He considered it personal.

Paul eased down the drive, crunching over the gravel and backed up beside the garden shed to face out again. He stepped onto the rounded slate outcrop, taking the carved steps carefully. Too shallow. He judged Wendell Sr.'s stone work.

For a moment he stood on the mounded rock, breathing in the glory of the harbor. He checked Wendell, Sr.'s dock below. The *Carnegie* was just tying up. The chutes were still lifted. The sun scudded across the harbor silhouetting the grain elevators; it gleamed on the web of rails lacing along Rice's Point and lit up each rill of water on the bay. Across the thin, long point, the great lake pushed the Minnesota and Wisconsin shores away from each other and finally out of sight to the northeast. Paul breathed the blue air flowing cool off the surface of the lake and looked down at the point with a smile.

Yes, Park Point, that long, thin breakwater that defined the harbor. "The finger of God," Wendell Jr. was fond of quoting, "pointing the way out of town." Paul had never seen it that way, but he enjoyed Wendell Jr.'s stab at the city.

Paul turned back to the house. Roger's screen was shut, but he had left the inside door open to the warm night. He's dead to the world, Paul thought. Maybe Memma's worry is on something else. He ignored an odd tug at his senses as he swung round the stair post and up the steps to Berta's porch door. She was waiting for him.

"Paul, thank God."

He kissed her cheek. "Is that coffee I smell?"

She talked as she led him to the little table. "I couldn't sleep. After they came, I didn't know what to do. But, you know, I told him I wouldn't snoop. I have to trust him."

"Slow down, Memma! You've got me lost."

"I'm just so glad you came." She pushed a piece of streusel toward him and filled a mug with coffee. "Sugar and cream are on the window sill," she said.

Berta sat down, smoothing her print housedress over her lap. She stirred her coffee and took a bite of the cake.

"Now, who came and what happened?" Paul asked. "Roger is downstairs sleeping. I peeked in."

"Thank God."

Then she told him about the carpet and the whispering.

The tugging he'd felt sprang forth strongly. Paul stopped her. "What carpet?" He was up from the table. "You sit. Let me take another look."

Ingstrom

That guy waved out the window. A Buick. Ingstrom swayed along the sidewalk but fixed his sight ahead.

Thank God, if there is one, he thought, it wasn't dear old Dad's car. I should have left through the cemetery. Well, ignore him. Keep walking.

The scare crept through him in a confused blush. Think, you tired-out scabby, he told himself. Daddy is gone.

"Your father would like a word with you, Reese," his mother had said. She summoned him from his room.

There was little choice. Ingstrom shook his blond curls back and followed his mother down the hall.

"He's packing," she said, pointing to the master suite.

Ingstrom vaulted the railing that divided the entry and family room.

"Oh, Reese," she said.

He looked back on his mother's consternation with a wide grin. With a finger he poked his round glasses up on his bridge and swung across the front hall to enter his father's realm. He swaggered past the home office, squared himself at the antique firearm display his father treasured, and passed into the master bedroom beyond.

His father leaned over a leather suitcase, carefully placing a shaving kit among the pressed and folded undershirts and socks. The senior Ingstrom straightened, hiding, his son noticed, the hem of a pinstriped pair of boxer shorts below the tails of a starched white shirt. His father had cinched a blue necktie beneath his stiff collar. His freshly ironed slacks hung primly from a dressing stand beside the closet.

"Come in, son, you won't see anything new here."

Ingstrom approached the corner across the bed from where his father was working. He stood and waited. *Here comes the-I'm-concerned mantra.*

"I'm concerned, Reese."

The boy did not move or reply.

"Don't you want to know what concerns me?" His father was slipping into the slacks.

"Yes, sir. Of course I do." *This'd be his I'll-be-out-of-town spiel.*

His father buckled the belt against his taut belly. "I'll be out of town for the next couple days, Reese, and I'm concerned. I hope you'll make yourself available to help your mother."

Ingstrom watched his father carefully. "Yes, of course I will." *She'll never tell him anyway,* he thought.

"Good." His father lifted a foot to the rung of the dressing stand and tied his shoe. "I've heard some things about you."

Ingstrom waited.

"Don't you want to know what I've heard, Reese?"

"Yes, sir. Of course I do." He knew this was to be a repetition of his father's hanging-out-with-West-End-toughs warning.

"I've heard you have been hanging out with some West End toughs lately." He'd slipped on his suit coat and now parted the jacket, spreading his hands at his hips. "Someone named Frizzy?" His father's mouth formed the word as if spitting something bitter.

"Fizzy," the boy said. "It's a professional name. He produces light shows. Daddy Fizzy's Light and Bright." He volunteered nothing more.

His father buttoned the coat and faced Ingstrom. "Look, Reese, we've talked about this before. Those people are trouble. They're different than we are. They play by different rules. Rules you may not understand. You owe it to your mother and me to behave properly."

"Yes, sir. I do not believe I've done anything wrong."

"Wrong and improper are not alike," the senior Ingstrom said. "We do not mix with the workers, Reese."

"I hear you, sir."

His father clasped his hands before him as if to start a prayer. He studied his hands. He ground them together, sifting his thoughts, and sighed.

"Look at the mess Skaansgard's daughter is in. She's stuck with an upstart crank who can't provide properly for her— the son of a bootlegger, maybe a murderer, who is tied to the crookedest judge in the county. She married into trouble. Don't get involved out there, son. Even beyond the laborers, there's nothing but misery there."

Here comes the you're-too-smart-for-this lecture.

The old man lifted the lid of the suitcase and stood

looking inside; perhaps, Ingstrom thought, for inspiration. "Reese, you are too smart for this. You have a bright future, if not in finance, then in law or politics. You can out-think the best of them. You're quick, personable, and you have the right connections. Please don't squander your opportunities. Holding a smoking gun is bad as killing someone. Even though you've done nothing wrong, people will sense trouble. "

His father zipped the suitcase and offered his son a hand. "I know you'll behave yourself."

They shook hands. "Yes, sir. I will."

So it was not his father's Buick. That had been parked at the airport since yesterday afternoon. Dear old Dad was in New York.

There was plenty of breathing room, and he didn't need much more space or time. One more transaction and he'd be gone: free from those lectures about West End women, college grades, propriety, the responsibility of his birthright, and on and on. All the trappings of family history, money, and status meant shit to Ingstrom.

He swung down the sidewalk, swaying blithely to the cadence of the trees that towered over the London Road palisades, guarding the estates that lined the Lake Superior shore. Ingstrom let his care fall away on the fresh lake breezes, as if he were already sailing on the sea.

Do your thing, man, he told himself. Let the establishment find out when it's too late. It's the '60s, for Christ's sake. Let the old man harp all he wants.

Ingstrom had other plans.

3

Central Hillside

A SKYDIVER TUMBLED AND SPIRALED DOWN THE WALL. Another twisted and dove below the first. Strobes pierced the room, making silhouettes of jubilant dancers and wavering waifs that came to life on the wall, blacking out the skydivers' fall. They took bites from the whirling, advancing landscape below the divers. *Ragas and Talas* wove invisibly through the live dancers and celluloid divers. The strobes quit. Yellow and red light flashed across new scenes: bare trees hung with frost; a laker breaking out of fog, its bow surging high above the camera; a bouquet of writhing, bodiless arms; then blue and orange flashes. The skydivers were back, holding hands, circling above tilled fields on an upended horizon. Up jumped the dancers in the strobes again. An endless archway of elms reeled past echoes of Gregorian chanters. The notes stretched around twirling graces wreathed with smoke. Among those watching from the pillows, the pipe went around again. Now the camera was tied to the wing of a biplane, looping, diving, twisting toward the ground. It would crash. Screams broke loose in the room. The pilot pulled it out. The party crowd cheered.

It was Daddy Fizzy's light show.

Word about Fizzy's show had gotten around. It was one of those Hillside Happenings. People from East End, from the working-class flats, hippies from the hillside, even a few down from Two Harbors twenty-five miles north. Lots of young kids.

41

That worried Skip.

He'd know most of the people. Still, he wanted to keep a lid on it. Randy had tipped him on narcs coming to town, and some of these people he couldn't vouch for. Janey thought it'd be fun.

"We don't have parties often," she said.

Skip had reluctantly agreed. He thought highly of Daddy Fizzy.

Fizzy was the legend of the Denfeld class of '66. He was one of the artists from the West End who understood what was coming down. Skip liked him. He was into the art, not the drugs. He was solid, in control, even at nineteen. The mix of people, Skip supposed, would be good. Fizzy attracted lots of attention from the college crowd out east. Good people to know. Fizzy looked like a hippie, so the cool heads on the hillside also gravitated to his shows. Yeah, the Hillside was a budding community. It felt like a new thing. No downers. No snooty crap. Everybody could get along. Harmony. "Peace and Love," they said. They were all headed toward a new world. It was a good mix.

Outside Skip's, from under a forty-foot acacia canopy, images of aviators and skydivers flung themselves across two sheet-covered windows sheltered beneath the branches. From inside, silhouetted dancers' arms shot across the panes; and shadowy, curled torsos beyond the sheets stretched over the "longest wall on the hillside" to cut wildly over the window openings. Below, at the trunk of the tree, a knotted trio talked low. They glanced around, keeping alert but often gazing up at the show going on inside Skip's second-story living room.

The central, mustachioed figure produced an envelope from inside the fringed leather jacket he was wearing. He held it out to the thin, blond fellow.

"It's good stuff," the moustache said, "culled from a real aficionado's stash." He waved the envelope. "But be careful. It is potent, 80 per cent."

"For the price, it better be," a third put in. He looked young, nervous.

Moustache shook his head at the blond. "Is he okay?"

"Fine," blondie said, "don't worry."

Colors burst through the two sheet-bound windows. "Wow," the young one said.

The curly-headed blond reached into a loose front pocket, splaying his legs and swaying in time to Shankar's music from upstairs. He stretched the pocket mouth, reached in, and pulled out a clip. His skinny rump defined a rhythm that furled his bell-bottoms like sails. "Okay, I've got three parties." He peeled off bills from the clip; his sway rippled like a sailor's, feeling the music of the sea.

"Got a fit?" the mustachioed dealer asked.

"Someone will."

The dealer took the money, delivered two more envelopes and moved away. He rounded the corner and was gone.

The two customers watched Daddy Fizzy's Light and Bright show careen past the windows above. When they heard a car start down the alley, they headed up the stairs.

Skip met the pair at the door.

"Ingstrom. Randy with you?"

"Haven't seen him," Ingstrom lied.

"The show looks really cool from outside," Ingstrom's friend said.

"Shit. You can see it through the windows," Skip was alarmed.

"Yeah. Cool."

Ingstrom wove a figure eight in place. "Don't worry. We're the only ones looking. It's not attracting a crowd."

Skip felt better. "Who's this?"

"Friend. Skip, this is Roger. Roger, the house-master."

"Cool," Roger said.

"Yeah, cool," Skip said without enthusiasm and let them in. "One of the projectors flashed out."

They moved to the living room. Fizzy was working on a machine. Donovan was singing *Mellow Yellow*. A dozen or so people lounged on pillows, sitting cross-legged on the floor. The smoke of incense and dope was thick.

"Hey, Rog," came a call from a group in the corner. Roger went over, whirling his long hair. "Wow," he said, and sat.

"Janey here?" Ingstrom asked.

"In the kitchen. They've got some hash." Skip nodded ahead and returned to looming at the door.

Ingstrom sashayed through the room, greeting people. He knew everyone.

The kitchen was candle-lit. Four women circled a pipe. "Inggy!" Janey broke from the group. She hugged him. "Wan'a hit?"

Ingstrom toked on the pipe while Janey held a lighter to the cube. "Thanks," he croaked, holding his breath. "We got something stronger. You have your fit?"

Janey passed the pipe to the other three. She shook her head. "It's packed up."

"Sure. This stuff is smooth and powerful. A party present. Just let me know." He touched her shoulder. "I'm going to see what Fizzy needs."

Ingstrom moved into the living room. He talked to a clean, freckled blonde lounging between the legs of her snoozing boyfriend. His hair was tied in a paisley bandana. The girl wore a peace sign on her cheek. Ingstrom waggled above her chatting, his hands in his pockets. She shook her head and raised a thumb toward her sleeper. Ingstrom reached down, stroked her hair and smiled. He went to Fizzy, who was still fussing with the projector.

Daddy Fizzy wore a tight-fitting belted jacket over bellbottom jeans. His legs were stuffed into Oxblood English riding boots that towered inside the bells of his pants. His black, straight hair swooshed around his handsome, chiseled cheeks and squared jaw. It fell into place as he straightened up and shook it away. Under dark, full brows, his eyes were large and wide open behind the perfect circles of his wire rims.

"Need something?"

Fizzy stood back from the projector and shook his hair aside again. "Inggy. No, Marly went for another bulb. Blew two. Had one." He looked to the turntable. "Hey, this one's for you, *The 59th Street Bridge Song.*" He put on "Feelin' Groovy."

Ingstrom danced away. He pointed at Roger and held up a finger. Then he slid down the hall and stood at the closed bathroom door. In a minute a couple emerged, intertwined, oblivious.

Ingstrom slipped the slide latch into its hasp and quietly turned the door bolt, too. He cleared the tank top of its toiletries and moved a candle off to the tub rim. From his vest pocket he took a small unframed mirror, and from his back pocket a thin jackknife. Carefully he set both on the toilet tank lid, with his three purchased packets beside them. He produced four new packets from his left pocket, set them opposite the mirror and straddled the toilet with his skinny backside protruding.

Hunched like a watchsmith, Ingstrom worked carefully. Over the mirror he emptied half of one packet into a new empty one, sealed each and put them into his vest pocket.

He added half the next one to an envelope he'd partly filled with baking soda. He shook the bag, turned it over and shook it again. He held it to the light, gazing hard at it. He emptied baking soda from another packet into the other half, performed the same ritual and then slipped both into his left pants pocket. The last bought packet he emptied onto the mirror and split it into three piles with his knife. He matched each pile with a larger pile of soda and pushed each coupled amount over the edge of the mirror into an envelope. These three he pushed back into his right pants pocket.

Ingstrom inspected the mirror. He licked it, licked the knife blade, and put them away.

"Bingo, bango, bongo," he said as he tapped his vest and pants pockets. He tongued and washed his hands, smiled at the mirror, and let himself out to the hall. Janey was loitering near the door.

"Okay, I won't look a gift horse in the mouth," she said.

Ingstrom smiled at her. He took a packet from his vest pocket. "Special just for you. Roger has his own stuff."

He turned to the living room. "Let me get him and John, too. Bedroom?"

"Yeah, if it's unoccupied." Janey kissed Ingstrom's cheek and smiled.

The light show was on again. Ingstrom had to duck under the beams to get to Roger. He stood over him, "All right, man, ready for the ride?"

"Ride?" Roger looked up. He was out of it already. "Oh, yeah. Come on, John." The two rose and bent under the projector lights. Ingstrom walked erect and then danced through the show, watching his silhouette against the sheets. Cries rose from the cushions: "Come on, man!"

Ingstrom flashed peace signs on the sheets and pranced after Roger and John. "In there," he pointed. John entered but

Ingstrom held Roger's shoulder.

He reached in his left pocket, bringing out a packet. "This is for you." From the other side he brought out another. "This is for John. First-timer-mix. Got it?" Roger nodded. "I'll work point out here," Ingstrom said.

Inside, Janey was cooking the spoon over the candle. "Got a fit?"

Roger nodded. John said, "No."

Without taking her eyes from spoon, she said, "You two can share." She set the spoon down, squeezed the nipple, drew the cooked fluid into her syringe and carefully set it on the nightstand. She nodded at the water glass. "Use that. You can have the residue."

Roger licked the spoon and produced his fit. Janey removed her bandana, rolled it and tied it around her right arm, cinching it with her teeth. Roger dribbled some water into the spoon through his syringe. John stared at one, then at the other. Janey pumped her fist and took up the fit. Roger tapped out powder from his packet, heated, and stirred.

"Are you addicted?" John stammered.

Janey had found a vein. She squeezed the fit's nipple, released, and drew blood into the fit. John gaped.

"Not right now," she answered without looking at him, "I have been, but it's been a while." She flushed, drew once again, and emptied the syringe into her vein. "Pull that bandana," she told John. She gently put the fit on the stand next to her packet. She sighed. "It's good stuff."

Roger had finished his preparations. "Can I use that?" he asked, indicating the bandana. He tied off and shot. John stared. Roger sat for a minute, humming *59th Street* off key. "Not bad, not bad," he mumbled. John stared at Janey.

Roger roused up. "Hey man, I haven't forgotten you. Let

me demonstrate. Cash?"

John looked dumbly, reached in his pocket, and handed Roger a clutch of bills.

Roger found Ingstrom leaning over the freckled blonde, his hands on the wall over her shoulders. He nodded as Roger slipped him the cash and closed the bedroom door. "It's a three-way. I'd join but I don't like one of the guys."

The blonde was lost in his smile. "I'd prefer one-on-one."

He gyrated over her and lifted a thoughtful finger, "Always thinking school, aren't you."

She blushed. "Well, Daddy wants me to be a professor."

"And what does Siiri want?"

"You know what I want," Siiri said.

Someone fumbled at the bathroom knob. Then again.

"Slide the latch back, Matty," Ingstrom said to the door.

The latch slid. The boyfriend with the paisley bandana lurched out. "Wow. Siiri. Ingstrom. Cool."

Siiri took paisley by the arm. "Let's do one dance, Matty. Then we're going home. I work tomorrow." She turned her head as she steered him down the hall toward the show. Her eyes said: later, Inggy.

Ingstrom rested a shoulder on the wall, angling across the closed door, smiling and shaking his head. Siiri was gone. A long, moaning voice from the bedroom made him stand straight. His smile faded. He waited for the moan to stop. He pressed his ear to the door. As if confirming a fear, he said to himself: John.

"Okay, John, I'm going to do you this one. You'll learn in time." Roger held the fit to the light, tapped the glass and watched two bubbles glide toward the nipple. "Tied off? Let's see those veins."

"You got those bubbles out?" John said. He was tense.

"Doctor H will relax you, Johnny." Roger soothed.

Janey watched, languid, amused. "First time is the best," she assured him.

John's first time was not the best. As soon as Roger loosened the bandana, John widened his eyes and began to moan. "Air bubble. I can feel it."

Roger laid him back on the bed. "It's nothing. Relax."

"No, I can feel it. It's moving. It's moving up my arm." John stared at the ceiling.

"Be cool," Janey cooed. "It's your first time. Go with it."

"It's moving again. It's at my shoulder. Do you think it'll flatten my heart? Am I going to die?" John thrashed on the bed. "I'm going to die!"

Roger laughed. "No, no, no. That's not going to happen. You're all right, man."

"Get Inggy," Janey said. She moved over John. She straddled him on the bed, dropped down, and held his shoulders with her extended arms. "Listen, John. I'm going to save you. I won't let anything happen to you. I know what it's like, and you'll be fine." John calmed.

Roger watched from the door. "Should I get Inggy?" Janey nodded without looking away from John. "You're not going to die. I won't let that happen. You're fine," she said.

Roger glanced at the nightstand. He cracked the door to look out. Ingstrom was not there. Roger looked to the bed. Janey was massaging Johnny's chest. Roger scooped up Janey's fit and packet and went out. The hallway was empty. The light show flashed wildly. A million strobes fluttered off the walls and ceiling. Roger softly let go of the bedroom latch. It clicked in place. He slipped into the open bathroom, shut and bolted the door, and leaned against it.

4

Oliver

Something was moving beyond the reeds lining the river, out past the willows that hung over the lawns. It seemed familiar, probably not dangerous. She cocked her head to look at the fish waving their tails in the slow current at her feet; then craned again at the motion beyond the willows. Something was burning. That could be pernicious. She spread her wings, cast off with a spring from her backward hinged knees, and sailed above the water hidden beneath the shifting fog that piled over its surface. She rose as a caution, leaving the smoke, the movement and, in avian regret, those fish behind.

Cindy was about to stub her cigarette when she heard a whoosh of heron wings. She held still and looked toward the river. Nothing. Too much fog. Then she spied, just for a moment, the sleek form of the heron rising through the mists to glide off toward the island beyond the bridge. She snuffed the butt in the sand. Nasty habit, she thought. Here's to quitting! She took her last sip of morning coffee and turned to the kitchen entry. Maybe I'll quit this year, before winter. Who wants to stand out here in the drifts?

Cindy had taken up smoking just after high school, when she started Duluth Business University. All the girls smoked, and it comforted her. The cigarette became her friend, someone to be with when she was lonely. I was lonely then. She sighed.

Grow up, Miscevich. You were lonely then! Hah. Get over

it. Not everyone marries her high school sweetheart, ya know. Why are you so different? You got him back and you still didn't quit. Crybaby!

Cindy twisted her mouth, took a last look across the lawn to the willows that hung over the river's edge. The fog would lift by the time she crossed the bridge. She considered. Don't be so hard on yourself, Cindy decided.

She unplugged the coffee pot and lifted the lid, then the basket by the percolator stem. She brought the pieces to the sink and carefully rinsed them. Out the window the sun was breaking through, glinting off the sluggish flow of water in the reeds.

Cindy lifted the receiver of the kitchen wall phone, listened, looked over her shoulder and dialed.

"Morning, Mom." She shot a glance toward the bedrooms. "Yeah, me too." Her words were crisp but hushed. She turned and twisted the coiled cord around her elbow. "I don't want Tommy to hear. He sleeps so lightly." She covered the mouthpiece as she talked. "Yes, I'm taking the bus." She listened attentively. "Don't ask. Just meet me at the 27th Avenue West stop. I'll give you the bag. It isn't large or heavy."

While she listened, Cindy placed the basket, tube, pot, and cover in the dish drainer. "I'll catch the 6:05. It stops around 7:00. Okay, see you then."

She traipsed down the hall, shuffling in slippers. She stopped at the boy's bedroom door, tightened and retied her robe front and tapped lightly before opening. "Hey, working man—happy birthday, sweetie," Cindy said, nearly singing it. "Time to rise and shine! Give me a ride to the bus."

Tommy stirred, turned, and smiled a crooked, sleepy grin. "Already?"

"It's Monday morning, and concrete waits for no man."

Tommy sat up. "Mom, whatever happened to taking your

birthday off?"

"Oh, did you do that in school?" she asked.

"No, not really. But we celebrated."

Cindy put her hands on her hips. "Just be sure to shower after work." She pointed. "I left clean clothes in that bag. And drop by Grandma's. I'm sure she has a cake for you. She ordered it from Berta West, too." She smiled, held the robe to herself, went to him, and kissed his cheek. "Come on. Up and at 'em."

Eighteen years, she thought. The shortest time on earth. She had Tommy nearly nine months to the day after her breakup.

Happy Halloween.

It was happy.

Sure. He was happy.

Yes, I let my guard down.

You did no such thing, fool. You wanted it.

Cindy took a final look at her son, his angular body still thin but growing muscular with the hard work. He had a body like Paul's.

He'll be a catch at college, she thought.

Yeah, he'll break a heart just like yours.

She'd lost her first job because of the pregnancy. There was no hiding it, of course, and it wouldn't do in a Lakeside lawyer's office.

"Cindy, this isn't what I would want, but you understand that in a practice like ours, we can't seem to sanction out-of-wedlock liaisons," he'd said. "After you have the baby, well, we'll see what our needs are. I can give you a good recommendation on the work you've done. And we hate to lose you. Good luck."

It had felt like a death sentence. After two years at the

business college and all her sacrifice, to be turned out like that hurt horridly.

She had not told Paul, either about the job or the baby. He'd hear, of course, and she had a story ready if he asked. It took him nearly eight years, damn him. At first more distance between them, the better. Even so, she had been lonely.

The glow that Tommy radiated from within and the warmth of her family in the West End kept her safe and glad. Life pulsed inside and around her. The women loved to pinch her cheeks and listen at her belly, to watch it move as Tommy rolled over or stretched in a yawn. No one asked the obvious. They never mentioned Paul, not even Berta. The ladies, especially Berta and Betty, fattened her on their cooking and were constantly throwing come-as-you-are parties.

"Cindy? This is Berta. Come as you are!"

She and Mom trudged up the hill in their pj's or house coats for the famous coffee cake and laughter. Hair up in curlers and half-made-up faces were common. One next-door neighbor came in a negligée under her husband's overcoat. Berta's dining room table roared and shook that day. All the ladies poked Cindy's belly under the pajamas and rubbed it for good luck.

Damn you, Paul. You were so thick. So treacherous. Without the women of the West End, I would not have made it through.

Of them all, Betty seemed the happiest. Three months after Cindy was fired, Betty said over morning coffee: "This 'condition' is going around. It must be catching."

"No, Betty! You, too?" Cindy guessed.

"Plumped up as a pullet," Betty said.

"And happy as a clam," Berta added, hugging her daughter. "I haven't heard her humming or singing for years."

"Yeah, not since I married old what's-his-name," she

laughed. Betty had only half a man—the bottle had the other half—but right then she was young and full of joy.

It had been hard to lose Betty. They did have years together, raising their boys without fathers. Even when Betty's drinking went out of control, Cindy had stayed close, as near as she dared.

Tommy and Roger were different, but they played nicely and cared about each other. Those were the joys of the neighborhood, Cindy remembered.

Yeah, and the troubles of the "friendly" West End.

Troubles are what we had, she countered.

Troubles are what you made, came the reply.

Cindy sighed again. If it weren't for the neighbors, I wouldn't have survived.

There you go, sniveling.

They are good times to remember, she pronounced, concluding the repartee.

Cindy buttoned her skirt, slid it to the side, and zipped it. She donned her best ruffled blouse, left two buttons open, and slipped on her light pinstriped vest. It's like drawing on a disguise, she thought. Professional? No, just cold and legal.

"Breakfast on the double, honey," she called to Tommy.

The boy emerged in jeans and work boots, a sweatshirt pulled over his tee.

"Comb your hair, Tommy."

He slapped a Twins hat over the mop and grinned. "I lost my comb."

"Sit." She pointed to the bacon, eggs, and toast on his plate. "Eat."

"And what's this?" He pointed to two boxes wrapped and tied together with ribbons.

"Not really birthday presents. Some things for college."

He smiled broadly. Between bites Tommy unwrapped

a pen-and-pencil set and five spiral-bound notebooks. "Thanks, Mom. You're sweet." He leaned over to kiss her cheek.

"It'll save money for other things. I got them at UMD, so they're college quality."

"Yeah," Tommy said, opening his arms to the tiny kitchen. "Nothing but the best for college-bound West Enders."

"You mind your words, birthday boy." She smiled. "We're in Oliver, in case you didn't notice."

"Yeah, a rural, lowbrow West End. Just fine for me."

"And for me, too."

She watched him negotiate the s-shaped bridge, rumbling over wooden planking. So tall behind the wheel. So handsome.

"Those glasses make you look like a professor," she said.

"Yes. Without them I look more like the fuzz."

"Don't denigrate the police," she said. Always hinting around, she thought.

Yeah? Wouldn't you? There it was again. And when are you going to tell him?

All in good time, Cindy thought. In time to do some good, I hope.

Tommy let her off at the corner.

Cindy leaned down to kiss her son through the open window. The day was already warm.

"Hey, lady, what you got in that bag you took out of the trunk?"

"None of your business. Just clean up after work. And be on time."

"Naw, I thought it was come-as-you-are, straight from the shower, birthday suit!"

"Funny." Cindy saw the bus a ways down Commerce

Street. "Here's my bus. Drive carefully. Bye."

From the bus window, she saw him still waving at her. She looked straight ahead. I'm headed for work; Tommy has to be going, too.

Yeah, you have to let go, and fast.

We'll see plenty of each other.

Okay, 'Mom,' time to move on.

Not all at once.

Milk-sop!

Cindy checked her watch - 6:05 on the dot.

Cindy Miscevich had been riding the Number 3 bus for seventeen years. Even after she bought the car, mostly for Tommy to drive, she preferred the long bus ride to downtown. It gave her time to think. Sometimes to dream.

She had moved to Oliver at first because she could afford it. She rented the house, which gave her the yard she wanted and—important, with Paul—the privacy the West End lacked. In time she was able to buy the place.

After Skaansgard hired her, when Tommy was a baby, she could catch a ride with a neighbor who worked at the wire mill over the bridge and the two of them bussed it to 27th Avenue West, where Grandma met them and took Tommy. Cindy continued on the bus to downtown. Summer, winter, sweltering, cold, freezing, or storm, it didn't matter. "Grandma will be there, don't worry." And she was. The few times she was sick, or when she sprained that ankle, Berta was there to stand in. Always, the West End cared for its own.

The drivers—just three in all those years, the union way— knew where Tommy got off. Each one learned to speed past the earlier stops to give little Tommy more time to climb down and meet Grandma. I could have sent him alone with those drivers, she thought. And on the return, Tommy was waiting for her. Tuesdays or Wednesdays she got off and stayed for dinner, sometimes overnight. Tommy needed to see her doing a little neighboring. She often stayed for the weekend and bussed it back to Oliver on Sunday. And now he's driving, she mused.

This time, the driver stopped for Grandma to get the presents. He waited while the two of them hugged and said a few words.

"Top of the morning to you, Mrs. Miscevich," he said.

"And to you, Mr. Putman," Grandma returned the driver's greeting. Her voice took on her father's brogue. "There are just a few things here. Did you get the cake?"

"I'm going up there next. It's only seven, dearie."

"You bet I know. Better get back on. Bye."

Her mother waved as the bus passed. Cindy looked ahead at the rocky hillside. She couldn't see Berta's house from down here but looked up the cliffs anyway. The bus moved around the curve at the base of Observation Hill, revealing the buildings of downtown.

After Tommy's birth, Skaansgard and Bullock had hired her.

"You have an excellent recommendation." The lawyer looked at her pointedly. "I know about your baby," Skaansgard said, "but as long as you work hard and stay healthy, we'll keep you. I won't be telling Mr. Bullock. Maybe you'll get married."

She didn't plan on marriage. Paul had wed this lawyer's daughter, but Cindy wanted the job. So even when she or Tommy was sick, she worked. She worked hard. She came in through snowstorms. Cindy was smart. Quick to anticipate. Closed-mouthed. Proper. Trustworthy. Everything a law firm valued. So she stayed. She prospered. She advanced.

Skaansgard took her on as his personal secretary after four years.

"You've done well here, Cindy. I put my trust in you."

Even though he was East End stock, Skaansgard admired the work ethic she and the people in the west of town marshalled. He did have a heart—that was apparent when he hired her—even though he stayed distant. He never asked about Tommy. Did he know Paul and I dated in high school? She was sure Paul had nothing to do with her hiring, and his father-in-law would know nothing of their history from her.

She'd worried about it when Paul turned up at the office. He hadn't known; that was certain. Paul dropped his jaw and stammered, "Cindy. What . . . I didn't know you worked here . . . How?"

"How long?" she finished for him. "Five years." She was matter-of-fact and kind. "It's good to see you, Paul. You look fine." She pressed the intercom, "Mr. Tuomi to see you, sir." She rose and saw him to the door. Like a muddled sleepwalker, he passed close to her. The scent she caught intoxicated her; nearly sent her reeling.

A few minutes later she asked Evelyn to sit in. "I need to stop in at the drug store for Tommy. I'll be just a few minutes." When she returned, Paul had already left. She didn't see him at the office again. Three days later, Betty—Paul's go-between and heavily into drinking by then—called her at home. He and Pamela had lost their son that year. Cindy thought it was pity that moved her.

5

Joe Huey's

INGSTROM WAS LEAVING. "Hey, Skip. Got to meet some merchantmen. Nice party." He slipped out the door before Skip had had a chance to say "Boo" and clambered down the stairs waving goodbye behind him as he descended.

He took the alley to Lake Avenue and swung his sea legs downhill toward Joe Huey's. If the Central Hillside was the mixing bowl of the city, Joe Huey's was the spoon. Into the egalitarian steam of his Chinese kitchen came the city's high and low, the fancy and plain, the drunk and sober, feeding together on fried rice and chop suey. Much of the nefarious business in town was handled in the booths at Joe's.

Ingstrom stepped lightly down the steep sidewalks along the avenue. At the canal below, the monstrous steel web of the Aerial Lift Bridge beamed like a static Fizzy light show. The complicated trusses, toothed armatures, and arced span combined in a jumble of mechanized commerce out of scale with everything near it but the salties and lakers that dieseled beneath the raised bridge, sounding "Thanks" in *voci bassissimi*. With any luck, Ingstrom thought, he'd be aboard one of those ocean-going salties within the week. All he needed was a seaman's card and a birthday. Both were coming fast.

The avenue flattened out beyond Superior Street onto the steel post-and-beam viaduct that passed high over railroad tracks and Michigan Street. Ingstrom kept to the wooden plank sidewalk, absently tracing the filigreed curlicues of the iron rail's balustrade. He stopped over the tracks, looking down into the industrial darkness as if peering into the iron past of the city, a past from which he was detached in time and breeding. His eyes traced the railroad sidings that led off to the huffing steam plant looming four stories behind him on the opposite side of the viaduct. The siding rails carried coal to the maw of the plant. Like the bridge, the rails below, and the viaduct on which he walked, the steam plant stood as a monument to the unmitigated gall of 19th-century "Big Men"—men who, steeled with the strength and servitude of early immigrants, were capable of stripping the forests, gouging the hillsides of their ore, suppressing and dashing the hopes of other, smaller men in order to build their own big dreams.

Like the "Big Men" themselves, those dreams were big, industrial-scale. One dream towered behind Ingstrom, a plant feeding huge boilers to send steam throughout the entire commercial district—enough steam to heat every hotel, office building, and warehouse in the fifty-block downtown. A mighty pulse along a mighty arm, controlled by a single mighty mind: such was the patriarchy of the city. He turned, leaned back on the rail to survey the steam plant stacks. That's what, he thought, dear old Dad wants to share with me.

Ingstrom hated it. Even if the power had weakened, the grip remained—steady as a hand in rigor mortis grasping one's collar. He hated the opprobrium, the venal slights and slanders, the business of business. He wanted to escape the destiny of the comptroller's son, and his flight lay right before him—beyond the behemoth across the street—on the magnificent lake that floated ships to the sea to adventure beyond the confines of a city thirty miles long but as narrow as the smallest mind in town.

Ingstrom shook off his reverie, swayed over the late-night tracks below, and again swung into motion. He passed the iron stair leading to the street running beneath him, passed the Metropole Hotel housing sailors and whores, and came to the door of Joe Huey's Cantonese Restaurant.

The green and orange neon from the sign announcing "Joe Huey's" echoed off Ingstrom's glasses, hiding his eyes beneath psychedelic hues as he examined his reflection in the restaurant window. He smiled at himself. He looked good. He was cool. He reached for the handle and flung the door wide. A torrent of spice and soy greeted him even before the birdlike man in suit and tie came from behind the counter to claw up a menu and ask, "One? Two? How many?"

"I'm joining some people, Joe." Ingstrom realized his error. One kept one's words terse and businesslike with Joe. "One," he said holding up a finger. Then he pointed to a booth where Carlos sat waving to him.

Joe Huey grinned and gestured his welcome, jammed the menu into Ingstrom's chest, and trotted back to his counter. Ingstrom made his way through racing bus boys amid the thick clatter of dishes to the booth where Carlos waited.

"The Wizard," he said. "Peace, brother."

Ingstrom felt startled but remained composed. Across the booth from Carlos—hidden before by the high dark lacquered seat back—sat a very black man and the whitest woman Ingstrom had ever seen. She was far beyond blonde: her skin, maybe powdered, was more platinum than her momentous, tumbling silver curls. She wore a white satin ensemble and a string of luminous pearls.

"Hey, this is Mike Light," Carlos offered. "I know him from UMD."

Mike offered his hand with a huge smile and a deep greeting. "Peace, brother," he said. His smile turned sly and his eyes narrowed. Ingstrom took his hand. "This is my girl, Lilly. Lilly, Mr. . . . ," he paused and cocked his head.

"Ingstrom. Reese. Reese Ingstrom."

"Sit, Inggy," Carlos indicated the seat next to him. "We're just about to order."

Ingstrom felt uneasy. "Make mine pork fried rice. I'll share." He looked to the man. "So, you're a student at the college?"

"Not exactly," Mike said, nodding at Carlos. "This guy's the book hound."

"Oh, you read plenty," Lilly said.

Mike shot out a massive, muscular arm along the table, then gently, softly stroked Lilly's cheek. "Darling, you know what I'm good at."

"Oooh, Mr. Light," she giggled.

Carlos looked at Mike. "Actually, Mike works in the studio. Art."

"He's a model," Lilly said.

He slapped her gently. "I do a lot of different things," Mike said. "How about you, Reese? What're you up to?"

Ingstrom kept in mind what Randy had told him. He kept his guard up. "I'm a seaman. Shipping out."

Carlos clapped Ingstrom's shoulder. "You got the card. Congratulations."

"That's just a formality. I have to wait for a ship. About a week."

"What kind of seamen are you?" Lilly wanted to know.

"Darling," Mike said, "that's seaman, not semen." He snubbed her chin between his index finger and thumb.

"I know. I know."

"A common swab. A merchant marine," Ingstrom told her. "I do what I'm told, but I plan to sail clear around the world and see it all. Especially India."

"They have some uncommon hash there, I'm told," Carlos said. "Maybe you'll send some, hey?" Ingstrom frowned.

The waitress was standing at the table. "You order?"

As the food came—six steaming platters of rice, egg foo young, chop suey, and sub gum chow mein—two sailors weaved their way back and past the booth. Ingstrom lifted a finger to one of them as he passed.

"Those guys are smoothing my passage," he said. "Leave me some rice, please." He slid out of his seat, followed the two to their places in the last booth, across from the head, and sat. "Treat time," he said.

"Who's the spade, Reese?" asked the sailor sitting opposite.

"He's at the college."

"Known him long?"

"Just met. Something wrong?"

"Let's just say something isn't exactly right. Probably nothing."

"I heard he works in the art department." Ingstrom said.

The man slid a fold of bills across the seat to Ingstrom. "Welcome to the club, man. Check with the steward on Monday. You're all right."

"Good," Ingstrom said as he took up the bills. "I've got to hit the head." He nodded to each. "Gents."

Once in the toilet, Ingstrom laid out the three packets in his pocket. He peeled the paper off a Band-Aid strip and taped the packets to the back of the tank lid. He tested the assembly gingerly and flushed the toilet.

When he emerged, one sailor got up and said in passing, "You didn't wash your hands."

"You can wash them for me, and don't forget to flush," Ingstrom replied.

The other man pushed him gently as they passed. Ingstrom

made like a wave on the ocean, giving softly. "Later," he said.

Ingstrom sat at the edge of the booth once more. "How much is the steward asking?"

"Another grand," the sailor said. "Cash."

"I have resources," Ingstrom smiled.

When he returned to his rice, Mike Light and Lilly were leaving.

"We have places to go," Mike said, making friendly. "Good meeting you, sailor."

"My pleasure, man. Peace. Lilly, take care of him."

"Oh, she does. That she does," Mike said, rising. Standing next to Carlos, Mike seemed even taller. Ingstrom looked up at him. Lilly rose in a flourish of Chanel No. 5. "Bye-bye," she said.

"Later," he said.

The two strode to the front, the waitress and busboys stepping aside. The whole place watched. Mike towered over Joe Huey, who was working the ancient cash register. The three of them, Lilly the white, diminutive Joe, and magnificent Mike played the crowd for a minute. The place buzzed with cheap amusement. Joe skewered the tab on his spindle, gave change, and returned to his accounting. The couple went out the door without looking back.

"Where did you find them?" Ingstrom asked, sliding in across the booth.

"Actually, Siiri met Mike in her figure drawing class, modeling."

"He's the model?"

"All of him, yes. He bares it all."

"Well, I hope she doesn't sample some of that. It's too weird."

"Maybe she can't help herself. Anyway, there's Lilly." Carlos raised an eyebrow. "You score?"

"Big. Not a lot, but high quality."

"Is that what 'they' got?" Carlos nodded back toward the seamen's booth.

"Do you know me?" Ingstrom widened his eyes behind his glasses. "They got their cut. You get yours."

"Okay, okay, just asking. It's on your seat."

Ingstrom didn't look down but slid his hand over the seat and found the envelope. He folded it and slipped it in with his jackknife. "I'll leave the tip," he said shoving a packet and two dollars under a plate edge.

"No, no. Leave it to me," Carlos said sweeping up the bunch. He put down a five.

Ingstrom felt relieved. He picked at his rice with the chopsticks.

"So is the card for real?" Carlos asked.

Ingstrom and Charles—Carlos to everyone on the hillside—one year apart at Duluth East, had been neighbors all their lives. Carlos was a fixture of Ingstrom's life, a known and trusted, if not trustworthy, friend. He told him only what he wanted put out on the street and trusted him with a few unrepeatable truths, like his dealing. This also was for the street.

"The card is as real as it comes," Ingstrom answered. "But I'll count it only when they hand it to me."

"Shipping is way up this year. You should be able to go right out."

"I'm not counting on it. Have this stuff tried out and, if anyone likes it, take some orders. I have to pile on travel cash," Ingstrom said. "I won't be paid on the ship for two months."

"I have some friends."

"You do, you do."

"Did you see Fizzy's light show?"

"No, missed it," Ingstrom lied.

"Well, it must be over. There he is."

Ingstrom turned to peer around the side of the booth. Damn, he thought. He had never seen Fizzy at Joe Huey's before. Actually, he had never seen him in a restaurant before. Fizzy kept to himself, mostly in the West End house he shared with his mother and sister.

Fizzy saw him and came straight back. Ingstrom met him halfway. "Let's go outside," Fizzy said.

Cool but upset, Ingstrom thought.

Outside he said, "What's up, Bob?"

"Let's walk," Fizzy said, "Marly's below in the car." He moved past the Metropole and turned down the iron staircase that led into the darkness of Commerce Street below the viaduct. Marly was sitting in the driver's seat of the station wagon. Fizzy opened the back door for Ingstrom.

"What gives?" Ingstrom asked.

"Let's get in first," Fizzy said.

As soon as they shut the doors, Marly moved off. Though she was going on sixteen, she had been driving nearly two years. Fizzy turned toward Ingstrom, talking over the seats.

"We had to break down the bathroom door to get to Roger. He O.D.'d. He's dead."

"Shit! How did that happen? Even if he shot everything in his bag, it would have barely gotten him off."

"He swiped Janey's bag when she was talking John through it."

"God! He did it all?"

"There was nothing left. He left a mess too. Skip is freaking out."

"What now?"

Marly said, "We figured you'd know what to do."

6

Bluestone

PAUL ROSE FROM THE TABLE. Breathe, he thought. Not in his trained detective's mind but in his long-preserved little boy's imagination, he saw the carpet roll being carried into the apartment below. The vision knocked out his wind. He guarded it, kept it to himself. Don't let her see, he thought. Breathe.

Since joining the force almost twenty years ago, Paul's ability to visualize had gained him a reputation of having the nose of a bloodhound. Sometimes, he had led an otherwise confused search or pursuit directly to the lost child or offender on the run. Though publicly he said it was hard work, in his own mind he credited his rapid rise in the department to this talent. It scared him, especially since it came upon him unexpectedly and unbidden.

Paul threw the kitchen screen door aside and took two steps at a time. Whoa, get your professional on, he told himself. At the turn of the stair, halfway down, he paused, dizzy.

He sorrowed for Berta. This woman has gone through enough. He touched the cool stone of the high foundation wall that the stair followed. It steadied him. As he had done as a boy, he pressed his forehead to the stone framing Roger's apartment door. He drew a breath and let the bluestone—Duluth gabbro quarried right there on the hill—anchor him, just as it had grounded the house itself for eighty years atop the massive outcroppings.

Breathe. Do it right.

At the porch door above, Berta whispered down to him. "Please, Paul, knock first."

Paul could only try to hide things from her. He took the last six steps slowly. Method. Method, he coached himself. He felt the far-and-old reach of the neighborhood and his love for this motherly woman spring up in defense, but he curbed the feelings with the orderliness learned through his years of study and self-regulation. College and the academy should handle this, he decided, not the affections of the 'End. Care, he reasoned, but be careful. His gut twisted. He felt a traitor. Educated and from the West End. Like snow under a July sun. But there he was. He came of the friendly West End, and now at once he felt barred from it and above it. Foreign. Longing for it from outside. He pressed the stone.

Paul stood firm now a step above the concrete landing that formed the last stair and the entry to Roger's apartment. He had stepped on this same porch ten minutes earlier and could still see his shoeprints in the residue of risen fog. Now there were others, not marked in dew but in traces of soil from the back yard. Those prints will tell a story, he concluded. He was sure, even without a team to work it. More cautious now, Paul sat on the stair and removed his shoes. Treat it as a crime scene. The thought scared him; but he sensed, just as Berta had, that something was "terribly wrong."

Paul stood on the final step and rapped softly on the screen doorframe. Nothing. He hinged the screen open, touching only the top corner of the frame. He curled an arm inside and knocked loudly on the door itself—for Berta and, he hoped, for Roger.

Stillness hung at the door like the fog that had crouched there. He called through the open doorway. "Roger?" He waited. "It's Paul. I'm coming in."

He shouldered the screen wider and swung the open door back. The spring creaked its complaint to the placid air. It sounded like a scream in the quiet of morning. *I shouldn't do this alone.* He warred with himself.

It isn't a crime, he thought. *Not yet.*

But you suspect, no?

Yes. But it's personal. Memma has to know.

Paul entered in stocking feet, watching each step. He kept up on his toes.

He remembered the room as a workshop and tool shed from years ago. Wendell, Sr. had partitioned it from the rest of the basement, some of which was still dirt and outcropped stone. As the hill bulged up toward the front of the house, the joists in that section grew lower until they sat on the bedrock itself. The furnace and water heater stood just behind the partition.

Wendell, Sr. had covered and plastered all but the entry wall, even the ceiling. Paul could still hear his clipped, musical voice say: "Ja, keep da natural stone, 's good." Wendell, Sr. stretched the word "stone" and rounded the "o" broadly. Once more Paul heard the bright, Norwegian rise he gave to "good."

The bluestone wall held the door and two windows deep-set in its bulky thickness. Three years ago—when Berta, after a lot of grousing, decided to allow Roger to move down there—Paul had painted the interior stone white. "I know Wendell Sr. will turn in his grave, but it'll brighten the place up," Berta said. "I want it nice for Roger."

"All right," he'd finally agreed, "but only the inside of the wall. The outside stays." It took two full gallons of paint to cover the gabbro. He had to admit the rough, faceted stone looked handsome with its white enameling.

And it had been bright inside, but Roger turned it into a

den. He covered the windows in a dark paisley print and the walls with bold-colored rock posters. The back partition wall he had painted a deep purple. Four light bulbs alternating blue and red studded the bared ceiling fixture. Roger had used the fixture lens as a dry bowl. A worn carpet of dusky Middle Eastern design lay, corners upturned, over a hall runner placed on the cement floor. The carpet leapt at Paul's senses. It was foreign. He closed his eyes. Odors of death rose from the rug. He saw the carpet being carried in again. "Evidence."

Oversize pillows were strewn around the room. A steel-gray amplifier, turntable, and dark speakers sat on navy blue painted pine boards lifted from the floor by concrete blocks against which, as if it had been tossed there, the rug curled up. Black leather beanbag chairs slumped on each side of an industrial wire spool. A lamp, its shade covered with the same paisley of the windows, lighted the spool-table.

In the far corner, on a pallet, Roger lay exactly as Paul had seen him earlier through the screen. He lay on his stomach, his face buried in pillows, his long brown hair disheveled over his shoulders and back. He was fully clothed except one bare foot stuck out at an odd angle. Roger's face was to the wall. He doesn't look right, Paul judged.

Paul looked to the ceiling. He heard Berta moving about the kitchen above. The click of dishes in the sink and the whir of an eggbeater distracted his thought. He followed her movements and fought the stinging in his nose and eyes. She's always had her baking, he recalled; always she had the kitchen. He forced his attention back to Roger.

Keeping his voice within the room, Paul said, "Roger?"

Careful to disturb nothing, Paul tiptoed around the carpet to the pallet. When he saw the needle and spoon laid neatly at the head of the pallet on a low table whose legs had been sawn short, he squatted, still on his toes. He crossed his arms over his knees and bent. He thrust his chin forward. A box of matches was spilled on the floor over a small, transparent plastic bag right below the syringe. Drugs, Paul knew. Oh, Roger, Roger.

Paul wrapped his knees with one arm and reached out to Roger's shoulder with his hand. One touch told him. He checked his watch: 6:15. The boy was dead. The body was stiff and cold. Dead for hours already. Sixteen years old. Almost.

Untrained feelings rose and filled his chest. He held his face in his hands.

Paul crouched there a long while. Could one blame the neighborhood, the working poor, the kids of kids of immigrants, the bad habits brought by oppressive work demanded by oppressive bosses and owners, the lack of a future? Paul vied within. No, drugs were everywhere now. The East End was rife with marijuana and LSD. That's where the money came from. High-class drugs. This is amphetamine or narcotics, he decided. A plague on the poor.

Paul pulled himself back through courses of training. The swirl of angst receded, evaporated as the fog had. He looked. He examined the odd angles of Roger's body. He studied the tidy lineup of the needle and spoon in parallel to the table's edge. He scrutinized the room. It was wrong. His inward and outward eyes both saw the same thing. Even the matches spilled over the little packet seemed wrong. He looked at his feet, around and under the periphery of the short table. He straightened at the ankles and pushed his hands against his knees to look from above at the table, into the ashtray, on the floor by the bed. He saw nothing on the carpet. He crouched again.

I don't see it, he thought. Maybe the team will find it. Yes, the team might find the burnt match.

Paul stretched up fully, stood looking down at Roger, stood surveying the room, the pile of clothes waiting for laundry, bowls and spoons stacked crookedly inside one another, a fork half under the carpet, and spilled popcorn. He looked back to the nightstand.

Wrong. It's just not right.

He tiptoed out the door. Paul removed and stretched one of his socks over his hand and gingerly pulled the apartment door to its former position. He let the screen bang shut. Paul sat on the stair, slipped on the sock and tied his shoes. He had two duties. He had to tell Berta, and he had to call this in. The first would be quite a measure harder.

When Paul entered the kitchen again, Berta was at the bread table working over a cake. The two layers were raised on a small pedestal. She held a spatula full of chocolate frosting aloft as she caught his gaze. She bit a tremble from her lower lip and wiped her free hand across the saddest eyes he had ever seen but stood firm and kindly as ever. "Sit, Paul. You've had a shock," she said.

Helpless before her, he took his chair. "Memma," he started, but she interrupted.

"Wait, Paul. Pour a coffee for us. I have to finish this frosting first. I'm right in the middle." She acted as if the frosting were the most important thing in the world at that moment.

He poured the coffee and watched Berta apply the frosting with deft flourishes. "This is for Tommy, you know," she said.

"Oh. Yes," he said absently. "I have a present for him out in the trunk. He's college bound," Paul murmured, sleepwalking atop his words. He watched Berta. She took the pastry bag up, trimmed the edge of the cake in shell-like waves, and set the bag down. Suddenly she looked tired. Very tired and very old, Paul thought.

She came to the table, stirred a spoonful of sugar into her coffee and swirled some cream into the brew. "Tell me now, Paul. Here at my table. This is where I get my best and worst news."

Paul opened his hands to take hers across the table. Yes, she had heard the news of Wendell Sr.'s death and Betty's, too, right here in the kitchen, probably at this very table. Sudden sorrows were enameled over the table's steel top, one layer on another, spilling over the edges, coloring Berta's apron. Death had shrouded her family life, though it couldn't dampen her gentle cheer. She placed her hands in his.

"I knew it," she said. "As soon as that car rolled backward over the gravel there, I knew something was wrong. And that carpet. Oh, Roger. Roger. Poor Betty's boy."

He let her cry, let loose her hands. He sat at the table where he and Wendell Jr. and Betty, too, had devoured cookies, pies, and cakes after school; where he had learned a mother's love unknown to him at home; where he drank milk and answered questions about history, mathematics, and English. Too, it was where he heard the laboring history of the town, the stories of the West End, of Finns and Norwegians banding together at Woodman's Hall; of workmen sweeping through the streets gathering strength in numbers, and standing firm, even under billy clubs and gunfire, for the right to a decent life. Those stories thrilled him. On that small table, stamped out of a single sheet of steel, rounded by a raised lip, spread a world as vital and sweet to him as Berta's cakes and as bitter as her strong black coffee.

Paul breathed in the enormity of his debt to Berta. And in her need, now, he could do little. Short comfort. Cold investigation. He rose unsteadily, went round the table, and, leaning over her chair, folded his arms around her shaking shoulders.

"Oh, Paul! I'm so happy to have you." She patted his arms. "God blessed me with a second son. You give me hope." Her comfort flowed without end. It was she who deserved it, who needed it. But it was she who sent it forth. He felt ashamed.

Paul let go her shoulders and returned to his chair. Berta blew her nose. "Is he really gone?"

Paul nodded. "Drugs, I think."

"I'll call Father Lucci."

"Yes, but I'm afraid there will be some police business that has to come first."

She looked at him, a sweet admiring gaze.

Paul spoke in the kindliest detective-voice he could muster. "I don't think Roger died here," he said. "Other people were involved. We need to find them."

She nodded like an obedient child. "You'll handle it, won't you?"

"Yes," he said and took the opportunity to get up. "I have some work to do outside to secure . . . the scene. Can someone come over to be with you?"

"I'll be fine. I have to finish the decoration. Elma is probably on her way to get the cake now. Later, we can walk down to her house."

"I'll give you a ride."

"No, a walk would be good." Berta rose and went to the cake. "You do your detective work, Paul. I have mine."

Berta followed Paul's movements, comforted by the sounds he made. He went out the front door this time. She heard him crunching down the gravel driveway. She thought he came to a sudden stop below her bedroom. She didn't hear him again until he closed the Buick door out by the tool shed.

"Must have taken it onto the lawn," she said.

She returned to the cake. She knew he'd be calling for help. I hope they don't come with those sirens, she thought. There's no need for that. Wendell Sr. wouldn't have sirens, at least at the house. Berta thought of that muffled knock at the door, the front door. So formal, she recalled. I knew something had happened. Wendell Sr. was late. It had been Carl Skoglund, the shop steward at the docks, and Enzo Rossi. Enzo didn't say much. He had come along, she supposed, to give Carl support. He only mumbled an "Our Father" in Latin–or was it Italian? Berta straightened over the cake. Realization shot hot across time. That's why Carl brought him. Italian. In eighteen years, she hadn't thought of that. An Italian Catholic. Wouldn't do to send just a Protestant. And a Swede at that. She smiled thinly and shook her head as much at the collective kindness of those men—Wendell Sr.'s union brothers—as at the connection she had just made. They remembered Mother was Italian.

Berta was doing concrete blocks in gray and black, a path in gold-ish tan leading to a college building—she had taken inspiration for the columns and façade from the Teacher's College in East End. She had seen it only on a calendar picture. June. The path to success, hard work and education, arced below three-color lettering: Happy Birthday, Tommy. Good Luck. How many have I made for him? She wondered. Eighteen. Two less than for Roger. Berta moved away from the cake. She brought her hands up. One held her apron. Oh, don't cry honey. Let sorrow turn to joy. It's the miracle of Christ. She prayed. She heard Paul's trunk slam shut.

Berta went to the window. She saw Paul carefully stepping down the slate stones toward the landing. He carried a roll of yellow tape. Police tape. "Oh, my," she said. Her house had become a crime scene. She dabbed with her apron fringe.

Berta returned to the cake. She moved it from its pedestal to the platter and carefully placed the steel dome over it, settling the cover into the groove on the plate. She folded the strap harness that Wendell Sr. had fashioned over the dome and clipped it to the handle at the top. Wendell, you were such a handy man. Eighteen years? He'd never held Roger. Still, he didn't have to see Betty all banged up and beaten. Berta took up the cake-saver by the fancy handle Wendell Sr. had made, and brought the cake to the dining room table.

Through the front room windows she watched Paul outside. He had moved his car to the street and was tying a rope across the driveway on posts he had driven into the lawn. Good. No yellow police tape up at the street. Paul looked up from his work. Elma came up the sidewalk. Berta moved to the front door and through the window watched them talk out front. Abruptly, Elma looked to the house. Her face drained of color. She ran up the walk.

Paul followed Elma to the front door. By the time he entered the porch, the two women were in each other's arms, sobbing.

He stood a moment in the doorway. He couldn't enter that feminine world. Even more, he was now out of the greater one bounded by the ore docks across the flats on one side and the outcropping of the western hillsides on the other. He had left that neighborhood—crossed a line that could not be crossed again. He wondered. What made it so final? Was it the university? Was it Pamela and the East End? Or the connection to the Skaansgards? No, it was more than all of that added together. Standing in the entry, watching the two women comfort each other, Paul felt it even more strongly than in Cindy's arms. Was it the past itself that had receded?

No, Cindy doesn't feel that.

She has Elma, he reasoned. Still living in the same house.

So, you have Berta.

True, but the distance is far greater.

To Memma Paul said something about finishing up outside and turned to go.

"We'll be fine," Memma said. "We have each other now." Elma, too, looked at him and nodded. He could see they had more than each other, more than the neighborhood, its history and their long lives, as painful as they'd proven to be.

"Yes, I can see that," he said, and went.

Being outside in the freshness of the morning was better. He had already done pretty much all he needed to do. He had taped the door, landing, and parts of the backyard. He had located the apartment key on its nail in the porch joists and locked the doors just in case. He'd called the desk sergeant, given him the address, and reported Roger's death. The last item was a request for the lab unit to sweep the scene and apartment.

"What're you looking for?" the sergeant asked.

"Anything. Take photos, prints, collect evidence. I'll brief them when they get here."

He knew he'd have to wait. At least until eight. It was half past seven. Have a look around.

Paul walked along the lot's boundaries. He looked hard before he placed his foot. He didn't want to compromise evidence. When he had worked his way back to the garden shed he sat on the bench that he and Wendell Jr. had been allowed to build while Wendell's father raised the shed. They worked from a sketch Wendell, Sr. had made with the help of a pattern maker at the roundhouse in Proctor. It showed the connections, some of the shaped details and dimensions. They'd been twelve and thirteen at the time. The war effort hadn't yet begun. They built, as did Wendell's father, out of scrap scavenged from worksites around town. Some of it might have come from the DM & IR Railway. The old dock worker didn't say.

Paul heard Wendell, Sr. whistling and singing in Norwegian. His handsaw barked in rhythm at the lumber he cut. Sometimes he laughed out loud. Paul and Wendell Jr. looked at each other and grinned. They never could tell what went through the old man's mind. What he laughed at was only a guess.

Sirens sliced through the echo of Wendell, Sr.'s songs. Paul had stood and climbed on the bench to see. That's not coming here. Then he heard more, at least three. Headed out east. He jumped off the seat.

Paul looked toward the bay. The *Carnegie* was loading. The chutes were lowered and swinging over the hatches. Ore spilled down the chutes into the ship's hold. Mostly, now, the operation was automated. Safer than Wendell Sr. had had it. When once more than seven hundred men had earned a good living delivering, loading, and trimming the ore into the holds, now few were needed. No wonder Wendell Jr. had left.

Paul's own father had seen it coming long before. He pushed Paul. "Get an education," he said, "don't be like the rest." He knew that the unions couldn't last, that the jobs would leave or be removed, a carpet pulled out from under everybody. That he had been correct didn't make it right, though.

Without feeling superior—even before he was a beat cop on West Superior Street—Paul had learned that he was lucky to have escaped the camaraderie of despair that hung around Curly's and The West Ender. "Let them drink down their own bile," his father had said. "They thought nothing would ever change."

82

Even now, his father was calling to him across the yard. No, it was Berta's voice. Paul jerked around. Berta was leaning out the back door, calling his name.

"Paul, it's the phone. For you."

"Okay, I'll go around the front."

It was the chief. "How did you find me?" he said and immediately felt stupid. These are detectives, idiot.

"Didn't you call the desk forty-five minutes ago? Look Paul, we have something big happening. I want you to take charge."

"I've got a death out here at the West's."

"I know. But this is big. A double murder at Brookside."

"I just went by there. Around five."

"Well, get yourself over there again before the squads trample the place. I need an experienced detective there, and you're it."

The Chief sounded angry. He seldom ordered anything. Paul didn't try to argue. He pushed the receiver button down and dialed.

"Bushy? Paul. Listen, I know you're off duty, but there's been trouble at Berta West's. Her grandson. I'm here now, but I've been pulled off. Can you be here until the lab arrives?"

Bill Buczynski lived nearby, was an underclassman from Paul's high school, and a passingly good friend. Bushy knew Berta.

It'll be all right, but Paul felt at sea. This was not something he wanted to leave to others.

Berta did not show her disappointment. She patted his arm.

"I'll be back when the lab crew comes," he said. "Don't worry; Bushy will be here before I leave. If you want to go down to Elma's it's fine."

Bushy arrived on foot. He lived on Fifth, two blocks up the

hill. Paul told him what he had found and showed him the key. He said to call when the lab crew arrived. Berta brought Bushy into the kitchen to feed him.

Paul went to his car and got behind the wheel. Before starting the engine, he radioed the desk sergeant again. "Can you call the coroner for the West residence?"

"All hell is breaking loose down here. You haven't heard?" The sergeant sounded frazzled.

"I've heard. Still . . ." the desk interrupted.

"I'll do what I can," the sergeant barked.

Paul ended the call. Already, he was holding his breath. He started the car and jammed it into gear. "Sure, 'do what I can.'"

7

Downtown

CINDY FELT AN ODD UNEASE. The bus curved around the huge belly of Observation Hill, which separated and sheltered the West End from downtown. Why she should feel restive today she couldn't tell. Maybe it's the party. Cindy hadn't been in public with Paul for almost eight months. That might be it. Even at her mother's house she feared someone would see. People talk. They talk too much.

That might account for it. The damage that discovery could bring would never be repaired. Cindy was sure of Paul this time—he had learned what loss felt like. That was a great lesson—but both their careers would be on the line. She'd lose her job, no doubt. Paul would never again be promoted.

Other couples have weathered that storm.

Oh, yeah, fool, and were they happier in the end?

Some were, yes. Definitely.

Tell me that when you're on unemployment pay, fool.

Cindy worked to quiet her voices. She opened her compact case, applied her lipstick and touched up her cheeks. She reached into her purse, finding the heavy horn-rimmed glasses, swung the beaded lanyard over her head and flipped her hair back over the chain. She placed the glasses on her nose and took a final look in the mirror.

Professional girl, she thought.

Yeah, pro-fresh-on-all was the refrain.

The bus was passing the house-sized granite blocks of the promontory. Berta's was just above her atop the Point of Rocks. She wondered where Paul was this morning. Idle thoughts. The monumental outcrop sent Superior Street off its course to merge for ten blocks with Michigan Street which in other places ran below it. Behind, the West End bustled on with its homey existence. At this point in her daily journey, Cindy took her last relaxed breath of the morning and got ready for business.

As she was passing below, Paul unfurled yellow crime-scene tape and started to wind it around the stair posts at the rear of Berta's house. Dreary concern splashed down the face of the rocks onto the bus as it passed. Cindy's own feelings were already shadowed.

Ahead, the morning sun had stanched the fog and was baking the backsides of the buildings. The shadows of the office towers reached as far up the hill as Second Street and kept Superior Street dark. A little gloomy today. Cindy wasn't sure if that described the street or her mood. Instead of getting her usual cheer-me-up cup at the lobby café, she moved directly to the elevators. Might as well get on with it. The doors opened immediately when she pushed the button, and there stood Skaansgard, coming up from the parking garage. He was very early, fumbling with his necktie.

"Mr. Skaansgard." She was now at work. "Can I help you with that?" Cindy shouldered her purse and finished the knot for him, smoothing it and sliding it carefully toward his collar. "I'll leave that last button for you, sir."

She could tell he had hurried out of the house. "Did you get some coffee yet?" she said. "I can go back down to the café."

He shook his head. "There isn't time. I have a huge call list for you."

Cindy knew better than to talk business in the elevator. She waited until she turned lights on in the suite and stowed her purse under her desk. She entered his office with the steno pad. He was on the phone. Bullock, the partner, was already there. He was saying, "Tell them this is our best chance to get those bastards." Skaansgard crooked a finger at Cindy as Bullock cut his tirade and paced.

"Hold a moment, please," Skaansgard said to the phone. "Cindy, get Paul Tuomi on the line for me. I'll discuss the list with you in a minute." He handed her a list of names. She recognized the first names as trustees of the Crosley Family Fund. She did not leave. She hovered uncertainly. Skaansgard raised an eyebrow, "Please hold again," and to Cindy, "what is it?"

Paul Tuomi junior or senior, sir?"

"My son-in-law, Cindy, please."

The firm of Skaansgard and Bullock had on rare occasions used Paul's father on investigations, ones they thought wouldn't require a court appearance. Cindy thought hers a reasonable question, but his "please" burst out irritated, unusually nasty coming from her boss. Did I react personally? She had never had to call Paul at home before. She could usually leave Skaansgard's message at the station, but this was clearly urgent.

It was 7:35. He'd still be at home. Cindy let it ring. The receiver was knocked off its cradle, someone swore, and in a moment Cindy was talking with Pamela. Her heart raced, but she held her voice steady. "Mrs. Tuomi, this is Mr. Skaansgard's office. Mr. Skaansgard would like to speak to Mr. Tuomi, please." The "please" caught and dried in her throat, coming out as barely a whisper.

"He's not here. Who's this?"

"Mr. Skaansgard's secretary, Mrs. Tuomi. It's important. Can you tell us where we might reach him?"

"Call the station," she said. "No. Yes, I know where."

Pamela's voice grew sharp, acid. "He's up at that Berta's house. Berta West." Cindy felt burned by the other woman's acrimony.

"Thank you so much, Mrs. Tuomi. I am sorry to have wakened you."

"You didn't. I've been up for hours."

Cindy wanted to get off. "Thank you again," she said and disconnected.

That was unprofessional. "Sorry to have wakened you."

Watch it, babe.

Okay, but no one should fault Memma. Cindy nearly broke a sweat dialing Berta's number. It was busy.

She turned to the list of trustees. She took a file from her bottom drawer. All their numbers were listed there. Skaansgard buzzed. "Yes, sir?" Cindy took the file to his office.

Bullock had gone to his office across the private hall. Skaansgard watched her approach the desk. "Sit down Cindy. Are you feeling well? You seemed pale before and now you're flushed." Mr. Skaansgard had forever been the great observer. It made him the veteran trial lawyer he was.

Cindy kept standing. "I'm fine. I have a birthday celebration later. I might be a bit flustered by it."

"It's not yours, is it?" He regularly remembered her date.

"My son's." She swelled a bit. "He's 18 today."

"Congratulations," he said, and indicated the chair. "You'll want to sit for this, Cindy."

She wondered, am I being fired?

Here it comes, idiot. He's found out. What did you expect, huh?

Skaansgard continued, softly, almost gently, as if breaking very bad news that could cause pain. "Cindy, early this morning there was a burglary at Brookside. The intruder turned killer. I'm afraid Miss Martha is dead. Her housemaid was also killed."

Cindy tried not to look relieved. The news was terrible, but it wasn't at all what she feared. "Who would do such a thing?"

"Bullock suspects Miss Martha's son-in-law and daughter," he said, "but that is quite farfetched."

"What can I do? I couldn't reach Mr. Tuomi."

Skaansgard handed her another paper. "Keep working on Paul, but I want you to phone each of the trustees and read this message to each. I want everyone to get the same message. Then screen my calls. Let me know who is on the line. Cancel any appointments I have."

She went about her tasks as she usually did, detached and efficient. When trustees expressed shock and outrage, she echoed their sentiments and agreed coolly. In between, she tried Berta's again, still busy, and left word at the station for Paul. At exactly eight o'clock, the phone queue filled, and she had to help the receptionist. All three television stations, the *Tribune,* and the radio stations were calling for interviews. It was nearly an hour before she called Berta again. She let it ring but put down the receiver when a man entered.

"Excuse me, sir. Can I help you?"

The man handed Cindy his card. "Mr. Bullock called me this morning." He was a private investigator she had never seen before. She didn't recognize the firm.

"Let me tell him you're here. Take a seat, if you please. Would you like coffee?"

He shook his head and sat while Cindy rang Bullock.

The partner appeared almost immediately. "Crandahl, thanks for coming down."

"Is Tuomi here?" the man said.

"Not yet, but we've gotten him on the case. We'll have the

91

inside track." He held the door for Crandahl and the two went to his office. The third mention of Paul that morning flustered and confused her. The phones were jammed again. This one was Pamela.

"Mr. Skaansgard," she said.

Cindy stiffened. She treated it as a newsroom call. "I'm sorry, but Mr. Skaansgard is not taking calls right now. May I be of help?"

"Are you the one who called this morning?" Pamela was angry. "Just put me through to my father." In seventeen years, Pamela had made no effort to know the office staff. A kind word from her would have gone a long way.

She's a bitch.

Now, now.

At the demand, though, Cindy grew cooler, "Let me see if he can take the call." She punched hold and thought a moment, then buzzed her boss.

Skaansgard responded, "Yes?"

"Your daughter is on the line, sir."

"Not now," he groused. "Tell her I'm in a meeting. I'll call back."

"I'm going for coffee, sir. Would you like a cup?"

"Yes, yes. Get some pastries for three and get something for yourself."

She knew it was wrong, but she took satisfaction at turning Pamela away. She used her firmest voice, touched with kindness. "He's just finishing his meeting and will call right after."

Pamela cursed.

Cindy checked out at reception. "Just take messages. Mr. S. will call them back when he wants to. Say nothing to the news people. If Mrs. Tuomi calls for her father, tell her he's still in a meeting." The receptionist smirked and held up a thumb.

Cindy needed the break more than she wanted the coffee. The constant mention of Paul and two conversations with Pamela had unnerved her. She took the stairs down. After ordering and leaving the office coffee urn at the café, she slipped into a phone booth in the lobby. She never made her personal calls from the office. It was her rule.

She dialed home, her mother's number.

Elma answered and immediately announced Roger's death.

The phone booth pressed closer. Cindy grasped the edge of the little table under the phone and pushed herself hard against the seat and wall. The cubicle floor gave way. She grew faint and broke into a full sweat.

"Cindy, are you there?" her mother said.

Cindy cried. "Yes, Mom, yes." She couldn't stop the tears.

The gloom she had been feeling all the way into downtown now fell heavily on her shaking shoulders. "Oh, Roger! Roger!" She had easily absorbed Skaansgard's announcement, even though she had met Miss Martha and thought she knew the housemaid. But not this. Not this. Her taunting voices were silent. "Mom, let me speak with Berta."

Cindy didn't know if she'd be able to speak, but she had to try to comfort Berta. Then she realized that she had gone to the older woman to receive rather than to give. That's the way with Memma. A well-lit one-way street. Berta cheered her with her praise of Paul and her thankfulness that he had come.

"Oh, honey. He took over. It was lightness to my heart."

Cindy immediately felt better. Berta was good enough to realize she was still at work and had duties to fulfill.

"I'll come as soon as I can, Memma. I don't know, with all the hubbub." She stopped short. This was no time to add to Berta's troubles or to counter them with someone else's business. "I'll call at lunch for sure. I'm sorry, Memma, so sorry."

"What happened?" Sherry, the café owner, said. "You've been crying."

The question startled Cindy. "It's all the tragedy today." She couldn't talk about Roger.

"I heard. It's all over the news this morning."

"I'd better get upstairs," Cindy said.

"Take a minute in the biff," Sherry said. "Tell 'em I'm slow today."

She did the best she could with her face. Though her eyes showed the hard cry she'd had, Cindy felt better. She put her purse on the coffee cart and wheeled it into the elevator.

Maybe they won't notice.

Yeah, blame it on the Crosleys.

She settled outside the office door, sighed deeply, and entered.

The private eye was with them both in Skaansgard's office. Cindy was glad that they were discussing the murders and hardly looking at her. Skaansgard noticed nothing. He was talking. "We should not be directing this thing. Be reasonable." It seemed he was arguing against his partner.

"We have to be sure they don't inherit," Bullock said. "They have gone too far."

"Let the police do their job," Skaansgard argued. "We'll cover our bases, but it's their show. Thank you, Cindy."

She poured the coffee, murmured something about Sherry's slowness, passed the pastries, and left. They took no heed.

The phones were still brisk, and Cindy was glad. It kept her busy. Every time she looked at Tommy's picture, she felt like crying. That he and Roger had been so close as children worried her. How Tommy would take it—and on his birthday—she didn't know. He couldn't be reached at the block plant. She wanted to be the one who told him.

She got rid of another radio newsman. All the lines were lit. She picked up one of them.

"Paul!" She held back tears and felt about to break her own rule. "I talked to Memma . . . No, no. She said to keep the party on. That's her way. It's for the best . . . Yes, five o'clock." Her chest burned, filled to bursting. "Oh, Paul, I don't know." She wanted him badly right then. I'm losing my senses. Hang on to something. "You have your hands full, I know. We are flooded here, of course." Then she realized he was returning a call. "Let me put you through to Mr. Skaansgard." The professional voice helped her compose. Before transferring him, she whispered, "I'll see you at five."

8

Brookside

INGSTROM HAD HAD IT. People, he brooded. Get away from people. He needed to be alone. "Pull over here, would you?" Marly was driving him home. Daddy Fizzy was asleep in the back seat.

"Here?" she said. They coasted down the rail overpass from the London Road strip. The street had turned residential and dark.

"Right here, if you would," Ingstrom said. "This'll be great."

Marly looked at him as if he were just slightly crazy. "It's a couple of miles."

"I need the walk," he said. "Don't worry." He toyed with her hair and squeezed her tiny, shapely arm.

The last two hours had been horrid. From Joe Huey's Marly had driven them back to the apartment where Skip was going bonkers. He had grabbed Ingstrom by the collar, "What the hell was in that stuff? You really screwed me over."

There was little Ingstrom could do except stay cool. Skip was a tall, tough guy, too nervous and excitable for his own good. Ingstrom just went with it, didn't resist.

Janey spoke up. "Leave him be, Skip. He's here to help."

The big man put him down. "Sorry, I'm all worked up about this." Ingstrom nodded.

"I mean, Christ," Skip was off again, "I'm having a party and suddenly some little shit is dead in my bathroom, and we have to break down the door and clean up the mess, and now what the hell are we going to do?"

Ingstrom didn't want to look at Roger's body. He didn't have to. He had already worked it out. He was just waiting for Skip to give him an entry. "Can we sit a minute?" he said.

The whole bunch of them took to the pillows around a coffee table. They were all looking to Ingstrom.

"First off, that shit was clean. You had a first-timer and a beginner and an old head. Janey got the purest stuff. The other two had cuts according to their experience." He looked around the little circle. Skip queried Janey with a glance.

"He's right," she said. "I was working with John, and Roger slipped my bag into his pocket. I thought he was out looking for you." She nodded at Ingstrom. "He must have gone right to the bathroom."

Even though he was the youngest one in the room, Ingstrom moved on with the assurance of a chairman of the board. This was what Fizzy had come to him for. "Okay, let's solve our problem." He was careful to emphasize "our" for Skip's benefit. "This is what we're going to do."

Skip didn't want to take part in moving the body, but he didn't want Roger's corpse in his house either. Ingstrom was calm, in command. Skip sat with his head in his hands.

"We roll him up in this rug. Move him in Fizzy's wagon across Mesabi Avenue to his apartment up the hill. We put him in bed. His grandmother lives upstairs, but she's real old. Bring his needle and bag, the spoon too, and we'll leave them there. Got gloves?"

It had been gruesome, with Skip complaining all the way, especially about the carpet. Janey poked her head in the car to kiss Skip on the cheek before they left. "You're getting an assist here, darling," she said. It didn't help. On the way back he wouldn't shut up. "So I'm minus a rug now. A broken door and no rug."

Janey wasn't there to smooth him over it, so Marly, all of fifteen years old, put him in his place. "You've got your life, don't you?" Everyone murmured thoughtfully. "Anyway, I don't think you want that old carpet hanging around." After that, Skip kept his mouth shut. They dropped him off in the alley and drove east to drop Ingstrom at home.

Ingstrom watched Marly. The glow of the instrument panel made her look almost pretty. She's too young to be as mature as she acts, Ingstrom thought. Nothing fazes her. Probably she's seen a lot, he considered. She wasn't the type to say much, and like her brother could be counted on. Good breeding, Ingstrom decided, then at once reflected that his dad would soil his pants to even suspect he'd had that thought.

Ingstrom didn't have to say anything to Marly about keeping it quiet, so he just said, "Thanks. See you around."

He shut the car door and stood back. Marly pulled a U-turn and cruised quietly away. Ingstrom watched her taillights move up and over the WPA-built railroad overpass on the way back to the West End. The red eyes sank below the hill into the glow of the strip.

"Nice girl," Ingstrom said.

The relief of darkness closed over him like a sigh. He moved off the curb toward the high wrought-iron fences lining the wide sidewalk and began his swaying gait toward home. He walked deliberately, brushing the grass beside the walk with the toes of his deck shoes, sweeping up the fragrance the night had laid down. He patted the stiles of the fence with a loose hand and breathed deeply the cedars' oily scent rolling off their flat fingers. He rubbed the scruff of the lofty brick pilasters and counted the steps between each: four, five, four and a half.

Ingstrom peered through the gloom of the cedars and

pines looking across the broad, woodsy grounds of the industrialists' old estates that lined London Road. He paddled the bars of two shut gates he passed with a comb he took from his hip pocket. Locked up for the night, he supposed. He caught a glimmer off the lake down one driveway. Lake Superior was far off, across "private property." Ingstrom snorted the words. He resented them. He resented the fences, even the low one that surrounded his parents' house, and these gates, barring people from the lake. Fences make good neighbors. Ha. But they can't contain greed. He shook his head. He caught a strong pine-pitch scent from the huge trunk that nearly touched the fence. The sidewalk swelled and lifted over the roots. The groomed woodlot he allowed if only for the fusilade of its fragrances. But the rest stood in the way, blocked the view.

The huge pine lifted the sidewalk for three paces. Ingstrom caught a toe on an upturned, broken slab but danced away instead of tripping. The fencing here was low-built, coming only to his waist—doubled wrought-iron arches between widespread spear-tipped stanchions. He pitched forward and grabbed an arced rail to cant over the barrier. Why had he vaulted that fence? Had he felt a tug from the midnight lake? Did the cedar fronds wave him over on a current of sharp breath? Did he actually stumble? Perhaps he leapt the fence when car lights rose behind him at the hill and beamed his way. Indeed, he had not wanted to be seen. Whether it was magnificence, intoxication, accident, prudence or curiosity, he knew it was not the opulence of London Road living that drew him in. He hated the money "they" —his family and others—had tried to buy him with. Let them choke on it. Anyway, he already had nearly enough of his own, and fairly earned. He felt quite sure.

Once over the fence, Ingstrom stooped behind an erect

stone slab, crouching as an oncoming car passed. Was it a police cruiser? He waited for his eyes to readjust to the gloom and surveyed the grounds he could see from that spot. Christ, I'm in a cemetery.

The trees were thick toward the road and along each side of the graveyard, but they thinned out considerably toward the lake. He drifted from headstone to grave marker toward the water. Away from the street, crypts and mausoleums blocked the sound of passing cars.

Ingstrom had been there before. He recalled Willy and him smoking a joint back there in 9th grade. Somewhere was a bridge they'd crossed from an adjoining mansion. Yes, and Gus is buried here, he remembered. His great-grandfather's grave lay toward the back of the cemetery, near the creek on a hillock overlooking the giant lake. Ingstrom was drawn to that grave through memory of the internment. Was I six? Seven? I'll find out. He recalled the heaped soil leeching its acidic odor from under the tarp. To Ingstrom it became the reek of death. Piney decease.

He rambled through the necropolis, stroking walls of monuments, springing over a few low headstones, weaving his way toward water: the muffled gurgle of Tischer Creek flowing down to the lapping chill of Lake Superior. Through the maze of stone and trees he spotted the tall granite slab— the penny he had called it, for the giant copper medallion set deep in its surface—surging heavenward between twin pines. Gustav Ingstrom's monument to himself and his accomplishments towered above the family plot, a roughhewn ton of stone taller than any man, housing on its huge copper coin the larger-than-life noble profile of an industrialist's banker. Ingstrom bristled at the clear resemblance to his father.

I was seven, he thought, checking the dates on stones

below the monolith. Great-grandpa Gus had the pillar erected long before his death. Smaller slabs set at its foot told of family births and deaths. Ingstrom hadn't known the wife. He ran a deck shoe over the dates. He stood swaying before the dolmen shaking his head slowly.

"Sorry, Gus," he told the metal profile, "this is where it stops. No more Ingstrom bankers to kowtow to the gods of industry, none to count their golden beans. I'm hopping a different freighter, one that floats on water, not on the backs of men." Using people isn't my style, he thought. "The times they are a-changing," and I'm changing with them. Leave business to people like you or dear old Dad. I want a life, not a monument.

Standing on tiptoe, he reached up and patted Gustav's copper cheek with his fingertips. "So long, old boy, I'll stop by if I come this way again. Lest you forget me," he said and unbuttoned his fly. "Unto Caesar render what is his."

Ingstrom left the family plot. He heard the creek talking faintly to itself below, and he smelled the mosses that grew alongside it. He followed a sharp-gravel path leading toward the sounds and found the stone footbridge arching over the ravine. He paused over the stream, leaning on the stone side rail, looking down to the sound of water hiding in the dark. He heard rustling. A deer? He listened for the animal's passage, but it must have stilled itself. He followed the bridge and stopped beside a soaring mansion overlooking the lake beyond.

Another deer?

He couldn't be sure. He'd turned with the sound. Had he seen someone up near front of the house? Had a figure ducked into the bushes at the corner above the creek? Ingstrom moved cautiously along, carefully placing each foot in soft grass or matted needles. He worked his way through trees, from trunk to trunk toward the front of the house until he could touch the dark corner rising above the bushes. He peered out on a driveway defined by an avenue of elms. He was sure now which mansion it was.

He had been brought there by Willy, whose great aunt or some such lived there. Maybe his great-grandmother's second cousin. Ingstrom smiled at that thought. They'd explored the house and its secret passages. Were we ten then? He wondered. Fun. He looked along the façade. No one was there.

Ingstrom returned to the trees and worked his way back down until he stood below the house in the shadows of pines nearer the lake. He looked behind him. From the lower side, the house rose a long and imposing three stories over grounds that sloped open and wide down to the lake. He knew the boathouse stood behind the white pines over there on the shore. Ingstrom crept down toward it, keeping within the pines' darkness until he reached the rocky beach. Out of sight of the house now, he picked his way across the felsite rock, smoothed over centuries by the waves, to the hewn-stone dock alongside the boathouse. He sat. He watched the night play on the water. He leaned back on the cut-rock breakwater and dreamed of sailing.

Out across the water the Wisconsin shore streamed away, disappearing beyond as the lake spread to the south and east. The land and water seemed to push the constellations into the sky, wheeling around the North Star. Ingstrom looked over his left shoulder for Polaris, but it was hidden somewhere beyond the tallest elms at the far end of the house. He stood, rolled his shoulders back, and bent his neck to gaze high, straight up to where his pole star floated.

"Alpha Cygni," he whispered drawing the sibilant sounds of the name around the fulcrum of the hard g. To Ingstrom the name breathed a rhapsody of the sea. It called him to the ocean. He pronounced the name again. Still stretching back, letting the intensity of the star and its partners in the triangle burn into his eyes. He barely breathed, "Deneb," an older name, a heavy, blunt sound. He wanted to remember the romance of the summer triangle when, for him, it would fail to rise above the southern seas of the Indian Ocean. He chose the names as well as the stars he followed. I'll take the Roman Swan over the Arabic Tail any day, he concluded.

Though he yearned for a new sky that he thought would bring him back a childhood—one that had been despoiled by family and social obligations, by seven-thirty dinners that for him were as regimented as a military academy, even if the mink-trimmed women and their dandy bankers made them fluid, bantering affairs—Ingstrom wanted to carry far off with him the vision of northern stars. His wonder at the stars had led to his affection for the sea. He craved the Southern Cross and places that no one he knew had visited. Yet he understood that nothing could outshine a night like this along the shores of this giant lake.

The rumble of the foghorn down by Joe Huey's brought him back to earth. He lowered his gaze to Wisconsin to find it had disappeared behind a swelling cloud bank. In no more than six repetitions of the horn's blast that felt its way over three miles of its soupy wetness, the fog bank had grown high and thick. Like a damp cloth lowered to a feverish forehead, the mist touched Ingstrom's skin and sent a chill through him down to the fingertips and toes. In the moments the vapor first rolled across the dock, shortening its length each second, out of a sole Norway pine that grew at the side of the boathouse doorway, high up from a bough that stretched toward the lake, an owl that must have been eyeing Ingstrom spread wings as wide as the reach of his own arms, swooped low from its perch, and moving directly over his head sailed without shadow over the lawn then rose steeply above the dormers of the house to disappear into the gloom beyond the mansion's roof. Standing silent as the fog, Ingstrom breathed with the swooshing sound of the owl's wings, in and out, following the bird, disappearing with him past the bastion's walls.

Through the murk that also seemed to have followed the flight of the owl while growing denser as it advanced, the house extended its dominion and intimidation across the open lawn. The behemoth from a long-gone age cast its piercing profile toward the lake as if to examine and chart each ship that sailed by toward the harbor, that it might extract its fees for the right of passage and safety. As he watched the darkened mass of the house dissolve into the gray mist, Ingstrom caught a dash of light that flared from a basement window of the house. Like the owl, the flash drew him. He walked, invisible now, across the open lawn directly to the spot he had seen emit the light. As he neared that end of the house, its windows took shape, watching sternly through the gloom. One lighted casement far up and away from him shone steadily. He slowed, moving cautiously, without sound. Across a stone walk, down a short brick stair, he saw a lower-level door ajar.

Ingstrom crouched. He was ten feet from the door. He felt himself flow into the fog, into the silence, into the stillness. He waited for a sound. None came. He crept further. He moved toward the dark opening. Ingstrom, dissolved in the haze and the darkness of the house's shadows, removed his shoes, placed them amidst a growth of snow-on-the-mountain that bordered the foundation. He rose and padded down the brick stairs. He slipped into a long vestibule that ran along the basement wall. Right then—or so it seemed to him—he ceased for a time being flesh and became a shade unseen, hollow, inexistent. He was out of himself.

Inside, a long line of windows placed at the top of the outside wall broke the shadows of the gloom below, geometrically dividing the floor and far wall into luminous rectangles. The depth of the dark in here made the billowing brume outside seem bright. Ingstrom slid his stocking feet across the floor of what was—he remembered from his visits with Willy—an underpass sunk beneath the veranda above, plumbing a distance a few feet below the grade of the lawn. He moved to a half-open window in this passage that led into the basement of the house proper. At the window, he pulled on the gloves Janey had given him. Was it just tonight? It seemed a year ago. He swept shards of broken glass off the windowsill and levered himself through the raised sash. He stepped on a davenport placed just inside, below the window. Ingstrom was in.

He was ten again. He knew the house. In pitch darkness, he moved through the large room he'd entered. To the door opposite the huge central fireplace of the room, he put an ear and listened intently. The fog-sailor knew someone else, maybe a night watchman, was moving through the house. Up by the gate, he had seen something. A man? Then the light had flared from the porch.

In the basement, he heard nothing through that door. He opened it a crack. It was darker in this room than on the porch and beyond the door darker still. Ingstrom squeezed through the smallest opening he dared make and, once through, he pressed into a corner of the blackness on the other side. Of the pitch dark asked, a watchman? Why would he break that window? That doubt tensed his spine. Silently, he reached back to close the door behind him. Ingstrom waited in the corner, listening.

The house abode silently in its vastness. At this end of the corridor, Ingstrom stood stock-still. Can I be seen? At the other end, sixty feet or more away, a faint glow from an electric light fanned out from behind a partition wall. He knew that was the kitchen stair. He slid down the one wall of the corridor past a closed double door, a closet door, and on to an alcove. In this area, toward the back of the house again, he saw the central stairway, leading to the great main hall above, a hall that had overwhelmed him on his first visit as a young boy. Its austere grandness had dwarfed and humbled him. He had soon pushed that feeling down as his friend Willy strode confidently through the space. Now, Ingstrom paused. Yes, this was stair he and Willy had played under. They'd found old toys in a cubby beneath the flight that led upward.

Halt. Ingstrom's voice sounded in his mind. Above him, a creak on the stair stopped his breath. He melted to the wall. Yes, there it was again. Weight had shifted on a step. Someone was going up the stairway above him. As if tuning a console radio in the night, he shut his eyes to let the sound clear, become distinct. The movement was slow as stealth itself.

This is no night watchman, he decided. He breathed in, expanded his psychic reach to the floor above him as if gazing into a night sky. He sensed another creak as faint as mist passing through an owl's wingtips. A six-foot man, on the heavy side appeared to his closed eyes.

Then, as if swinging down the sidewalk as he had done earlier, Ingstrom opened his eyes, left the alcove, and swayed silently down the hall to the kitchen stair. His stockinged ascent raised no alarm.

Now he was sure. The house opened to him like a blueprint to a builder. He scooted up to the kitchen without hesitation—left, left, left again, right—then bounded up the servant's stair to the second floor. He was light, fast, silent. He knew the heavier man was still working his way up the main flight, now just creeping across the landing, making his final turn. Ingstrom squeezed through a heavy door to the second-floor hall and boldly moved toward the head of the main staircase. A tread creaked loudly, and someone stirred in a room opposite the head of the staircase. For once, Ingstrom had no thougtht of what to do. He felt intoxicated but lucid. He saw as an owl and moved as bravely.

In the upper hallway, he glided toward the sounds, pressed to the wall, his senses wildly alive, his reflexes alert. He sensed the stair-walker had paused at the rousing in the next room. Had he stopped halfway up? A grunt, as someone rose from a chair or bed, sounded through that door opposite the balustrade. Two steps away, Ingstrom froze. He backed through a partly open doorway behind him. In a bedroom there, an old woman slept in a hospital bed just feet away. At once Ingstrom pivoted and hid behind the door.

The door across the hall opened. "Who is out here?" a woman's voice said. She may have glanced past his door at the old woman in bed, and Ingstrom listened to her stump toward the main staircase. "What're you doing here at this hour?" she cried out to the man on the stair. Then, as she scrambled back across the hall, Ingstrom softly guided his door closed.

The woman in the hall abruptly stopped. Then she screamed. Something tumbled down the stairs. As Ingstrom turned the door bolt, the woman in bed stirred. He turned to find her awake. Her immediate aplomb just arising from sleep returned him to flesh, from hollow shade back to physical existence.

"Reese," she said, "what are you doing here?"

Later, he thought the obvious and intense mayhem out in the hall had led him on. His name, even used with such familiarity, had seemed foreign to him. That didn't matter, but he couldn't dismiss those other thoughts.

The grand bedroom, its furnishing and fireplace, woodwork crafted by carpenters on site, the spacious, sprawling house higher than the trees that circled it, the vast property with gardener's, boats', and caretaker's houses, servant quarters, and, beyond, the investments: land, timber, paper, ore, office buildings, and a spate of castle-like homes strewn across the entire country, all surrounded this one old woman. For what? To protect her? To entertain her? To dignify her? Ingstrom wondered. At what human cost? At whose expense? These thoughts sprang forth spontaneously. He had conjured them long before. Now, the musings by themselves formulated an idea.

Ingstrom couldn't ignore the bile that rose in his throat, the pressure that grew in his chest and arms, the clarity of his teeming mind.

The woman pushed up a little on an arm. "What is going on out there, Reese? What are you doing here?" she said.

Ingstrom moved to the bed. He looked with calm eyes directly into hers. "I came to help you," he said and reached for the pillow.

Ingstrom felt something thump in the staircase landing the other side of the fireplace wall. He let go the pillow. The old woman was still. Stairs creaked. He heard a heavy tread in the hall. His heightened senses told him the watchman had just entered the room across the hall.

Ingstrom put an ear to the door. He heard water running. Was the man washing? Ingstrom turned the door latch and opened the door a crack, then wider. The water stopped. He listened. Rustling, rummaging, movements advanced. If he waited longer, he'd meet the watchman face to face. He repositioned the pillow. The stair? The closet? Under the bed? Those were his options. He heard keys. He slid under the bed.

In seconds the burglar had entered the hall and then the old woman's room. He closed the door quietly and came straight to the bed. Ingstrom saw his shoes, heard the satin swish of the pillow. The bed moved as if the man were pressing down hard, pulsing through his shoulders, bearing down with might. Ingstrom found himself holding his breath. It went on a long time. Finally the watchman let up. It was as if the entire bed frame relaxed. The man did not move from the bedside. He was fumbling with something in the bedding. Ingstrom breathed ever so softly. The watchman wandered about the room while Ingstrom curled away from his movements. He shifted by inches, keeping out of sight.

The man was noisy, opening drawers, digging in the closet, spilling boxes on the floor. His movements seemed aimless, random, without purpose. Ingstrom listened and shied away when the burglar seemed likely to discover his hiding place. Otherwise he held still, breathing guardedly and lightly. The man again approached the bed, and his shoes showed below its sheets inches from Ingstrom. The man tossed something atop the covers. He went back and forth three times carrying things, it seemed, to the bed and throwing them—into what? A suitcase? After what seemed an eternity, the watchman secured his cache and left. He walked out the bedroom door, down the main staircase, and further below to the basement. That is where Ingstrom lost his sounds. He would wait.

Ingstrom lay directly beneath the old woman. His rage had left him, whether through his own or the watchman's actions, he couldn't tell. He felt drained. He thought he heard the muffled barking of a dog. He lay still. He decided it came from outside, far off.

Now the house was absolutely still. He drifted. He thought he heard a car start. He stayed put. He waited. He let his tension flow out and soak into the carpet under him.

He was thinking of sailing. He was thinking of the money he needed. He was thinking of the ring and the watch the old woman wore. He knew Randy would have a market for them. Twice he felt ill. He thought about shipping out, and the sick feeling drifted away. He waited and thought.

He couldn't have slept. But he must have. Daylight had crept into the room. The sun wasn't yet up, but it was not far from rising. Ingstrom slipped from beneath the bed. He stretched. He turned to the woman. The pillow now covered her face. He didn't touch her. The ring and the watch were gone. Ingstrom wanted to go, but he surveyed the room. Jewelry was spilled on the floor over by the windows. He approached to look out.

The lake was still hidden by cloud. Mists clung to the lawn and billowed halfway up the pines. He thought he saw a ship headed toward the harbor through the murky haze. He leaned over a glass case at the window to get a better view. If it was a ship, he wished he were on it. Going the wrong way? He wondered. The fog was too thick to tell. He looked down at the curio case on which he was leaning. The rows of artifacts inside, disheveled and strewn with broken glass, looked more valuable than the jewelry. He picked a coin out of the shards. It looked old. Leave the rest, Reese, he told himself. Avoid greed. He moved to the door. Ingstrom pocketed the coin and slipped through into the hall.

He took the main staircase. It was a gory mess. He had been right to hide. The watchman was a brute. A woman lay across the window seat on the landing beaten, bloody, and stiff as Roger had been. Ingstrom's gut revolted. He held his mouth, retraced his route outside and spewed onto the snow-on-the-mountain. That's enough for one night, he thought. He felt for his shoes and, stepping to the grass, put them on. He was unsteady. Twice he went to his hands, jamming his knees into his stomach and retching. Dry heaves.

The fog was lifting. He needed to hurry. But he was careful to keep to the cover of the trees. He climbed down to the creek below the house. It afforded the best shelter. A car engine started. He flattened against the creek bank. Listening intently, he tracked the car as it turned around and moved up the drive. As it passed, Ingstrom popped up to see who might be driving, but bushes blocked his view.

He followed the stream up close to the road and climbed a brick staircase to the open driveway gate. The car had just turned toward town and was gone. Ingstrom brushed himself off, removed the gloves, and folded them into his back pocket. He took the coin from his pocket and held it as he swung around the pilaster to the sidewalk along London Road. He commenced his swaying gait. The sun had risen and the fog lifted. He was alone on the sidewalk.

Swinging down the sidewalk, Ingstrom felt better. He was tired, but that wouldn't last. He had plenty of time to sleep. His nausea was gone; he felt stronger with each stride. Two blocks up, a car turned onto London Road coming his way. He kept his gait. The driver shot an arm out the window and waved. Ingstrom kept ambling on.

West End

Paul Tuomi parked under the maples a block and a half from home. He was looking for a patch of shade and a moment of peace. The day had been a hot one. Even through the filter of the trees, the sun baked his bare arms, and the turgid air stuck his shirt to his chest.

It was yesterday's shirt. When he'd thrown it on that morning after Memma called, it had already cried out for laundering. All day he'd worked in those clothes dashing back and forth through downtown, between Brookside and headquarters, between headquarters and Memma's.

Paul wasn't just smelly and hot. He was angry. He'd yelled at his staff, at his boss, even at the coroner, and if he went home now he certainly would bellow at his wife. He had hoped to out-wait her, parking up the hill so he could watch her leave. But time had nearly run out. He needed to be at Tommy's party soon and wasn't showing up there un-showered, without a shave or clean clothes.

He'd been watching the house for twenty minutes. Pamela's Fairlane crouched in the drive. At least her mother wasn't parked at the curb. That would have cost more time and caused more trouble.

He could almost hear her complaints and Pamela's, too. "A bigger house may not suit you, Paul, but a bigger driveway should. I have to park on the street every time I visit." He couldn't handle the two together. He found he'd married them both. His mother-in-law half suggested joining them on the honeymoon. "I've never seen Port au Prince." She had taken over the wedding, of course, and six years later stepped in to direct Alex's funeral as well. "You have too much on your minds. I'll take this on." And she did, both times running up bills he was still paying. When he asked to see receipts for the grand wake she said, "He's your son, for god's sake." He kept his response short: "Was."

Heat and in-laws, a marriage marred and soured weren't Paul's only problems. It had been toward noon, and only after he blew his top at the desk staff and then with his boss had the investigative team been dispatched to Memma's. All that time Roger lay face down with the morning sun beating on the paisley curtains, heating the room.

"Christ, it's been nearly six hours since I called that in. And everybody dropped the ball." He straightened, put his hand on his chest and hung his head. "Including me." In the crush of the press and the large team he was expected to manage at Brookside, he had actually forgotten about Roger. He couldn't believe it and couldn't forgive his own lapse.

After leaving Memma and Elma with Bushy standing guard, he'd sped down Second Street to the Brookside scene. Though his house sat only blocks away and he had thought to shower quickly and change, he was lucky he didn't stop at home. Already, Brookside's driveway had been jammed with cars and vans, the press was crowding the gate and a television crew was setting up on the sidewalk. Men brandishing microphones tried to get by the squad car parked astride the gate. Inside, all sorts of people—house staff, fellow detectives, the district attorney, and patrolmen—had walked around the landing where one body lay, mucked around the entry point in the basement and tramped through Miss Crosley's bedroom. Even the FBI had beaten him to the scene.

Paul didn't know why he was chosen to lead the investigation, and at that point he didn't care. On the drive over, he had been consumed with Roger and Memma up on the rocky hill overlooking the West End. Once he was back in the East End, death actually seemed sunnier, more a public spectacle, less personal, and far less lonely. The only thing the scenes had in common was his disciplined point of view. Get control of this, pronto. He told the two detectives, actually his seniors, to call in all personnel and vacate the house while the three of them surveyed it. He invited a fourth, the federal agent, to join them. Christ, he'd thought, it's like flies to dung here.

He was uneasy about the number of intrusions at the scene, but took it from where he found it. In the three hours he spent there that morning, he felt he had gained control and moved the investigation in the right direction. He made a list for his team. He had officers combing the grounds— look for trespass, he told them, though to Paul's mind they were looking for anything that might connect the young man he had seen walking that morning. He felt sure the kid either knew something valuable or might be involved is some way.

In the middle of all this, he thought of Memma.

When a call to the desk revealed that nothing had been done with Roger's room, he handed his list to one of the senior detectives and calmly excused himself. "I'll be back in an hour." He sped to City Hall, siren on, fuming, and had it out with the desk sergeant and his boss. He then went to Memma's to relieve Bushy and wait for the promised team.

"Sorry, Bushy, all hell broke loose. You know, when something happens out east, we drop everything and run."

Bushy nodded. "Same time, same station," he said. "It's no problem. I'm always willing to help." They threw a hug at each other and patted backs.

The head of the investigative team arrived. He told Paul who had been assigned the case. Paul was off it. "Boss says you got enough to handle out east." He knew the man and, though he'd rather handle it himself, said nothing.

Something in his chest burned. It made him cough. I suppose yelling at the chief didn't help. I'm over my head.

"All right, I'm leaving it to you," Paul said. He showed the lab team his early morning efforts and took the key to Roger's apartment from its nail.

"I'll let you draw your own conclusions. Drop a report copy on my desk, would you?"

Paul looked down the street. Pamela's car had not moved. He sighed and started the Buick. Better get this over with before Mommy comes around, he thought. Paul knew the two women were to attend some gala event this evening, and Pamela usually went to her mother's house beforehand. That way they could arrive in the Cadillac. Pamela's plans gave Paul cover to attend Tommy's party, and he hoped the Brookside thing wouldn't quash her event. No, he decided, it's too good a chance for heavy gossip. I'm just as bad, Paul thought. He had already thought to use the murder investigation as an excuse, just in case. And it was true. Pamela would expect him to work overtime on this one. The truth was that Paul was going to make a few visits out west later on. He needed help and had some favors to ask.

Paul put the Buick in gear, pulled from the curb, and cruised down the hill toward home. He parked across the street, crossed, and walked up the drive. Pamela did not come to the window. He slipped in through the garage and tried to make it to the shower before she caught him.

Too late: Pamela was standing in the bedroom, fists on her hips.

"You didn't even call," she said without preamble. "I waited here for hours, and you didn't even call. And look at you. You're filthy and stinking. Of course, you don't care what people think. Here you are the lead detective on the biggest case in Duluth history and you can't even put on a clean shirt!"

Paul roared. "What? Who told you that?" He took a step toward her.

"Well, Daddy . . . ." She stopped short. "I mean it is on the news, you know."

He let out the anger and frustration that had been building all afternoon. The press had been insufferable, doing everything but climbing the fence. One crew had approached by boat and had to be chased back by the Coast Guard. He had to try to undo mistake after mistake his colleagues had made at the scene. And now Skaansgard? What was he up to? The lawyer had put calls into the office—had probably talked to his boss—and finally phoned the mansion itself. Suddenly, Paul saw the hand of the trustees in this.

"So now we're working with Daddy? Sure, he's got to keep his finger in the pie, doesn't he?" Paul advanced toward her. "And you're no better."

She backed around the bed, cowering before his rage, but reversed direction when he seethed at her.

"Someone has to look out for us. And so what? You won't do it. Listen. This is the biggest thing you'll ever see. You can get the promotion we need—the one you've worked so hard for. This will be a feather in your cap." She looked at him, playing Daddy's sweet little girl, but she acted as if he were about to blow. "Be reasonable, Paul."

Her coyness fueled his heat. His shirt was soaked, his whole body felt tight. "Oh, no. Get your head out of the sack. It isn't about me or about us. It's about the money. It always is and it always will be with you people. Money, money, money," he shouted. She pressed against the wall. "I know what Daddy wants. He couldn't help telling me. He tracked me all over town today to make sure I got the message. He probably called here."

Paul was rolling now. He thrust out his chin and looked hard at his wife. "Yeah, I'm right. He called here first, looking for me, didn't he, didn't he?" He'd taken her by the shoulders.

"No, he didn't." She glared into his eyes. "It was that snotty office girl of his. She woke me up," Pamela said, nearly shrieking it. She writhed in his grip.

"I wish someone would. I've been trying for years," Paul yelled. "Snotty? I bet. Isn't that usually your department? Didn't you win Miss Snotty of East High School?" He let go her shoulders. "I'm taking a shower."

He shed his shirt and pants along the way and headed for the bathroom.

Never one to lose an argument, Pamela followed, picking up his cast-off clothes. "No, it's you who are stuck up and selfish. Always running out west. Always thinking about yourself and your long-lost friends. Living in the past. You've thought of no one else since, since Alex got sick."

Paul shook his head but didn't turn around. "Don't even mention his name. Don't bring him into this." He slammed and locked the bathroom door, dropped his shorts and climbed into the shower. He could hear Pamela shouting in the hall.

When Paul emerged from the bathroom, Pamela was gone, the driveway empty.

The shower had helped. He felt clean and new. Soaping up cleared his mind. He thought through parts of the day. Now he was sure. Skaansgard had pulled strings to get him appointed lead detective. The lawyer hadn't admitted it, but during the call it should have been clear to Paul that that had happened. "Listen, Paul, this is big for you," Pamela's father had said.

Paul had been pulled off the case most important to him and redirected to the one that mattered to the bigwigs downtown. Shit, Paul thought, they didn't even know about Roger. And they didn't care. These were people who thought they could control him and his investigation. Once a traitor, are you always one? He wondered. Paul was not as sure as his father-in-law that he had left the West End behind.

His call back to Skaansgard had been taken on a speaker, he could tell. Bullock and maybe others were listening in. The lawyer didn't pick any bones about it. He wanted to pin the murders on Miss Crosley's daughter and her oddball husband. Now that he had a chance to put his mind to it, it all made sense to Paul. If they could get that conviction, it would save the trust a couple of million, maybe more. Skaansgard worked it smoothly.

"I heard you were assigned the case and thought you should know what others are saying," he'd started out. Paul could just see the trial-lawyer-turned-trust-manager striding past the desk speakerphone as if before a jury. He could see Skaansgard pacing in his office turning the imaginary jury against the defendants, the wayward daughter and her husband. "We're with you all the way, son," Skaansgard had said. Paul had been interested but not convinced.

He hadn't told Skaansgard his suspicions about the young man he had seen that morning walking the London Road sidewalk. He had a hunch about the boy, but he avoided argument and didn't show his hand. It wasn't really Skaansgard's business.

"It is too soon to draw conclusions," he told the lawyer.

"We are still collecting evidence." Now he was glad he'd kept it close. His father-in-law would manipulate everything to get what he called justice. It wasn't long, though, before Paul found out Skaansgard's ideas had spread, for, when he brought his idea to his boss, the chief was quick to dismiss it. Everyone seemed to be on the same page: the daughter did it.

His boss squared his shoulders and spoke carefully to Paul. "Look, I don't want to overlook any evidence, but a hunch isn't much to go on and the description of this kid could match a hundred, maybe two hundred boys in town. It isn't a crime to walk in the early morning."

Paul insisted. He wanted it checked out.

"Okay, okay. But don't lose sight of the obvious. Crosley was rich. And her will is full of suspects who had a lot to gain when she died. Some of them are flat broke and in debt to their eyeballs. Do you see a connection?" The chief stood, brushed his suit with his hand, and said, "I've got a news conference to prepare for."

Nothing more was said. Paul eventually assigned a junior detective to the "morning walker" part of the probe. He wanted to question the neighbors. Maybe someone could ID the kid. That would be a start.

Paul pushed his hair back, running his fingers over the tops of his ears. A haircut tomorrow wouldn't hurt, I suppose.

He was going to be late for the party. Just twenty minutes, but he pushed the Buick down Third Street as fast as he could. He waved at the one patrol officer who recognized him immediately and let him speed past. Paul drove over Observation Hill, taking First Street below Memma's and back up Piedmont to Third, to the house where Cindy had been born and lived half of her life. He parked in front and took the present out of his trunk. He tossed his coat over the service revolver that had sat there all day. The evening had yet to advance. It was still hot.

Paul didn't know what to expect inside, but he felt more relaxed than he had all day. This is where you belong, he told himself. He entered without knocking and made his way toward the kitchen. Cindy met him in the living room.

"Oh, Paul! You've come," she said.

She came to him. He gave a quick lookout for Tommy and folded her in his arms. He held her not like a lover but more like a family friend who was sharing tragic news. "I wanted to do this all day," he said.

Cindy turned her face to his. "It was as if no one cared about anything but Miss Crosley. I couldn't even talk about Memma or Roger at the office. Poor Roger!"

"Poor Memma," he said.

Cindy held his gaze. She wanted something, he could tell.

"Could you bring Tommy out of the bedroom?" she said. "I think he's been crying. He's only just heard about Roger. The East End news was all anyone talked about at the brickyard. So he's been in there half an hour. I wanted to wait until you came."

He patted her back and hugged her again. "Let me see what I can do."

Since Alex's death, Paul had let his feelings for Tommy grow stronger. After Alex, he was a father looking for a son, and, even though Tommy was a few years older than Alex, he needed a father. The transfer of affection amazed Paul. It was so easy he'd felt guilty. The comfort it afforded also drew him more and more back to the West End, to his early life there and, of course, closer to Cindy. In effect, Paul became Tommy's dad.

Paul entered the bedroom. It was on the morning side of the house that stood just a few feet from its neighbor, so the blinds were shut and Elma had draped the window. It was dark inside. He closed the door and let his eyes adjust.

Tommy greeted him. "Hi, Paul."

Paul located Tommy sitting on the far edge of the bed, hunched over, twisting his face over his shoulder and up toward him. "I suppose it's not going so good," Paul said.

Tommy straightened up, "Yeah. Some birthday, huh? I feel bad for Memma."

Paul moved around the bed and laid a hand on Tommy's slim shoulder. "She'll be all right, at least in the long run. She's tough but with a heart of gold." He squeezed the boy's shoulder. "Say, you're putting up some muscle here."

Tommy didn't pull away. "Loading cement blocks all day will do that." He seemed pleased. "Paul, they're saying it might have been suicide. I hate to think that."

Paul hadn't, in his rush, stopped to see the report. It might not have been on his desk yet, and though surprised at the idea he stood steady for Tommy. "Who is 'they?'" he said.

"I guess the officers up the hill, maybe the coroner. Some people talked to them and came down with the news." Tommy shook his head, "I don't think so, though."

More sloppy police work yakking with passersby. Paul was more ashamed than angered, though he knew he should have been hopping mad. "Did they talk to Memma? I mean the detectives?"

Tommy shook his head, "I don't know. You can't tell anything about her. It's as if my birthday was the only thing in the world she's worried about. She wants everything to be happy."

"That's Memma, Tommy," Paul said. "It's police business now, but I can tell you this, Roger's death was an accident, probably an overdose, and he didn't get back home on his own. So other people know exactly what happened." Though Tommy was likely to know the people who hung with Roger, Paul fought down the urge to ask police questions. "It was not suicide," he said.

Tommy looked relieved, reassured. "Rog was a lot of things, but he wasn't a quitter. He was just reckless."

Paul agreed but didn't say so. He sat on the edge of the bed next to Tommy. He put his arm over the boy's shoulders. "Let's just join Memma and your grandmother and have us a party. No matter what has happened or when, you're still the birthday boy. I brought you a present, and I for one want a piece of that cake."

Tommy nodded. They both rose. Paul, in a rush of emotion he had suppressed all day, wrapped Tommy in a tight hug and pulled him close, stroking the back of his neck and shoulders, "Hang in there, son, you're a fine young man."

Tommy tightened his own arms around Paul. His chest heaved twice, then he let go. He stood back and smiled. "Let's party," he said.

The party went well. The five of them ate Elma's fritalja, a fish paprikash she made with walleye and spaghetti, topped with Berta's sugo.

"Got to have pasta," Berta announced.

Tommy had a couple of friends stop by for cake afterwards. The next-door neighbors from each side joined in to sing. No one mentioned Roger, but he was in some way there.

Paul was there as a family friend, and he tried to keep his distance from Cindy. Whenever she came near, he was tempted to touch her, even to hold her face and kiss her. That was something he'd not do in public.

At dinner he sat across the table from Cindy, next to

Tommy, which sent the women into a discussion of how handsome they both were. Paul caught a few words they shared at the stove while ladling sauce over pasta: "They look just alike," Berta said.

Elma tried to hush her and said something about Cindy. This happened often. Sometimes Paul felt irritated. He knew what they were talking about. Cindy, though, never joined them, so Paul said nothing. This time, at Tommy's 18th birthday party and with the undercurrents of another youthful death sweeping darkly through, he was touched. Paul glowed. He basked in the attention because he and Tommy shared it. Many times over the last few years, when he'd thought of Alex, Tommy's face appeared. In that way, he had to admit, Tommy had taken his own son's place. And for all his absence from Tommy's early life—Paul had broken with Cindy to marry Pam—Paul was Tommy's unacknowledged father.

When the time for gifts came, Paul produced his roughly wrapped package. "For the college man," he said, "Happy Birthday."

Tommy put on great bravura, holding the package high and extolling the virtues of the colorful paper, the weight of the present, the mystery of it. He tore the wrap open. When he found a pen-and-pencil set tied to a stack of college notebooks, Tommy lifted his wry grin, glanced a second at his mother, and turned to look Paul directly in the eye. "This is special," he said. "Thank you, Paul. I'll think of you when I take notes." He added, "And when I doze off in class." They both laughed. Everyone did.

Berta made a great to-do of the cake. She placed candles along the golden road that led to college on one side of the cake, and she made Tommy eat the piece from the other side that depicted a concrete block wall. "You're going to eat that brickyard, young man," she said. "I hope you'll own it someday."

"I think I'll buy the ore docks first," Tommy countered. Everyone cheered.

The party went well. Cindy had a surprisingly good time. Seeing Paul and Tommy together seeming so close played a soothing tune to her warring heart.

Should I after all this time?

Yeah, after ten years mum, you'll become a blabbermouth.

He should know for certain.

So, are you willing to lose him?

That won't happen.

Oh, little Miss-I-know-the-future, huh?

No, but I know Paul.

It was for Tommy, not for Paul or her that she worried over the past. Still, Cindy was proper. She might carry on with the man she'd always loved, but she wouldn't work to trap him in any way. The time to stand up in public will come, she promised herself.

She took her place at the kitchen sink drying and storing the dishes. Cindy ignored the older women's protests. "You have company," they said.

"Company can wait," Cindy told them.

The three women worked in sympathetic silence that Cindy finally broke. "Memma, you stay here with Mom tonight. I don't want you alone up there."

As if in answer to the questions Berta wasn't going to ask, Cindy continued: "Tommy is going stay with you two. He'll sleep on the couch and drive himself to work in the morning. I'll catch a ride home with Paul. He's going to drop in at his dad's on the way back."

Berta tried to be cheerful. "Oh, I'll be fine." She put her

sudsy hands on the sink rim. Her straightened arms shook, and her shoulders heaved. "It'd be nice to have my lovelies around." She took the dishtowel from Cindy and dried her eyes. "Tommy is so handsome." Berta bit her lip and pressed her eyes tight. When she opened them, tears had been replaced by worry. "I have to tell Paul about Father Lucci."

Cindy's spirit was moved. She nearly cried herself. She had hardly ever seen tears from Memma. But the look in Memma's eyes brought out her hard, protective instincts, the kind that had bonded Wendell, Sr. and her own father together on the pickets. The Norwegian and the Serb had stood together, nose to nose with police and Pinkertons, with only that same protective determination that fired Cindy at that moment. "What did Father Lucci tell you, Memma?"

Berta drew in the kitchen air deeply, sighed, and looked to the floor as she shook her head. "He has to see the police report before he can say the Mass. It has to say Roger didn't kill himself." Berta fell on Cindy's shoulder. Elma leaned against Berta's back. The three stood as one at the sink. They let Berta sob a long time.

Cindy stood firm. She determined to protect Memma from any more hurt. From the church, too. She worried.

Yeah, the Roman Catholic Church, her skeptic chimed in.

Whichever it is, they have no right to hurt her.

Toss them all to hell, I say.

No, no, it can be made right. She believes.

Yeah, like all the dupes.

Stop it. Just stop it.

Cindy fought back the cynicism. She strove to be kind. "Memma, don't worry, Paul can deal with Father Lucci."

Berta took the towel again. "Oh, I hope so. Talk to him, will you?"

"Of course I will."

10

Allouez

CINDY LOVED PAUL TAKING HER HOME. The warmth of the evening moved her hair and brushed her arm as he drove her toward home. It was at once sweet and exciting, like so many of the evening drives they'd taken before he left for college. College. And now it's Tommy's turn. She was pleased.

"I loved the way Tommy chummed with you tonight," she said. "Even when his friends came, he stayed next to you."

Paul didn't answer right away. They were climbing up the approach to the High Bridge on their way to Superior. It was one of his favorite routes. The view would be spectacular from a hundred twenty feet up. The night had stayed fine and fog had yet to form over the water. He kept his eyes on the road and waited for the view.

Cindy tried again. "You must have had a good talk in the bedroom. Tommy snapped out of his blues."

Paul looked at Cindy and past her to the bay, sparkling with dock and pier lights way below them. Some ship traffic moved toward the Arrowhead. "You know something?" he said. "Tommy is a fine young man. He impresses me."

Wanting to string the conversation on a less formal thread, Cindy reached her hand out to his cheek. "He reminds me of you. Excited and brave to go off to school, bursting with ideas and ambition. He's very much like you were at that age, Paul." She loved the comparison, but to bring up those old days, especially the later times, when Paul stayed in Minneapolis, raised sore memories. Cindy pinched his cheek a little.

"Things will turn out better for Tommy, I'm sure," Paul said. Cindy drew him to thoughts of his college days, and he regretted the distance he had put between them by following his father's advice to get out of town.

The first years had seemed all right. He and Cindy were just the same as ever, together. She was finishing high school. He bussed the 150 miles for some dances, the prom, and Cindy's graduation. That summer he shipped out. His second year, he spent fewer weekends in Duluth and, why he did not really know, discouraged Cindy from coming down to see him after she started at the business college. Thanksgiving his junior year, he stayed at school, preparing, he said, for some tough finals that were coming in December. Actually, he had accepted an invitation for the holiday from a classmate from Chicago where her parents threw a huge party every year. She was classy and glamorous. Paul grew confused as, by comparison, Cindy started to look less sophisticated to him. Cindy was hurt that they missed the holiday together. He never told her the details, but his evasiveness told her all too much. Senior year he'd met Pamela. She sat next to him in labor history class. "Aren't you from Duluth?" she said. He hadn't realized that the meeting was not accidental. Pamela had no interest in labor history.

Paul looked again at Cindy, who was watching the ships below. "I was awfully stupid for a college boy," he said. He hadn't shaken the guilt even after he and Cindy had taken up with each other again. He had been cruel. They both knew at the time that their Halloween night together could be their last. Neither admitted it.

Cindy had thrown herself at Paul, desperate to feel the past love once again. He welcomed her advances, his own despair prodding him. He followed right along. They didn't speak or write at all during the following month.

Then the *Tribune* published his engagement announcement. He hadn't remembered taking that picture. He didn't know where the Skaansgards had found it. He and Pamela looked happy, smiling out at the camera. Paul had told Cindy nothing.

Cindy snapped him out of his reverie. "It feels good to get out of town," she said. "I want only so much of Duluth." The view of the Superior entry and the lake spreading broadly beyond soothed her ancient hurt and angst.

Paul smiled. She's so beautiful. "Let's take a detour. Let's go out to Allouez. Just for half an hour." It had been one of their favorite spots in high school. Even the ship traffic and metal-to-metal groaning of the trains up on the ore docks added to its beauty. Paul knew that Cindy loved their secret spot on the bay just past Barker's Island.

She clapped her palms to her lap and gave a quick nod. "Yes, let's," she said.

Paul let go his fretting over the past. He talked of Tommy again.

"You were right about Tommy. He had been crying," he said.

"But he was smiling when you two came out, so you must have said something good."

"We just agreed that it was important for Memma to see us happy. Tommy really cared about Roger," Paul said.

Cindy nodded. "Those two boys were a cute pair. Tommy always watched out for little brother."

The boys had been inseparable since Roger was born. For years Betty lived two doors down from Elma, and the boys played in her back yard almost daily. Two years in age didn't make a difference. Then, after Betty died and Roger moved up to Berta's house, the boys' paths crossed less frequently.

When Roger entered eighth grade, he started getting into trouble and took up with boys from Central. Tommy stayed on course out west at Denfeld. They seldom saw each other.

"I think he feels just a bit guilty that he wasn't closer these last few years," Cindy said.

"Less guilt. More sorrow, I think. He didn't give up on Roger. He just went his own way," Paul said. "He's worried."

"About what?"

"That it might be called suicide."

Cindy bit her lip. Tommy kept confidences well. She hadn't heard it from him.

"He trusts you, Paul. He didn't even tell me."

She didn't sound disappointed. Paul felt a little bit more like Tommy's parent. Yes, he had taken care of Tommy right then. "I tried to dispel the notion," he said.

"Memma brought it up to me. She's worried that they won't say a Mass for Roger. The priest wants to wait for the coroner's report, I expect."

Paul banged his palm on the steering wheel. "That's what comes from loose talk. No one on the force knows how to keep the mouth shut." He didn't want to duplicate the errors of his colleagues. He'd tell Cindy little more than: "I'm working on it. It'll turn out right." Given what he had seen over the years, and even more today, he was not at all sure.

Cindy leaned on his shoulder. "Paul, I know you will."

They continued in silence through the flats of Superior. Cindy thought about how sure Paul had grown since those long-ago days just after college. Of course, she had known he was seeing Pamela and expected him to be hesitant and uncertain around the West End. She'd held out hope that he would see the woman as others did: as another social-climbing East graduate out looking for a handsome conquest. Cindy had hardly seen Paul, then a senior early in his fall semester. He had called her, telling her again that he wasn't coming home for Thanksgiving. When she sent him an invitation to a Halloween masquerade ball at the business school, Cindy was surprised he accepted it. It felt like a last chance.

Paul had dressed as a brakeman, in striped trainman's hat and overalls, with a blue wash shirt and heavy boots. He borrowed a signal lantern from a neighbor. He had drawn on a mustache that made him look comical, but he acted morose the entire evening, dragging his feet during the dance numbers and drumming his fingers at the table the rest of the time. He didn't say much at all. Cindy had grown desperate.

Is that why you took him out here? Yeah, you tried to out-pussy that cake-eater he was seeing.

No. It wasn't like that.

Oh? It wasn't, huh?

No. I was honest.

Vamping him?

I wanted Paul, no competition, even for just that one time.

Yeah, and look what you got.

Yes, it was inelegant. That's youth, always a bit awkward.

But Cindy had been honest. She felt right. If she was going to lose Paul, she wanted to do it openly, giving herself to the very last. When his engagement announcement shocked her after Thanksgiving, she already knew she was pregnant. It made her decision easy. They hadn't spoken since that Halloween at Allouez. He didn't need to know. Years later, though, when she saw him at the office that once, she couldn't stop thinking about Paul losing his son. Then Betty called a month later just as Paul had asked her to do.

Paul drove past Barker's Island and pulled up near the foot of the Allouez ore docks that towered now above them like giant oceangoing ships heading straight out to the natural harbor entrance and to the big lake beyond. Sixty feet above them, the huge timbers and steel truss-work rose and spread wide like the cross-section of a ship's hull. Hundreds of supports soldiered in file, strong enough together to lift fifty rail cars full of iron ore up the tracks laid at the top of the docks. Surrounded as they were by marshes, the woodsy end of Park Point, and the forested shore line to the south, the Allouez docks loomed even larger than their brethren in Duluth. In the midst of gulls wheeling over and between them, the four docks stood at once erect and solid though isolated and ghostly in the dusky evening.

The heat had left the sky. The bay cooled the air. Mists began to rise. Paul and Cindy sat quietly in the car. Neither touched the other. They watched wisps of fog twist round each other, entwine, and rise off the surface only to fade again, together into the air. The slough of air felt sad. More swirls of fog rose and advanced across the water from the woods on Park Point, floating past the foot of the towering structures like workmen, crane operators, and car tenders shuffling to work. Paul imagined them to be spirits of the hundreds of workers who had daily swarmed there, especially during the war years, to dump the ore into ships' holds. "Remember how busy these docks were during the war, Cindy?"

Cindy had been thinking of other things but tried to move with Paul's train of thought. "Yes, I do. Everything was busy then."

Paul reminisced. He could just see train after train dumping loads at every minute of the day. Ships arrived, filled, reversed engines, and immediately headed back down the lake. He hadn't loaded here that summer he worked the lake. Only at Wendell's dock in Duluth.

Why he was uncomfortable, sitting here with Cindy,

he didn't know. He might not have been fully aware of the distance between them, but he didn't reach for her. Instead he made awkward conversation. "You know a strike started right here with an accident just like Wendell Sr.'s? Two men died and the company didn't bat an eye."

Cindy went along, nodding. "Yes, 1913. How could I not know?"

Paul gave voice to it. "We've both eaten labor history at breakfast every day of our lives, haven't we." In their childhoods, the 1913 dockworker's strike had been recent history. That sort of history was forever kept alive over Swedish pancakes or Serbian potatoes. It didn't matter where you had come from, only that you pulled the same load the next worker did.

Though she was relieved by his chatter, Cindy hadn't come here to talk history or labor. She turned to Paul and moved closer. He heaved a sigh as the tension he had felt growing since they parked by the docks released like dew into the grass. He drew her close and kissed her.

"I've wanted to do that all evening," he said. But Cindy still sensed reserve and stiffness in his movements. Her look questioned him, and he folded back on the door behind him. "I heard Pam talked with you today."

"So that's what it is," she said. Now Cindy understood his reticence and distance. "I wouldn't say 'with' is the right word, Paul. Maybe 'to' would fit better."

He played with the steering wheel and shifted in his seat, trying to get comfortable. "She accused you of being snotty to her. We fought. Not about that, though."

"She was probably right. I didn't think it was so obvious. Anyway, Paul, she gave as much as she took. What did you fight about?"

Paul thought. It seemed complicated. He wasn't so sure he

knew. "East meets west again, mainly." He chose his words carefully. "I think your boss and his partner had something to do with my appointment to the Brookside case." That sounded straightforward enough.

She'd suffer mention of Paul's wife occasionally, but Cindy never talked about work with him. "I'd imagine that didn't feel too good," Cindy said. Paul would rather earn everything that came his way. She approved of the ethic. They'd shared it.

Even though she knew quite well, Cindy asked. "What do they want, do you think?"

Paul shook his head. He didn't want to discuss business that involved Skaansgard, but he could say what was obvious. "They want Jessica Esterwald's head on a platter."

"Oh, the daughter. Do you think she did it?"

"Maybe. But I think evidence should run the case, not preconceived notions or wishes."

"They want to protect the trust," Cindy said, opening a little, "and they aren't very fond of Mrs. Esterwald and her spending habits."

Paul grew silent once more. This was just the daily truth about people. He could deal with it. But in the background was something else, something tougher that made him uneasy. Cindy was waiting for him, he knew.

"I feel pulled in two directions at once," he said. He smiled at her. "Not surprising, is it?"

His infidelity to Pamela didn't bother him that much. The secrecy did. He wanted to be more open. "It all felt simpler years ago, when I felt a part of the West End. A community member, maybe."

"That's youth, Paul. We get to believe it then."

"Still, I'm always torn. You know I want to be with you. I'd leave Pamela in a second if you'd let me. I wouldn't have to deal with façades and manipulations. Maybe I could feel like

I had the West End back. That feels good, doesn't it? You've never left it, really. You brought Tommy up there at your mother's house."

It was time to say more. "You can't go backward, Paul. Think of what could happen. Stealing the boss's son-in-law? I might not be fired outright, but I hate to think of the 'little talk' Mr. Skaansgard would want. He'd allow me to leave, perhaps with severance, maybe not. And I would, but I've Tommy to think of. Who would support him at college? Without a job I'd need ten West Ends to keep him there. And, Paul, what about us?" She looked at him sitting before her now and from across those nineteen years past. "Would I have you?"

Paul looked off to the bay. The fog had built up, obscuring the foundations of the docks. They seemed to be floating inconceivably over the water unmoored by the dense vapor. The docks reminded him of aircraft carriers spreading their wide decks over dark seas. He understood these structures. Even if they seemed uprooted by the fog, they were rock-solid. To Paul it was the human world that remained obscure, its purposes and wiles hidden beneath a mist, a swirling mess of trouble rising on mystic currents from the cold, deep waters of the lake. The pressures laid down in that world squeezed the air from his lungs.

Cindy, still close, took his hand. "Listen, Paul. There's something I want you to know."

The chill currents felt as if they were pushing him away; the dense haze seemed to rise between them, with Cindy calling out to him from a far-off shore. A single word was all he could manage. "What?" he asked.

Cindy stroked his cheek, and smiled sweetly. "It's nothing bad. Don't look so grim." She patted his chest and left her hand there, warm and light. "Today is a special day."

"Sure. Tommy's birthday."

"Yes," she said, "the day I gave him birth."

Paul nodded and waited.

Cindy drew a breath. "Tommy's life began here, though. Right here on this spot, Paul. On that Halloween. On the last night we were still really high school sweethearts." She looked at him warmly. She expected no answer.

Paul felt the vapors clear. He bobbed to the surface—able to breathe, able to swim, he felt, to her nearby shore. Her admission was less like news than confirmation of something he'd known a long time. The stories Cindy had put out about a desperate fling after they'd split never had a true ring to him. That did not sound like Cindy.

He said what came to mind. "Does Tommy know?"

Cindy stretched her arm round his neck and brought her head to his chest. "That's why I love you, Paul. It's others you think of, always." She pressed close, hugged him, and pushed back to look him in the eyes.

"Tommy does know. Just as you have. But I haven't told him. I always felt that, if he needed to know, his father would be the right one to tell him."

"And you waited all this time?"

"Today seemed right. Tommy's eighteen, and we came here after nearly nineteen years."

The gulls wheeled through the post works and crossties of the docks, over the rails and rail cars lining their lighted platforms, and down over the water, swooping around the lone car parked on Barker's Island. For a long time Paul and Cindy pressed the most contented embrace they had shared since taking up with each other again nearly ten years before.

When their warm plaiting was done, Cindy caressed his face. "Paul, take me home."

11

Fond du Lac

ROYAL FRAISER SAID, "Well, well, if it isn't old PS!"
It didn't matter that he had seen the headlights coming down the long drive or that no one but invited guests ever came onto the property for fear of the dogs and the shotgun Royal kept by the front door of his ranch office. He always said the same thing, "Well, well . . ." That was because, at least in Paul S. Tuomi's mind, he was Royal, the royal Fraiser. He was—in his own mind as well as in that of many others— king of all he surveyed; monarch of the Duluth Bar, of the municipal courts, and a judge to boot.

PS stood before the portly, white-haired lawyer in his ten-gallon hat. The man's belly pressed over the huge belt buckle presiding from beneath his embroidered western shirt. He always wore the hat while on his ranch, indoors or out.

Not cowed in the least by the regalia, PS gave as good as he got. "You knew goddamned well it was me even before I got to the fence. Didn't you just call me at home?"

Fraiser grinned and ignored the comment. "Well, well," he said.

PS flipped a cigarette from his palm to his lips.

"Don't you go lighting that thing in here," Fraiser said.

"Might make the horses sneeze?"

"Emphysema," Fraiser said. "Watch out or it'll get you, too." He eyed the cigarette and PS warily. When he was sure his visitor wouldn't light it, he indicated the rocker across the oversized desk from him and leaned back in the leather judge's chair, with the hat brim just clearing the chair's top. That was his signal: ready to talk.

"Well, well. How's the wife."

PS's wife had been in the lockup at Moose Lake for years. "Same as ever, I expect."

"And that detective son of yours?"

"You listen to the radio just like I do. You know," PS said.

"He's got himself a humdinger of a case now."

PS looked around the ranch-house office. The rustic touches would fool some who didn't know the man: lassos draped on pegs, a couple of saddles hung over mock stall slats, gas lanterns fitted with electric bulbs illuminating the open trusses of the roof. All were stage props for the old, wise geezer-cowboy, who, as a lawyer, gave the lie to the no-rattlesnakes-in-Minnesota story.

"Paul will handle it," PS said, naming his son for the first time that night.

"No doubt. No doubt," Fraiser said.

PS wondered, is he mocking?

"Say," the lawyer plunged on, "have you been working for the SOBs lately?" It was Fraiser's name for Skaansgard and Bullock.

"You know I can't tell you that," PS said.

"Sure, sure. Just like you tell no one you work for me. Everybody knows, though, don't they?"

"That's their business. They don't find out from me."

Fraiser put on his best Arizona twang. "Simmer down now, pardner. I've got a job for you. Concerns a certain family in town that the SOB's might be interested in. I just need to know you're not working for them right now."

PS lit his cigarette. "I'm not working for Skaansgard and Bullock right now."

"Snuff that thing, will you? Or open the window there."

PS rose and went to the window. He slid the sash up to the top of the casement.

The moist, pungent air from the river sifted through the screen. PS listened to the mewing whine of mosquitoes hovering at the screen. He puffed and blew smoke at them. He leaned on the sill. From the window he lifted an enquiring eyebrow at Royal Fraiser. He continued to smoke.

Fraiser gave an obligatory cough and pushed back a bit to raise a boot to the desk. He grunted and lifted the second leg over the first. The boots looked brand new.

"Well, well. This conversation has now become confidential. We agreed on that?" Fraiser waited.

PS nodded.

Fraiser toyed with a bridle strap he kept coiled on his desk. "Mid-morning I received a very interesting call from a certain member of a prominent family in town. This party was concerned, you might say disturbed by recent events and, in particular, by pointed accusations that had begun to circulate."

PS knew Fraiser couldn't be hurried. He smoked quietly at the window. It was clear to him who the call came from and what it was about. He could see why Fraiser had summoned him. The mosquitoes charged the screen again. He met their advance with smoke.

"You know how it feels, Tuomi. Something happens and suddenly everyone is looking at you." Fraiser smiled a lipless, rattlesnake grin. "This party felt the need for representation. Naturally, it won't be found with those SOBs. That is why I was called."

PS tapped the screen to send the insects buzzing off. "Couldn't have happened to a better fellow." He smiled into the darkness. "Exactly what is Mrs. Esterwald worried about?" They were playing cat and mouse. Fraiser thought he was the cat, but PS fed him a little cheese just to see.

Fraiser only sniffed. "So, so, it's about the Crosley killings. I need to know everything the police are finding and everything they aren't finding. There are a couple of private dicks the trustees saw fit to send snooping around. I need to know what they find and what they don't. Everything, everything."

PS lifted the screen and snapped his butt out the opening. Three mosquitoes slipped in.

"For Christ's sake, shut that screen. Those damned things will get in here." Fraiser scratched the back of his hand, looking PS in the eye. "There's big money in this."

PS shut the window and returned to the rocker. "Don't get me wrong, Royal, the money is fine, but I'm not going to pump my son for information. He's got enough to worry about. The rest I can do."

"Pump? Did I say 'pump'?" Fraiser swung his legs from the desk and pulled himself forward. "If you had a conversation with the lead detective on the case, would that be a crime?"

"I can't do it," PS said.

Fraiser put on his snake grin. "I understand." He sighed and took off his hat. "Mark," he called out too loudly, "bring that file in here."

Mark Fraiser looked exactly like his father twenty-five years back. He moved from behind the huge cochineal blanket suspended behind his father's chair. As PS knew, they kept a second desk back there, not as grand as Royal's, where a secretary sat when Fraiser interviewed clients. Mark was dressed in a business suit. He nodded to PS and placed a leather-bound file on his father's desk. Royal rested his hand on the cover.

PS Tuomi had seen this file several times before. He glanced at Mark, who lurked in the shadow that Royal's lampshade cut across the blanket behind.

Above that cone of light, Mark's face had a peculiar glow, as if bathed in Earthlight, at once faintly fearful and dimly surprised. Forty years back, a younger PS had seen that look on Mark.

Back then Mark's odd aspect was mixed with superiority of the snotty, unearned kind. On that night long ago, PS had loosed himself from the tussle he and a Canadian trucker were engaged in, when over the roar of the rushing river outside the truck, they heard the shot. PS shoved his opponent back, climbed over whiskey cases and fish crates, and jumped off the truck bed to the ground. He poked his head around the truck panel to see who was still standing. Then PS stepped out. Mark was staring at him, open-mouthed and afraid.

Beside PS, the Canadian trucker, his opponent of seconds before found voice. "Jesus, you killed him." The man ran across the road into the woods. The gun Mark held and had fired belonged to PS, a war souvenier and the only thing of value PS's father had left behind.

No matter how he justified his behavior afterward, PS boiled it down to two simple things: power and inexperience. Mark's father was sitting on the bench; he had the power, while PS had the lack of experience. So when Royal promised to protect him, PS hadn't caught the meaning. After all, it was during Fraiser's bootlegging operation that a man had been killed. PS and Mark provided the muscle; PS not enough, Mark way too much. Later PS understood that Royal was simply protecting himself and his son, while using PS more than sheltering him.

Once, when he objected to his assigned duties, Royal brought out the file. It contained news clippings from the *Tribune* archives and pictures of the scene where Mark had shot the foreigner. "German gun kills Canadian," one headline read. The damning information in the file was the description of the gun. The rare Mannlicher 1900 used a single load. Who besides Fraiser knew he'd inherited the souvenir from his father, PS didn't know. Royal had the firearm hidden safely. It was blackmail pure and simple.

Fraiser hadn't used the file on him in years. He had brought it out only twice before. Royal Fraiser knew when to twist an arm and how much. He knew a spring too tightly wound becomes dangerous.

PS didn't care about himself now. His career was near its end, the case was old and would be tough to prove, even with help from Fraiser; and Mark was a weak link for Fraiser and Fraiser, partners at law. He'd be a failure as a witness. It was his own son PS had to protect. A scandal would hurt Paul's career for the next twenty years. He'd never live it down. The nightmare of possible headlines plagued PS: Police detective's father linked to grisly murder. He had given up looking for the murdered man's partner, the one who ran. The man had disappeared, likely changed names, evaded PS's searches – while Fraiser had probably helped the man vanish.

PS rose, looked down on Royal Fraiser's bald head, and threw a glance at Mark. "All right, partner, you keep the cash, but I get the gun this time," he said.

"Fair," Royal's expression said in return.

Neither of them wanted to shake on it. That was for amateurs.

12

Hotel Duluth

THE SQUABBLING OF SQUIRRELS in the oak that shaded his window from the late morning sun worked its way into Ingstrom's dreamless sleep. He heard the two scurrying in fits and starts around the old trunk as the couple scolded each other, scraping the bark, galloping up the limbs, jumping over the low eaves, and thundering across the roof. He could easily have slept through the squirrels' inconstant commotion and antics, but when the lawn mowers started, one at his neighbor's and one in his own yard, their constant drone, moving nearer then away, only to return loudly and recede again, lifted him ingloriously to complete wakefulness. The yard crew had arrived. Burnt oil and gas vapors sifted in through the corner window screens, poisoning any hope of more sleep.

Five hours are enough, he decided. Ingstrom studied the shifting spangles of sunlight and shadows of leaves on his ceiling, allowing one thought, then another to filter into his mind and settle onto the path his day would follow. The seamen's office would be one stop. He stretched his bare torso along the narrow confines of the nautical-style bed his mother had indulgently presented him two birthdays ago. The sheets were crisp and clean against the skin after his brief sleep. Yes, the seamen's office. Ingstrom lifted his shoulders and legs, balancing in a V and thrust his hands and arms forward to hold him there. He returned to supine and then lifted again, stretching his back and compressing stomach muscles. On the last repetition, he buttoned the fly of his pants that he had loosened in the night and swung off the bunk.

The temperate oak floor proved how warm the day already was. Ingstrom slipped his hand into his trouser pocket and only then remembered the coin. I'll have to see Randy about this, he thought.

He allowed only the shadows of last night's lake and the owl to flow into his morning mind. The rest he shut behind a door of daylight. Still, Ingstrom set the coin under his wallet on the nightstand, unbuttoned his fly again, and stepped out of the bellbottoms as they fell. He picked them up and examined them front and back, systematically drawing his vision down the legs and up the crotch. He scrutinized the tee and the denim vest he had worn yesterday. These look fine, he mused, but you've got two reasons to wash them. He stood naked and attentive in his room. No one was home, he knew, but listening and checking had long been part of his practice.

He brought his clothes to the laundry room and started the machine. He read his mother's note taped to his breakfast bowl. "Sorry, Mom, I can't make the time," he told her in a note that he left on the refrigerator under a magnet styled as the Eiffel Tower. He crossed the family room to the so-called adult wing of the house. He checked his father's bedside drawer for cash. He took half of what he found there.

Ingstrom heard the muffled ring of a phone. The sound came from his room in the so-called children's wing. He sprinted, leapt over a love seat in the family room, and vaulted the divider rail to the hall. Ingstrom bounded down the hall to his room. It was Daddy Fizzy on the line.

"Hey, man," he said, "what gives?"

Fizzy sounded oddly tense. "I waited as long as I could. Were you sleeping?"

"I've been up for hours," Ingstrom lied. "I was just doing pushups. What gives?"

"Bad news, man," Fizzy said. He sounded dismal.

Ingstrom thought of Roger for the first time that morning. Shit and jingles. "Already?"

Fizzy sounded just a bit confused. Then he seemed to snap onto Ingstrom's train of thought. "No, no, it's not about last night or anything like that."

Ingstrom waited. Splaying his legs, he swayed his bare buttocks.

"I got a letter from Uncle Sam this morning."

"The draft?"

Fizzy read the beginning of the notice to appear. He had been called for an induction physical.

"What? You have to go all the way to Minneapolis?" Ingstrom said.

"Yeah. Fort Snelling. Jeeze."

Fizzy wanted something. Ingstrom guessed it was advice and stepped into his role as the man who knew what was what. "Listen, Bob, I imagine you have a while yet, so don't worry. Let's meet this afternoon. I'll lay out your options. I have some literature and phone numbers."

Fizzy didn't sound relieved. He was struggling. "Do you think I should go?"

"Hell, yes. You might flunk the physical."

"No, I mean into the army."

"What? Volunteer?"

"Maybe. Isn't that longer?"

"Yeah, four years. Double the trouble and chances to die," Ingstrom said. He gave it a sing-song cadence, and regret winced in his throat. Fizzy took this stuff seriously. "Listen, Bob, you don't have to do anything. Let's meet up in Woodland. We can talk quietly."

"When? I don't have the car until swing shift starts. I drop mom off at two-thirty."

"I'll call you after three."

The situation annoyed Ingstrom. How could a cool guy like Fizzy be so stupid? Ingstrom had had a draft plan for two years, and he was only eighteen. Nineteen next week, he reflected, old enough to sail. He returned to Bob's problems.

That was just like Fizzy. He'd graduated high school, nearly twenty; he'd registered for the draft as he was supposed to, and hadn't given it another thought. Now he's in trouble, Ingstrom mused and felt disgusted. I'll make the connections for him, but I know that Fizzy will likely go, probably enlist— even though that seemed too active an idea for him. No, Bob would wait until it was too late, get his hair cut, and board the bus. That plan's not for Ingstrom. By the time I'm on the list, I'll be on the high seas, far out of reach.

He answered the laundry buzzer. While his clothes were drying, he showered, wrapped himself in a towel, and ate breakfast in the dinette. He wrote another note to his mother, adding an explanation of his absence from dinner tonight and placed it over the one pinned by the Eiffel Tower. He counted his stash, folding in the bills he'd filched from his father and the ones he'd collected from the sailors and from John, Roger, and Carlos last night. The thought that too much was going on in too short a time came and went. He let it pass. Full steam ahead, he thought.

Ingstrom left the house by the front door. He saluted the lawn guys, Serbs or Italians or something, he suspected, and wheeled onto the sidewalk up the hill to Superior Street. He'd catch the one o'clock Lakeside-Lester Park to downtown and still have plenty of time to make his rounds.

The summer air clung to his clothes. The morning breeze

had died. Afternoon would be still and hot. He removed his vest and stuffed it into the sack he brought for the evening. He swung the sack over his shoulder like a sailor and stepped up the hill, springing with each stride. Ingstrom looked jaunty and light, a neighborhood kid on a summer outing. He smiled and waved to people out in their yards. He knew most of them. They certainly knew him—the Ingstrom kid was going to be a big success like his father. That's what Ingstrom imagined they said. Won't they be surprised, he reckoned. "Hey, shove your stodgy ideas and attitudes," he wanted to say "This kid isn't wearing a tie."

Ingstrom passed a two-story house with a large stucco porch rising high above the sidewalk. He waved at Julia there.

"Hey. Peace, sister. You're looking fine." Julia glanced up from her book, tossed her hair back and smiled. "Inggy. Going downtown?"

"No, up to UMD," he lied. "Checking out the library."

"Don't get lost in the stacks, babe."

At the corner a couple of old ladies stood waiting. They were overdressed for the heat, but for all their wraps they still looked cold—cold and frail. They'd be shivering in furs, Ingstrom concluded. They each clutched a large purse. One of them shouldered her bag as he came up the hill.

Ingstrom passed behind the women, put a foot on the bench and hoisted himself to perch atop the backrest. He let his sack slide to the seat and tapped out the rhythm of "Sailor's Hornpipe" with his tennis shoes on the slats of the bench seat, slapping the toes flat, thudding his heels. The women huddled closer together and shuffled a few inches away.

He scanned the street for buses. Nothing was coming yet. He jumped down, did a little of the jig as he landed, and sat on the bench. One of the women said the word "murder" in a hushed voice. Ingstrom looked away but zoomed in to listen hard. He couldn't make out anything more. He thought he might walk the two blocks back to the grocery and check the paper, but as soon as he turned to go, the bus came into view.

The bus was nearly empty; his stop was near the beginning of the run. He shied away from the women, who took seats up near the driver. Bolder in the presence of the driver's authority, they talked over the noise of the engine and wheels, the creaks and squeaks of the bus, loud enough to be heard plainly. They addressed their comments to the driver.

Ingstrom learned that the two bodies had been found around seven that morning, when he was sound asleep in his bunk. Too late to hit the *Tribune,* he suspected. Radio stations, the bus driver said, were calling it a burglary. The news was all over town, the ladies shouted. The wire services carried word to New York, they agreed. The driver mentioned a name, "Miss Crosley's daughter," he said. Ingstrom didn't recognize the name. Nothing he heard worried him, though he idly fingered the coin in his pocket. He relaxed in the dappled sunshine moving on the bus along the tree-lined streets of the East End. He felt loose and at peace with the world.

Moving along the East Hillside, the bus took on passengers and filled at the hospital stop. Everyone was chattering about the murders at Brookside. When Ingstrom got off the bus two blocks past the hotel, the two women were still talking avidly with the driver and everyone else who got on. Those two have become experts on the case, Ingstrom decided. They must be headed further down to Glass Block for a midsummer sale. Maybe some new pillowcases.

Ingstrom smiled at the women as he got off the bus.

He strolled back past a theater. Nextdoor, he looked in the window of The Coney Island to see if an afternoon paper had been left behind. No luck. The dapper little Greek who served hot dogs was leaning near the grill behind the counter, reading a copy of the *Herald*. He looked up when Ingstrom paused but returned to the paper when he resumed his stride. Ingstrom swung past the front of the hotel and turned up the avenue to enter by the side door.

Ordinarily, he'd go up to the mezzanine to ride the elevator unseen; but today he took the stairs down to the main lobby where he could get a paper at the cigar stand.

The girl behind the cigar counter jumped off her stool. "Inggy!"

It was Siiri, Matty's girlfriend. "Hey, long time no see," he said. He searched his memory of last night. He was sure Siiri had gone before he left. "I heard you worked here."

"Really? How?" she said. "I just started last week."

Ingstrom went round to the side of the counter to stand behind one of the ornate columns that supported the mezzanine. He leaned over to her. "Word gets around, you know."

Siiri blushed as if to say 'What do you mean?' but uttered nothing. "You visiting?" she said.

"No," Ingstrom lied. "I rolled in to get a paper and see you."

Her blush deepened, and she arched her back as she stood fully fronting him. "Sorry. You can look at me all you like, but the papers are all gone. The *Trib* sold out fast this morning even though it had nothing in it. The *Herald's* early edition went like hot cakes. It's the murder out on London Road."

Ingstrom thought to get away, then looked again at Siiri and changed his mind. "Yeah, I heard something on the bus. Weird."

"I don't like that kind of stuff. I just sell the papers. I don't read them."

He leaned closer to her. "Hey, I met a friend of yours last

night."

She looked a bashful 'who' at him.

"Saw him down at Joe Huey's," he said, watching for her reaction. "Mike Light."

Siiri's cheeks colored more than he thought possible for the freckle-faced blonde. "Yeah, well, I don't really know him," she said. "He's a model in the art department."

"Oh." Ingstrom stood back. "Is the buxom blonde modeling, too?"

She looked confused. "Who do you mean?"

"The brash one he was with last night, Lilly or something white sounding."

Siiri was displeased with him or with Mike Light, Ingstrom couldn't tell which. "I'm fooling," he lied. "He was alone with Carlos."

"Oh," she said, looking away. She appeared relieved.

Siiri straightened some magazines. She waited on a tall, bald man who bought a fistful of expensive cigars. He lined a silver case with them and asked for matches. He stood there, lighting and puffing, staring at Siiri. He dropped a two-quarter tip into the tray, pointed a finger at her, and left. He hadn't looked at Ingstrom once.

Ingstrom watched Siiri handle the sale. "I've got something for you. How about I stop by your place after work?"

Siiri fidgeted with the magazines on the counter. "Well, when? What time?"

She must get off at three, he thought. "Three-thirty? I want to catch you in the shower."

Siiri responded in kind, "Yeah, you can join me there. Matty gets home at five-twenty-five."

"Ever so prompt," Ingstrom said. "Until then, ma chérie."

He shouldered his bag, swayed across the lobby—the consternation from the wing-backed-chair set of lobby-sitters lay thicker than the plush carpet—and skipped up the steps to the side entry. Ingstrom pushed the door open and stepped back inside, letting it close heavily on its jamb. He leaned against the radiator in the hall and waited. After a minute, he took the steps up toward the mezzanine elevators, kept away from the rails and the view below, and, opting for better cover, ducked into the stairway leading to the floors above.

Ingstrom slowed toward the tenth floor. He stopped in the stairwell to smooth his breathing. Be relaxed with Randy, he told himself. His dealings with Randy made him nervous though he worked hard at not showing it. Randy Belisle was not a man to be crossed or toyed with.

Belisle was all business. He moved around a lot. Mondays he was at the Hotel Duluth, most but not all the time. Different rooms, different names. Other days, Belisle did business at the Radisson or motels downtown. Sometimes he met his people at the West End house he kept, but he never stashed dope there, having a depot in Superior. Randy did nothing to jeopardize his relationship with the Duluth police department. He disappeared often, sometimes for a week or two to San Francisco or to Mexico, Ingstrom guessed. Only once had the High Octane 66 been mentioned. That was Belisle's stash-house in Wisconsin. Ingstrom had made a point to discover the location.

Everyone knew about punk dealers who had tried to finagle in Randy's absence or who'd tried to renege on a deal. Usually they were busted by the fuzz not long after, or they left town in a hurry when Randy reappeared.

Despite his reputation of playing hardball, Belisle was jovial, sometimes downright friendly, but always held a reserved, judgmental eye on everyone and everything. Ingstrom knew he was still being sized up. Randy had dated Ingstrom's older sister years before. That formed the background check. But Belisle wasn't sure how steady Ingstrom could be. He'd let time tell. Until last night, things had been going well.

Settled, Ingstrom moved into the hall. He found the room Belisle had indicated last night and knocked once. He heard nothing from behind the door. Down the hall, around the corner, the maid was vacuuming, but no one else was around. He waited as he had been told to do. He was being watched, he knew, so he held still and stood tall. With no sound preceding, he heard the deadbolt thrown. The door opened a crack. Ingstrom waited. Finally he pushed on in, entered a little vestibule, and bumped the door shut with his tennis shoe. He set his sack down just inside the door. He passed the bath and closets into the main room.

Randy lounged at a glass-top table set between two overstuffed chairs. Wearing a silk printed robe, he was having toast and coffee. A newspaper sat neatly folded on one end of the table. Randy remained silent but opened his palm to indicate the second chair to Ingstrom. The volume of the room, the twelve-foot ceiling above them magnified the quiet of the plush. Randy took the paper from the table, folded it in half, and slipped it between the cushion and arm of his chair.

He looked stern. "Things got a bit out of hand last night."

Stay cool, Ingstrom thought, keep the defenses quiet. "They did." He wasn't going to offer much unless he had to.

Randy shook his head and smiled. "At least someone kept his head or the cops would be all over Skip's place right now." He tapped the paper. "No matter what else they have to think about."

Ingstrom could tell Skip had been busy on the phone already. Maybe he had come down in person.

160

He needed to say something. "Except for Skip, all parties are cool."

Randy gave him a hard look. "At least he made sure I knew. That was pretty cool. Who's the girl?"

Which girl? Ingstrom had to keep up with him. "The driver?" He was right. "She's Fizzy's sister. A solid citizen."

"We'll see," Randy said. "Anyway, too many people know."

Ingstrom sensed that excuses would be unwelcome. "Suggestions?"

"You didn't come for this," Randy said. "Were you thinking of reloading?"

The man didn't mince words. Ingstrom reached into his pocket and brought out the coin. "There are a few things I'd like, but mainly I came for this and to see about last night."

He offered Randy the coin. He hoped curiosity set on the coin would shelter his half-lies from Randy's scrutiny. At least he removed his polygraphic eyes from Ingstrom's face for the moment.

"Where is it from?"

Ingstrom kept as close to the truth as he could. "The Crosley mansion." Randy, he could see, thought of dropping the coin right then. "I've had it for years. I used to play with Willy there. She was family, twice removed or something. Maybe a great aunt."

Ingstrom didn't like the sound of what he was saying, but he was into the lie now and had to continue. "I'd actually forgotten I had it until I heard about the burglary this morning. I'd like to get rid of it, but it is worth something."

Randy set the coin down on his saucer. "It's worth less today than it was yesterday. You realize how hot this little baby is, don't you." It wasn't a question.

The other man sat back in his chair and considered the coin, while polishing it in the folds of his silk robe. Ingstrom watched him think. The man was fast, thorough, and unpredictable.

"Get me that envelope on the desk, would you?" Belisle asked. He sounded a bit friendly.

Randy took the newspaper, put it on the table and dropped the coin onto it. When Ingstrom came back with the envelope, Randy said: "Just slide the coin inside. Don't touch it."

That done, Randy said, "Seal it, would you?"

Ingstrom was uncomfortable, but in no position to object.

Randy examined him. "You're going to hear this anyway, so I'm telling you. I'm sending this to someone who doesn't want to see it right now. Someone who stiffed me big-time," he said in warning. "It's off your hands. It benefits humanity."

Ingstrom couldn't ask for anything. He wanted to make it right with Randy, at least for the next few days. Until he shipped out. He sat again.

He felt the heat of Belisle's gaze on him. Don't flinch now, boy, he told himself. Stay cool.

Randy finally said, "I'll give you a hundred. It's a rip-off, but I'm the one with the risk."

"Fair enough," Ingstrom said. "Throw in two hits of speed and a couple of joints if you would, kind sir." He smiled his best genuine grin.

Randy got up and went into the bathroom. It was a five-minute wait. Ingstrom pinched the corner of the envelope with his thumbnail and wiped across it twice with the tail of his tee shirt.

Randy emerged fully dressed. He put two fifties and the extras on the table. "Listen, Reese," he said, "you might want to make yourself scarce for a while. You don't want to be answering any questions."

Ingstrom thought of holing up at home. Belisle had other

ideas.

"I've got a cabin for the rest of the month out at Grand Lake. You can use it. I'll send word if it's okay to come back earlier."

Ingstrom could easily cover on the home front. A cabin sounded nice. The weather was fine. Maybe he could convince Siiri to come out with him. He scanned Randy, now sitting back in his chair with the coffee cup raised to his lips. "Deal," he said.

As soon as Ingstrom had left the room, Randy picked up the phone. "Swing round in five minutes. Yeah, out back."

He pulled on gloves he took from a desk drawer. He consulted a small book he took from his pocket. He circled a pen over the envelope as if stirring an inkpot, then smoothly scrawled a name and address on the letter. He dampened the stamp on a bath sponge and fixed it to the corner. He slipped the envelope in a leather case he carried and shouldered its strap.

He hung the "Do Not Disturb" sign out and left the building by the same stairwell Ingstrom had just descended.

Ingstrom was back on Superior Street. His interview with Randy had left him wary. He wanted to look over his shoulder, to back up to the building and check to see he was not being followed. Instead, he remained loose as a way to keep panic at bay. He got what he had come for; the added hundred dollars gave him enough to pay off his card and have seed money for his travels. He could ship out quickly.

The Superior Street-Grand Avenue bus swung to the curb, and Ingstrom boarded. He moved to the rear and scanned the sidewalk that fronted the hotel. Everything seemed fine. Careful is good, he coached himself. Paranoid is uncool.

He sat behind some high school girls who were heading to the Park Point beaches to enjoy the fine weather. He knew of them from school, but they'd graduated behind him this June. Ingstrom held little interest in underclassmen like them. If they only knew, he thought. I won't be around their little college come September.

One of them glanced and smiled at him. "Going to the Point?" she said.

"Naw. Headed out west to see a friend."

"You look like you're going to jump a ship."

"I just might do that," Ingstrom said.

The girls got off on Lake Avenue after questioning the driver about transferring to the Park Point line. The friendly one waved at him as the bus pulled out. Ingstrom kept his eyes on the driver up front. Peace sister, he signaled. He did not look after her.

The ride to the hall was short. All the conversation in the bus seemed to be about the robbery and murder out east. Ingstrom focused his own thoughts on the call he'd make to his mother later in the day or maybe that night. He railed inwardly at her.

He resented the firm grip her love held on him, her well-intentioned interference and protection, her insistence on what she called "good communication." He regretted his need to avoid her caresses but not his escape from her supervision. She'll be hurt and angry when she finds I'm gone. But it couldn't be helped. A future marked by more college classes and a stultifying profession repelled him. "Let me live life, Mother. For God's sake!" He had actually said that to her once. She'd lectured him for an hour, and after that he kept his sentiments to himself.

Now that he was on the final leg of a journey he had planned for two years, he didn't want to blow it by carelessness where his parents were concerned. All the other stuff he could handle, Randy included.

He got off two blocks ahead of his stop and walked the rest of the way. The West End Bakery lured him. He was hungry. Inside, the store was hot. The linoleum squares oozed an oily sweat onto his sneakers. Ingstrom listened to the women behind the counter while he peered into the glass case making his choices. They weren't talking about the Crosley news but about a suicide. He decided on a half-dozen assorted cookies. "Yours are the best in town," he said.

The attendant beamed. "Thank you, young man."

He asked her. "Everybody's talking about the Brookside deaths. Did they decide it was a suicide?"

The counter maid brushed some crumbs from her white uniform blouse. "I hadn't heard about that. Where's Brookside?"

He explained.

She shook her head and turned to him confidentially, "It was Berta West's grandson."

"I'm not sure I knew him," Ingstrom said.

Almost afraid to utter the name of the dead, she whispered, "Roger Sillanpaa."

Ingstrom shook his head. "Never heard of him. But I'm sorry."

She seemed surprised. "He was about your age, maybe a year younger. Drugs, they say," the woman confided.

Ingstrom feigned surprise. "Oh, that's bad." He lifted the little bag she handed him. "I'll stick to sweets, myself."

"You do that, young man."

Ingstrom left the bakery feeling all right. He hadn't worried until Randy mentioned it, but since then he'd been wishing he hadn't gotten involved in moving Roger. If it was suicide, that was better. What good would the truth do Roger or his grandmother? Their little neighborhood would take care of the survivors. He liked that. They didn't even know about the Crosley thing or, if they did, they didn't care. It probably seemed disconnected and remote from them. There the neighborhood news took precedence, as it always had.

He veered at the corner, headed down to Michigan Street and the hiring hall. He'd be able to get the card, sign up, and make it back to Siiri's by the time she left work. Everything was working out fine.

Max at the hall expected him. Ingstrom passed him the cookie bag he had emptied and then stuffed with cash. Max went into an office behind the counter. When he returned, he slid the card over the counter. "Congratulations, mate."

The card was typewritten and laminated in plastic that was still warm. Ingstrom's picture showed on the left. At last, my ticket to ride.

"I see this is effective August 1. Can I sign up before that?"

"You in a hurry?" Max said.

Ingstrom swayed at the counter. "No, just eager."

Max consulted a logbook. "No lakers until next week. They're usually filled at this time of year anyway." He flipped through another book. "There's an Indian vessel coming in two or three days. It won't be fancy, but they almost always need someone."

"Put me down. Got to start somewhere."

Max made a notation. "Call me day after tomorrow."

"Aye, aye." Ingstrom said.

Max crossed his eyes. "Good voyage, mate."

13

Smithville

IT ISN'T VERY FAR FROM Fond du Lac to Smithville, just
five miles, and Paul S. Tuomi needed more road than that
to blow off the steam he had built during his visit to Royal
Fraiser. So at the top of Fraiser's drive he hung a left, spraying
gravel up against Royal's gate, and laid enough rubber on
Highway 23 to silence the crickets and frogs singing in the
ditches beside the driveway. Headed south away from home
across the river, he floored the big Oldsmobile. He was doing
ninety up the grade.

PS gripped the steering wheel and yelled. He yelled at
the top of his lungs, louder than the roar of the V-8 engine.
He invented the most obscene names he could to call out
Fraiser—fantastic, demeaning monikers he'd never utter
before a living person. The speed and the cursing helped.

By the time he'd reached the top of the long, steep hill,
his head was feeling lighter, less pinched. PS let out a long
controlled breath between tight lips. He made it last until the
air trailed out softly and pressed his lungs to exhaust the last
smidgeon of breath. Then he drew in deeply.

On the flats above the rise, the engine pushed the
Olds faster. He was going a hundred and five. When the
doe pranced out on the road, turned her nose toward the
headlights, and froze there, her eyes glowing like eternity
and luminous as death, PS refused to panic and eased the
Olds just a degree to her right. He floored the pedal again
and sailed past close enough to give her a kiss. Then he let

the gas up all the way. He hadn't hit the shoulder, used the brake or nicked the deer. He forced his eyes away from the mirror—don't look away doing one hundred, he instructed himself—cradled his good luck and his skill together in his palms at the bottom of the steering wheel and coasted the engine down to twenty-five. His shirt was soaked and sweat seeped through his eyebrow, salting one eye. His heart raced in counterpoint to the slowing engine. In a long minute he pulled off to the Nopeming overlook.

PS Tuomi, he judged himself, you're an idiot. He rested his forehead at the top of the wheel and pushed the footbrake tight. He mopped his brow and worked at slowing his breath. But he felt fine or better. He'd stayed in control. I don't have to kill Fraiser or anyone or anything else. I can still make it. PS switched off the lights and got out of the car.

Sitting on the hood of the Olds, the engine idling under his buttocks, PS looked over the valley that held the St. Louis River on its rock-strewn course from Thompson toward Lake Superior. Somewhere to his right, on the shoulder of the forested hill, nestled the sanitarium where his father had died. He lit a cigarette, held it out away from his face, and looked at it as if to say: What the hell, something's going to kill you. He watched the cloud of tobacco smoke drift over the steep descent.

PS pictured the south-facing screen porches of the three-story brick wing his father had lived in. The wooden casings and newel posts were painted a yellowy cream. It looked trim against the ruddy brick, colonial in a way, almost like an Adirondacks resort. On those screen porches, patients wrapped in white sheets rested on lounges and breathed the piney air as deeply as they dared. His father had been short of breath since returning from the war. Until the end, which came in winter when he seldom visited, his father had insisted they meet on the grounds below the compound, at picnic tables far from the other tubercular patients. His father had never seemed sick but appeared very unhappy; certainly frail, but mostly sad. A lousy waste, PS had thought. Lives sifting away through those screens.

PS took a drag on his cigarette. His father's unsuccessful life, and particularly his dismal death, steeled PS against dependence. He'd never become, as his father had, a vassal of the rich or a ward of the state. He had sworn he would stay close to his son, to be around when he was needed.

His posture on the Olds's front fender—one foot steady on the bumper, the other dangling casually off the side—seemed to say: Maybe I haven't done things in the most ethical way, but I've always stayed my own man. PS did what was called for, in a way that always spoke of strength.

Now, he looked out across the valley that hid the river cascading hundreds of feet down from the reservoir. Thompson was the place. He considered his youthful folly. Forty years seems like a day, he decided.

Back then he and Mark, working gladly together, were to collect a thousand dollars from the Canadians with whom Royal traded. The two Canucks had been slow to deliver, and Royal's payments had jumped ahead of shipments. The whiskey was good; it just wasn't flowing fast enough.

"If they don't have the full shipment, rough them up a bit," Royal had told them. "I don't want to cut the ties, just get better results." It sounded easy; but Mark, though not a small man, was not up to the task. He was a second-year college boy who had grown up in the shelter and shadow of his father, not, as PS had, in the alleys and on tough streets.

"Let me have your gun, Paul," Mark had said. "It'll make me feel safe."

PS didn't agree. "We'll leave it in the car. There's no need."

His memories of that night appeared like dreams slowed to a crawl—disjointed, electric with horror, and always, always tumbling into a mist that drew him down to a sure, disastrous end.

The lettering on the high panels of the truck flashed in their headlights: Pucci and Sons – Lake Superior Fish. The driver swung open his door and stepped down.

"Jesus, look at the size of that guy," Mark said, already trembling.

"Don't worry, I'll handle him," PS said.

A second man, a Mutt to the other's Jeff, rounded the front of the truck. "That's your man, Mark." PS killed the lights. "Stay in the car a minute."

PS got out and approached the men. "The Queen sends her greetings," he said.

"As does the Duke," the smaller man replied.

The code sounded corny enough for Royal to have insisted on it. Paul waved his flashlight beam at the truck box. "We should inspect the catch," he said.

He followed the driver to the rear. The fish sign, he saw, was removable and gave Knife River, Minnesota as the home of the company. Likely it said Port Arthur, Ontario underneath.

Sometimes in dreams PS saw the sign's stay bolts unthreaded by a ghostly wrench, letting the placard come loose to dangle on a single bolt, revealing the *Tribune* headline, "Gangland Murder, Inc." Underneath was his face from a police lineup photo.

The driver had opened the rear doors and fastened one of them on the truck's side. PS tapped Mark's window as he passed and hoisted himself up into the truck. Mark was to watch his back as he inspected the load and settled the account.

He and the driver crawled over blocks of ice and huge crates of fish, working their way toward the front of the truck bed where the cases of whiskey were stacked.

At night, sleepless at 3 AM, PS often saw their flashlight beams playing over the ice, bouncing off fish scales and clear frozen blocks, shining coldly back in bent, oddly colored rays.

He'd carefully counted the cases, opened several, and held a few bottles to the beam of his flashlight. The rays turned from white to amber running through the bottle. PS unsealed one of the bottles. He sniffed the product and took a short swig.

Since that night he couldn't brook the taste of whiskey, but that shot felt pure and warm in his throat. It burned with a rounded aroma of newly split white pine logs, powerful and sustained. He re-corked the bottle and put it in its case.

The driver's shadow loomed huge above him in the confines of the truck. PS knelt by the open case. "It is good stuff, but where is the rest?"

The driver shrugged his shoulders. PS stood, reached over the stacked cases and thumped three solid beats on the truck wall. Mark would know the deal was sour. Then he showed the driver his full height, a head taller than the other, grabbed him by the collar and raised his flashlight to club him.

The driver struggled but PS held. "Hey, I just do the driving. He's the money man."

PS held and turned the beam on the driver's face. He didn't hit him. "Well, the King is feeling a little cheated. You might have to walk back to Canada. Give me the keys."

When the man handed them over, PS pushed the driver down on a fish crate. "Sit until I tell you to come." He climbed around the ice blocks to the tail gate.

That was when he heard the shot.

PS was at the door, stepped down the bumper and hit the ground instantly. The second shot sounded. He strode to the right side of the truck and beamed the light ahead toward the cab. The second Canadian was on the ground, lying oddly crooked.

PS swung the beam to Mark's face. He saw a face that seemed to be made from bulges of the very oldest birches in the woods—a stretched, tattered growth screaming fear and confusion. Mark was a white mask dumbly gaping back at him.

"What the hell did you do?" PS said.

At his elbow he felt the driver's bulky heat. "Jesus, you killed him" was all he said. Then he ran. PS let him disappear into the night. Mark was still too stunned to think.

In the end, PS drove the truck half full of whiskey cases and fish to Royal's warehouse in Gary-New Duluth; while Mark, still carrying the gun, took the car with him back to Duluth, leaving the Canadian, or so PS assumed, by the side of the dam road.

Mark, though, had dragged the body to the river and dumped it in. The newspapers loved that: "Gangsters send body through state park rapids." The beating the corpse took in the river—one arm was never found—couldn't hide the lead lodged in its spine. "Dammed Murder," the *Herald* quipped. Hundreds of gawkers drove out to the park that spring to view the torrent. They stood on the swinging bridge, pointing at the razors of slate that stuck out of the river's foamy brine.

PS tossed his cigarette to the gravel and pushed off from the fender. The memories that the overlook stirred were not all bad. He and Illja had spent their courtship watching the sun set over this valley. They had soaked in the fall colors from here and had watched the river shimmer through November trees under moonlight. Those had been good days.

Within the panorama stretching south and west over a twenty-five-mile sweep of forest and farmland to the horizon past Carlton, he had lived much of his life. When times were tough, he lost himself in the woods along the Nemadji and Blackhoof rivers, sometimes on the reservation land near Net Lake. He carried a fishing rod more as an excuse to tramp the woods than as something to use. He had scaled the Duluth gabbro above Smithville until he knew the best routes up the escarpment to Skyline Drive and higher. The world of rivers, lakes, and trees was one he understood, one that soothed troubles as they came. The encroaching world of people, always more and more of them, was confusing, forever changing. It irritated him. Out here, the long view and stillness under stars coaxed him into a stillness of his own.

PS stepped on the glowing butt, twisted to grind it out, and walked around the car. He felt pleasantly tired. He was ready to go back home.

When he pulled off the road and up the drive, his son was there waiting for him. Paul had turned round and parked the car to guard the approach. He was sitting inside the car, the glow from the radio weirdly lighting his face. PS pulled up to the garage and walked back down. I still like the '50s models, he thought, looking at his son's car. This one looks boxy. Paul had left his seat and was standing by the Buick.

"You're up late," PS said.

Paul opened his arms to embrace his father. "I was about to say the same."

His father felt hard and bony in his arms, far from frail, but Paul thought he had lost some muscle. "You should be getting more sleep," he said.

PS gripped Paul's arms and looked at him in the yard light. "Looks like the lead detective's job is treating you well. You've been working out."

"Not enough, but it gets me out of the office and home."

"Pamela is up to her usual, I guess." PS wanted to ask about Cindy, but he always waited for Paul to bring her into the conversation. "What brings you way out here so late? Cup of coffee?"

"It won't keep me up. Sure, thanks." On the way to the house, he told his father about the party and bringing Cindy home.

PS did some calculation. "Either it was a late party or you dallied a bit with that sweet thing. It's past 11 o'clock."

Paul smiled. They'd few secrets from each other and Cindy wasn't one of them. "We had some talking to do, yeah."

His dad held the door open. "I like the way you talk." He slapped Paul on the back and guided him through the doorway.

PS had always been fond of Cindy, and, though he had said nothing when Paul announced his engagement to Pamela, he had felt disappointment and misgivings. Still, he kept his peace. A father can't shelter a grown son, he'd thought. And over the years, he judged he had been right. "Taste life for yourself," was his adage, "no one can tell you what it is like." And when Paul brought Cindy back into his life, PS was perhaps as glad as Paul himself. The regeneration of Paul's romance was far more genuine than his own affairs had been, those that had started even before Illja grew ill. Paul's had proven a life-long love.

He felt warm and talkative now that his son was with him. As he loaded the percolator and brought out sugar, cream, and some flatbread and butter, he grilled Paul with his jovial humor. "So, how is Cindy? Tommy's eighteen now, isn't he? How was the party? Sorry I couldn't get there." He kept it personal and avoided asking about the Brookside case.

Paul answered each query briefly but in an open manner. He had a great deal to share but didn't want to jump right to it.

After PS poured the coffee and sat down, they both started talking at once. They laughed.

"No, you first," said his dad, "you're the one who came by."

"I've got good news and bad. Which do you want first?"

PS smiled at their old-time lead-in. He always answered the same, "Well the good, of course. Bad new can always wait."

Paul felt his face flush with pleasure. It was news so good he had to share it. "You're a grandfather."

PS did his best to act surprised and pleased, though he wasn't quite sure exactly what was coming. "Tell me more."

He had known about Tommy for a long time and, like Paul, had loved the crossing of paths with Cindy and her son. Even before Paul and Cindy reconnected, PS had done a few things for them; the latest were the block-factory job and some college funding, but he had waited for Cindy to confirm to Paul that Tommy was his. Sitting there with his happy son, the older man thought: I'm not blowing it now.

Paul studied him as if reading his thoughts. "You knew, didn't you?" He understood his father was the better detective, and maybe Paul himself hadn't wanted to be told at first.

PS feigned ignorance. "You mean Tommy?" He smiled back broadly. "I suspected. 'Knew' is a bit strong."

"Maybe. But that's where the college fund came from, didn't it?"

"Blood's thicker, my boy."

Paul stood. PS followed. As if he had just left the delivery room with the good news, the son embraced his father. PS stroked and patted his son's back. "It took eighteen years for her to tell me," Paul said.

"She's an independent woman," PS said. "Cindy makes her own time." He faced his son squarely, "You have been a father to Tommy. Knowing won't change that. You couldn't improve on it, either."

Paul hugged his father again. "Thanks, Dad." They sat again and sipped their coffee, a bit uncomfortable, having disengaged.

Father broke the silence, "So now, give me the bad."

Paul told his dad about Roger's death.

PS, of course, didn't let on he knew. After all, he had known Berta all his life. Different schools, ages, and languages, but she had always been the golden-hearted girl in the neighborhood. "Poor Berta," PS said. "She has had her share and more of tragedy." He stirred his coffee thoughtfully. "Is Wendell Jr. back yet?"

"I called him at his lunch break. He'd drive up after work. He's on the road yet."

PS was, no matter that he hadn't lived there for twenty-five years, still from the neighborhood. "I'll make time for the funeral," he promised.

Paul had come for advice on Roger's case. It troubled him, and he laid out for his father everything he knew about Roger's death.

Like the consummate detective PS was, he listened intently and scribbled in his little book. He was an excellent researcher, but more importantly he kept an ear on the street and knew pretty much all that was going on in Duluth, from Fond du Lac to the Lester River thirty miles north. By the time Paul had finished, his father had already put the pieces together and asked the central question. "So, is it more about nailing someone or about getting the padre to say the Mass?"

Dad was quick on the uptake and knew the answer already. "They committed a crime, but Roger was dead already. Obstruction of justice, I suppose. But for Berta's sake I want nothing more than the church service."

PS knew that this was not why Paul had come, but the old neighborhood saw 'give some, get some' fit his present need. He still had Royal to deal with.

"Listen. I've seen a couple of the guys Roger has been hanging with recently. A mixed bag, like the kids say. There's John Limmer, a loser who stays around on the Central Hillside. A kid named Bob from the West End who goes by the name of Daddy Fizzy. He won't be hard to find. Then there's a blond kid from out east. I don't know his name. So if you want fast and good results, Fizzy is the one."

Paul noted mention of the blond kid, but he simply tipped his cup in acceptance.

"You want help?" His father asked.

"Yeah, that's the other thing, I'm not on the case, you probably can guess." Paul went slowly now. This was the main reason he had come.

"Hang on there." PS didn't want to backtrack and had decided to practice honesty first. "We both have news, right?"

Paul nodded. He waited.

"I know about your appointment. Everyone knows." He searched for the best way. "Including Royal Fraiser."

"Oh, not that sleazebag again! Why do you keep dealing with him? I don't get it."

"This time I'm going to tell you why. But first, I want you to know the reason he called me."

"Because of me?"

"Sure. I told him I wouldn't talk with you about the case, and I meant it. You owe me nothing on that score."

Paul shook his head. "I owe you everything. What does he want?"

"First, let me tell you what you really want to know. Why I keep on with Fraiser."

Paul sat quietly. He let PS tell it the way he wanted it told, straight up, without questions, matter-of-fact. That Fraiser had been a bootlegger was no secret. Judge Whiskey had been notorious even in Paul's childhood. That PS had worked for him, he knew. His father's involvement in the shooting and dumping of a Canadian transporter was the news. It had occurred before he was born. That, and the blackmail. Though anger rose in his throat, he didn't threaten to shoot Royal. Paul kept his feelings dressed in an objective jacket. He wanted to listen. He had learned that much from his father.

"What is ironic is that my dad left me the gun, a fancy German weapon he salvaged from the trenches."

PS buttered some hardtack and crunched it as he mentioned his father. Paul waited for him to swallow. "What Royal Fraiser wants is the inside dope," PS said. "He wants a running total of the evidence, including what people are thinking and all the mistakes that are committed by your department and the DA."

"Let me guess. He wants to get a leg up on Skaansgard and the trust."

PS did not say no.

"There's more." Paul liked showing off to his father. They were playing the "I know" guessing game his dad had invented. "He's representing the Esterwalds."

"At least one of them, I'd guess." PS had always been the master of the game. "The one with the money."

Paul wasn't surprised. The case was destined to be a pressure cooker. "You must have taken a long drive on this one."

PS smiled. His son knew him well. "Just out to the overlook and back."

"And pretty quick, too," Paul added.

His father didn't mention the deer.

Paul took a deep breath. "I'm not going to let Fraiser come between us. What you tell him is your business. I came tonight to spill a bit. You're still the only one I can talk to. And, believe me, I need to talk."

Even as he said it, Paul knew it wasn't true. He'd edit his comments on the case. But he also knew that this would be a two-way street—that he'd give some and get some from the talks he and his father would have. It would be good to know what Fraiser was thinking, if that were possible. But now Paul had new questions to ask, ones that were more important. He wouldn't let the opportunity pass. "What happened to the second Canadian?"

"Believe me, I've looked. He disappeared, probably changed names, probably with help from Royal. He may not be living." As if PS had guessed what came to Paul's mind, he said, "It's not worth your time."

Paul, for his part, proved stubborn. "Maybe. But give me what you've got. Maybe I have friends you don't know."

"All right. But don't spend any time on it. You have bigger fish to fry." PS offered more coffee.

The two talked until nearly one o'clock. Paul shared his hunches and thoughts about Brookside and Roger's death. They reminisced about his childhood, father and son. Discussed Illja's condition. Paul wondered aloud about Pamela and their future. About Cindy. What do to? He confessed the pressure he felt leading the Crosley case, the anger at being manipulated by Skaansgard.

His father encouraged him to follow his hunches,

agreed that the rush to judgment on the Esterwalds was a mistake, though inevitable. He guessed Roger's death was an unfortunate accident.

PS was a good sounding board. As from an echo along the Blackhoof valley, Paul heard only what he put out, undistorted, clear. Because he received encouragement and not advice, Paul felt good about sharing his train of thought. He knew his father wouldn't enter his life as a guide; but listening to himself echoed by his father led him down a trail he hadn't walked before.

Paul recounted his fight with Pamela. "I blew it, of course. But like father, like daughter. I get tired of the manipulation."

PS echoed the sentiment. "That crowd invented intrigue, and they don't have any conscience."

"The only way out is out," Paul said.

"Sounds like you want to leave."

Paul pressed his lips tight and shook his head. "I have to do it on my own. I have to protect Cindy's job, Tommy's future."

"You thinking you shouldn't fly from one nest to another?"

"Yeah, something like that." Paul was working out an idea. The coffee ran out, and they were still talking. "I was sitting at Berta's table—what, nearly twenty hours ago—saying to myself, Paul, you've got to do something for this woman. Then the department called."

"You feel you owe her."

Paul touched his father's hand. "No offense. I do owe her. She was the mother I couldn't have."

"Illja wasn't made for mothering. That's true. And Berta always wanted another son."

Paul nodded. "It'll be good to see Wendell Jr., despite the circumstances."

PS remembered the two as boys and young men. They worked different angles on the same problem: What do you do when the world you thought you'd inherit faded away and disappeared? The West End had changed during the war, losing some of its ethnic edge and the unifying struggle of labor strife; Illja had grown worse, then much worse; Wendell Sr. died on the docks; jobs both boys thought would sustain them had already started disappearing. Paul chose college. Wendell Jr. changed venue.

PS knew how fast expectations could be dashed. Tubercular consumption and, two years later, public consumption had changed his life. His own father faded away. The bootlegging business floated PS down a new stream. Even the connections with the neighborhood loosened, flowed away. Yet nothing had changed inside.

"You know they say 'the more things change the more they stay the same.' Everything is different now from when I was a boy. But I feel it's exactly the same. The neighborhood lives. All the people gone, Wendell Sr., Betty, in effect your mother, Wendell Jr. and now Roger, but they live on. In us. Still, I'm not sure what to do with it." PS laughed. Waxing philosophical was not his strong suit.

Paul pushed his chair back. "It's too late for this." He was drained; dog tired and one more stop to make.

They moved outside. Paul reached in and turned off the porch light. Immediately, the stars sprang to life. Between the trees lining the drive and above the forest that surrounded the property, the Milky Way lay strewn across the sky, unchanged in a lifetime, rolling in the same apparent circle night after night, shifting only with the seasons. Each man craned his neck, breathing in the brilliance with the summer air. Neither said a word. Then Paul gripped his father's bony shoulder, squeezed, and turned loose to descend the stairs.

With less than a warm sensation, he felt his father's eyes on him all the way down to his car.

14

Railroad Street

PAUL PULLED OVER. The road a few yards ahead dived into the woods that would obscure the view down the ridge, and he wanted to take in the panorama. The view wasn't pretty, but it enchanted him in the uncomfortable way that fit him well after a midnight visit to his father. Looking out toward Oliver over the sleeping streets of the company town, United States Steel's Morgan Park and at the steel plant itself, he could make sense of the grim and grinding struggle he felt inside. Through the fatigue of sleeplessness, trouble swirled around him, coal grit driven in wind. His scrambled feelings foamed hot inside him like an acid bath in the plant below. That's where I should have been, he said to himself, tending a furnace or drawing miles of wire through a die.

Below, sixteen stacks angling off in three separate files spewed smoke toward the west that in daylight shone white, yellow, or gray but in the night glowed orange and shiny black: the plumes lit from the furnaces below and coated darkly on top by the night sky. The steel plant sprawled like a gigantic cat—a Bengal tiger striped like industrial night. It loomed so large in the distance that the squealing of steel on steel, the compression and sudden release of steam at the boiler house, the roar of the ship-sized open hearth and foundry furnaces, even from a half mile away exploded loudly over the clank of metal on harder metal, the scraping of iron ore clods and coal bricks on conveyors, and the banging of presses rolling steel sheets—the gargantuan feline, exhaling in an arrhythmic, faraway but powerful *huuhh-huuhh* of breath, the force of which even from high above Paul could feel on his skin.

He tracked two trains, ore and coal, winding through the plant, shedding their loads at the feet of conveyors that fed the beast. Hard coal made it breathe. It seemed he could feel liquid heat from the hearth radiating his forehead and cheeks, hot and abrasive at once, warming and warning alike. The creature's power overwhelmed, frightened, and mounted a threat. Yet it was unimaginably collared, controlled by men—not those who scurried between conveyors and pistons, who broke the dam for the molten pour. Those were mortal men who could be burned, scraped, crushed, or sliced. The igneous cat was leashed by steel men, giants who stood clean and away in East Duluth, Cleveland and New York. These men were invisible, invincible; they did not bleed. They, whose souls had been scorched barren not at the two-thousand-degree open hearth that blackened and sooted the faces of the leprechaun-men scrambling at the furnace but by the mammonish glow of money and mounds of wealth—it was they who made it purr, in unmitigated gall, *huuhh-huuhh*.

His father had angled, contrived to escape that beast. He wouldn't stand at the gates of a ferric hell as his own father had before tuberculosis laid him out; nor would he see his son put in the traces of a laboring life. PS had kept his distance from the work and the politics and the wars that had destroyed his father's health. He insisted that Paul seek a clearer, cleaner way. He had derided the puny comforts Labor had brought to the ardor of work—gains that were forever worn away by manipulation and chicanery of the steel men who juried the trials of working people. That, he had sworn, would not be for his son. So, despite misgivings about the primacy of education, PS opened the way and pushed Paul hard in that direction. College was a chance for Paul to free himself from the smoke-respiring monster that he gazed upon this night from the Smithville ridge. To Paul, that escape now seemed futile.

Paul felt still under the heel of the steel men far away. He had crossed over by going to school; he'd never have to trim ore or channel red hot steel into molds or crawl inside machines to repair or lubricate their bearings or have to scoop six tons of coal at a time into hoppers that fed the furnaces. He had left behind, too, the common share of suffering camaraderie that he saw bind the West End together, that coated over differences in language and customs—Finnish, Serbian, Swedish, Italian, Polish—that had made separate nations but had here found common cause pitted against the cat, the beast, and the steel men.

Paul had gained and given up. He would not feel at home at a Finnish Hall dance. The talk of milling, pulping, moving ore, and pushing ten-ton cars would leave him out. The boisterous and drunken release from labor was not for him. His aches were of another kind, cleft from pals and proletariat.

Paul looked down to the plant. Yes, he was high above it. He had followed PS and climbed the ridge, but both were still held in thrall by the force of steel—PS by cold iron ordinance and the connivance of crooked law, he himself by the machinations of an East End marriage, downtown politics, and his misapplied ambition. His gut churned sharply. The bile of injustice rose in his gullet, choking him with the taste of rusted iron. He got out of the car. He wretched but nothing came. He doubled over gripping the front tire, panting between heaves until his shirt stuck to his back with sweat. The wooziness subsided. He spat acidic rust on the dirt of the road and propped himself against the Buick. Things have got to change, he brooded. Paul was not sure how that would happen or who would cause it, but he was certain he could not go on in the same old groove.

The day had made that much clear. Roger would be as easily forgotten as Wendell, Sr. had been. His life, his death would make little difference. That he had to fight against. Pamela and her parents would continue the press on him, doing what they knew best or perhaps the only thing they knew. He could no longer stomach their cloying, mincing words and remain himself. He didn't relish running away, either.

Miss Crosley's murder would grow larger than life, he knew. Her death could overpower his life. It was sad, Paul thought, but the passing of an eighty-year-old woman was less tragic than the death of a fifteen-year-old boy with a life ahead of him, robbed by a needle. Money, Miss Crosley's fortune, would fuel the voyeurism of the press and public. Though the flow of that case already was wrong, he'd stay the course.

Tommy's birthday, Allouez, and Cindy herself had brought him back in review of the eighteen years past. Can I reshape those years? Can I live down my mistakes and free everyone involved? Paul cringed at the thought of himself as hero. The past couldn't be relived, but the future might be made much more right. He could not continue as he had been. Maybe, through it all, he could undo the crime that kept his father in the shadow of a corrupted judge.

But as he looked back through the twenty years since his startling idea to leave the West End for good—it had occurred to him on a spring morning, walking to class at the university—as he gazed beyond to his father's shock at the Thompson dam, with Mark standing over a Canadian's corpse, and even further back, well before he was born, to the last breaths his grandfather took on the screened porch of Nopeming Sanatorium, or even twenty years before that, to the torch-lit mob of Finnish and Swedish strikers, his grandsire included, swinging clubs at scab-driven street cars and pistol-armed deputized sheriffs and, once more, looking further toward the cold Atlantic seas and Baltic frosts his great-grandfather had shivered over—Paul saw that he had wandered away from what mattered most to him, had always mattered, and without which, he decided there on the Smithville section of Skyline Drive, he could not go on.

If Cindy had waited for him through the early years of his marriage to Pamela, if his father had stood by him in his decisions, good or terrible, if Tommy adopted him as a father until he knew he was one, and if Memma had nourished him with her cakes, breads, and cheer all these years, he not only owed them but he also belonged to and with them solidly, wholly, openly, and forever.

Paul pulled onto the road and turned down the hill toward Morgan Park. After years in the West End, he had entered adolescence nearby in Smithville but had escaped the regimented life and narrow thinking of company-town lives and minds. PS had him in a private school for several years but relented and allowed Paul to attend Denfeld with Wendell Jr. and, though they never spoke of it, with Cindy too. Sometimes he stayed at Berta's to keep the travel time shorter. The Morgan Park crowd didn't notice. He was a neighbor but an outsider. They hardly knew he existed.

Paul drove by the concrete, architectural gates of "The Park," catching just a glimpse of one of the two churches US Steel had built for the community. It was a miniature of a gothic cathedral, not stone but concrete like everything else in the town, including the houses, shopping and community centers, streets, and alleys. As intended, the addition was a world unto itself—protected, inward-looking, and completely dependent on the company for everything including heat, electricity, and upkeep. Paul had to chuckle every time he drove by. The Steel Trust had solved one problem: how to keep the laborer "happy" at his job.

If the company owned his house, provided heat and electricity, how could he agitate or strike? It was an expensive idea that for years kept the Duluth Iron Works an open shop, free of serious labor organizers. When wages were eventually forced upward by Labor, the company "made it possible" for the workers to own their own homes in Morgan Park. They were dumping old houses on well-heeled workers who bought the idea and the houses with open arms. They also had to buy their own furnaces or boilers. The best views in "The Park" were of the plant itself, the source of all.

Paul drove on. He had made almost a complete circuit of St. Louis Bay from Superior, through Oliver and Gary, stopping in Smithville and passing Morgan Park on his way to West Duluth, the business district serving these far-flung communities. He cruised West Grand on his way past his old high school.

Denfeld brought Wendell Jr. to mind, and Paul wondered if he had made it to town yet. Probably not, Paul decided. Wendell Jr. was a careful driver. He'd stretch the seven hours into nine easily, stopping frequently, driving below the limit. I'll see him tomorrow. Paul rubbed a fist in his eye and smoothed his hair back, slowly passing his palm over his forehead. Hell, it is tomorrow.

His dad's coffee held his exhaustion at bay. He could make it. Just one more stop. He detoured to Cindy's old house and looked for Wendell Jr.'s car, which he knew could not be there. A light shone in the living room, but he didn't stop.

Paul turned up the hill, taking Third Street to glance at Berta's house. It was dark. He had wanted to be sure. Of what, he did not know, but he revisited the house anyway. He drove on and dropped down Lake Avenue to make his final stop. His "street source" would be at Huey's at this hour. Paul would do his own kind of smelting tonight. He'd seine the truth from the river of lies that floated on Randy's words. To Belisle it was a game. To Paul it was his work.

No matter what the weather, the atmosphere inside Joe Huey's was the same, a steamy babble of voices seasoned in soy, even on a very early Tuesday morning. Joe didn't work this late, but his brother Howard, a rounder, plumper, less animated version of Joe, calmly tapped on the change mat the lustrous gold seal ring he wore on his fat pinkie. Howard had a grace and warmth Joe completely missed. His reserve seemed to balance Joe's quick, effusive greetings. Paul enjoyed seeing them together in the hour they shared between shifts. That hour was long gone.

He paid in advance at the counter. "The usual, Howard," Paul said. Pork fried rice in the back room.

Howard handed a waitress the order and bowed pleasantly down the row of lacquered booths, past the end of which hung a curtain beaded to represent a dragon. Paul moved past the booths, in second nature checking their occupants as he went, and swept through dragon's mouth to enter a room divided into three red-curtained booths. In the last one, next to the stairway door, sat Randy Belisle. He faced away from Paul's advance, watched the back door, and sipped Chinese tea from a lotus-blossom-decorated cup. Paul slid onto the seat across from Randy and pulled the curtain cord. He wanted to get this over with.

Randy was decked out. His fringed cowhide coat was an

191

expensive one. He wore gold-rimmed John Lennon glasses tinted enough to obscure his eyes. The embroidered V-neck of his white cotton smock framed the triangular Navajo amulet that matched the bracelets he wore on either wrist. Randy never wore a watch. He was well groomed; wisps of facial hair and a faint moustache softened slender, pretty rather than handsome lips and jaw line. He wore, Paul decided, a ridiculously large-brimmed vaquero's hat.

Though Randy came out of the West End, Paul had a hard time liking the guy. He found that unusual. Randy's mother, like Paul's wife Pamela, came from upper-crust parents and never ceased ranting over the "clods and kikes" she had to live with in the neighborhood. When her husband dropped dead on the grain exchange floor in early morning trading, she packed up and moved east the day before the funeral. So Randy's view of the old neighborhood was filtered like the light thrown by the Chinese lantern above his head through his greenish glasses. He saw only ways to make money there. He entirely lacked the familial grounding of the West End and wanted, too, the stiff uprightness of the East End. Those two traits, in their absence, left him venal and vacant.

His ethical emptiness made him a perfect snitch. Randy could steal with a smile. Buy from him, fine. Buy from someone else afterward, he turned you in. His easygoing manners were calculated. He housed a saber up his sleeve. His movements he kept hidden and unannounced. Paul was even a bit surprised to see Randy here as planned. Ordinarily, he kept his next play secret.

"Good evening, Mr. Tuomi."

"Hi, Randy."

"Tea?"

"No thanks, I've got some rice and water coming."

Paul glanced upwards—through the spindles high above

Randy's seat back—at the ceiling of the next booth. He could tell the booth was occupied by the shifting shadows. He pointed and made a zipping motion at his lips.

Randy grinned; his teeth glistened white, accenting the pride of his Mexican tan. He nodded.

A small, muffled voice said, "Pork fried rice."

Paul pulled the curtain aside. The waitress put the platter and his water on the table. "Soy and oil at the table," she pointed.

He proffered a dollar and said, "Thanks." He fixed the curtain again and looked at the steaming heap of rice. "Want some?"

Randy beamed another lustrous smile. "Never touch the stuff." He laughed and sipped his tea.

Paul inhaled the lush vapors. He heaped a serving for himself from the platter. He doused the rice with hot oil from Joe's container and dug in with relish. He ate in silence, eyeing Randy and the booth ceiling behind him. Randy was smooth. He had no telling habits or ticks, even when being surreptitiously observed. He had a remarkable ease in his movements and demeanor. I should be so smooth, Paul noted. Was that envy? He wondered. Paul figured, though, Randy's suaveness was as much façade as it was nature. He knew Belisle had much more going on underneath than one could guess.

Paul slowed his eating deliberately. He swallowed a little of the water between forks full of rice. He wanted to press Randy with silence, just to see. Demure as ever, Randy sipped his tea. He wasn't going to fidget. Paul finished half his plate and wasn't hungry anymore. He pointed at the booth behind and said, "Let's step downstairs for a smoke, hey?"

Beyond the door was the iron landing of a fire escape. The stairs led all the way to the curb of Railroad Street a story below. More than a few backroom customers used the Railroad Street stair to get to Joe's without being seen. "We'll have some privacy," Paul said.

When they reached the bottom Paul led the way around the corner and out of sight of the street. He didn't want to be seen with Randy, and he knew Randy felt the same, even though he'd not complain no matter where they talked.

Once round the back, Paul removed an envelope he had tucked in his pocket. "I think you know where this is from," he said. He didn't want to open it or see how much was inside. The vice squad was setting up a bust, buying a list from Randy. It would have names and addresses of low-level users and a few local dealers that had crossed Randy somehow. Paul was just the messenger, doing a favor for vice. It was not his bust. Randy pocketed the envelope without looking at it and handed Paul a folded sheet of paper. Paul looked down the list.

He looked up at Randy, squarely and suddenly. Roger's name and basement address had been scratched from the list. That electrified Paul.

"What do you know about Roger Sillanpaa?" he said.

"I heard he was dead," Randy answered flatly. "Happened yesterday."

"What else?" Paul wanted information and wasn't going to give before he got. "Who'd he been hanging with?"

Randy didn't like to be pressed, but he stayed loose. "Let me see the list again."

Paul gave it to him.

"Limmer. John Limmer. He's right here. Crashes on different couches but he's most likely to be there." He pointed to an address on Fifth Street. "For the next week, anyway. Might be at any of these hovels." Randy only hinted derision in this last word. Even in speech he stayed cool.

"Who else?"

Randy thought, or pretended to think. "Nobody else, as far as I know."

He's lying, Paul thought. Sure, but he needed other information from Belisle and could wait until Limmer was picked up in the bust for the other. "Ever heard of Fizzy? Daddy Fizzy?"

"Who hasn't," Randy said. "He's the light-show impresario. He's not on the list and isn't likely to be. The guy is an entertainer. Stays clean."

"Ever see him with Roger?"

Randy sounded defensive, on purpose, "Hey, I don't see these people. I source them."

"Well?"

"I know nothing more." Randy was done with it.

"Okay. I have one more question. Not about this, either."

"Shoot, detective," Randy made a pistol of his hand. He pulled the "trigger" gaily.

"You know I'm on the Brookside case."

Randy sounded genuine. "Big case. Right man to run it."

"Flattery accepted. This morning, no, yesterday morning, early, I was passing by on London Road before the deaths were discovered and saw this kid walking along the fence. Maybe he came out from the gates. Five-seven. Curly, long blond mop. Thin slip of a guy. Wearing a tee shirt and a denim vest. He had an odd walk."

"Hair to his shoulders or shorter?"

"Shorter."

"Glasses?"

"Yes."

"Walks like a sailor?"

"That's what it was," Paul said. "You know him?"

"I did. Not now, though. I heard he was pedaling coins.

Friends were suspicious."

"What kind of coins?"

"Old coins. Foreign, they said."

"You know his name?"

Randy kept it factual. "Ingstrom. First name Reese. Lives in Lakeside or near."

"Thanks. Anything else?"

"I don't know where you'll find him, but when you do, ask him that."

Randy wasn't going to say anything more. Paul could tell that. He didn't push it, but Belisle didn't move toward the street or the stair. He seemed to want to say something but was holding on to it.

"Something else?"

Randy took a steady, even friendly look at Paul. "You'll remember me at the right time." He continued to size Paul up.

"You have stored manna in heaven. Yes."

"Ever heard of a guy, Roland LaPrairie?" Randy said.

Paul shook his head.

"I think you'll find him interesting. He's lived out at Solon Springs for a long time. Big guy. Uses the name Robert Larson." Randy's eyes grew round behind his circular lenses. Circles within circles, Paul thought. "He's about your dad's age. Look him up sometime."

Paul felt like leaping on the punk. But whatever the information was, Randy was through giving it. His cryptic mention of PS rankled Paul. At once he had to strangle the fierce anger. Obviously, Randy felt he had something valuable, something that would help him down the road. If it weren't worth that, Randy would have volunteered nothing. Paul let it go. "I'll make a note of it. Thanks."

They were done. Randy moved to walk away around the

corner. "*Hasta luego, Señor.*"

Paul took the street stairs to Lake Avenue, where his car was parked. When he looked down on the road and the tracks, Randy was not in sight. There were no cars down there.

Fatigue ground at Paul. The break he got from Randy tonight, at least in the Brookside case and maybe more, buoyed him, but now sleep bore down on him heavily. Though he dreaded going home, he needed to rest. And on the long drive from Oliver and Smithville, he'd formed a plan.

At the house, the kitchen and hall lights were on. She's up, he decided. Pamela minded the bills and didn't waste on utilities. She was up waiting and surely loaded for bear. He sat in the Buick for a minute, moved to the garage, and then took the time to lock his revolver in the tool chest. Keep it out of reach, he concluded. He stared at the blank kitchen door and pushed it open.

Paul was barely into the kitchen when Pamela spoke from the dark of the living room. "Paul." It sounded like a command.

He wanted to be civil. He had decided. There was no need for shouting or mean words, at least on his part. But he couldn't resist parody. "Pamela," he said mimicking her tone.

She entered the lit kitchen. Her hair was up in curlers, of course, and she had wrapped herself tightly against the summer night in her winter robe. She shuffled along in her furry slippers. God-awful pink. He gave her a once-over and lowered himself to a chair at the café table.

"Oh, you must be tired, dear. You poor thing." She was mean. It didn't matter to Paul. "Where in the hell have you been? And don't tell me on police business, either."

Again, he couldn't stop himself, "On police business." He

let it sink in. "Yeah. I saw my father."

"Ah, the great detective, Mr. Paul S. Tuomi, master of disguise."

Paul was tired. The day had been long, but the marriage had been longer. He wouldn't fight to defend anything, not even his father. "Yes. That one. I found him helpful and friendly."

She wanted a row. "I'm glad he has at least one friend. No one else finds much use for him."

"Sad. True, but sad." He wouldn't rise to her baiting.

"What is?"

"My father, but you too, Pam. You make me sad."

"Screw you, Paul. If anyone is a sad case here, it's you and your godforsaken West End cronies and cranks. What the hell do you think I should be doing while you gallivant around town in your big car? Knit? Hold come-as-you-are parties?"

Years ago, Berta had made the mistake of inviting Pamela to one of her impromptu neighborhood coffee klatches. Pam arrived an hour afterwards, dressed to the nines and made up like a doll. The party was just breaking up and all the other women were in the nightgowns, scrub clothes, or flowered aprons they'd been wearing when Berta called. That was the last time Pamela responded to anyone in the West End.

Paul didn't return the jibe. He simply rose from the table and went to the linen closet in the hall. He heard Pam ranting in the kitchen.

When he passed the kitchen doorway with bedding in his arms, she yelled. "What do you think you're doing?"

Paul put the sheets and blanket on a chair in the hall. He stood in the doorway to look directly at her. "Right now, Pam, I'm going to sleep on that couch over there. In the morning, I'm packing my bags and leaving."

"It's about time."

Even though she didn't deserve an explanation, he softened and gave her one. "Listen, Pam, I need some space. I'll be working most of the time anyway, until this case goes to trial, if it does. Together, we aren't doing each other any good."

"You've got someone else. Don't you."

He shook his head, not at the accusation, but at how long it had taken him to make this move. "I need to be alone. I'm not moving in with a lover. Take the rest as it comes, will you?"

She stood. He could see her working through a speech, but finally she stamped her furry foot, gathered the robe tighter and, like a homecoming queen, strode from the room. The heels of her pink slippers flapped down the hall. The bedroom door hit the jamb, hard.

Falling sleepward as he made his bed, moving softly, Paul hummed the last refrains of "Sentimental Journey." He knew he'd sleep well.

15

East Hillside

INGSTROM STEPPED DOWN from the bus right in front of the funeral home. He did not take it as an omen. He found it funny. He recited to himself: You go from the dowdy apartment building down the street to the geriatric hospital next door to the undertaker's at the end of the block! All that's missing is the cemetery.

That was miles away. As close as he had been to it last night, he had little fear of death or fascination with it. It was the irony that tickled him. Anyway, he'd alighted there to avoid being seen at the stop nearer Siiri's. It was a practical consideration.

He turned down the steep, public stairway beside the mortuary. It would bring him to First Street below. There he could walk under the sheer granite cliff that supported the foundations of the hospital. He'd double back and cross into Siiri's alley two blocks away without the conspicuous fanfare of the bus stop.

On First Street, trucks were lined along the curb waiting for service at the garage across the street. They shielded him from the view of businesses on the other side. No one could see him. The sidewalk was empty. Like most things in his life, Ingstrom took his recently born caution with a bouncing step and cooling attitude.

He kept to the shadow cast by the escarpment below the hospital. At some points, the stone towered four stories above him. It was as if giant children had been playing with gabbro building blocks and, called to dinner, left abruptly. Squared masses piled up the rock face and, despite crevices and cracks between them where screening trees had here and there taken root, the monumental outcropping muscled aloft in a prominent tumble of stony plinths. Ingstrom was glad of something natural and bigger than himself. The man-made seemed to grope and irritate him. People made him uneasy, but in the shade cast by the looming adamant, he felt as comfortable as if he were sailing down the shores of the lake. He was carried along. He could be more a witness than an actor. Somehow that removed a nagging whisper about responsibility. That he could do without.

He was cutting it close. The Central High clock, which he'd seen from the bus, told him he was late. Ten to four. Matty would come at five thirty. Enough time. *I feel like another shower. It's all good.* He was looking forward to Siiri.

He rounded the corner, marched quickly up the hill and crossed the avenue, striding directly to Siiri's back door. He entered the covered stairway and climbed to the second floor. He stopped at the window, checking to see that no one had followed. From the landing, he could hear the water running. *She must be in the shower.* Ingstrom tried the knob. The door was unlocked. He took a step into the kitchen.

"Peace, sister," he said.

Siiri poked her head out of the bathroom door. "Inggy. I'm glad it's you! Was the door unlocked?"

He didn't like her games but understood her need to play them. Her hair was dry still, so she had likely watched him crossing the avenue. Running the shower was her ruse.

"I just got home," she said.

He produced a joint from his pocket. "Care for an after-work, pre-shower doobie?" He lit the thing.

"Let me shut off the water."

She came out in a towel. "Well, sure. You're so thoughtful." She moved close.

Ingstrom handed the joint over. Siiri drew deeply. Hedonist, Ingstrom thought. Siiri passed it to him and exhaled the thick, bluish smoke.

"Whew! That's good stuff."

"Pleasure-seeker," Ingstrom said on the intake. "You love the high."

Siiri pushed him gently to a chair. With a hand she held the towel to her chest, wriggled between his knees and straddled his thigh. "I need one more hit."

She took the cig from his hand, brought it to her lips. Ingstrom stroked her towel, feeling her chest rise as she inhaled the smoke. He massaged her breasts softly and let his hands descend along her sides and thighs. Siiri held the joint to his lips.

"I think we should get clean. Then we can get dirty," she said.

Ingstrom felt the rush of the high rise to his head. He held the smoke in his lungs and slipped a hand under the towel at her knee to stroke her. Then he removed his hands from her. He wet a finger and thumb with his tongue and snuffed the hot end of the joint between them. He flipped the little cylinder on the table.

Ingstrom returned his hands to her hips, sliding them along her flanks now, and pushed her up to standing. He steadied both of them as he rose from the chair. Once standing, he moved his palms under her breasts, lifting them and letting them fall as he parted and unbound the towel with a twist of his wrists. They let it fall to the floor. Siiri leaned onto his chest and pressed close.

"Maybe you want to get that water running again," he said.

She kissed him fully, tonguing his teeth and mouth,

parting from his lips with a sigh. She turned, swept the towel from the floor and trailed it behind her as she moved to the bathroom. "Come along, sailor boy."

Ingstrom followed, shedding clothes as he went.

They finished the stubby doobie in bed. They'd toweled each other drier than they needed to be and slipped between the sheets. They lay satisfied both from their bathing and their coupled desire and let themselves drift along on the grass. Siiri mumbled through a litany of incoherent hopes and dreams for her art and, still muttering, drifted off to begin snoring lightly. Ingstrom listened to her and studied the molding at the ceiling, the plinth blocks at the window. A light breeze moved the shade in and out of the open sash. For an apartment so close to downtown, the quiet impressed him. A couple of robins chirped to each other outside, and the trees on the lot next door wove silhouettes across the translucency of the drawn shade.

Ingstrom needed the quiet. He felt peaceful now. It had been good. He had flirted with Siiri over a few weeks, mostly on a whim. He didn't like to think her reputation was what drew him to her, but he had to admit it had helped overcome his usual reticence to get close. With anyone. Siiri was devoted to Matty, but she also had a tough time keeping her pants on. He wondered if she had had Mike Light over once or more than once.

Free love. Ain't it grand? The thought rankled him. Nothing's free, he reminded himself. He preferred to ignore what didn't please him. But wasn't he here because he saw Siiri at Skip's and then heard her name from Carlos down at Joe's? Yes, she can't help herself, he thought. Then, no, she can help herself. He smiled his private little smile.

He thought about having a woman in every port. Ingstrom

longed for the sea, but it was the adventure he wanted more than the ocean. Got to get away. That's always been my aim, he mused. Now, it's more urgent than ever. Things were unraveling here, that was sure, and with one more little stumble this adventure would cease to be fun. Randy was right about keeping a low profile, and Ingstrom had already decided to take Belisle up on the cabin idea. A few days at Grand Lake would rest him well. The ship might be in port by then. Maybe he could board early. Don't be too eager, he considered. That's suspicious.

Ingstrom looked over Siiri for the stub of marijuana. The clock read five. He remembered. Fizzy!

Bob was waiting for his call. Ingstrom got up, going quietly to the phone hung on the kitchen wall. Daddy Fizzy was waiting, but he wasn't worried. Worry wasn't his style, except, Ingstrom thought, about the draft.

"I'm late but on it," Ingstrom said. "How about I buy you a burger at Somebody's?"

Bob sounded reluctant. "There?"

"Hey, it's the best in town."

"Can you include Marly?"

A warm flush came over Ingstrom. "Yeah, sure. Bring her along." He liked Marly. Her cool the previous night had charmed him, though she was younger than Roger. Even than Roger. Yeah, Roger.

Then he was back with Fizzy. "I'll wait for you at Second and Third Avenue East," he said. "Just stop at the corner. I'll be looking for you."

Ingstrom went back to the bedroom. It was five-ten. He woke Siiri by sliding atop her.

"Oooh, mister, you back again?" She ran her arm down his back and between his buttocks. "What a nice ass."

His thoughts of Marly had incited him. Siiri enticed him. "I am made for you, Inggy." He ravished her again. This time it was fast.

"What time is Matty back?" He had rolled away from Siiri.

"Shit." She was up and dressing. "He's getting off the bus right now. Grab your clothes. You can dodge down the front stairs. You can leave that way."

Ingstrom needed no prodding. He bundled up his duds and headed naked to the door.

"Dress on the stairs. He's here!" Siiri, opening door for Ingstrom, said, "Debajo, Señor." Then she raced to the kitchen door.

Ingstrom heard Matty coming in. "Hey, hon, whose sack is that out there?"

Ingstrom sat on the fifth step down, drawing on his trousers and shirt without a sound. He'd have to go around the back for the sack. He smiled to himself. It didn't bother him. He stepped bowlegged down the steps, placing his feet solidly at the ends of the treads. Not one creaked. He slipped on his shoes. Outside, he kept close to the house and circled around back.

Though he deliberately slammed the back door on his return and tromped up the back stairs again, the two didn't hear him coming. They were shouting.

"Where did you get it?"

"At Skip's. You were out of it, remember?"

"Why are you smoking alone?'

Ingstrom wanted to hear her story. She was doing well.

"It relaxes me. The job is a drag."

"I think someone was here. It's obvious."

Ingstrom intervened. Even though his bag was there for the taking, he knocked.

Matty came to the door.

206

"Hey, Matty. I came back for my bag. Thought I heard your voice."

The wind left Matty's sails. He was aghast.

"Stopped by to use the phone and just skipped out the front without thinking. Smells like dope in here. Got some?"

Matty shook his head, still speechless.

"I do." Ingstrom produced the second reefer Randy had given him. "Should we light up?" He put a foot on the step up to the kitchen.

Matty muttered something about studying, but Ingstrom swept by him into the kitchen. "Hi again, Siiri." He lit the joint.

Siiri smiled her admiration at him. "Matty's the one should toke up." She took the reefer and passed it to him.

"All right, just one," Matty said.

The three sat at the table and smoked. It's the least I can do for them, he decided. He wasn't one to crow about conquests and didn't want to get one up on Matty. He kind of liked the guy, even if he was a dupe. Ingstrom had wanted to save the grass for the cabin, but this was a better use of it. He saved half of the roach. He looked out the kitchen window for Fizzy. He wasn't there yet.

Matty looked at Ingstrom in an odd way. "I heard Roger Sillanpaa OD'd."

Siiri took her hands to her mouth, "He's dead?"

Ingstrom brought horror to his face, "No!" he said.

Matty doubled his frown. "I heard you gave him the stuff."

"I ran into him at the light show but he didn't get anything from me. What was it?"

"Horse, they said." Matty watched Ingstrom's face intently. "Weren't you there?"

"At Skip's? Yeah," Ingstrom said.

Matty wouldn't leave it alone. "No. At Roger's later on."

"This is the first I've heard about it. Did it happen at Roger's house?"

"Skip says . . ."

Ingstrom broke in. "Yeah, that's where Roger got it, from Skip's girl. She used to mainline."

Matty wavered. Siiri broke in. "Yeah, Skip was acting real nervous even when we arrived. Remember, Matty?" He did not remember. "Standing at the door like the fuzz or something. Like he wanted to check ID's."

Ingstrom was acting now. "God, this is awful," he said. "I wonder how his grandma is doing." He hoped reference to family might change the direction. "Do you know her?"

Matty shook his head. "I know of her."

"She's got to be hurting," Siiri said. Though Siiri herself was not of the West End, coming from thirty miles up the north shore, her voice quavered with concern and sadness.

Matty was looking pale.

"Yazoo. My ride is here," Ingstrom said. "Thanks for the use of the phone. He didn't take long. Got to go." Ingstrom headed for the front door again. "No. I need my bag." He turned to leave from the back, picked up the sack and waved a peace sign at the door. Siiri waved it back. Matty just stared.

Ingstrom was down the stairs and out the door fast. He didn't want to miss Fizzy and Marly, and this had been a scene that, even though he handled it well, he didn't want to extend. Siiri could handle his sexual visitation; she must be used to it. But Matty connecting him with Roger's death was a bummer. Matty liked listening to talk and didn't mind that Skip was a creep and a rat.

Marly was parked in the bus stop. Fizzy had just got out of the car to look for him when he bounded up the hill, his sea bag over his shoulder. "Bob. I'm here."

Fizzy held the door for him. He got in the back and moved to the middle. He leaned forward touching Marly's arm. "Glad you could come, girl."

"Sure. Thanks for the invite."

On the way up to Woodland, Ingstrom asked his favor. He was buying dinner and giving valuable advice, so he wasn't shy about calling in his chips.

"Hey, a big favor. I have an invite for the night out on Canosia Road. Can you give me a lift? I've got gas money."

Fizzy looked at his sister. She nodded.

"Okay, but I'll have to bus it back to the West End early. Marly can take you."

That's fine, Ingstrom thought.

Somebody's House

POSH WAS NOT AN APT DESCRIPTION, nor was tony a fair critique, of the restaurant that Ingstrom, Marly, and Daddy Fizzy entered. Like any creation, Somebody's House grew in the first place as an expression of its owner and chef, but immediately afterward became a reflection of a clientele that varied according to the time of day you entered but mostly matriculated from the university just across Woodland Avenue: students and parents, professors, college brass, and clerical staff, but there were others, too.

Lunch served women on shopping dates with neighbors and friends. For early dinner came mothers and school kids who left behind the uneaten halves of their huge burgers. Later, couples in casual trim spoke low, leaning over clothed tables, occasionally lifting their voices to greet arrivals in like polo-ish attire, all talking savvy. At night the sweets and European coffees turned Somebody's into a true café, a mellow, candlelit coffeehouse, lingering through the evening just above the edge of respectability. In the evenings the student clientele housed throughout the Central and East Hillside trickled in.

That the patrons were seldom residents of the Friendly West End was why Fizzy had raised a mild fuss over the suggestion. Still, Somebody's, even though far from a late-night, egalitarian mixer like Joe Huey's, carried enough panache to provoke Fizzy's desire to show the place to his sister. He had heard wondrous descriptions of the burgers served there and of the campy descriptions of them in the menu; but more than the food, he wanted to taste—wanted Marly to taste—the Café Borgia, a rich, hot, and creamy coffee-chocolate combination that couldn't be had in the West End for any price but had gained a reputation amongst what he called the munchies crowd, pot smokers on the hillside. On a winter evening, high and extolling Borgia's virtues, they piled six and seven into a Volkswagen bug to spin and slide their way up Mount Royal to Somebody's, hoping to arrive before closing. Fizzy hadn't been party to those excursions, but had seen them brew hunger and pour hippies out an apartment door to flow up the hill.

It's the name. Café Borgia. To his mind it spelled exotic, European romance. He didn't admit that to Marly and certainly not to Ingstrom, for even though this visit tickled infatuation, it also framed him as a rube of the village below. Though more accomplished and mature, he did not think of himself even as sophisticated as Matty Melting, who felt no conflict leaving his home town for the university. But to Daddy Fizzy the leap from worker's housing to the dormitory was too wide to manage. He hoped Marly would be able to clear the chasm he had shied from. She was capable, intelligent, adaptable, and unafraid. Even if he would not, she could. That was why he brought her along.

Fizzy was here for counsel. He had all but made up his mind to respond to the draft call, but he did want to hear what Ingstrom had to say. Inggy was hip and definitely informed. He didn't put down patriotism or duty, but he was dead-set against killing and war. He had already helped two graduates from East High get some sort of special status, and another Inggy knew well had emigrated to Canada. Yet another was hiding out, some said, in New York City. Fizzy couldn't see himself doing those things, but he also didn't relish cutting his hair and trading riding boots for a combat pair. I'm no hero, he mused. Already, several brash patriot volunteers he'd gone to school with in the West End had come back in body bags.

They took a table off alone by the front window. "Hey, you two," Ingstrom said, "it's my treat."

Fizzy looked to Marly. "Why don't you try a Café Borgia?"

"Cool," Ingstrom said, "but have a burger too. Look at all the choices." At the moment he was his father, magnanimity wrapped in worldly knowledge. He liked the role. "We'll be here a while. Have what you will." He sauntered away from the table to wash and to leave them to study the menu.

Marly was charmed. "Bobby, thanks for bringing me," she said. She pointed at three different burgers on the list. "Which should I get?"

"Any one of those sounds good. Don't forget the Café Borgia, though. I think you'll like it."

"Have you tried it?"

He had to admit his innocence. "No, but I've heard a lot about them. Inggy has the cash, don't worry."

Ingstrom had already visited at several tables on his way to the bathroom, and just before he reached the back of the restaurant, an older woman at a table with a younger one, both dressed expensively, stopped him.

"Good evening, Reese."

He had seen them back there and had hoped to pass without talking to these neighborhood gossips. "Good evening, Mrs. Skaansgard. How are you on such a fine evening?"

She looked him up and down, less with disapproval than with hope for his reform in years to come. Her eyes said as much. "You remember my daughter Pamela, of course."

"I wasn't even born when you left our neighborhood, Mrs. Tuomi, though I know we have been introduced. How are you?" The woman looked pained and haggard. Of the two, Ingstrom thought, impossibly, she seemed the older. He knew she had lost a son years ago.

"Fine," she said.

If this is fine, don't show me terrible, he concluded.

"Are you off to college next year, Reese?" the mother asked.

Let me be, woman, Ingstrom thought. "Oh, no," he said, "I have a year under my belt."

"Ah hah! You'll do fine. Follow in your father's footsteps."

Ingstrom nodded. "Accounting is where the money is, for sure." He kept his expression earnest, thoughtful.

"Don't become a cop," Mrs. Tuomi said.

"A detective, dear, Paul is a detective," the mother corrected. She looked at Ingstrom. "He is heading the Brookside investigation, you know."

"I didn't know. You must be proud."

The daughter looked startled and a bit confused. "Yes, yes, I'm very happy about it." The mother smiled, smug and superior.

"I had best wash and rejoin my friends. Good to see you."

He heard the older woman say, "Such a nice boy, don't you think?"

"He looks like one of those hippies. His friends certainly are. Oh, don't turn around, Mother."

Ingstrom smiled. God, get rid of them. He went to the men's room. He inspected his smile in the mirror. He shook his head. It hadn't been a good idea to come here with Fizzy. Too many people knew him. But so what? Who cares about the neighbors? He splashed water on his face. He felt better. I need something to eat. That's it. Food.

On his way back to the table, he nodded at the two ladies. "Give my regards to Mr. Skaansgard. I haven't seen him lately. Oh. And to Detective Tuomi as well." Ingstrom muted the note of derision he felt rising in his voice. He smiled broadly.

At the table, Marly and Fizzy were bent over the menu, pointing and talking. They looked at each other and smiled, but when Ingstrom approached they grew silent. Fizzy didn't look so cool, being the big brother to Marly, but Marly looked all the more cute and demure. She's an exceptional girl, he decided. He plunged his hands into his pockets and swayed up to the table standing behind her. He leaned over to see their choice. "Ah, the Alpenburger. Goes well with a Borgia." He kept from touching her with Fizzy right there, but leaned close enough to sense the heat of her frame. He sat to her other side.

"They have great fries, too. Get some."

When the waitress came Ingstrom ordered. "I'll have the same as Marly here," he said. Her name tasted good in his mouth. Looking at Fizzy, he said, "And give my friend here a Café Borgia."

When the waitress left, Fizzy looked at Ingstrom. "What have you heard about Roger?"

Ingstrom's stomach felt queasy for a moment. He didn't want to talk about Roger, but he could see Fizzy was bothered by something.

"Other than Skip blabbing all over town about it, I've heard nothing."

"I figured he couldn't keep it to himself," Fizzy said.

Ingstrom was annoyed. But they could do nothing. "Let him draw attention to himself. We'll stay cool."

Fizzy leaned in. With Marly between them, Ingstrom followed suit. She was sweet and he moved his cheek close to hers. She didn't retreat. "I heard the priest isn't going to say funeral mass over him," Fizzy said.

Ingstrom was a little confused. He hadn't anticipated this and didn't understand what it was all about. "Why?" he asked, baffled.

Fizzy whispered the answer. "I guess he thinks it's suicide."

Ingstrom gave a blank look. Marly cut in. "In the church, suicides are damned to hell. A priest can't say Mass or bury one in the church cemetery."

Fizzy fidgeted. "Berta, Roger's grandmother, is all upset over it. The whole neighborhood is talking."

"That's a bummer," Ingstrom said. It was a rare thing for him to be at a loss. He withheld his anti-religious rant as out of place here, but he couldn't understand the worry. "Can they hire someone to do a service? Like a funeral director?"

Both Fizzy and Marly frowned. That wasn't the right thing to say, Ingstrom thought. The siblings seemed mystified, maybe disgusted. "It isn't the same," Fizzy said. Marly pulled back. She slouched against the high chair. She left sourness on his cheek.

Ingstrom regrouped. "What's the story from the coroner?"

"Nothing yet," Fizzy said. "If he says accidental death, it'll be okay."

"Don't you think it was an accident?" Ingstrom said.

He expected a sudden protest. But each of his companions was thinking of something to say. Finally, Fizzy opened up. "Skip was saying the dope was bad."

Ingstrom had regrouped and was ready. "Listen. I'm truly sorry about Roger. He didn't deserve to die. All Skip is doing is covering for Janie, and it isn't even necessary. She knows the dope was good. So do I. It was too good. What Roger and John got was cut just for that reason. Janie's was practically pure. You know that was what Roger got hold of. He knew it was potent and went for it."

He stopped and looked at them. They were with him. "Roger was looking for a high, not a way out. It was an accident. Can't the minister"—Ingram searched for the word—"priest, see that?"

"Someone from the party would have to come forward," Marly said, "and that ain't likely."

"We're not going to squeal," Fizzy said, "but it's a shame if Roger can't be buried decently."

They both looked at Ingstrom. He usually had a plan, but this was out of his bailiwick. Priests, even protestant ministers, were beyond him. He'd use them if he had need, but Ingstrom stayed away from what he called mumbo jumbo. "Let me think about it." It was the best he could do right now.

Thank the gods, Ingstrom thought as the food arrived.

They all let their hunger lead them away from talk of Roger. Ingstrom watched Fizzy and Marly with appreciation and amusement. The aroma of the beef and the trimmings on the burgers clearly pleased them. When Fizzy sipped the chocolate essence of coffee through the Borgia's whipped cream, Ingstrom thought he'd levitate from his chair.

Fizzy looked at Marly. "This is fantastic."

She tried her own and agreed. Ingstrom watched her sweep her tongue over her lips. Her delight warmed him again.

The food and hot drinks took the edge off the angst over Roger. Ingstrom's anxiety over the West End talk subsided. Neither Fizzy nor Marly would snitch, even if it came to an investigation. He could count on them, but he couldn't see himself influencing the priest or the coroner. He was stumped. Let it be, he told himself, and turned to Fizzy's draft counseling. "What about this draft notice?" Ingstrom asked.

Fizzy brought it out. Ingstrom read it.

"The first thing to remember is that you don't owe them anything. This war isn't like World War II. We aren't liberators in Viet Nam. We are the aggressors." He liked to start with the faraway politics of the situation.

They were listening to him. "We're over there on false pretenses, killing babies and children along with Viet Cong. We don't even know who our enemy really is." He liked to accuse the military of baby-killing. No one could favor that. "The soldiers don't really know what they're fighting for."

Fizzy raised a finger. "Isn't it about communism?"

"No, it's about power. All about military power."

The political argument was lost on Fizzy, he could tell. He switched to make it more personal. "Look, Bob, I know you. You don't want to go over somewhere and shoot people. You are for peace."

Now he had him nodding. "Your art is more important than what some army recruiter would call duty. You enlighten and entertain people. You want to delight folks, not kill them."

Ingstrom moved into his usual spiel. "You don't have to do what they say you have to do. You have options. First, you could disappear. Lots of guys are doing that. Go to San Francisco or New York and vanish into the scene there." Something told Ingstrom that this option wasn't for Fizzy, but he was covering the bases.

"Problem is, you can't let anyone know where you are," Marly said. She was following it closely. "I wouldn't like that."

Ingstrom thought to defend it briefly, "True. The guys that tell their family where they're living usually are the ones who get caught. It's not the best option. Then they do time."

Fizzy broke in. "In jail?"

"Usually, they can serve in the Army or go to prison. It costs them a year or two.

That is the second option. Just refuse and do the time in jail."

Marly was on it. "You'd have a criminal record then."

Ingstrom had to agree. "Yeah, that's why so few go that way.

But it is one option. Some leave the country. Go to Canada. I've got a couple of friends in Vancouver now. They have apartments and jobs, girlfriends. You know. A life without war."

"I'd miss home," Fizzy said. "Can they come back after the war?"

"I'm not sure but not right away in any case. You have to consider it a permanent move."

The siblings turned to each other. They looked sad.

Ingstrom continued. "I don't recommend blowing off a finger or laming yourself. A few guys have done it. They might have gotten out on psych issues anyway. Some go to the shrink and play crazy. It could work, but it's not best."

"What is the best?" Fizzy said.

Now they were getting to the good stuff, what Ingstrom wanted to suggest in the first place. "Conscientious objector status," he said.

"What's that?"

Fizzy seemed interested, finally. Maybe I can get him to do this, Ingstrom thought. "It's a legal classification based on moral objections to war."

"How does it work? What do you have to do?" Marly had perked up. Now she was asking friendly questions.

"Usually, you have to have a sponsor. I turned two friends on to the minister up at UMD. The minister talked with them and wrote letters to the draft board," Ingstrom said. He didn't flout his experience but was pleased with it. "One was granted CO status. He had to serve in the Peace Corps or something like it, but he didn't have to fight or kill."

The mention of the college agitated Fizzy. "Do you have to go to the University?"

"No, you can talk to your regular minister. Your priest, I guess."

Fizzy looked to Marly. "You think Father L. would listen? I haven't been there much since catechism."

Marly sounded hopeful. "It wouldn't hurt to try."

Ingstrom dug in his sack. He had grabbed his last pamphlet on CO status that morning as he left the house. He wouldn't be counseling much on the high seas. He handed Fizzy the information. "You can get an application from the draft board."

Ingstrom could see this might be the best way for Fizzy.

"See what you can do. I see you as an objector. You're more peace-loving than anyone I know, that's for sure." It was worth a try. Ingstrom felt good about it.

Fizzy took the papers. "Thanks, Inggy. I really mean it. You're a great friend."

Marly looked at Ingstrom and smiled. "I don't want to lose Bob. I owe you," she said.

"Hey, I haven't done anything, just talking."

Ingstrom paid the bill with a generous flourish and left more of a tip than called for. He was feeling good. He had a warm feeling about the evening and the coming night. He had helped Fizzy and thought Marly had warmed to him considerably. That was good.

He and Marly dropped Fizzy off at the bus stop and turned up Arrowhead Road toward the lake. Ingstrom asked her to pull into the Holiday station for gas.

"I've got plenty," she said.

"No, no. I insist. Let's fill the tank."

A burly man limped out to pump the gas. "Check the oil?" he said.

"Sure. I'll pay inside," Ingstrom said. The attendant was eyeing Marly as if to say, are you old enough to be driving this boat?

"Driver's training," Ingstrom told him and went into the store.

Inside Ingstrom went straight to the phone. He dialed two of Randy's numbers before he reached him at the third. "Hey, man. I'll take you up on that Grand Lake offer."

Randy gave him directions and the location of the key. "It's good until the first. Keep a low profile and don't burn the place down."

"Very funny," Ingstrom said. Randy was a jokester even when he sounded serious.

Randy wanted to know how he was getting out to the lake. "I'm hitchhiking," Ingstrom lied. Randy had noted Marly as a name he knew, and Ingstrom wanted to keep her out of it.

Belisle was always cautious. "Have them drop you off past the lake and walk back to the turnoff. It's only half a mile in. Mind the mosquitoes."

"Sure. I'll dodge them all."

When he got back to the car the attendant was standing against the pump with folded arms. His look reeked of judgment.

"Hey, sis, slide over. I'll take it from here," Ingstrom said. The gas jockey looked less concerned. "Thank you, sir." Marly got the drill and slid across the seat. Ingstrom eased out of the station. He was not at all used to driving.

"The place is out on Grand Lake. Feel like a swim?"

Marly smiled. "I didn't bring my suit."

"It'll be dark by the time we get there. Do you need one?"

As cool as always, Marly looked him in the eye. "I guess not." She folded her legs under her on the seat and, turning, moved over toward him. "Let me teach you how to drive."

17

Point of Rocks

Mema was sitting up late with Tommy. "That was Paul," she said.

Tommy craned his neck and just caught the taillights of the Buick. "It could be. How do you know?"

Berta had been up since 12:30 and found the boy awake. She patted his legs, stretched out on the living room couch. "When you get to be my age, you just know things without knowing them." She knew Paul had stayed some hours at Cindy's and had circled round to talk with his dad. "He's looking for Wendell Jr., even though he understands him well enough to know he couldn't possibly be here yet."

Tommy wove his fingers together and stretched them and his arms behind his head. He leaned back on the pillow. "Why would he be looking for him when he knows he's not here yet?"

Berta smoothed the blanket over his legs. She gently pushed his skinny rear over to make more room and brought the blanket over his chest. She laid her hand there. "You'll see when you're older."

Tommy smiled. "What will I see, Memma?"

Berta looked past him out the front windows as if watching scenes from years ago. "You'll see Paul coming by looking for Wendell Jr. very early in the morning. Sundays, usually. 'Is Wendell Jr. up yet?' he says. And you tell him once more what a sleepyhead Wendell Jr. is and that he, Paul, is better off as an early riser. You feed him coffee cake and, once he

223

is twelve, a small cup of coffee, too." She gazed fixedly at the windows. "Month by month, year by year, gallons of coffee and a hundred pounds of cake later, you just know that in a minute Paul will be by, looking for his friend who is still fast asleep, and you're glad you're an early riser and have coffee on the stove and cake in the oven."

Tommy rose at his waist and threw his arms around Berta. He kissed her cheek. "I won't be seeing Paul, though, will I?"

"Not as the boy I knew. You'll see other people that way," she said.

Tommy held her tighter. "But him, I won't see him, will I?"

Berta pushed back, taking his face like delicate dough in her baker's hands. "I think you will. Everything has its way, though sometimes it takes a while." She drew him close again and squeezed.

"Now you get some sleep, Mr. Block-thrower. You have work to do in the morning." She softly pushed him to the pillow and once again smoothed the blanket over his chest. "Paul is a fine man, just as you are turning out to be. Give each other time."

She kissed him as if she were his mother, stood, and turned out the light. Berta left the darkened room and felt her way to the kitchen. She wept over the sink.

"Life will break your heart," Berta whispered to herself. "And love will do the same." She trailed her hand over the kitchen table and looked from the window. In the back yard the swing set and sandbox Tommy and his friends used years ago stood out against the dark lilac bushes. "They are waiting for a new boy to come along. Tommy's boy." She thought a moment, her shoulders slumping a little. "That'll be a while."

Berta missed being in her own kitchen, even though it had not yet been a full day. She'd go back home in the morning with Wendell Jr. There she could see the bay and the lake.

Those were a comfort.

She was waiting for Wendell Jr., even though she knew he'd be at least two hours more arriving, even though she knew he'd be of little help or comfort, even though she knew he'd leave again right after the funeral, maybe not even staying for the wake. That was Wendell Jr.—always leaving, always on his way somewhere else. He didn't seem to need much mothering. He left a lot of it for Paul.

Even though Paul was more a support, more a son to her, Wendell Jr. had never been jealous of him. He didn't begrudge Paul her affection. He himself was too busy to want it. Still, she waited for him. That was it. He could change Father Lucci's mind.

She wondered. How could Roger's confessor believe he had taken his own life? It was all a horrible accident. Yes, drugs, she had to admit, but her grandson didn't seek his own death. She was sure. But she couldn't tell that to the doubting priest. Wendell Jr. would do that.

Berta found it curious. Though she didn't feel troubled, it intrigued her. After so many years in the church, so many prayers, hundreds of candles lit, so many ladies' circles, and the cakes she served there, she did not question. She felt she had no right to object. Not that the priest was infallible, like the Pope. She knew better than that. Years back, a priest had run off with Sister Margaret. They had children somewhere; Milwaukee, she thought, or Chicago. No, the good Father Lucci had erred. They'd just have to show him how Roger made a terrible mistake and died by accident—just like his mother, who everyone said would kill herself. But Betty's had been accidental, too.

Berta fingered her rosary beads. Betty hadn't said prayers for years before that night. Fallen away, Berta thought. Oh, Betty should have accepted the protection, a St. Christopher at least. Berta had told her, "Have faith. That will save you, Betty. That will keep you from harm." But no. Her children did not listen to her. Neither cleaved to the church after Wendell, Sr. had been killed. That broke their ties. Wendell Sr. had converted just to marry her, so, once he was gone, Betty and Wendell Jr. thought they should leave the church too. She looked for a crucifix. Elma didn't keep one, at least not in the kitchen.

Berta took up each death like a holy medal to be examined—her daughter, her dear husband, her grandson, her own parents and grandfather. Papa Enzo lived the longest. She had been his favorite and knew the whole story of his voyage to America. *Sul molo*, he said, *c'erano due navi.* "At the pier were two ships"—the two ships she had heard about since she was a girl. One went south to Argentina, the other to America. *Ho avuto la fortuna*, he said, his voice wavering. He was lucky to get the ship north.

Berta wondered. She knew little about the Italians who went south, just that they were accepted and that they prospered. The languages were similar. Papa Enzo might not have suffered so in Argentina. Here he was dark, suspect, undesirable even amongst the other immigrants, among Swedes and Finns like Wendell Sr.'s parents, but he stood *fianco a fianco*, side by side, in the lines and on the wildcat pickets gaining the admiration of the rank-and-file. Even so, he had the toughest, dirtiest, and most dangerous jobs for most of his working life. He might have fared better on the other ship.

None of this would have happened had he gone south, Berta thought. Then she laughed out loud. I'd be speaking Spanish. I wouldn't understand myself! She might have been a Romero, had children named Juan instead of Wendell, Beatrice instead of Betty. Berta could not conceive of it. You take life as it comes, she decided, good and bad. She didn't doubt the bad. She knew better, she had had too much of it to naysay, but there were so many people to love, to laugh with, to bake for. They fill my world, she admitted. So, Berta, you just have to keep rising early.

She sat in the kitchen and brought her hands to her cheeks. "Love will break your heart," she said, "and life will do the same."

She swept the few crumbs from the table into her palm. She brushed them into the sink and went to the pantry to see what Elma had to bake up for Wendell Jr. She couldn't sit still.

Wendell Jr. drove carefully. He watched for deer trotting out from the close woods that hugged the road. He stopped each hour to rest and to walk a little. He eyed the few oncoming cars, sure to dim his lights as they neared. He was on the lookout for wavering, drunk drivers. His sister had taught him that. Six sheets to the wind, she had plowed into a semi on a road like this. The truck driver who survived said she hadn't tried to swerve, "Just came straight on." Betty had to be pried from the wreckage of her Chevrolet.

Wendell Jr. didn't grumble. He prided himself on being a practical man who took care of business, did what he had to do, worked on behalf of others, and tried to stay safe. Even before his father's accident, since childhood actually, he had been cautious, some said calculating to a fault. But here he was in one piece, had good work, had never been injured on or off the job. His father's death only reinforced his meticulous heed. One slip can mean the end, he reminded himself. He supposed it was his prudence that got him the votes for shop steward. He thought things through before he acted or said much. Wendell, Jr. was known to be able to see from the other's point of view. That made him ideal to listen to and present grievances. Being a successful shop steward was Wendell Jr.'s glory. He knew his father would have been proud.

He took his foot off the accelerator. Something caught his eye. "Sure enough, a doe," he said. Wendell Jr. touched the brake. "Watch for the second one or the fawns." And as he said it he saw the spots of the fawn move from the tall grass of the ditch fully onto the road. They often have twins. By this time he was at a full stop with his emergency flashers lighting the road. Again, he was right. A second fawn emerged, trotted onto and across the road. Wendell Jr. was looking in his rear view mirror for cars approaching. He had moved to the narrow shoulder but occupied part of the pavement. As quickly as they had appeared, the trio melded into the woods on the other side of the road, and Wendell Jr. pulled back onto the road.

"That could have been bad," he told himself. He had seen the wrecks—like hitting a pregnant doe at 60 mph. Of course it killed the deer, but it also demolished the car. The driver took six surgeries and two years of physical therapy to recover. He shook his head. "Speed kills," he said, "and so does stupidity."

He thought of Roger. To Wendell Jr., Roger was still seven, his age when Betty was killed. Wendell Jr. had a hard time seeing him as one of those hippie kids. He had been clean-cut and tearful at his mother's funeral. Berta had since told only enough for him to know that Roger was trouble, though the drug thing was new. He hadn't heard much about that. And it was through Paul that he lately got most of his news. Paul didn't make excuses or sugarcoat things. That was the way Wendell Jr. liked it: straight on.

"So Roger did something stupid," he said when Paul gave him the news.

Paul had kept to the facts. "I wouldn't say that, but it isn't an unfair assessment."

"Don't worry," Wendell Jr. said. "I won't say it in front of Mom."

Paul was still shy about protecting his Memma, but it had been a long while since Wendell Jr. had thought it odd. His friend's love for his mother was as familiar as it was welcome to him. He didn't share the feeling in particular; Wendell Jr. acted after his father's death as more a guardian or caretaker of his mother than as a devoted son. He had done it at a distance. So Paul's affection was something good, Wendell Jr. thought. His mother seemed to need it, and his childhood pal's devotion freed him to move ahead. Even though Paul's phone call at work startled him—he thought it was about Mom—it was a comfort to have his best friend giving him the news.

The second call, just before he left his apartment in Bettendorf, was harder to manage.

His mother had been crying. "Wendell, you've got to come."

"I'm coming, Mom. I'm sure Paul told you." He wanted to sound comforting, but he couldn't keep annoyance out of his voice.

She blubbered into the phone. "Father Lucci. He won't say Mass, he told me. You've got to talk to him. He has to change his mind."

He kept calm before her stormy emotions. "Mother, I've already left a message with his secretary. He was teaching when I called. I have an appointment at ten tomorrow. Don't worry."

She would worry, of course. But the fact that he'd taken some action should ease her anxiety. Wendell Jr. could see the priest's point. He had his set of rules to follow. To Wendell

Jr., it did not matter. A funeral home could just as easily bury the boy as the church. He hadn't seen anything special in the funeral Mass said for his father or Betty. They were just as dead as could be. Wendell Jr. didn't believe any of that church crap, as he called it. The church had been as much the oppressor as management, City Hall, or the Pinkertons. They were all in it to get the little guy, any way they could. That was Wendell Jr.'s gospel.

He had passed through Eau Claire nearly two hours ago and expected to see the lights of Superior and Duluth at any moment. Eau Claire had been asleep, like most of the countryside. Wendell Jr. had the road to himself.

When he topped the hill at Pattison State Park, he took his last break. Out of the car, he walked well on the shoulder past the crest of the hill. Off in the distance, still miles away, Duluth glittered jewel-like across the hillside. Wendell Jr. could see why the town had always been touted as a crossroads that would someday prosper. It was beautiful and well situated. The lake lay dark and huge before the hills of town. He was almost moved by longing, but refused the sentiment. "A place is a place," he said. He reminded himself why he had left. Duluth is a heartbreak town. It never was what it could have been. You were right to leave. The future's elsewhere.

He returned to the car and started the last leg of his trip. Soon he was coasting down the north side of the High Bridge—the Point of Rocks dead ahead. Of all the landmarks in town, this point held special meaning. It was as hard-headed and sturdy as the Norskies who had settled on it and always, Wendell Jr. thought, stood for the people. It couldn't be uprooted, and it had to be dealt with. Often in his meetings with John Deere management, he brought the Point of Rocks to mind. Don't waver. Don't give in. Having been born and bred atop the pile of Duluth gabbro, he drew strength from it. He knew it was just rock, but it felt alive, supportive, and durable, everything he wanted to be.

Wendell Jr. came under the shadow of the point. He took it in, still the same as when he left, as when he was born, and the same as when the town had been settled. It had outlasted the rich and the poor, stayed in place during puny sweeps of city history and the country's wars. It would be right here even when glaciers slid again down from the north.

He turned along Superior Street then off to Elma's house, where he suspected his mother was already up making ready coffee and rolls for his arrival.

18

Grand Lake

THE DRIVE TO GRAND LAKE was not a long one, but
Ingstrom deliberately kept his speed down. The slower
the better, he'd decided. He didn't want any attention from the
authorities. Marly, curled up beside him, coached him gently
through the motions. Fortunately the car was an automatic,
so he had little to do but steer it around curves.

Marly sat close and dangled her arm over his near shoulder,
lifting her hand to his hair and occasionally twirling a few
strands of curl around her finger. As long as she was doing
those things, Ingstrom was going to keep it quiet and enjoy
himself. Too much talking had already been done.

The road rose gently away from town and rolled between
birch and poplar woods close on each side of the two
lanes. The shoulders were narrow and plunged down to
drainage ditches that met the woods steeply at the roots of
trees bordering the road. The trunks rose through dense
undergrowth of bushes and grass. The July evening breezed
through the windows, moving Marly's hair and ruffling her
cotton top across her boyish chest. The dark air breathed
sweetness around them and stirred full-leafed boughs that
crowed over the road, reaching toward each other.

At one point the trees grew thin, then absent, and the vista
widened on the right over an inlet to neighboring Pike Lake.
The stream swept narrow at first, then opened to a piney
point past a small bay where cabin lights shimmered on the
water near shore. The bay gave way to the lake proper on the

other side of the point. As he drove slowly past the inlet, the air splashed coolness across Ingstrom's face.

"Oooh," Marly said, "I've got goose bumps." She rubbed her arms and crossed them over her chest.

Ingstrom took his arm off the window and reached for the crank. "Want the window closed?"

"No. It was just the lake breeze," she said. "We must be close."

"It's just ahead." Ingstrom switched hands at the wheel, slipped his arm around Marly's shoulders and caressed her bare arm. "You're chilled," he said. He stroked her skin with a warm palm, chasing the bumps away. Her softness grew smooth. "There's a long-sleeve pullover in my bag. Put it on."

She turned, sliding her body across his arm to reach into the back seat. She brushed her erect nipples on his skin as she canted over the bench seatback. Ingstrom watched her narrow hips and backside gyrate as she searched. Rifling through the sack, still bent over the seat, Marly found the shirt and drew it to her. He had moved both hands back to the wheel. She pulled her head through the shirt and smoothed its body over her chest. She spread her arms to model the shirt. "It's a perfect fit!" she said. "We're the same size." She laughed and folded up once more against him.

While she was fussing with the pullover, Ingstrom had seen the turn but had driven on. "I'm parking just ahead. Now that you're warm, I think we should walk in."

Marly shrugged. "Not that I mind, but why?"

Ingstrom had an answer ready, "I don't know the neighbors and would like to come up quietly. I'm not sure about parking either."

"I could use a walk after that meal," she said.

He pulled onto a wide spot past the shoulder where graders piled snow in winter. Bushes sheltered the area from the road. Ingstrom pulled on the brake. "Anything you want to bring with you?" He locked the doors, dropped the keys into his sea bag and slung the sack over his shoulder. "Let's beat the mosquitoes," he said pulling her along by the hand and striding off. Marly scampered right along with him. Both glowed in the softness of the night and of each other. Ingstrom wanted it to last.

The dirt drive that led from the main road was dark. Here the trees touched each other across the way and formed a tunnel through the woods bounding the lake. Now and again a two-track path led off the gravely road they followed.

At each of these, Ingstrom paused, struck a match against the pitch dark and read the names posted ladder-like across parallel poles sunk into the ground next to rutted road. *Bergstad, Berman, Otterson, Peters, Tilinen,* the signs read. Through the trees they could make out a few lights. At one spot, they heard a screen door slam; at another, some people laughing. They continued hand in hand, cautiously feeling their way with their feet.

They were having an adventure, exploring both a strange landscape and each other, dark and unknown. They came together, Marly rounded Ingstrom's waist with her arm, he her shoulders, and they walked gingerly through the dark, Ingstrom's sack bouncing off their bodies as they moved along. It was hard to manage. They separated, holding hands, and found the going steadier. They laughed at their stumbles. The cooler air near the lake muted the mosquitoes, but they occasionally swatted their arms, Marly her bare legs as they went along. The buggy annoyance was just part of their fun.

At a particularly narrow wagon-rut road, Ingstrom found what he had been looking for: *Andrews, Gullickson, Lambert, Mattson.* "Lambert, that's it," he said. They turned in, each falling to in a parallel track, dangling their hands together over the grassy median of the narrow road, brushing hazelnut, spirea, and grasses that bent over from each side. The woods swelled pungent, full, and fresh. An arrow inscribed with *Lambert* guided them off to the left, and as the trees grew thinner, the bushes less close, the road widened into a treed clearing that led to a wide esplanade of beach at the lake. A few stars and cabin lights shimmered on the water. There was a moon that lit the water but didn't filter through the woodsy canopy.

The cabin was off to the right, surrounded by lilacs, watched over by taller birches. It was a summer cottage raised on pilings, skirted with a white-painted crosshatch lattice. On one side a wide deck, railed and latticed like the foundation, opened to the lake. The white clapboard shone in the night. The cabin, the lot, the lake, and neighboring cottages behind the lilacs seemed empty, silent under the summer's night sky.

"The weekend crowd's gone home to work," Ingstrom said. It was past eleven.

Ingstrom went to the lone white pine off to the left. He slung his sack down and swung himself up on a large low branch. Standing on the limb, he found the key hung discretely atop a higher lakeward limb. "Bingo," he said.

They went in, lit a single white-gas lantern, and had a look round. The room adjoining the deck extended through a living room, small kitchen, and dinette. The furnishings were Spartan: wood table and chairs, a slatted couch appointed with thick cushions, and three upholstered rockers. Magazines were spread on the several tables. Two small bedrooms opened behind a knotty pine-covered wall at the back. The beds looked comfy and plain. The kitchen had a hand water pump at the sink. The outhouse they'd passed back toward the road.

"Looks like we have to bathe in the lake," Ingstrom said.

Marly kicked off her shoes and pulled the long-sleeved shirt and her tank top over her head. She sprinted out on the deck. "Last one in is a silly."

Ingstrom followed to watch her bound toward the shore. He slipped his shoes off and unbuttoned his bellbottoms, letting them slide to the deck with his briefs. Marly's slender prancing frame glowed white against the navy stillness of the lake. She clambered onto the dock. He threw his t-shirt on top of his pants.

Out in the moonlight at the end of the dock, Marly, willowy and pale, turned to wave him on. "You're the silly," she said. He was picking his way through the trees, halfway there when she dropped her shorts and dove into the water making nary a ripple. He was standing at the end of the dock by the time she surfaced. He crouched, carefully setting his glasses on the seat of the rowboat tied to the dock, stood, pushed off and arced into the water.

The lake felt warm from the long, sunny day, a counterpoint to the cooling air. Ingstrom took two underwater strokes and found Marly treading water four yards out. He rose to the surface, slipping up along her torso. He took her hands, and facing each other they stirred the lake with their feet.

"It's toasty," she said.

"You're toasty." He pulled her toward him.

She circled his hips with her legs and his shoulders with her arms. "Peddle harder," she said.

Their lean torsos rubbed each other as they bobbed along toward shore. Ingstrom struck bottom and could stand. He bent an arm and took the nape of her neck in his hand to guide her down to his lips. She slid down, holding him between her thighs and kissed him tenderly, taking his lower lip between hers and pushing her tongue into his mouth. He tasted of the lake and the night and the dark.

Over Ingstrom's mind, Siiri's kiss that afternoon blew like a cloud across the stars. Her body now seemed like a fetish to him, a lust for flesh without fulfillment. Ingstrom shut the memory out. Right now, stay here with Marly.

Marly's lips explored, curious, without heated desire. Behind her search he felt a giving, not a longing, a wide, comforting stillness moving from back in time like a flow from the springs that fed this very lake, formed long ago, persistent, natural. He had not felt this in encounters with any other girl; certainly not from the nervous, protective classmates at East High, nor that afternoon in Siiri's uncontrolled waywardness.

Marly's tenderness rooted itself in fertile social plains of the West End—fed, he supposed, by that sureness and certainty of what life would bring, from an uncomplicated tradition barely realized in thought. There, Ingstrom thought, love was not a flirtation as it was understood amongst his East End cake-eaters, nor a lascivious celebration as those newly liberated girls on the pill seemed to think, but a sworn legacy like a neighborhood code or like this lake itself, held in a basin filling, seeping out and refilling, weathering winters, nourishing new life in spring, and feeding all it contained through a summer, such as this one, from sediment laid down in fall.

Marly's natural cadence in a kiss, wrapping his lips and hips and member as gently as a leaf taking form on a small branch, flowed back to the roots that reared it and made it full, solid, salubrious. Ingstrom knew the source at once and feared its strength.

Suddenly, he didn't have to worry about that vast darkness overwhelming him. Parting from his lips as sweetly as she had first touched them, Marly with a swift seizing of his shoulders slipped her calves to his knees and forced him to crumple and tumble forward through her bowed legs, submerging fully beneath the surface. She released herself to push him down and followed him lower, then let loose entirely and sprang away, trailing her belly and legs over his head. He felt as if he could drown.

Coming to the surface he blurted out his surprise. "What did you do that for?"

She was sloshing her way to the shore end of the dock. She turned, put her hands on her bare hips and said, "Because you were the silly, silly." She stepped onto the dock. "Come on. The air's cold." Then she laughed and extended her hand, waiting for him to shake off his fright and the water.

They sprinted to the cabin, naked and shivering, to search out some towels. Ingstrom retrieved his clothes from the deck. Marly put on his shirt again.

"I left my shorts on the dock," she said, "but this works fine." She spread out her arms, the shirt tails rising to reveal her pubis, and then she tugged the hem down. "I'll get them later."

Ingstrom feigned magnanimity. "You can wear my pants."

She teased him. "I'll only have to take them off again."

He slipped on his briefs and reached into his pants pocket. He found the roach he had saved from Siiri's. He struck a match.

"We don't have to do that," Marly said.

He lit the three candles on the coffee table. "Is it against your rules?"

"I just want you to know that it won't make me easy. I'm ready to be your lover without it." She watched him hold the burning match. "You won't tell Bobby, will you?"

"What?"

"That I smoked with you."

He lit the joint and toked.

He found the strictures of her family odd. Sex was okay, but smoking grass violated mores. "I won't tell. Have you tried before?"

She didn't admit it, but took the joint, drew deeply and held. She passed it back to Ingstrom. Her aplomb bewitched him.

Even though the grass filled them with heady lightness, Ingstrom knew it was superfluous to their time together. The night brought him alive. Something new was rushing into his life, greater though akin to his first inhaling of marijuana which, he'd thought at the time, opened possibilities he had never before dreamt of. And Marly so close, so alike him in body and character, was a thing he had never experienced.

If I weren't leaving so soon! No, he dismissed that. If things weren't so balled up right now. He thought of Roger and what had happened at Brookside. His resolve sprang strong, but he didn't harden. I'm going to sail, he promised. He had lived too long with that dream to scuttle it. Still, the nag of this new conflict harrowed his thoughts. For her, it's worth staying. With that idea, music from the transistor radio flooded the room, and Marly began to dance.

Her hips swayed, her arms arcing to one side and the next. Her chin rose with her gaze to the ceiling. She stood momentarily on a single limb, bent the other and sprang to that side, pivoting on the ball of her foot. Now turned away from Ingstrom, she lifted both arms, bent one to the other, trailed a single finger of one hand back along the opposed arm, and holding out that hand lithe with grace, she tweaked the dial of the lantern hanging above her head. She spun away, rose on the toes of a single foot, and as the lantern light dimmed, fluttered, and glowed its last, she bent supplely back, reaching far with arching arms and spine, kicking high, over and up with one leg then the other. She finished the cartwheel flip with a coy curtsey, stretching the pullover out like a skirt and down as she descended, her fingers delicately pinching the garment's hem. She lowered her head as she straightened and, turning her face in profile to him, opened her arms as if for applause.

Mesmerized, Ingstrom shook free of the paresis she induced, disregarded the tightness inside his briefs, leapt, and vaulted over the couch to land at her side. He struck her very pose in opposition, lifting his chin, spreading his arms. She joined her hand to his, dropped the other to his shoulder, his to the small of her back, and they danced together slowly, feeling out the next move together.

"Oh, you're leaking a little," Marly said.

Ingstrom pressed to her. She crossed her slender arms and pulled the shirt up over her head as she leaned back on his hand. They continued their gliding dance but sought each other's mouth to resume that deepening kiss they'd started in the lake.

Marly kept her lips bound to Ingstrom's, leaving her breath and spirit to rise free in flight. Reese stirred her life in magic. To her sequestered West End sympathies, he was exotic and promising. She was attracted to the one and demanding of the other, for Marly was in her self-confident and quiet way quite ambitious. She wouldn't leave the ground; when she flew, she'd take it with her. Ingstrom had traveled over lands she wanted to explore. The drugs and cavalier escapades she did not need. She knew that they were the trappings of his immature genius. The intelligence, ease, and precocious knowledge he tapped from his privileged life was what she admired and could use as she vaulted from a world so old as to be worn out into a new one she saw building at a close remove.

Leaving the West End was not her goal, but she'd bring it with her if she did go. That was her grounding; but Ingstrom, she knew, was not just geographically close to the university, he was there by expectation. And he was already beyond it. That she could sense. One step at a time. This night she didn't want to waste. The bond was not premeditated but would be permanent, she knew. Their marks were already on one another. It was the other things beyond this covenant that she wanted more: prosperity, validation, expansiveness. Marly would burgeon. She'd be known. Her life would breathe in the marvelous world. Best, Marly thought, she was to bequeath that wellspring of Slavic wisdom her grandfather had brought to and planted in Duluth.

Ingstrom, too, held the kiss. This time, no one but Marly lived in his thoughts. It was not even the girl; it was a presence, another self, moving along on a doubled track. And he was acceding. He was already making his promise to return. If he left, he'd come back. Of that he was sure.

Together they swayed, followed, and led by turns. Not knowing the waltz, they waltzed through a bedroom door. They left the candles burning and disappeared behind the knotty pine wall. The cabin, the yard, and the lake lay quiet, as if holding their breath.

Ingstrom had lain between the sheets listening to the night for half an age. Marly breathed softly in the paralysis of her dreams. His own breath had lessened in cadence with hers, but he hadn't slept. The silence of the night had been broken. He couldn't tell what it was; he had heard no step, no motor, no cracking twig, or the brushing of a leg across hazelnut leaves. But he sensed something there, outside the cabin. It was not the shift of the breeze, but he felt it respire. It was not the quiet lapping of waves at the shore, nor the tapping of the rowboat's gunwale on the dock. Whatever it was drew his thoughts away from Marly's mysteries. He pictured the dome of the night sky above arching above the cabin as wide and open as over the sea. For the first time in his life Ingstrom feared that vault, as deep as it was vast.

For a long time he struggled between a creeping agitation within and the silky placidness of Marly asleep at his side. Twice he turned the sheet back; twice he smoothed it again across his chest. She hadn't stirred in the least. Outside, the presence persisted. It grew along with his thoughts of the dank darkness in the woods. He was staring at what he knew lay beyond the bedroom ceiling, the stars, the galaxies that drew him into the center of their wheeling flight. This floating feeling didn't lull him to sleep. It held him awake, fighting a nauseated torpor. Again, he folded the sheets back.

He eased out of the bed, tucked the sheets double over Marly and snugged his pillow next to her. He brushed the light waves from her temple and softly kissed her there. Carefully, he picked his way to the other room.

He stepped into his pants and, not seeing his tee shirt, took up the top Marly had tossed off in her run to the beach. Ingstrom stepped over the shoes he'd left on the deck and walked toward the dock in bare feet. His glasses were there. Those would help.

His arms prickled, as did the back of his neck. He moved toward the lone pine where the key had been hung. Ingstrom stopped. Someone was there. He saw the figure fade, not duck, behind the trunk. He swung wide and approached, carefully toeing the roots bulging from the ground. Despite his attempts to stay calm, his breath rasped between the rising thunderous beat of his heart against his chest. Again the figure faded back.

"Who's there?"

He pursued it, coming close to the trunk. As he rounded the enormous tree, what he saw shifted him into reverse. Around the spreading roots, Ingstrom stumbled back and tripped over the sea bag he had left under the limb. He went down.

He scrambled to his feet and ran, swinging the sea sack like a mace, fleeing toward the dock. Without his glasses and in such dark, he hadn't seen the figure clearly. Was anybody there? He was still high; his imagination might build and vaporize forms at will. He was afraid to wonder. Was it Roger? The idea hit him in the back as he ran. No. Not Roger. Almost to the dock, he turned. Yes, Ingstrom decided. It is. The phantom was now plain, out from under the trees, advancing in Roger's trudging tread. It looked ghostly but followed as if solid, weighty.

Ingstrom sprinted to the end of the dock. He slipped the boat hitch off its post, swept Marly's shorts into the boat, and tossed his sack ahead of his dive onto the stern thwart of the rowboat. The little craft lurched from the dock, gliding yards away into the lake and, as Ingstrom paddled he propelled it farther and farther away. He lifted himself fully into the boat and clambered to the oars. Immediately, he pulled against the water and scooted away eight feet at a stroke. Roger—that apparition or whatever it was—had steadily advanced but now stood confused and wavering at the end of the dock. Ingstrom reached behind to grab his glasses, which had fallen to the bottom of the boat at the bow. He stretched out, caught the spectacle's nose rib and slipped the pair on. When he came up from his supine tautness, Roger was gone.

Freak out, Ingstrom thought.

He continued to pull those oars. The work helped calm

his panic. The sailor rowed nearly to the middle of the bay. The cabin was lost in darkness under the trees, and the dock was one tiny white mark among others along the shore. Everything seemed quiet there. He boated the oars and held his head in his hands. Am I losing my grip? Don't let this happen, he pleaded. He shivered cold. His pants were soaked in lake water from the crotch down. He peeled the trousers off, dried his legs and thighs with a woolen cap from his bag. He wrung the pants out and set them on the bow. He slipped on Marly's shorts. They fit nicely. He felt good in them.

Was it the grass? Had it been laced with something? No, I smoked some earlier. He considered stress, worry, concern. They weren't things he usually admitted to his life. Stay cool, be real. He calmed himself. Moving down off the seat to the shelter of the boat's shell, he wrapped himself and the sack in his arms and breathed steadily. He felt the urge to cry— and rejected it. He shook out the cloche and stretched it over his head. Huddled in the rowboat like a shipwrecked sailor, Ingstrom curled up tightly and escaped into sleep.

The rowboat rocked lightly and drifted in soft night whispers of air. Ingstrom slept a fitful and brief sleep, but it washed his senses of mind-blown hauntings. When he opened his eyes to the night sky, it was the real night sky, still, magnificent, imperceptibly turning. He stretched out, draping his legs over the rear seat, lying now on his sea bag with his hands under his head. The sky was clear. He felt rested and calm.

He cleaned his glasses on the tail of Marly's cotton shirt and lay back to watch the sky. The stars were spread fine over the dark canopy. Their thrilling distance and sparkle connected like a net thrown over heaven and lake, keeping and comforting the creatures below, staying them to earth.

Ingstrom gazed at Alpha Centauri. He'd dreamed of sailing there through seas of space, eternal night. The small waves of the Earth's quiet night lapped at the boat, friendly hands holding and buoying him, guiding him along. He thought he heard a trout jump, maybe gobbling a summer moth. He looked to the north, where the Big Dipper lay upright and full. Past three o'clock, he calculated. He recounted the months and weeks. Yes, three-thirty. He thought of rowing back. Again, he watched the sky. His nap had stilled his nerves but hadn't erased his fear. No, he decided, it's still too dark. He laid back, letting the rocking and drifting of the boat move the stars around in his view, but now he was restless. His agitation had returned. He felt uncomfortable, uneasy, vulnerable.

Though Ingstrom might have dozed, he was not sure he could have. If he had, it did not restore him. He opened his eyes to a tapping, a scratching, and bumping along the bulwarks of the boat. Thin clouds had drifted over, obscuring much of the Milky Way. He didn't want to rise and look over the gunwale. Alert now, he listened intently.

The sounds came separately: scratching from the bow, tapping from the stern. Finally, he raised himself up and looked toward the bow. Reeds, cattails, and grasses rose above the gunwales. He had drifted to shore. He came fully upright and twisted to stern. Sure enough, another rowboat loose from a nearby cabin was knocking against his stern. They both had listed into the shallows of the reeds.

Ingstrom took an oar from its lock. He stood one foot to stern and the other on a seat to push the companion boat away. It was then he saw a shadowed bundle on the bottom of this neighbor boat. Is someone else sleeping out here?

He spoke. "Good evening. Are you all right?" Nothing but the wind and water stirred. He tried again. Dead silence. He prodded the bundle with the oar. The wrap fell open. He saw.

As in his fright at the tree, again he fell back, this time as if the figure revealed under the blanket had given him a push. This time he hit hard. His arm and shoulder smacked the gunwales; his head hit the bow seat. Hurt, he scrambled to his knees. He panted hard, his chest throbbed wildly. His boat was captive in the cattails, hemmed in by a ghost-boat carrying the body of an old woman. No, it can't be! Taking an oar, he tried mightily to pry the boats apart. Neither would budge.

There was no movement from the body he had prodded. It was a corpse. Shadows darkened her bruised face, but he was sure she was dead. He was pushing hard against the bow of her boat, but the reeds held its broad stern fast. It only grew more tangled. He fought down frantic ideas and thoughts. He sat and controlled his breath.

Ingstrom stripped again. He tucked his glasses between Marly's shorts and shirt and folded them on the seat. He sat on his boat's bow and slipped gingerly into the reedy water. The bottom was not deep but proved mucky. He held onto the anchor rope and threw himself flat on the reeds, using the bowsprit to propel himself forward. The cattails bent and flattened. The long leaves' sharp edges cut shallow slits in his skin. He pulled the boat behind him over the flattened reeds. Again he pushed off a little to one side and pulled. Over and over he thrashed in the tule brake. Bit by bit he turned his rowboat around, coming eventually to the edge of the reeds forty yards from the other boat.

The water deepened. On his back he finned, draping the anchor rope around his shoulders. The boat followed easily. The clear water felt good, cleansing the mud from his feet and cleaning the cuts all along his torso and legs. Reluctant to get into the chill air, he swam for a while on his back. He dove alongside the boat, lunged up to grab the gunwale, and hoisted himself aboard.

The night air was cold, and Ingstrom began shivering immediately. He flicked off as much water as he could, squeezed his hair, and used the hat, his damp pants, and the sack itself as towels. The rest he'd air-dry. Row! Row to keep warm. He retrieved his glasses, being sure to leave Marly's clothing as dry as possible, took his seat and poised the oars to dig into the water. He took his bearings by the few stars he could see. The cattail brake was a hundred yards away. He couldn't make out the boat caught there.

Ingstrom shook, just short of convulsion. God, please God, forgive me. He couldn't help himself. Cold, lost, naked, scared, he had nothing else to go on. He had no organized prayers to recite, only, "God forgive me."

He turned the boat toward the cabin, which proved to be two miles down the lake. The young sailor began to pull and rock with the oars. There might be some light by the time I arrive. He was not sure what he'd do when he got there, but whatever it was, it would include Marly.

The rowing cheered Ingstrom. Sculling into the wind, he grew warm quickly. His progress was slow, but he steadily gained on the point that marked Randy's cabin. He hoped Marly was still sleeping. That he didn't want her to wake and find him gone prodded him to put his back into the rowing. The winds would be lesser near the shore, but Ingstrom kept far out, moving parallel to the beach. He wanted to avoid being identified.

After a half-hour of rowing he was close enough to pick out Randy's dock. The cabin was still swathed in darkness under the birch canopy. Ingstrom brought the oars in and paused. He slipped into Marly's shorts and top. A glow rose to his skin under the garments. Looking over the bow, calculating his course with the wind, Ingstrom squinted and peered intently toward the cabin. Had he seen car lights? He wasn't sure. Then he was sure. The car was black and had just made the turn around the yard to the right of the house. He saw the flash of brake lights. He turned, dropped oars, and pulled hard. He was still at least ten minutes away.

He made good time and, when he neared shore and the wind dropped, better time still. Every fourth or eighth stroke, he threw a look over his shoulder, but the unlit cabin and the dark car were barely visible even in the coming dawn. His caution and concern fought each other as he neared the dock. Caution won. He anchored a hundred yards out and lay prone in the bow, raising only enough hat above the gunwale to let him watch. The swelling dawn kept Roger at bay. The cabin scene was solid, decidedly un-ghostly. But something was wrong.

At the side of the cabin nearest the parked car, the cross hatch-skirting protruded from the house. Someone had gone under there. Maybe a drug stash was hidden there. Ingstrom could figure no other reason for the intrusion. With Randy, one could be sure of nothing. You don't want to interrupt someone digging for a stash, even if it's Randy himself.

He watched. The rowboat drifted around the anchor. He saw a man crawl from under the house. He stood with his back to the lake. Ingstrom thought he lit a cigarette. A puff of smoke rose near his head. The man, a big man he saw now, knelt to the crawlspace opening and reached inside. He stood again and replaced the skirting. When he got in the car and started it, Ingstrom recognized the distinct cat-eyed brakes of a '59 Impala gleaming momentarily. The man drove off without lights. Ingstrom could barely hear the engine.

He immediately pulled the anchor and rowed to the dock. He hitched the bow to one cleat and ran up the path that he saw clearly for the first time in the predawn light. Approaching from the dock, he saw smoke drifting through the panel the man had replaced. Ingstrom smelled trouble—danger and wrong. He called out to Marly. "Marly, get out!"

As he ran toward the skirt panel, a flame flared through the lattice. Then he was on the ground for the third time that night. A wall of heat and flame singed his hair. His breath was sucked out of him, as if he had fallen into the vacuum of space. Still, he rolled and somersaulted on the wave of heat that pushed out from the fiery front wall of the cabin. He scrabbled across the ground and came to his feet behind one of the large birches whose bark, facing the house, flamed and sputtered. "Marly!" He screamed. No cries came out of the house. Everything smelled of gasoline.

Ingstrom sucked air down his rasping lungs and coughed. He sprinted from behind the birch to the deck steps. A second explosion blew the burning door off the house. Ingstrom found himself lying near the big pine. Propane! The white flames shot straight up in a giant claw, raking furiously along birch trunks surrounding what had been the cabin and what was now a blown-out inferno surrounded by collapsed walls.

Marly was gone. Ingstrom ran. In the boat again, rowing with all his strength, he was fueled by fear and hatred.

He watched the flames consume the cabin and was surprised how long it took before he saw tiny men scurrying before the conflagration. The wind pushed him out fast. He tacked on a course that would bring him to the car. There, he'd already figured, he'd set the boat free and be gone. He'd take the back way to town. He had to risk stopping home before doing anything else.

Ingstrom was just starting the car when the fire truck screamed by. He dove to the seat where Marly had curled next to him. On his scorched skin, he could feel the heat of her body seeping away and vanishing into the upholstery. He drove, wiping wet streaks of soot across his cheeks. And drove.

19

Denfeld

PAUL TUOMI AWOKE SURPRISED at how refreshed he felt. He bounced up, folded the bed sheets on the couch, and stowed them in the linen closet on his way to shower. Pamela's bedroom door was closed. Pamela's bedroom, he thought. The moniker had been appropriate for a long while. For years he had been a guest in that room—mostly unwelcome. He wouldn't invite himself there again.

Paul used the hall bath. He ticked off the chores he had ordered for himself sometime during his short, deep sleep. Pack some essentials; get research going on Fizzy, Ingstrom, and LaPrairie-Larson; see Wendell Jr. and Berta; lunch with Cindy. He didn't see how he could fit in a trip to Solon Springs until that night. He'd ask his father to do that one, maybe because Randy had mentioned the guy down there in concert with PS. What else? Leave time for Father Lucci and the coroner.

The last thing on his mind was his meeting with the chief, which would happen this morning. He was not looking forward to it. The Brookside case had taken on a life of its own; he was hardly in charge of its direction. That had to change. Nor was he happy with the pace or direction of the investigation into Roger's death.

He blubbered, his face under the stream of water. Loose talk in the neighborhood. He couldn't remember when he was as dissatisfied with his job. Still, something was buoying him. The weight of his worries billowed away out the window, like the steam from the shower. He sang, "Summertime and the livin' is easy . . . ."

Why so peppy this morning? Last night's argument: it was more one way than any he could remember, and it was going to be his last. If you're unhappy, change things. Why he hadn't realized it fully enough to decide before, he couldn't tell. Loyalty had bound him. Now wasn't the best time, but it was the time. The weight he'd carried since Alex's death had only multiplied year by year. His had become a house of the dead—a lost son, a moribund marriage. Throwing it all off, admitting the marriage was a mistake and moving on, felt good. There were living people to tend to. You're not running to Cindy. You're going out on your own.

Paul took the guest towels out and gathered his toiletries. He stuffed it all into a beach bag from the cabinet below. Hearing the master-bath shower running, he slipped into the bedroom to grab a couple days' supply of clothes. Avoid an encounter with Pamela if you can. He'd return later to recover what he missed. He was out of the house by 6:45 and turned up to Lakeside to catch some breakfast. Brookside would wait. And he'd confront the chief better on a full stomach.

The Busy Corner was just that. The mailmen reported for work right next door at 7:30. The banter was loud and familiar. It happened every morning.

His regular carrier, Mel, waved him over, "Tuomi!" Paul sat at the stool next to him.

"You're on the front page, my boy," he said thumping Paul's back.

It was unavoidable. "What did I do now?"

"You've solved the case, Detective!" a postal clerk three seats down said.

Kathy, the empress of the Busy Corner, saved him. "What'll

it be, Sherlock?"

"First," he said, "what's your recipe for staying so shapely? Especially around all this food."

She tapped her foot somewhere down below the counter. "Answering dumb questions does it," she said.

The kitchen was jammed with noisy cooking. "Let's see. Had pork fried rice at 1:00 a.m., so I'm already starved. Ham and eggs sound good. Extra toast." He was both jaunty and hungry.

She poured his coffee without asking. "Thanks, Kathy."

"Sure, Mr. Holmes."

"Okay, Mel," he said, "let's see the headlines."

"Burglary Motive, Police Say."

"Old news is good news," he said and handed the sheets back to Mel.

Mel was undaunted. "I've delivered that address for years. Plenty of mail to and from that daughter of hers. Packages and more packages. I bet she's involved."

Paul stirred in sugar and cream. "Keep that one on the down-low, pal. If I promise not to deliver mail, will you stop sleuthing?"

Mel had more. "Heard on the news this morning about an explosion and fire out at Grand Lake. Sheriff is talking arson investigation."

"All fires are arson until proven otherwise," Paul said.

"Yeah, just like we're all innocent until proven guilty."

"That's the saying," Paul said.

"They found something that's getting common around here, though." Mel waited for Paul's curiosity to rise, but Paul just mixed more cream into his cup. He knew Mel couldn't stand suspense or silence.

Finally he blurted it out. "The sheriff found a body in the ruins. Charred. Cremated. Couldn't even tell if it was a man or woman."

"That makes it murder," Paul said nonchalantly.

It wasn't his case, not even his jurisdiction, and he sure didn't have anyone to spare on an investigation for the county. "Right now, Mel, it's ham and eggs making headlines with me."

Paul's thoughts were miles away. He pondered his change of address. Mel would have the forms in his bag. Not yet, man, he decided. Keep it private for now. You barely know it yourself. He could forward his mail to the department, where he'd be living for the next six months anyway. He hadn't decided where to hang his hat. Hotel, motel, maybe Memma's.

Mel got up. "Seven twenty-five. The mail must go through. Ask around about that daughter." With that, he bolted for the door.

All the letter carriers were gone. The Busy Corner hushed. It was Paul and a couple of clerks from the hardware store lingering over coffee. He stuffed himself a bit more, paid, and stepped into the bright morning light. It was already feeling hot.

Paul drove. Seeing two cars from up on Superior Street, he pulled down into the parking lot at East High School. It's good to stop before school brass arrives. He got along with janitors and secretaries better than with principals. Anyway, he wanted to play down his visit. There was too much buzz around town already.

The office door was open; the school secretary was the one getting things underway.

"Hi, am I too early for class?"

"About twenty years too late, I think. How can I help you?" She got back to business.

"I'm wondering if I could look at a copy of your most recent yearbook." *The Cake-Eater,* he thought. "Is it *The Greyhound?*"

"*The Birchlog,*" she said, sizing him up. "Looking for someone in particular?"

He guarded his purpose. "Not in particular. I want to refresh my memory on a couple of pitchers, baseball pitchers."

"You're not proselytizing, are you?"

"Fall-ball," he said.

She came to the counter. "We keep yearbooks in the drawer, otherwise they might sprout legs." She placed three books on the counter and held them down while she took one more look as if to say, "I'm watching you, buster."

He raised his right hand. "I won't leave the room."

He leafed to the sports sections till he found the baseball team. The secretary busied herself unlocking files and disappeared into a back room. Paul smelled the coffee she was brewing.

He checked the senior "I's." Not there. He had looked young, Paul thought. He paged back to the junior class pictures and scanned the faces. Curly-haired blonds were common. Nothing.

He opened the previous year's book. Thank heaven for school photographers. Ingstrom's face leapt off the page. He checked the name below the picture: Reese Ingstrom, "Mystery of mysteries." Intriguing epigram.

He closed the book and waited for the secretary. "I thought Reese Ingstrom was on a team," he said.

"Baseball? Debate more likely. Mr. Ingstrom was not the athletic type."

Paul flipped to the public speaking pages. Not there.

"Oh, I think he was in the Young Democrats Club." She took the book, found the page and pointed. "I was right.

There he is."

Paul turned the book. The casual photo showed him untouched. It was definitely the young man he saw outside Brookside's gates. Randy had been dead on. Paul wondered what else Randy knew but hadn't told. This kid was definitely on his burn list.

"He graduated last year," she said, "Attends UMD. If he can keep it together, he'll be a college grad. Bright but not motivated." She sensed she had said too much.

Paul closed the book and pushed it to her. "Don't worry. Your Greyhounds are safe with me."

"Sorry I couldn't fill your team, Mr. . . . ?"

"Tuomi. Paul Tuomi." He extended his hand. She'd likely know later who he was, but for now he took short leave. "Thanks very much."

He turned to go, then came again to the counter. "Could I use your phone book a moment?" He did not want to show his badge. Paul liked to keep investigations light. Rousing more loose talk was not his desire. He did luck out. Though there were three Ingstroms in the book, only one lived in Lakeside. "Enjoy your summer," he said as he closed the phonebook on the counter.

Surprising, Paul mused, how easily the old ideas and rivalries come up. He had felt it as soon as he entered the school, even after all these years.

West-Enders had called the Greyhounds Cake-Eaters for as long as he could remember. Someone in his Denfeld High history class had said it derived from Marie Antoinette's ill-fated quip about the starving peasants. To the Hunters, his school's denotation, the Cake-Eaters were snotty rich kids too good to mix with the working-class Denfeld crowd.

It went further back than Denfeld though, well before

either he or the school had been born. The clash between workers, housed mostly in the West End, and management, all of whom lived on the east side of town, left anger and bitterness in the craw of immigrants who passed the enmity along with the mashed potatoes to their kids at the dinner table. PS had worked some to cull out the attitude—one that could hold Paul back from fulfillment of his promise—but Paul had had plenty of it. And when he'd announced his plans to marry an East Duluth girl, PS was far from ecstatic but supportive. If his dad had concern, it was for Cindy.

Paul had tried to cross over. He'd tried hard. But given Pamela's attitude and aspirations, Paul was now sorry he'd followed the delusion. When Pamela regarded him, especially after they had lost Alex, he saw nothing but "second-class citizen" written in her look. Cake-Eaters and Hunters didn't mix.

Paul parked in front of the Ingstrom residence. He sighed, a long breath. Here he was again, a Hunter on the east end of town. This call might not be easy.

It was Mrs. Ingstrom who answered his ring.

Paul showed his badge. "Good morning," he said. "I'm here to see Reese."

Mrs. Ingstrom looked ready to leave for the office or a charity board breakfast. She wore pearl earrings and a matching necklace beneath a stiff, white open collar. Despite the incipient heat, she wore a vee-neck sweater.

"Is that boy in some sort of trouble?" Her words dripped confidence and social control.

Paul brought out a smile. "I don't think so. I am just verifying a few facts this morning."

She glanced away from the door, looking inside then back again. "Let me see. Please come in." She ushered him into the kitchen. "Please, have a seat. I'll pour you a coffee."

Paul was surprised. The formal living room was what he expected. Was Mrs. Ingstrom keeping it informal and friendly, or did she not want to soil her white upholstery?

Appreciate the gesture, he told himself. Though he'd had had his fill at The Busy Corner, Paul did not refuse the cup.

"I'll wake him up." She left Paul at the table and went down the hall.

He couldn't help comparing the Ingstrom kitchen with Memma's. The spacious room seemed only lightly used, hardly lived in. Everything was stored away in cupboards. There was a package of jellyrolls on the counter. He recognized the brand. Not much baking goes on here. Memma did not have a dishwasher.

Paul heard Mrs. Ingstrom knocking on a door. She spoke Reese's name. Paul sipped the coffee and winced. Cold.

She returned looking bemused. "Well, he isn't an early riser, but he's not in bed now. He must have left already this morning." She went to the refrigerator, removed a note from beneath a magnet and sat at the table reading.

"That's my son." She smiled and shook her head. She handed him the note. "For chores, he doesn't have the time," she said, "but it is summer vacation, after all."

Paul read the note. "Sounds like a teenager, yes."

"Maybe I can help you," she said.

Paul wanted to give her something to play down suspicion. He recalled what PS had said: "Then there's a blond kid from out east. I don't know his name." Take a chance. "I wonder if you have heard the names Johnny Limmer or Daddy Fizzy mentioned."

"Daddy Fizzy? That's an odd one," she said, and paused. "No, I'm sure not. Reese spends a lot of his time alone, reading and, well, daydreaming. I don't think either is a friend of his. Strange names."

Paul had folded the note. "Yes. Youngsters from the West End." He smiled thinly and rose. He reached for his wallet, drew out a card, and while she glanced at it slipped the refrigerator note into the billfold. He brought forth his most polite words. "If you would be so good as to have him call me, I'd appreciate it." He wanted to put her at ease. "It's nothing to worry about. Thanks."

She showed him out. Paul strolled down the walk and, as he turned at the car, he saw her watching him, a curly telephone cord stretched across the sweater and pearls. He might find out later whom she had called.

He drove. Paul tried to keep his ideas factual, but his stops at East High and the Ingstroms' had fed his West-canted sensibilities. He had met too many Mrs. Ingstroms to be taken in by her appearance. Her son was privileged, the free-ranging progeny of over-indulgent, laissez-faire parents. He could be up to a whole lot they didn't know about. Paul was sure without checking the room that Reese Ingstrom had not spent the night at home. The note had been written the morning before. It referred to the weekend as just past. At least he knew that the boy had touched home Monday, maybe not long after passing Brookside. Paul had two points, the beginning of a time-line. He knew he'd find others when he looked. He felt he had something to jar the chief off his single-track investigation.

Paul resisted his impulse to drive by the house and instead went directly to Brookside. It was already past 8:30. He didn't want to appear lackadaisical, even though he had been working on the case already that morning as well as late the previous night.

Paul wasn't surprised this time at the scene he encountered.

The television crews had trebled, lookie-lous lined both sides of the road and policemen milled about everywhere, supposedly keeping a secure perimeter. He edged his car between reporters and crews, past gates where two officers moved a barricade for him while two others kept citizens and newsmen from entering as he drove through. He ignored the dozens of questions they fired at him as he passed. He had too many of his own and knew the chief had held a press briefing the day before. Limelight was not what Paul sought.

"The chief has been calling," a sergeant told him.

"I bet he has. Where are we set up?" He went to the phone bank in the police van. Before telephoning the chief, he made three calls. He invited Cindy to lunch; he arranged to meet Wendell Jr. afterwards; and he gave PS the two names in Solon Springs he'd gotten from Randy.

Paul took a briefing on the Brookside case: the autopsy reports, a missing items list, a list of employees at the property the previous night, a list of Miss Crosley's heirs and relatives.

"Where are the evidence photos?"

The sergeant shook his head. "The lab screwed them up. Chemical burn. We had to retake them."

"Get the chief for me," Paul said.

"No need. He's on his way."

Yelling at the crew would not help, but the loss of the pictures was damaging. Retakes at this point were almost futile.

"I'll be around back," he said.

Paul took a walk. The grounds had been scoured the day before, but he walked around the house, over the lawn, down to the boathouse. The lake swelled intense and blue, turning into a shimmering mist out where the Apostle Islands broke the shoreline as it turned south. The chill, lapping water at the dock dampened but couldn't cool the morning air that already promised a swelter. He cupped his hand at his eyebrows as he checked the sky and stepped into the shadow of the Norway pine that grew at the side of the boathouse. He turned toward the mansion. Though dour and purposely imposing, in the sharpness of the July sun it looked less like a scene of carnage. How had it looked in deadly night? He felt troubled within its borders, as if the money spilled to build the place had somehow ordained the slaughter that had been revealed yesterday morning.

Paul left the dock and walked across the lawns to the murderer's point of entry. He pictured how it must have appeared to a killer two nights earlier. The fog would have covered movement around the perimeter of the house. Paul already knew that the occupants of the house had observed no one. He knelt at the top of the stairway leading down to the door and the broken window inside. Between his thumbnail and index finger, he snipped a sprig of Snow on the Mountain from the bush hanging over the brick walk. He twirled it round in his fingers and tossed it on a trampled spot near the foundation wall. Someone had stepped there. Murderer, thief, or officer of the law?

He rounded the far end of the mansion. The chief had arrived and was fighting off reporters. He didn't look pleased.

The chief took Paul's arm and walked him toward the gardener's house. "Let's talk," he said.

Paul handed him the list he'd picked up from Randy. "The cross-outs aren't mine," he said. "Roger Sillanpaa was on the list."

"I'll give it to Dahlen," the chief said. He didn't want to talk about it.

They stood just out of earshot of the milling officers. The chief put his hand on Paul's shoulder. He was a short, burly figure and had to look up at Paul. "Paul I have great faith in you as an investigator. You know that."

It sounded like an opening of a firing.

"Thank you, sir." Paul knew there was more. The chief didn't mince words. That was good.

"But as far as handling this family"—he indicated the mansion—"I don't want you anywhere near. You won't like them. I don't know who does. And they won't deal evenly with you." The chief didn't hide his disgust.

"What's happening?"

"First of all, everyone in the whole damn family is coming to town. Some are already here."

Paul found nothing strange in that.

"Second, they're holding the funeral services here."

"At the murder scene?" That worried Paul. "We've still got a lot of work to finish."

The chief diminished, grew palpably shorter, and said with sadness: "When Lionel Crosley calls your home number at two in the morning to tell you what they'll do, you listen and say, 'yes.'"

"Thanks for running interference for me," Paul said.

"Honestly, Paul, for all your years out here you're still West End. I know you have crossed the line in many ways, but I don't think you can handle these people. I've trouble enough."

Paul thought of Mrs. Ingstrom and his mother-in-law. Yes, he'd rather run them over than have to deal with their sympathies. But he could certainly investigate them. "It doesn't bother me, sir," he said.

"I got the word early on this daughter and her husband. They're bad news. They'll likely try to get into the house as soon as they arrive in town."

Paul's indignation rose. "On my watch? I don't think so."

"Let them on the grounds, but not in the building."

Paul stiffened at the directive. "You don't have to tell me, chief."

His boss turned on him. "I think I do. Here's another thing." He had been waiting to unload. "I assigned you to this case and this case only. You've been mucking around in your friend's suicide too much. Did you think I wouldn't hear?"

Fury rushed up Paul's spine. "It isn't suicide."

The chief put his hand on Paul shoulder in a fatherly way. "There was a note, Paul."

It knocked him off center. "Where?"

"It was in the kid's pocket. Of course, the coroner will have to account for it."

Paul was shaken. "I can't believe it."

"Paul, leave the investigation to others. You're watching out for those people too much."

"Someone's got to." He spit the words.

The chief fired right back. "And someone's got to make sure we get a conviction in this case," he said. "This case is a career maker, but it can also smash a man. These people don't fool around."

Paul didn't like the drift. "Who's calling the shots here?"

Now the chief was pissed. "The DA. And don't think the Crosleys have failed to sit on his desk."

"Meaning?"

"We'll see. But the daughter and her hubby were involved. That's a given."

Paul pulled out the note. "I've ID'd the kid I saw here yesterday morning. I'm going to question him."

"You're a bull in a china shop, Paul," the chief said. "I already know you've been around this morning. Heard it from two sources."

Paul burned. "Sons of bitches."

"Hey, people talk. And they aren't where they are without fierce defenses. It isn't the Friendly West End here, Paul."

"Chief, I've heard you. But explain this: my source says Reese Ingstrom was peddling coins yesterday, one old one in particular. There are several on the missing items list. Are we looking for the truth of what happened, or are we hanging the most convenient patsy?"

Paul had hit his mark. The chief calmed down. "Between you and me," the smaller man drew closer, "I think you have something. But keep it between you and me. And, for Christ's sake, don't go barging around the East End so early in the morning! Be a little careful."

"What else, chief?"

"I want you to interview this couple when they arrive. We plan to search their hotel while they're at the funeral."

"Okay, boss." Paul said, standing taller. "I have a few questions for the coroner before he rules on Roger's death. No matter what, I've got Berta West to think about."

The chief sucked his teeth as he looked up at Paul. "Just don't ruffle any feathers in the department."

With that, the chief strode over to the reporters.

Paul reviewed the evidence collection with his second, Halvorson. He had to admit that what they'd found so far pointed to a large, strong man, a bludgeoner who chased the housekeeper down the stairs and bashed the life out of her with a brass candlestick. Paul tried to picture the featherweight Ingstrom doing that. No image came.

He turned to Halvorson and said: "Let me pick your brain, Nick. What have you noticed in the evidence that could point to two intruders rather than one?"

"You mean working together? The daughter and her husband?"

"Not necessarily. Maybe unknown to each other. Who knows?"

"First, the daughter was out of state at the time. Confirmed. Second, I don't think there's anything that points to two."

Paul tacitly agreed, but he wasn't through with the idea. He gave his orders. The house would remain off-limits until two hours before the funeral, and then they'd open only parts of it. "Keep everyone out of the house. I think we are done with the grounds. An officer at the front and back should do it. Lock all the other structures. Let me know when the pictures are ready to look at."

"You off somewhere?" Halvorson asked.

"I want to inspect the house again. I need to be in there alone."

Halvorson gave a knowing look. Paul was famous in the department for his bloodhound nose that, most had to admit, helped him crack puzzles and solve crimes.

Paul started again at the top of the stairs where the Snow on the Mountain crowded the sidewalk. He closed his eyes a moment, breathed softly some, then stepped down toward the door at the end of the stairs. Something wasn't right, but he continued through the door. It had been open. He couldn't prove that, but it was more than reasonable.

The sun shone hot through the glass, spilling patterns of window stiles and rails across the floor, but the light's intensity was dampened indoors. Paul removed his shoes. It gave him a better feel. The rhythm of his breath told him he was right. I'm on it. He examined the broken glass on the tiled floor. Yes. He swept over it. Once in Paul examined the window sill. He breathed, his eyes closed. The intruder wore gloves. "Yes," he said aloud. He added gloves to his mental evidence list. They'd have glass bits embedded in them.

Paul obeyed the police tape he had himself ordered after two officers had climbed through the window, demonstrating how it had been done. As much as he wanted to, Paul wouldn't call them idiots.

He entered a large room by the door further down the subway. He shut and opened his eyes, adjusting to the dim interior. He stood with his back to the window and the couch under it. How did he know where to go in the dark? Paul let his thoughts travel where they would. He knew the house. Yes. Does it mean one? The son-in-law would be familiar, but could there still be two? Paul could not rule it out. There could.

He moved slowly, carrying his shoes and listening intently.

On the floor above, Paul heard the investigators moving. The house staff was being interviewed in the far wing. He pushed all that away, listening for echoes murmuring still within the paneled walls. His breath led him to the double doors. He approached slowly. He sensed caution, alertness. Had it been fear? He pressed the lever and opened the right-hand door enough to slip through. No, it was excitement, he decided. He stood adjusting to sound and darkness. A shaft of sunlight spilled in the hall further down, but this corner was dark.

Paul moved, cautiously preserving the thin veneer he had built between two nights back and today. What had happened then concerned him more than what was happening now. And as he crept along the wall closer to the sunlit rhombus ahead, he smelled it. It clung to the wall, just as it had to the doorjamb in Roger's apartment. Positive ID. Sweat. More stagnant than acrid; truly singular. He hadn't noticed it upstairs at Berta's, but it had been smeared on the door jamb of Roger's apartment. Could it be this second person had leaned or lingered there. Paul built a loose time line from Roger's death, to the delivery of his body, to Crosley's murder, to sighting Ingstrom on London Road. Today, encountering the odor again, he knew. One and the same. There was a connection, but for now, he didn't worry it. He just kept moving. It was no use trying to smell it. Like the first scent of morning coffee that fills the kitchen air, this odor filtered in and instantly exhausted the sense.

Paul came to the area below the stairs. Fear hung there. No, not fear, a startling. It had been a realization. His gaze was pulled toward the steps above where someone, now, was dusting fingerprints. The stair creaked. As if it resounded in the air now and on that previous, darker morning, he imagined a duplicate sound muffled by many hours, one made in the night. A man had ascended the stair. But Paul sensed surely that, right here, someone had stood and listened to the stair complain. That made two.

He closed his eyes to move through the sunlight. On the other side of the main stairway he continued to hug the wall, opening to any sensation he might encounter. There was nothing. Maybe he took to the center, he supposed. The intensity of the light scorched the wispy presence. Paul strode now to the kitchen stair. As he rounded the first bend he heard the interview above him. Someone scooted a chair against the floor. He climbed past toward the second floor. Halfway up, he heard it—"left, left, left, right"—faint but to his senses certain. He followed the directions, up and through the servant's quarters to a heavy door and beyond. Paul found himself at Miss Crosley's bedroom door. The team was on the landing below, painstakingly observing and gathering whatever was there.

Paul stooped below the tape into the bedroom. Someone below said, "Hello." He ducked behind the door but just as suddenly called out, "It's Tuomi." Then his engagement with the daylight world snapped shut.

Behind the door that sweaty scent was strong. He snuffled

slowly. Paul saw Roger, then an old woman, both lying across a bed. Waiting for more, he stood still. He breathed slowly, deliberately, fended off with sealed skin the intrusions of the house, the investigation, his own concerns, thoughts of lunch with Cindy, curiosity about Tommy. No, it would not work. The odor of sweat was all he'd get, and that faded as suddenly as it had filled his nostrils.

Now, Paul felt foolish standing behind the door. He nudged it with his foot, and as the door clicked shut, plain as day, he heard a woman's voice. "Reese, what are you doing here?"

20

Rice's Point

THERE WAS STILL TIME before his rendezvous with Cindy, but Wendell Jr. and Memma had gone to the church, Paul knew, and he didn't have enough time to meet with the coroner now. So he took it slowly. He zigzagged up to First Street driving toward headquarters, sorting out what he had felt and seen at the mansion.

He had sensed a murderous furor at the head of the main staircase but resisted walking through that part of the scene yet another time. The physical evidence was enough, and preserving the faint but patent monitions he had encountered between the point of entry and the murder bed were more important. Paul couldn't, yet, prove there had been two intruders who entered the mansion at the same point at different times. One might have followed the other. The one was surely Reese Ingstrom. Miss Crosley had recognized him, but the chief would hit the ceiling if Paul, without hard evidence, even mentioned Ingstrom's presence in the old woman's room though he knew it was of utmost importance. So, on the circumstantial side, Paul wanted to know what the connection between Ingstrom and the Crosley mansion was, but even better, he wanted to trace the missing coin he was sure Ingstrom had peddled already. These were things Bushy could be doing on top of the other chores he had set him.

Paul circled the block and parked in the lot above City Hall and the Department. Do I dare require a thorough dusting of the wall behind Miss Crosley's bedroom door? The day was turning muggy, and he smelled rain. About that he was never wrong.

Bushy clambered up from Paul's desk chair when he entered.

"Relax, Bushy," Paul said. "I won't be here long enough to sit. What've you got so far?"

Roger's autopsy would be late today. The house would be cleared by one this afternoon. "Nothing on Roland LaPrairie, but this Larson guy is fairly interesting."

Paul rounded the desk. "Tell me."

"He's a plumber of a couple sorts, it seems. Does repair work in the Solon Springs area but has also been accused of breaking and entering in three states—Minnesota, Michigan and Wisconsin over a period of twenty-five years. Most wild, he beat an arson charge ten years ago."

Plainly, Bushy was enjoying the work.

Paul had an idea. "Who defended him?"

Bushy was a step ahead. He beamed. "Your friend and mine, Mark Fraiser."

Paul nodded. "Makes sense. Did PS call?"

"He's got all the dope," Bushy said. "He'll call you as soon as he knows anything."

"Good work, Bushy!" He clapped his shoulder. "Do one more on this guy."

"Anything, Boss," Bushy said.

"Cut the boss. But check Roland LaPrairie with Port Arthur and Fort William police, especially prior to '27."

"Juvenile records too?" Bushy was going to be good at this job. "The guy is just that old."

Paul felt comfortable. Not only could he trust Bushy, another Denfeld grad, but the guy was sharper than he'd expected. "What do you have on this Fizzy?"

Bushy handed Paul a card. "Lives off Fourth Street, near

27th Avenue West."

Paul briefed Bushy on Ingstrom. "You have to be gentle with these people. Work from a safe angle. But I want to find any family or work connection to the Crosleys, relatives, friends, acquaintances."

"Will do."

Paul handed Bushy his notes on the coins from the missing property list. "Put out a tracer with the local and Minneapolis dealers and pawn network. If any of these shows up, make a note and have it held wherever it is. We keep a list of private collectors too. You'll have to contact each of them. If they ask if it's the Crosley case, tell them nothing."

Bushy was taking notes.

"Call the coroner. Tell him I'm coming to the autopsy."

Paul had just enough time to pick up Cindy. He held the door open and paused as he was leaving. "You're becoming indispensable, Bushy."

Paul pulled into the underground parking lot of the Medical Arts Building. Cindy stepped out of the stairway as he pulled to the curb. The few times they lunched like this over the years, they met here, a block from her office. Cindy got in quickly. Paul pulled through to the cashier. "Hey, Frank, just cruising through." He handed him two dollars.

"Yes sir. Thank you." He knew their infrequent meetings were safe with Frank.

Paul drove Michigan Street, away from public view, then turned west on Railroad. The Cove was tucked down by the docks on Rice's Point. Sailors, longshoremen and a few West End retirees frequented the place. None really knew him, and the nautical and underwater décor with porthole windows threw little illumination over the tables. They could talk quietly at the back and not be noticed. A friend of PS's owned the place and would not say a thing.

After the turn onto Railroad Street, Cindy vented her irritation, "Okay, Paul, what is the big deal? I thought we were keeping a low profile. I had to lie to Doris to make it work."

"I've got a suitcase in the trunk," he said.

Cindy looked at him firmly. "Going somewhere I don't know about?"

"No—or yes—maybe," he said, stammering under her scrutiny. "I'm leaving—I've left Pamela."

Cindy waited for the story, her face as stony as the Point of Rocks. He told her about the previous night.

She softened a little, put her hand on his shoulder. "Have you thought this through? With all that's going on, is this the right time?"

Paul reviewed the twenty years he had spent trying to move eastward: college, his opportunistic marriage, moving up the ranks, having a child, losing a child, diving into work, making detective very young. But it seemed a waste. It seemed to him then that he had missed his own life—the life his was meant to be—and had been living someone else's existence.

"Enough already. It is the time."

He saw that Cindy was going to push him. "It might be the time for you. But what about Memma, your investigation, the Skaansgards? How is this going to make it easier?"

Paul noted that she omitted herself and Tommy from the list. "It's because of Memma and the Brookside case that I need to do this now. Of course, it'll take time to make our life together easier, but I can't straddle the line anymore."

Cindy looked concerned. "What line, Paul?"

"The line we both know is drawn at the Point of Rocks— the line between us and them—the division of west and east."

He saw he had lost her. "Look. Roger's investigation is just as important as the Brookside case, but no one cares about it because only money, fame, and power rule. And in that trio, the little guy gets the short end. It's Roger and Memma in this case, but it could be Wendell Senior, anyone who lifts a shovel for a living, or Tommy, even Tommy."

She was shaking her head at his argument. "Paul, keep it simple. You can't change the whole world, not by yourself."

"You're right. I can't," he agreed, "but I can change course and make headway, just like our grandparents on the picket line stood up to Pinkertons and hired thugs."

He struggled to make it personal. "Cindy, look. I blew it twenty years ago. I should have been with you. With Tommy. But I let myself be misled. I was excited to move east, to be on the side of the powerful," he confessed. "Maybe because of my dad's efforts to keep me aloof, I was fooled into thinking that I could shrug off everything I had known growing up in the west."

She pushed back hard. "Wake up, Paul. Tommy's eighteen now. I'm nearing forty. You can't turn the clock back, Paul. You can't."

"You think I should stay with Pamela?"

"I didn't say that." She looked sad. "I just think you should have the right reasons."

"I may not be able to express it in a good way, but I do have the right intentions. I owe it to Memma, to you, to Tommy, the Wendells, and to myself to be who I really am. The chief, Skaansgard and Bullock, the press all think I'm their patsy, their boy. Pamela thinks the same way, but she and the others are wrong. I just have to find the best way to show them."

"So, it's about politics?"

"No, it's about love. I love you. I can't believe I ever left you. It was wrong. It was stupid. Unforgivable. I want to set it right. Pamela was never my wife. You were. Always. Is it so wrong to want to fix that?"

Cindy hardened even more. "I know you better than to think you'll be moving in with me."

Paul could handle the nuts-and-bolts question better than the moral one. "I'm taking a room at the Arrowhead for now. It's crummy but affordable. I'll see if Memma might rent me a room later. I want to finish all this before we talk at all about reforming our future."

Paul turned full on Cindy, grasped both her shoulders, and held her steady. "When all is done, yes, I want us to be together, to marry, not to turn the clock back but to open to a future worth living."

They had parked behind The Cove. Cindy motioned to Paul as she turned the window crank on her side. She wanted some privacy.

Then she turned to him and touched his face. "I love you, Paul. I will gladly be your wife. I know how thoughtful you'll be." She kissed him.

"I've lost my appetite for food," he said.

"I don't need lunch," she said.

"Me neither."

They drove up Garfield onto the hill and across Skyline Boulevard to Enger Tower. They sat quietly together on the granite block wall, watching lake breezes turn the birch leaves, spattering light in all directions. They watched a couple of tugboats down on the bay, guiding a salty to dock. The lift bridge rose and descended twice, its horns making talk with the ships as they passed beneath. From the promontory the city spread out below all in one, continuous, quiet, and gem-like, west and east together.

If Paul had had any doubts about his reasoning with Cindy, joining Wendell Jr. and Memma at Elma's house put them to rest. It was like a Denfeld reunion.

They were eighteen again—lusty, jostling pugilists, jokers, guffawers, friends. Paul was half a head taller, still blond at forty. Wendell Jr., grown slightly stout like his father, showed traces of gray at his temples. Memma said it made him look distinguished.

Paul thought Memma looked worn, very tired. And after coffee and rolls, she excused herself for a nap. "Let you two catch up," she said and shuffled into the guest room where Paul and Tommy had talked. Elma shooed them out while she cleaned up, so Wendell Jr. and Paul moved to the living room.

"How did it go with Father Lucci?" Paul said.

Wendell Jr. frowned. "Things haven't changed in three hundred years in that church. They'll be Philistines to the last."

The priest had learned about the note. All Memma's testimony about men moving Roger's body hadn't overcome the good father's conviction that Roger had intended to take his own life.

"So, he won't say Mass," Paul said.

Wendell Jr. stood and paced. "Hell, he won't even let her use the hall and kitchen for the wake, for Christ's sake."

Paul moved to calm him. "Keep it down, Wendell. I understand, I agree, but don't let's disturb your mother. She's distraught enough."

Wendell Jr. plopped into a chair. "I see Pilate's point. I'd like to crucify the bunch of them." He kept his voice low, but the steely tension hadn't left it. "After all the wakes she has catered and worked at, not being able to even use the hall stinks. It just stinks. The man should be whipped."

"Look, Wendell, I'm meeting with the coroner in a couple of hours. It isn't a done deal yet."

Paul expected his friend to be skeptical. He wasn't wrong. "I don't know what you can tell him that he doesn't know already," Wendell Jr. said. "He isn't going to buy your visionary wisdom. Not at least on something so close to home."

"You're right about that, but I have a couple of things that at least might buy more time to investigate." He poked his sunburned nose toward his friend's swarthy face, "And it isn't based on hoo-doo. At least not all of it."

They both laughed.

Wendell Jr. gave Paul a love tap. "I have to admit, you always have had a sixth sense about things. Except for your own self."

Paul moved the conversation on to his marriage and his plans to dismantle it.

Wendell Jr. was sympathetic. "I know better than most what it costs to leave the West End. I'm never coming back, but that doesn't mean I don't miss it every day of my life. You learn that you bring it with you, anyway."

"At first I thought I couldn't shake it," Paul said. "Then I didn't want to."

They talked of Paul moving into the house. "I don't think she's going to leave Duluth," Wendell Jr. said. "I mentioned it. She just looked sad."

Paul treaded carefully. "She'll need some looking after through all this."

"I'll be going back in a couple of days. If the funeral can't happen before then, you'll stand in for me. I don't have the leave to come back." It wasn't regret, just fact. Paul agreed.

A little embarrassed, they embraced. "Come up to the house later, Paul. We'll sit out back on our bench."

"I'd like that." Paul fingered the card Bushy had given him. He still had a hundred things to do with the day half gone. "Take care of Memma, Wendell."

Paul cruised by Daddy Fizzy's. The house was typical of the West End. It resembled the house Paul had been born into, just a few blocks from Elma's. It was one of a line of row houses joined by a single long covered porch, divided into six spaces by spindled railings and newel posts at each of the units. Paul turned into the alley behind to look for the station wagon registered to Fizzy's mother, Lorraine Ustoff. He hadn't seen it on the street. He came round the block and parked in front. Before Paul made the porch, a long-haired young man in a tight-fitting jacket, bellbottom jeans, and ankle boots came out the door.

The young man tossed his long, straight hair away from his eyes. "Have you found her?" Daddy Fizzy said.

Paul was confused. "Who?"

"Aren't you with the police?"

"Yes. Detective Tuomi, homicide."

The young man paled. "No. She isn't dead, is she?"

Paul took command. "Hold on. I don't know what you're talking about. I'm here just to ask a few questions."

Fizzy looked relieved. He opened the door again. "Come on in then."

The apartment was sparsely furnished—not-too-recent Montgomery Ward, Paul guessed—but it looked neat and well cared for. Fizzy indicated the couch. Paul sat.

"Coffee?" Fizzy was courteous.

"Thanks. I just had a cup," Paul said, wanting to stay official. "First off, let me get things straight. You are Robert Ustoff, no? Known as Daddy Fizzy?"

Fizzy nodded.

"Now, who are you asking me about?"

"My sister, Marly," Fizzy said. "She should have been home last night. When she didn't show up by nine this morning, I

281

called the police. I thought you'd found her."

Paul took a note. "I'm from another department. I hadn't heard." Paul wanted to work with him. "How old is she?"

"She's about to be sixteen. But she's mature and wise for her age."

"Okay, that's good. Gives us less to worry about. When did you last talk with Marly?"

Fizzy thought about Ingstrom. He wasn't ready to reveal everything. "Yesterday afternoon, here." He didn't want to mention driving or their visit to Somebody's House.

"Was she with someone, or did she leave alone?"

Fizzy let it out. "With mom. She gave her a ride to work."

Paul noted the hesitation. He let the licensing issue ride.

"Didn't you say homicide?" Fizzy said.

Paul gave him a card. "I'm actually here informally. I'm a family friend of Roger Sillanpaa and his grandmother. You know about him, don't you?"

Already a bit peaked, Fizzy grew paler. "Yes. He comes— came to my shows— sometimes."

"Then you know he died night before last."

The shock treatment was working, but Fizzy resisted in the face of interrogation. "I didn't." Lying didn't come easily for Fizzy, but when others were involved he knew how to dissemble.

"You knew him, though. When was the last time you saw him?"

Off the topic of his sister, Fizzy worked to block the questions. "Maybe last week. When I'm doing shows, I don't always have time to notice who's there. It's pretty rapid fire." Fizzy shook the hair out of his eyes. It fell right back over his glasses. "That's shocking. How did he die?"

"It might have been an overdose. We won't know for sure until the autopsy. We haven't ruled out suicide."

Fizzy blurted out shock. "He killed himself?"

"Some think that, yes. So, he wasn't, didn't seem depressed or anything, when you saw him?"

"Roger? I don't think I could tell." Fizzy evaded the trap. "Some people hide it pretty well."

"You know a John Limmer?" Paul asked. Fizzy denied it.

"How about Reese Ingstrom?"

With Marly missing and likely with Inggy, Fizzy thought it best to confirm. "Him I do know."

"When did you last see him?"

Fizzy searched for the best lie. "I saw him night before last at Joe Huey's. He was with people I didn't know."

"Any idea where he might be?"

"None."

Though he wasn't making headway so much, Paul believed in giving as well as getting. He returned to Fizzy's concerns. "So, your sister. Anyone else responded from the Department?" They hadn't, of course. "You have a good picture of her?"

Fizzy was relieved to be off Ingstrom and Roger. He took a photo off the sideboard in the dining room. "Can we get it back?"

"I'll see to it personally. Thanks." Paul extended his hand. "Roger's grandmother will be glad to know he had good friends."

If Paul guessed right about Ustoff, this would bring more results than cross-examination. In the West End, loyalty to family beat loyalty to friends. Pushing him around would not be the best tack. Let him come forward. Paul ended the interview on a positive note. "I'll get copies of the photo circulated and drop it back here. Don't worry. Kids have a way of showing up."

Paul had missed the autopsy, but the coroner, Walt McConnichie, was still at St. Luke's writing his report. Though he needed to meet with McConnichie, Paul hadn't been so anxious to witness the exam of Roger's body. The results of the Brookside exams he had already seen but had some questions to pose there as well. He wanted to reconcile his visualization with the hard evidence. He broached that topic first.

"I'm curious, Walt. Your report on Miss Crosley indicates that some of the pressure marks on the deceased's face were made postmortem. What do you make of it?"

"That's your department," the coroner said. "I just tell it like it is."

Paul would lead him, then. "Would you say that the nature of the marks made after her death were different than those she suffered before she expired?"

The coroner thought about it. "Maybe. What do you mean?"

"It seems that someone came back to make sure the job was done. Don't you indicate more force needs to be applied to leave postmortem markings?"

Walt knew Paul's reputation both for thoroughness and for hunches. "You think there were two men involved?"

"If I don't have it wrong, isn't suffocation one thing and death by suffocation another event that can happen a bit later?" This was the place to try it out on someone neutral. "If Miss Crosley was suffocated but not yet dead—somewhere between spontaneous recovery of breathing and irreversible death—and the murderer returned to the bed, or another person entered, isn't it possible that more smothering was administered?"

"I can't say that it is impossible. Her suffocation did not take that much force, especially since she struggled. That uses oxygen, and the other marks, yes, were very forcefully induced."

"So say the first attempt didn't kill her outright, that she didn't look dead, just old and tired." Paul leaned toward McConnichie. "A second person enters the room to smother her, thinks she's sleeping and applies the pillow again, this time very forcefully. Is that possible? "

Walt had to smile despite the grim circumstances. "You weave a good tale. Yes, I suppose so."

Paul jumped on his words. "You could testify to that?"

"Paul, I'm speculating."

It was weak evidence but he felt he was on the right track. Paul left it and moved on. "Tell me what you think about Roger. Roger Sillanpaa."

"Cardiac arrest brought on by a second and massive dose of heroin."

"Two doses?"

"Yes. Two fresh needle entries, perhaps within half an hour of each other. The heart might have been weakened by the first. It was paralyzed by the second. The traces in the heart itself are strong. Stopped it instantly."

Paul wanted answers. "Is the bodily evidence concomitant with suicide?"

"There was a note, Paul."

"I know. But what about autopsy findings?"

Walt hesitated. "I realize, Paul, that you knew this kid."

"I want you to stay to the facts as you know them," Paul said.

"We know that few suicides 'pull the trigger' a second time if the first doesn't do it, but the fact that there were two injections, both hitting a vein, seems to indicated that suicide is a possibility."

"Even without a note?"

The coroner danced around it. "Not certainly. But there is a note."

"Seen it?" Walt hadn't. "So, ignore it."

McConnichie sighed. He couldn't get off Paul's hook. "One thing is strange. The residual heroin found with the body was not nearly pure enough to be lethal. It did not contain the fatal dose. I don't know what to make of it. I've said so in the report."

Paul told the coroner what he knew, what he had seen and sensed in Roger's apartment. "Also, it's struck me that under the odd circumstances, the so-called suicide note has to be authenticated. We need something to compare it to, and it'll need handwriting analysis."

Walt could see where Paul was going. "That isn't in my bailiwick, but I can hold the report for another seventy-two hours while blood analysis is sent to the state lab."

Paul knew that Roger didn't intend to die. Apart from the carefully orchestrated return of his body home and the placement of the wrong dope bag, Paul knew that a distraught soul would not choose a lively party as a scene for his death. The depressed wander off alone and hide their pain until it becomes unbearable. Roger's death had been an accident.

"Okay, Walt," Paul said, "that is the time I need. Thanks."

Paul checked into his room at the Arrowhead. He had a good view of the lift bridge and the lake. It was three blocks from his office. Convenient too, he reckoned. No matter the view, though, the less time he spent in that room the better. It wasn't going to be home.

Paul had been in the car all day, so he stretched his legs walking to the office. He wanted to check in one more time with Bushy and see what new had come to light at Brookside. He had more work for him, too.

Bushy was packing up, nearly out the door.

"Hey, detective, not so fast," Paul exhorted. "This isn't necessarily a nine-to-five job."

Bushy put his satchel down. "Want a report?"

"Of course," Paul said, "and I have a couple more items." He showed him Marly's picture. "Copy this and send it to Missing Persons. The description of the station wagon should go with it."

Bushy looked at the picture. "I've seen her. Underage driver for sure."

"And the wagon?" Paul said.

"Yep. She drives her mother to work, not far, all in the West End, harmless stuff." Bushy knew his beat. "I hadn't thought about it but the car also fits the description of one leaving the area of the arson fire on Grand Lake."

Bushy showed Paul the county sheriff's bulletin. Two cars had been sighted: one, a '59 Impala, dark color, no plate number; and two, seen after dawn, a Ford wagon.

"Have they identified the victim?"

"Not yet. The body was incinerated in the propane fire. Some clothing fragments blown clear say a male, 5'7", but they're not sure yet."

"Let them know about the missing teen and her mother's wagon. I was at the house. Neither the girl nor car has shown up."

Bushy had set his bag down and was at the desk again. "Sure thing. PS called an hour ago, said he'd be late coming back. He'll meet you at Huey's around ten."

"Anything on the coins?"

"Not yet." Bushy hesitated. "Skaansgard called. Twice."

Paul ignored it. Let him wait. "See if you can get me a copy of this so-called 'suicide note' of Roger's. You might ask if they have another sample of his writing."

Bushy was eager. "No problem." He handed Paul a folder. "Here's the poop from Canada."

Paul raised an eyebrow. "Canada?"

"Yes. On LaPrairie."

"You're great, Bushy. Slipped my mind." Paul was through. "Don't work too late, detective."

"Get out of here," Bushy said.

Paul walked to the Arrowhead and drove out to check in at Brookside. Sure enough, the family was descending on the scene the next day. The funeral would be the day following. Keeping them from wandering around the murder scene would be a chore. The state lab technicians would finish up tomorrow.

Evening and the moist coolness of a storm front had shouldered out the muggy afternoon air. The weather had yet to rush over them, but anyone could now feel the threat Paul had sensed earlier in the day. Standing in the circular drive before the front entry of Brookside, Paul let his professional and personal ruminations slacken in the atmosphere. He allowed the air, the scent of pines, and settling weather to smooth his tanned brow. The enchantment of grassy, piney, and mossy brume twined in his nostrils and spelled his thoughts. For an instant, the rarified air of Brookside Estate rested. It became the province of Everyman, streaming unfettered past the proprietors and laws that tried to contain it. Unleashed, it felt healthy; it had nothing to do with violence, murder, or theft. Paul sucked in the scents, held them until his chest chafed, and let loose with a grumbling rasp he felt humming through his lungs, throat, and jaw. Suddenly, he wanted to sit with Wendell Jr.

I've bought some time with McConnichie, so Father Lucci

can wait.

It was getting late. The thunderheads in the west blocking the early evening summer sun made it seem even later. Paul drove straight to Memma's house and found Wendell Jr. sitting on the bench they'd built together, his arms braced on the seat, shoulders high, watching the storm roll in across St. Louis Bay. He acknowledged Paul with a nod.

They sat quietly together, each counting the lightning strikes miles out across the water as thunderheads advanced behind a marching electrical army that would bring on the torrent. Black clouds piled atop gray ones, towering a mile above the hills. The air around them bristled before it flowed. Goosebumps stood out on Paul's bare arms. The temperature, like a falling sheet of rain, dropped twenty degrees in a second. Night was blown fast before the gale.

The two friends sat, boys again, astonished by what was bigger than them, grander than the hills, out-sizing the city spread out before them and behind. They stayed put until the first splatters of icy rain slapped their scalps and arms.

Wendell Jr. pushed himself up. "Come on. Mom is heating up some leftovers."

21

Mesaba Avenue

CARLOS WAS HOLDING FORTH on the latest news of the Hillside. He sat in front of dining room windows in the overstuffed chair, shirtless, waving his arms, demonstrating, emphasizing his points by thumping his chest. He was barefoot and had tied a blue bandana around his forehead. The dining room served as the hookah lounge. There was no high table, only a sari-draped, rounded half-sheet of plywood on a concrete block pedestal. Madras-covered pillows crowded three corners of this small room surrounding a machine-loomed Persian carpet. The water pipe stood in one bare corner behind the door to the hall.

Carlos draped his arm around an imaginary woman to his left. "So this real cool African guy shows up at The Caribe, starts getting friendly with Skip and Janey, especially Janey."

Matty, leaning on an elbow, rose up on his knees to break in. "Didn't Skip get uptight?" Matty and Siiri had been snuggling on cushions.

Siiri poked him in the ribs with a ringed toe. "Not everyone is so jealous, you know." She smiled.

"All right you guys," Carlos said. As a pair, they annoyed him. "The guy has narc written all over him. Looks like he dresses from the men's department at Glass Block. Short hair—no afro. Funny little gold chain on his neck that shouts out police, police. You know the works. Phony."

Johnny Limmer stirred and fretted. "Did you see him?"

"Skip told me all about it," Carlos said.

"So they drive him around the hillside?"

"He wanted to score some grass, he said. He was charming. A real nice guy." Carlos held both hands over his heart, wringing the utmost attention from his audience. "He told them he knew Inggy."

Matty flopped back down. "That jerk!"

Siiri pinched him. "Matty, don't judge."

Carlos came to Ingstrom's defense. "Inggy's cool. We all know that."

Siiri was quiet. Nobody disagreed but Johnny fretted more. Matty just glared.

"Anyway, that is what the guy said. It wasn't necessarily true, though it's feasible that he was a senior from East, like he said."

Johnny looked scared. "So they drive him around the hillside!"

"Did they come here?" Siiri said.

"Don't know. I just know they stopped at Skip's and a couple other places."

Johnny got up. "Here? Shit. Did someone sell to him?"

"I think he got a dime bag over at Mike Light's place."

Matty burst forth again. "There's another jerk."

Siiri rolled off the pillows, away from Matty.

Okay, Carlos thought, put this kid in his place. He's such a downer. "Listen, lover boy," he said to Matty, "take care of your own business and stay out of the other guys', will you?"

Matty got up and walked to the living room windows. That room was bare of everything except a blue-antiqued four-poster bed sitting square in the middle of another Persian carpet, itself centered in the room. Matty walked around the headboard and leaned out the window to see the Central Hillside clock. "9:30," he said.

Johnny Limmer returned from the back bedroom with a

bag slung across his shoulder. He looked very pale.

"Where you going?" Carlos said.

"For a walk."

"With all your worldly belongings?"

Johnny struck a thoughtful pose. Maybe he couldn't convince Carlos. "Yeah, I'm going to the laundromat."

"Cool," Carlos said. He lifted a heavy arm toward the door. They watched Johnny bungle around with the lock and finally let himself out. No one said goodbye. They sat quietly as he descended the stairway and shut the lower door. Carlos flattened his lips together, raised his brows, and rounded his eyes, "Paranoid. He'll sleep in the park tonight."

"Johnny can act pretty strange," Siiri said.

Carlos dipped into his pocket. "Hey, Matty, come on back here. Uncle Carlos has us a treat."

Matty trudged back from the living-bedroom. "What'd ya have?"

In a single motion, Carlos slid off the chair and knelt at the low table. For a fat man, he was amazingly flexible and spry. He carefully unfolded a quartered sheet of lined paper to reveal three lilac-colored pills. "Now that Johnny is gone, I present you 'purple domes,' pure and gentle."

Matty stared. "Huh?"

"LSD, my friends. Guaranteed to be a good trip. They have the Timothy Leary seal of approval."

Siiri moved closer. "I don't know. I have to work tomorrow."

"Takes you up, trips you out, and lets you glide back smoothly. You'll be perfect before daybreak." He licked his index finger, touched a tablet. "Put out your tongue."

He rolled the tablet onto Siiri's tongue. "Don't chew. Let it dissolve right there."

She flashed Matty a defiant frown and retracted her tongue.

Matty dragged himself to the table, reluctant and shamed. "Oh, all right."

Carlos repeated his ritual, placing a tab on his own tongue, and handed the paper to Matty.

The three sat together. Donovan sounded from the next room. "'Mellow Yellow,' that's right, slick." That's an old song.

Mesaba Avenue cuts diagonally uphill below the eastern face of Point of Rocks past the Bethel, an old sailor's home, angling up across Third through Ninth Streets to meet Central Entrance, the thoroughfare running up to form the eastern border of the Central Hillside. Together, these two roads define the Hillside as a neighborhood. Mesaba Avenue is also one of the few diagonals in a city that should have had many traversing its hills. The grid plan superimposed on the city despite its mountainous terrain forces avenues to soar steeply up, or drop precipitously to the lake. Despite the snow and ice that coat the inclines six months a year, denizens of the Hillside love to call their city the San Francisco of the Midwest.

Mesaba separates downtown from Observation Hill with a terraced boulevard along its trajectory. The upbound side runs ten feet below its downbound partner, divorced by wide lawns and stone retaining walls running in between, some ten feet high and two blocks long. The uphill, residential lots overlook the whole boulevard atop their own retaining walls, holding back trees and lilacs that soften the exalted shoulders of the mammoth thoroughfare.

Carlos rented his apartment high on the downbound side. His building soared above and back from the traffic. His two front rooms, living-bedroom and dining-hookah room, opened to a view of the bay, the lift-bridge, and Minnesota Point. The St. Louis County Jail and civic center blocked the sight of downtown.

At night, Carlos lit his candles in those windows.

Siiri was laughing. "What're you doing?" she asked.

Sitting in the overstuffed chair, Carlos had rolled up his ample belly toward his barrel chest, creating a fleshy shelf. He bent his head over and scrawled in ballpoint pen with one hand on the belly top, while holding the huge roll below with the other arm. He raised his quizzical acid-crazed gaze.

"I'm writing poetry," he said.

Matty had been wandering the room, peering at the Hendrix and Airplane posters Carlos had collected. "Read us some."

"Yeah, let's hear it," Siiri said. She writhed on the pillow giggling uncontrollably around her words. "Your stomach is speaking."

Carlos needed little encouragement.

Midnight on Mesaba
the wandering wizard
becomes the candy man.
Three are tripping
high on pills on hills.
The moon shines silver on Superior.

He stood and let his belly fall. The verses written on his stomach sagged upside down below his chest. Siiri was lost in laughter. Matty stood open-mouthed, silent.

Carlos weaved his way into the kitchen.

The couple stayed as they were, Matty erect and ghoulish, Siiri lost in the pillows, rapt, ecstatic. "White Rabbit" played from another room.

It could have been a minute. It could have been twenty.

Siiri's spell diminished with her laughter. She looked around a room full of writhing ghosts and dancing spirits. "Oh, oh, oh," she said. Nothing more. She gazed at the walls as at film screens. She braced her arms behind her and lifted her face to the ceiling, ooh-ing and cooing.

Matty moved to her, stood above her, looking down at her lifted face.

The two watched each other, gazing like strangers who spoke different languages and were suddenly left alone with each other at a party. Neither said a word. It could have been a minute. It could have been five. Siiri fell back and covered her eyes with her palms. Immediately she uncovered them again, as if what she hadn't wanted to see had stuck to her palms. She rolled away from Matty and sat up on her knees.

The two watched each other. As if for the first time, she realized this man was no one she knew.

"Weird," Siiri said again and again. Finally, she broke with Matty's gaze and looked to the empty chair. "Where's Carlos?"

Matty said nothing. He stood and stared. She crawled crabwise farther away and pulled herself up over an arm of the chair. A little unsteady, Siiri wandered toward the kitchen toward where Carlos rummaged noisily through the refrigerator. She stepped as if she were picking her way through a field of deep-growing mosses, uneven and spongy. She entered the yellow light flowing through the doorway and disappeared, as if she had merged into the sun itself. Matty stared at the empty doorway.

He looked around the room. For him, the posters had ceased their movement. Jimi Hendrix had stopped speaking to him. The walls, the paisley pillows were still. The candles in the windows burned with steady flames. It seemed perfectly normal, but he knew he had to hide. They'd find him if he didn't. Now Matty didn't know where he was. Fear washed over him in a sweat. He had to find a place to go.

He listened to a child's voice coming from behind him. That bed. Go, Matty. Crawl under that bed. Cautious, he entered the bedroom-living room and once again rounded the high headboard that stood four feet from the wall. He ducked behind it. He crouched on the floor, out of sight. New voices reached like tendrils through the house. He heard a man and woman clearly but couldn't make out their words. Addlepated? he wondered. Though it sounds familiar, could they be speaking another language?

Matty thrust his legs under the bed and wriggled beneath. He lay on the carpet, the bed hovering inches above him. He rested like a corpse, perfectly centered on the rug under the middle of the bed. The voices from the kitchen seemed to writhe along the wood flooring like heavy smoke or a creeping fog.

The voices laughed and chatted in a friendly way. There, now. The woman giggled. The man spoke low as if inclining his head toward her ear. Matty heard only a low rumbling sweetness. She giggled again. His stomach churned. He felt a knot below his kidney, as if he were draped over a baseball. He resisted his impulse to cry out. He kept still. He listened. The voices surged, twined, and filled the room. His own voice told him: Matty, you need to leave.

Across Mesaba Avenue, in the hearing room of the St. Louis County Jail, a young black man pointed to a map of the Central Hillside as a uniformed policeman read addresses from a list.

"525 Lake Avenue North," the officer said.

The young man fingered the gold link chain at his throat and shook his head. "They parked a car-length down the alley. She stayed in the car talking with me, so I can't with certainty ID the house he went to."

A gray-haired man dressed in suit and tie nodded. "We skip that one. Let's keep it clean."

Addresses on 5th Street, 3rd Alley, and Mesaba Avenue were read. Each time the young man pointed at the map, running his other hand over his forehead and close-cropped curls before he spoke. "Observed paraphernalia. Purchased two ounces of marijuana. Observed marijuana cigarettes in an ashtray." The man in the tie approved each one.

"Gentlemen, assemble your teams. We move at 5 a.m."

Under Carlos's bed, Matty wrestled and schemed.

Work out a plan. I've listened to enough. I'm through eavesdropping on strangers. I don't know how I came to this place or even how I find myself under a bed set in the middle of a room here, but I do know what I'm going to do. I'm leaving.

With that thought an empty pang pushed on his gut, but Matty ignored it. I've had enough.

Out from under the bed, at the door he fumbled with the passage lock. It should have been familiar but somehow was oddly different.

European, Am I in France?

He managed to turn a knob and slide a button up until it clicked. He turned the doorknob. The door opened.

Matty was four steps down when he heard his name. "Matty, where are you going?" It was a man asking him.

"I'm going for a walk," he said. Do I know this man?

Carlos came down to him. His voice was soft. "No, no, no. It's three in the morning."

Matty turned to go. "I'm a stranger here," he said. He didn't convince even himself. "I think I have to go."

Carlos gently took his arm. "Strange, but not a stranger.

Let's stay together. I want you here."

Matty didn't pull away. Carlos guided him up again. "We're all coming down. It's best to sleep some. Then you can go, okay? It'll be light in a couple of hours."

This man's kindness soothed the fear. Matty allowed himself to be led to a sleeping room someone named Johnny had used, adjoining a place the man called the hookah room. The man—yes, his name was Carlos, wasn't it?—gave him a blanket.

"Lie on the pillows, Matty." He knew his name. That made Matty feel better. "Promise me not to leave again."

Carlos himself moved to the living room and climbed onto the bed. Siiri was already dreaming in the back bedroom. Soon, Carlos was snoring at the front. Matty slid into sleep as into a new hiding place. The house grew still. No voices crept along the floor.

She was screaming. "It's Janey!" She pounded the door. Carlos had lurched up in bed at her heavy steps bounding up the stairs.

"They're busting!" she yelled. "They're busting!"

Carlos hit the floor. He yelled at Janey's voice. "Beat it! I'm out the back." Without bothering to open the door to Janey, he ran to the kitchen and opened the freezer. He took two tinfoil-wrapped packages out and jammed them into his back pocket. He careened into Matty's room to grab a shirt.

"Hey, man. Better get out right now. The cops are coming." He threw on the shirt and stuck his feet into sandals. He left Matty alone.

Carlos took the rear steps three at a time, loped across the back yard, and strode up a wooden stairway to the alley above the lot. He didn't look back until he had mounted the neighbor's porch across the broken asphalt and stepped into the vestibule. He stood quietly behind the duplex's door at the foot of the stairway, the first-floor entry at his back.

Matty and Siiri hadn't followed him. Carlos saw Janey walking nonchalantly up the hill half a block away. A squad car lurched across the parking entry at the front. Two uniforms jumped out and ran around his house toward his apartment's back door. Suits and another uniform leapt out. They burst right in through the front door. Far above them, Carlos heard them pound and shout.

Half a minute had gone by when Matty flew out the rear door. Siiri, holding her sandals in her hand, followed a few seconds later. They ran right into the arms of the police. Carlos watched the officers cuff them. They pushed them ahead and brought them to a newly-arrived squad car in front. Carlos sat on the stairs inside the neighbor's duplex entry. He waited for quiet.

Matty struggled with the policeman who had cuffed him. "Hey, don't do that to her." Siiri was yelling and slapping at the other uniformed officer who struggled to cinch the handcuffs around her wrists. "Goddamn you, leave her alone."

Neither cop said a word but pushed them ahead and around to the front of the building. One opened the door to the back seat of the squad car. A cage separated it from the front.

Siiri struggled. "Pig! Rotten pig!" She kept repeating. The officer pushed her head low to clear the door jamb.

"Well, hello darling," Mike Light said. He lounged in his pajamas against the far door. "It is a pleasure, but should we be meeting like this?"

Siiri stopped her screams. As if seeing her first surrealist painting, she simply stared.

"Hey, Jeff! Put the guy next to the spade."

Jeff yanked Siiri from the car and addressed Matty. "Okay, mister, you go in first. We don't want any hanky-panky on our little ride."

"Sir Galahad himself," Mike said. "Your damsel is in distress." He smiled widely. "I apologize for mixing my metaphors, but welcome to Harlem. They know how to treat you here."

Matty went stiff with anger. "Fuck you," he said.

"Oh, my! The English major speaks. Your vocabulary befits your present position."

Matty turned away. Siiri, uncuffed now, entered the car. "Bastards! Huns!"

Mike leaned forward and smiled. "They don't know how to treat a lady."

Matty tried to block his view. "Don't talk to her."

She turned her wrath on him. "Shut up, Matty! I'll talk with whom I please."

Matty retreated under his bed. Now, no one spoke.

Six hours later, Matty left the police station. He waited forty minutes across the street. Siiri did not come out. He walked across the hillside to their apartment. He was hungry.

22

Lake Avenue South

PAUL FOUND A PARKING SPOT a block down from Joe Huey's. He didn't need to cover his tracks. After all, he was meeting his father. Nothing could be more normal.

Across the street the steam plant, even in summer, hissed and pulsed bursts of power behind the tilted wire-glass windows of its silo. The six-story smokestack towered above the brick building. Against the Lake Avenue side, a man leaned back in the recess of a window well. Steady puffs of smoke drifted from the shadow. When Paul approached Huey's, the man pitched the glowing stub of a cigarette to the street and stepped forward.

"Hey, Paul. Over here." It was PS.

Paul dodged a few cars to cross the street. "Hey, Dad. Still prefer cloak and dagger, huh?"

PS made the motion of turning up his collar. "Let's walk. I'm not hungry." He raised his arm southward and turned to the lift bridge five blocks down. They walked.

PS kept close to the buildings. "You don't like dogs much, do you?"

Paul tucked his chin to his chest and frowned. "What kind of thing is that to say?"

His father ignored the consternation. "I don't either, but it's lucky they like me." PS was playing his mystery game, and Paul's part was to let the suspense build.

"Dogs love you, Dad. So at least somebody does."

PS smirked. Then he turned serious. "Who turned you on

to this LaPrairie guy?"

Rising to the sky overhead, two blocks away, the lift bridge sounded its horn. Just after, warning bells clattered between the warehouses lining the street.

Paul waited for the cacophony to cease and named his source. It was safe with PS. "Belisle."

His father picked up the pace. "Let's try to catch a peek at this ship. It's from India."

They strode the two blocks to the causeway that formed one side of the canal. They walked lakeward toward the approaching vessel. The pier was mostly abandoned. A few tourists lingered far down under the bridge. PS and Paul rested against the waist-high wall that ran the length of the canal. The oceangoing ship had made a five-day sail from the Atlantic. Out on the lake, romance and mystery streamed from its stacks.

PS lit another cigarette. "Belisle. It figures. Makes it more interesting."

Paul waited. It did no good to probe. He watched the approaching ship. It was five minutes away from entering the canal, though its diesels were driving it much faster than it appeared.

PS took a drag, lifted his chin, and exhaled to the stars. "Randy knew it. This is the guy."

Paul played the game. "Okay. Dogs like you. You needed to know my source, and 'this is the guy.' It all makes sense to me."

PS smiled. "The only question I have is, why?"

"Why indeed? Why what? Why whom? Why why?" This was Paul's part of the script.

"Let me tell you."

Exasperation was also part of the game. PS thrived on it. "I can't wait," Paul said.

PS had driven to Solon Springs that morning as soon as Bushy called. He located Larson's place: a converted gas station south of the town, a little off the main road. The faded billboard over the parapet said *Larson's Plumbing*. A homemade sign. The front windows were soaped. The place looked disused. At the house sheltered amongst elms behind the station, no one was home. PS turned around. He pulled off the road, drove up a dirt trail and parked in an old apple orchard on the hill facing Larson's garage. He worked a few crosswords while he waited. Stakeouts were old hat for PS.

"Within an hour comes a black Impala, '59. I note the plate and put binoculars on the driver. Right away I knew. When he gets out of the car, I say 'bingo.' I haven't seen this guy for forty years, but I'd never forget him."

Paul sensed PS was close, so he kept quiet.

"Last I saw him, he was standing next to me after Mark Fraiser shot LaPrairie's partner. He's the guy from the Thompson Dam. The driver of the truck. My witness." With an air of finality, he pitched the cigarette butt into the canal.

Paul saw Randy Belisle's face again, circles within circles. Last night's anger flared and subsided. It was Paul's turn to lead the game.

"I thought he was from Canada, not Thompson."

PS cocked an eye. "You know something. What have you got?"

"What got Royal started in the whiskey business?"

"Oh, you have questions, is that it?"

"I may have answers," Paul smiled.

PS preferred to hold the cards. "Okay, smiley, he knew some people in Port Arthur."

Paul pursed a sage's mouth. "Yeah, he knew some quite well. Let's say intimately."

"Family?"

With just a few hints, PS had put it together. Paul couldn't tell how he knew, but maybe it was intuition.

"According the record, our man LaPrairie was born to Madeline Fraiser LaPrairie."

"Sister. Yes, the good Uncle Roy kept it in the family."

Paul finished his father's thought, "By hook or crook. He did."

The bridge, now a hundred feet above the water, sounded its greeting to *Bisnu's Dream*, the name stenciled below Bengali script on the ship's prow. The ship replied with a shaky double blast. It was still three hundred yards from entering the canal and didn't look as if it would fit. More tourists had come to the causeway.

"I want to climb to the lighthouse to see this rust bucket up close," PS said. They moved toward the approaching ship.

Paul had figured why Randy led him to this guy. It was a favor he could call in later. One he might desperately need sometime, Paul theorized. PS thought about it.

"That might be the 'why.' But it's only part of it."

"Larson left the Impala running and ran into the house," PS went on, emphasizing 'ran'. "He was big forty years ago. Now he's huge. Running isn't something he usually does." PS had watched Larson bring up the wing-shaped trunk lid and place a box inside. He returned to the house, again on the run, and brought another box, then another. He slammed the trunk lid and threw gravel out to the road as he pulled out, roaring away.

Paul formed a picture in his mind. "This guy is in a hurry to hide something."

Father and son climbed the twenty steep steps to the lighthouse platform. *Bisnu's Dream* was plowing down the center of the canal. The Dravidian sailors lounged at the bow and waved to the two on the pier. The ship rolled lightly and creaked.

"Rust bucket," Paul said.

"I'd say decrepit," PS rejoined, and went on. "As soon as the dust settled, I went down to the house. I checked the garage, too. My longtime friend has the fire-bug, and he's got it bad." PS tapped out a Pall Mall from his pack. "I didn't know what he got rid of, but there was plenty left to tell his tale, including The *Herald* story on the Grand Lake fire, sitting plain as could be on his kitchen table. It was only a three-inch story, but he'd cut it out. Maybe for his scrapbook."

Paul's head was spinning. "An Impala was sighted early this morning near Grand Lake."

"I thought he was connected. It gave me a leg up, besides the surprise. That's why I decided to stick around."

PS had hidden his car behind a lilac hedge on one side of the house and waited for Larson's return. He called Bushy from the garage to check some details and confirmed the arsonist's history. Bushy told him Fraiser had defended the guy.

"I figured I had him where I wanted him, so I did a little composition while I waited." PS patted his shirt pocket.

Bisnu's Dream sounded its salute and thanks. The bridge responded. The lake waters smoothed the ship's wake, lapping the concrete sides of the twin piers. In the bay, tugs were waiting to guide the *Dream* to berth. The bridge lowered its twenty-ton bed neatly over the water and causeways. Bells summoned the waiting cars to cross. PS was taking it in.

Like a driver impatient to mount the bridge and be on his way, Paul drummed his fingers atop the concrete wall. The relationship between PS, Larson, and Fraiser was clear. Why PS had not discovered it long ago puzzled him, especially with the prosecution, though it had happened in Michigan.

Still more enigmatic was Belisle's connection with this guy. The bridge bells rang Paul's questions into gear.

His father watched the bridge descend and watched his son's eyes flash inquiry. "It's a setup," PS said.

"How so?"

"With Randy Belisle it's always a setup."

Paul didn't want to play the game. "Just tell me what you think."

Like the bridge and the ship, PS would not be hurried. "You read too much detective fiction, my boy. I can tell you what I know. The rest is speculation."

"Okay, okay then, just suppose."

PS was in his element. He loved his audience and gestured with his unlit Pall Mall, "First, you don't cross Randy Belisle and get away with it."

"Granted."

"We can assume, then, that Mr. LaPrairie did something Randy didn't like."

"Or that I did something he did like."

PS shook his head. "He doesn't work that way. He's too East End."

"Okay."

"Randy gave you the tip before the Grand Lake fire was set."

Paul agreed. "So?"

PS cocked his head at his son. "Think. What does that tell you?"

Paul felt eight years old. Still, he ventured a guess. "Randy hired LaPrairie and wanted him caught."

"Bingo."

In Paul's mind the voice of Kathy, the empress of the Busy Corner mocked his investigative prowess: What'll it be, Sherlock? As easy to follow as PS was, the connections only now started to make sense to Paul.

"I'm fairly thick," he admitted, then took over. "But now it's elementary. LaPrairie and Fraiser are connected. It's Fraiser that Randy is after, but he can't get at him directly."

PS carried it along. "Old Mark is a junkie in a bow tie. The judge's son is just that, the son of a bootlegger turned trafficker in his own right. He and Randy are partners. But Mark has a weakness: dope." PS extended his hand and pressed Paul's arm. "Partners outside a family always split. Randy doesn't want survivors."

"So Fraiser and LaPrairie go together."

"Up in smoke, so to speak."

Paul reviewed the little he knew about the fire. "So who was in the cabin?"

PS shrugged. "Whoever else crossed Randy recently. Someone not on the 'bust list' for tonight."

"Hey, I should ask you what's going on downtown. You know more than I do."

PS grinned. "I thought you might be able to solve the equation. I figured you might know."

And Paul did know. Randy said, "When you find him, ask him." Randy was much too open about the kid.

"Reese Ingstrom," Paul said, "the blond kid. Ran with Roger."

Sadness crept into his dad's eyes. "It's a mean world out there," PS said.

"I hope I'm wrong. I want to talk with that kid."

"Randy isn't as sharp as he thinks he is," PS said. "I think your boy might still be breathing."

Here we go again. This one, though, is worth waiting for.

With a grunt PS hoisted himself atop the causeway wall and finally lit his cigarette. PS drew deeply.

"He was leaving. The house was rigged. The garage, too. What he took with him must have been really hot, but I knew he'd be back. Otherwise he'd have lit the torch."

PS had waited hours. It paid off. In the garage cabinet he had found a file he was hoping would be there.

"If you could call it a file," PS snorted, "clippings and notes stuffed into large envelopes."

When LaPrairie roared back in just before dark, he was driving a rental car. He dashed into the garage.

"I heard him banging file drawers and rummaging like a madman. What he wanted was locked in my trunk." PS was now enjoying himself as much as he had out at Larson's. He had waited years for that meeting.

"When he came out, I was leaning against his car." PS was laughing. "You should have seen his face when I flipped my Pall Mall over toward the garage. He nearly dove on it, all three hundred pounds. Dropped his cash box. I says, 'If it isn't Mr. LaPrairie! It's been a long time.'

"He knew who I was, of course. With a lot of help from Mark, he had been avoiding me for forty years. So I tell him, 'I de-fanged your little firebomb in there. You only have to worry about this.' I showed him my Colt persuader. 'Relax,' I said. 'My deal will be good for both of us.'"

PS dragged on his smoke. "He says to me, 'I'm not dealing with you.'

"'Oh?' I say. 'Then tell me how you broiled that body out at Grand Lake.'

"He says, 'Who are you working for?'

"I says, 'Family.'" PS smiled broadly.

"He tells me it was a mistake. The kid who was supposed to be in the cabin was out on the lake. He tells me no one was inside when it went up. I say, 'That's not what the sheriff says. Must have been someone else.' Then he says, 'So what's your deal?'"

Paul held his hands wide. "So what was the deal?"

"Pretty simple: he signs my affidavit. I photo the act. He goes on his way. Fire or no fire, I didn't care."

"Sounds too simple. What went wrong?"

PS brushed a hand across the side of his head. "Just a few hairs singed."

"What happened, Dad?"

"He signed. I was backing away to turn the car onto the road and, Kaboom! The house went up like a rocket. It blew half the leaves off the lilac."

As PS had backed his car away, he trained the pistol on the big man. LaPrairie'd shuffled into the house. "He must have flicked the kitchen light switch. The ceiling fixture didn't light but something else did. He knew what he was doing."

"The garage went up. Torches blew in through a window."

"Why did he do it?" Paul said.

PS shrugged. "Maybe he was tired after 40 years of plumbing. For starters Fraiser, Belisle, and the sheriff would be out looking for him. Canada was out. Maybe he was sick."

Paul shook his head. "Dad, aren't you a little old for this kind of stuff?"

Throwing the half-smoked cigarette to the ground, PS landed on it with both feet as he leapt from his perch. "I can still run with the pack."

"Do you think a dead man's confession will help you?"

PS looked like a magician about to open an empty box. "It'll sure give me something to play with." He slapped his son's shoulder. "What do you say? Let's get some fried rice."

PS let Paul take a step down the stairway and stopped him. They were now eye to eye.

"Hey," the old man said. "We're good together, don't you think?"

23

Laurel Lane

SURE, I COULD HAVE called dear old Dad in New York. Mother wanted me to. I'd even promised to do it. I just cannot make the time.

Tangling with dear old Dad was not on Ingstrom's agenda.

That man is much too dangerous, Ingstrom thought. Dealing with Belisle was child's play compared to messing with "The Accountant," as Ingstrom's father was known downtown. Dear old Dad's specialty was winning through finance. Fiduciary murder, if it has to go that far. Kill a man, his money lives on. Drain away his money, and he's finished. Ingstrom smiled. No, dear old Dad should not be approached.

His mother was his intermediary. Her he could handle. This morning, he had done just that.

"Reese, you have an explanation to make," she had said.

Ingstrom had pulled on a tee shirt and come out in his pajama bottoms after Tuomi left. His mother was on the phone. "I'll get to the bottom of it and call you back."

"That was Dad, of course."

"Even if he's in New York, Reese, with something like this he has to be informed right away. Anyway, he knows the chief quite well. Now, tell me the truth."

Ingstrom sat at the breakfast table. He let his mother pace the room. It helped to calm her—that much he knew. "It's about the station wagon parked in the garage."

She hadn't seen it. "You didn't steal a car, did you?"

"Mother! How could you?" He said, letting indignation do its work, then waxing cooperative. Ingstrom knew that, with his mother, names were safe. She'd give nothing to the authorities. "No. I'm only keeping it for my friend, Bob, until tonight."

"Keeping it from the police? Start at the beginning, young man."

"It started at Joe Huey's Sunday night."

Ingstrom told her about Roger Sillanpaa's death. "I hardly knew him, but he was an acquaintance of Daddy Fizzy's."

"The police mentioned that name." She crossed her arms, crooked a wrist and toyed with her pearls. "Who is he?"

"You've met him, remember? Bob Ustoff." He lied about her having met him.

"No, I do not. So?"

"I like him. He's an artist—quite famous, you know."

"And?"

Ingstrom pieced his words together carefully, properly. "He and a man named Skip on the Central Hillside, at whose apartment Roger died, wanted to carry him back to his grandmother's house. It was mostly out of respect."

His mother was shaking her head. "And they needed your help?"

"Fizzy trusts me." He wanted to use that word. "Anyway, I was the one who knew where Roger lived."

His mother sat down. "I trust you too, Reese. It isn't pretty, but thank you for being truthful. Now, what about the car?"

He told her truth: Daddy Fizzy didn't have a garage. He bent the truth: fearing that Skip would blab about Roger, Fizzy wanted to hide the car. Someone might have seen it, maybe Roger's grandmother. Ingstrom invented: "Just long enough for Fizzy to find out what's going on. I'm turning it over tonight. He has another place for it."

His mother thinned her lips. "Reese, we'll back you one hundred percent, but I don't like this at all. You need to talk to your father and see Mr. Tuomi. Ask him what he wants."

He looked his mother in the eye. "I won't implicate my friend."

His mother shook her head, but Ingstrom knew it was understood. "You will, though, talk to the police."

"I'll visit Mr. Tombi after I return the car. Tomorrow."

"Tuomi is his name," she said.

Ingstrom reached across the table to touch his mother's hand. "I suppose it was wrong to help them out, but otherwise I had nothing to do with it. I wasn't there when it happened."

She took his hand and stroked his cheek with her other. "My sweet son, what happened here? Were you in the sun yesterday, Reese?"

"Well, I went rowing with a friend. I'm afraid I over did it."

"I have ointment for you to use. I'll put it out." She looked closely at him and touched his hand.

"You are a fine son, Reese. Your father was reckless as a boy. It's something you grow out of." She smiled at him.

He gazed through her smile and thought: I'm going nowhere near the police. I'm boarding my ship. He said, "Don't worry, Mother, tomorrow morning, I'll see Tombi."

She didn't bother to correct him again.

"I'm late for my club meeting," she said. "Bring the car to the curb for me, sweetie." She went to freshen up in her powder room.

When Ingstrom came back in, she was applying lipstick at the entry hall mirror. "I'll be at the golf club later, then at a university women's dinner. There's a plate for you in the fridge."

She caressed his ear as she left. "Stay out of trouble. You can reach your father at his hotel between four and six."

315

"Sure. I might be out when you come home. I'll have someone drop me off late," he said.

All that day, he'd kept out of sight in the house. He packed his sea bag, sewed his cash and his stash into his jacket lining, and read Alan Watts until the sun set.

All that day, he mulled over what had to be done about Randy Belisle. Randy had done in Marly, Ingstrom figured. Belisle's mistake would devastate Fizzy, maybe destroy him. That called for action. What would a West Ender do? Break both legs, I'll bet. Whatever happens, I'll be gone before anyone knows. At this point, I'm the guy.

Dark descended in that faint, thinning way it does in the northern summer, lingering on the opposite horizon for a spell, long after sunset, before dropping fully down. Ingstrom waited for full darkness.

He rolled the car down the drive, then to the corner before starting the engine. He drove the station wagon up the lonely Seven Bridges Road, where he turned west along the mostly ill-lighted and little-traveled Skyline Drive. It was lover's lane on a Tuesday night, empty all the way until he had to dip into and through populated parts of town. He kept to quiet residential streets.

Drive like a square, Ingstrom told himself. When he passed above her neighborhood onto West Skyline Boulevard, he felt Marly's warmth beside him. Once on the western hills of Oneota, on the darkest streets he could find, he made his way down straight to and across the Arrowhead, rumbling on the wooden plank bridge into Superior. He'd guessed where Belisle would be if he was still around. If he's not there, he thought, I can still do him some harm. Leave a calling card. He headed across town toward Central Park and the High Octane 66. What a stupid name.

Traffic had been light over the bridge and along 21st Street, an alternate route. Ingstrom avoided the downtown area and took residential streets past Laurel Lane to hide the car under wide oaks that sheltered one of the large houses set back along the adjacent street. He slipped out of the wagon and walked quickly across the street into Central Park. When he came to the stream, he left the path and followed the low creek bed until the angular roof of Randy's stash house showed itself between the trees. No one could see his approach. He waited and watched.

He'd learned where Randy's stash house was months ago. Now he congratulated himself. It's good to know these things. The structure stood stately, a corner house with deep lawns and a wide Victorian veranda at its base, all topped by a distinctive octagonal clerestory on the third floor. Four tall firs bordering the property towered above the house. Sixty-six Laurel Lane was the address. Randy had dubbed it High Octane 66 after the Phillips brand. Ingstrom snorted at the name. This is going to be fun.

The clerestory windows were lighted. Is someone moving in there? The light varied, shadows seemed to drift across what ceiling beams were visible. Someone is moving around up there, for sure.

He ducked down. A sedan cruised along the lane, lighting the hedges of his hiding place. It paused at the corner and turned down 9th Street. Ingstrom sat on his haunches and waited. He watched the house. I'm here, and what'll I do? It seemed that Belisle held most of the cards.

He surveyed the sunken creek banks, took up and handled the flotsam he found, elder and birch branches. The birch was too brittle, he decided. An elder branch nearly as thick as his wrist proved hefty and strong, but it was too long. He couldn't break it. Stuck in the culvert leading under the road,

Ingstrom found what he wanted: a thick, strong branch a bit shorter than his arm. He sliced three twigs off it with his pocket knife and struck his palm several times. He held the branch up. This might even things. Surprise him and act fast.

Clutching the club he'd made, he recalled his night walk with Marly, holding hands, laughing at the mosquitoes and their coming evening together. He squeezed the bat harder.

Ingstrom looked again at the house. Nothing seemed changed. He was ready.

Reese Ingstrom climbed to the lane and skipped across. He halted between two of the firs, scanning the house and its entry. He slinked beside the bushes along the porch railings, then tip-toed up the steps. He sidled to the door, checking it carefully, tried the knob, and found it unlocked.

"Where you going, sonny?" Behind Ingstrom, he stepped out from the shadows cast by the spirea bushes along the railings.

Ingstrom saw the gun. "I'm here collecting for the *Tribune*," he said.

"With a club?" The man laughed. "Must be in arrears." He stepped closer.

The man was familiar, but Ingstrom kept his eye on the gun. He knew the weapon. The safety was on.

They heard the footfalls on the stairs inside. The man looked toward the door. Ingstrom tossed the stick at the man's face, vaulted high over the banister and bushes, and ran. He stopped only after leaping off the culvert into the creek. He was sure the man had not followed.

Sheltered by the hedges, Ingstrom watched the house. Across the street, Randy Belisle opened the door and stepped onto the porch. He went down across the entry, shot twice.

As he loped away to Fizzy's wagon, Ingstrom heard a third pistol report. He sprinted.

Ingstrom left the opposite way he'd come, took the bayside streets, and drove through the lights of downtown Superior, heading toward the Oliver Bridge and far western Duluth.

He hadn't needed to visit Laurel Lane at all.

24

Saint Erasmo

THE BELL STARTLED FATHER LUCCI. He groped for his lap blanket, but the nice wool comforter had fallen to the floor. Even in the summer afternoons he felt chilly.

Father Lucci liked to grumble as if God were listening to his every word. "Dear Lord, so many years in your drafty churches. I never get warm." Fortunately, his shawl was still in place, and he gathered that around him. "Cold, cold, cold," he said. He listened for Maria's step and tipped forward in his rocker to reach the blanket at his feet. The bell rang again.

He blustered and fussed, even though she couldn't possibly hear him. "Sister, the door. Someone is at the door." He wrapped his legs and lap in wool. Who comes at this time?

Sister Maria's heavy heels pounded across the tile in the hall below. The familiar cadence brought Father Lucci back to the world. Oh yes, the young draft-dodger. He had made the appointment himself. How he forgot things, these days.

Father Lucci roused himself. He rose, holding the blanket against his hips. He folded it three times. "*In nomine Patris, et Filii, et Spiritus Sancti,*" he said. He doubled it lengthwise for the Holy Ghost and set it on his chair. The wrapper he hung over the high rocker back. The good Father scurried to his desk, sat, and lifted a pencil end to his lips just in time. Sister Maria opened the door to the study and announced his guest.

"Oh, yes, yes. I'll meet him in the chancellery, if you please, Sorella." Father Lucci preferred the formality of the church office, even though it would be like ice this time of day. In summer, the sun could not warm it through the heavy leaves of the oak tree. Yet the place instilled the proper respect. One must enter the sanctuary, see the altar, and pass five of the stations.

Sister Maria gave a nod that approximated a slight bow and turned on her wide heel. He had recommended the shoes to her. Yes, he supposed they were a vanity, but they brought her erect, taller, and a bit more imperious. He liked that. Father Lucci watched her close the door. Yes, Maria was his favorite over all the years.

Father Lucci stretched and yawned. He smoothed back his hair. Thinning, yes, but far from bald. He threw his black cowl around his shoulders against the cold office he knew he'd find below. He let the hood hang loose at his back, fastened a single button at the chest, and left his cozy den.

The western clerestory was ablaze in the summer sun. It spilled color across the aisle to the far wall. The baptistery bathed in rainbows of red, blue, and yellow. Aha! *Gloria Dei.* He loved the nave glowing in the light of God. Father mumbled a prayer. "Thank you, dear Lord, for giving me this parish. Yes, a small one, I know, but your cathedral is so grand."

The worry of a shrinking parish washed over Father Lucci. It wasn't his fault. His flock was growing older. Yes, it's the young who are forsaking the Church. They don't listen to their priest. Two years ago, Sister Maria had had to abandon the boys' choir altogether. There weren't enough voices to fill the church, even with the new microphones and speakers. Regret played the organ. He nearly forgot to cross himself before the altar. He cleared his throat. "Ahem," the nave repeated.

Sister Maria was holding the chancellery door open for him. She peered through her tiny glasses at the young man seated at the desk. "Roberto Ustoff has come to see you, Father." She italicized his name as much as possible.

Father Lucci brushed past her. "Thank you, Sister Maria. You may leave us." She took one more look at the young man and bowed deeply as she closed the door.

The office was clammy. Father Lucci gathered the cowl around his legs to sit at the desk. "Ahem. Mr. Ustoff," he said. "What kind of name is that?"

Ustoff sat stiffly. "Russian. My mother was a Chartier."

"Ah. So she raised you a good Catholic."

The young man tossed his head to flick back his hair. "Yes, Father, she tried. I went to catechism and attended Mass."

Father Lucci folded his hands under his belly. "Some years ago, I think."

"Not too far back. Father Arrivido was here then." It had been when Arrivido died that Ustoff and Marly had stopped coming to the church.

"*Poveretto,*" Lucci said and crossed himself. He wondered if he, too, would breathe his last on this cold hill. "You have come to . . . to what?"

Ustoff pulled himself more erect in the chair. "I received my draft notice, Father."

The priest nodded. He did not try to hide the contempt that washed over his swarthy complexion. "So, you come to the Church for help." Leave the choir to die, but for mercy you will cry. "Are you afraid, my son?"

The young man shook back his hair again. He sat tall and straight. "I'm not afraid to die, Father." He let the words sit on the desk. "I just don't think I want to kill."

"Yes, of course. Though this may be a time of need. To serve your country."

Ustoff leaned over the desk. "I'll serve my country, Father, but tell me: do I have to murder others to do so?"

Father Lucci didn't like this young man's tone or the question he posed. He'd take another tack.

"Are you a good Catholic, my son?"

"Not as good as I should be, no, but generally yes. I believe in doing good."

"Good deeds are not enough, my son." This boy's attitude deserved his paternal consternation. "If your city were attacked, say, like Pearl Harbor, would you defend it?"

The young man shifted in his chair. "I think I would. Yes."

"Would that include taking up arms? Say a rifle or even a club?"

Perhaps he saw where he was leading him. "I'd have to think about that."

Augustine had saved him the trouble. Father Lucci pushed on. "Would you defend your house, your mother?"

"What's your point, Father?"

"The church has held that societies have a right to defend themselves. That it is a just cause. And the good Catholic can follow that call to fight for a just cause."

"Viet Nam isn't a just war, Father."

Father Lucci's smile was tinged with a little cruelty. "Perhaps, but if you believe any war to be just, then you aren't a conscientious objector. At least in the eyes of the law, if not in the eyes of the Church."

He watched his visitor search. The young man struggled quietly in his chair.

It seemed time to turn the conversation. "When was your last confession?" the priest said. Father Lucci loved to ask this question. It always turned things powerfully to his side.

It seemed that Robert Ustoff had anticipated the question. He spoke without hesitation or shame. "Five years, Father."

"Five years. Ahem. Don't you think that might be a better place to start? To clear the air?" Lucci folded his hands on his lap and sat back in his chair.

The young man had been untroubled for years as Daddy Fizzy the entertainer; but now, with Marly missing, the police asking about Roger, and Ingstrom involved with everything that looked bad, Ustoff's door had darkened. He had decided before coming to Lucci that some repentance would be in order.

"Yes, Father. I think it is time."

Lucci raised his hands to his heart. He was pleased. Swift on the wings of victory, he thought, and pushed further. "Afterwards, you may take communion. Then we can study your problem more carefully. Clear your conscience and accept Christ anew. That is our way."

Robert let Fizzy fall away. "Yes, Father. That's a good idea."

Father Lucci was glad. His side of the confessional contained a little portable heater to keep his feet warm. He should have turned the heater on earlier. He rued the oversight. "Well, well, it can't be helped," he said.

Robert was following closely, nearly at his side. "What can't be helped, Father?"

The young man's proximity startled him. "Nothing. Nothing. I was just thinking," Lucci said.

They crossed themselves and bowed before the altar, then moved to the confessional. The light above the booth was lit. "*Ave, Maria,*" Father Lucci said. Maria had overlooked nothing. The heater would be on. Thank you, Lord, for my little Maria. *Compassione Dei.*

He entered the booth. It was toasty warm. Yes, his Maria had been busy. Father Lucci took his time: shifted the pillow on his bench, arranged the length of his robes to trap the heat rising from underneath, and leaned back with a sigh. I must not dwell on my desires.

After a minute, after he heard Robert Ustoff stir again in the next booth, he slid the partition only part way from the grate so less heat would escape. He hoped the confession wouldn't be long.

Ustoff intoned his part. "In the name of the Father, and of the Son, and of the Holy Spirit. My last confession was five years ago."

In Latin, Father Lucci recited his favorite parts of the Prodigal Son story. He was pleased that it fit the circumstance. Often it did not, though he'd recite it anyway. This time he gave the story a short translation.

When he was sure the good Father was finished, Daddy Fizzy began. "Father, forgive me, for I have sinned." He began a litany of minor offenses.

The priest listened listlessly. He basked in the warmth of the heater and the drone from the other side of the confessional. Over the years he had attuned his ears, listening for the words: "I firmly resolve with the help of your grace." At these he would awake fully and answer in absolution. Father Lucci drifted on the glow of the heat and the cadence of Robert Ustoff's confession. He began to dream.

Was it something the young man had said? Into his warm trance the face of Berta West materialized at the confessional grate. Oh, how they ruin their beautiful names Anglicizing them, the good Father complained. Poor woman! She was one to take all the sins of the world on her shoulders. "That apostate son of yours should follow your example," Lucci said to her dream face. His words brought out more confessions of fault and sorrow. She wept.

It was a sleepwalking Berta—Roberta—crying at the grate. "Should I have called the police right away when they carried him in? Was I wrong to wait, Father?" The apparition sobbed. "This is my fault."

He spoke dream-words of comfort, words he hadn't spoken at the time of her actual visit. When Berta had come seeking the Mass and Christian burial for her grandson, he told her no. "He has taken his own life. It is a mortal sin. He died without repentance, without forgiveness."

Now, asleep in the confessional, he comforted Berta. "God will protect him even where we cannot."

She wept thanks to him, and in his dream the partition disappeared. She washed Father Lucci's feet in her tears and dried them with a big swath of her abundant hair. This phantom was a younger woman. The dreaming Lucci blessed her and waved his hand over her head. When she tossed her hair from her face, he saw the phantom was not Berta but little Maria. He reached down to stroke her hair.

Father Lucci snorted awake and bumped his head on the wooden wall behind.

Ustoff was recounting something Lucci had heard about. " . . . We put him in bed to make it look like he died there in his grandmother's house. Isn't that bearing false witness, Father?"

Leaning toward the voice, Father Lucci bumped his head on the grate. He couldn't help himself. "What?" he said. Indignity. You fool! Compose yourself. "Please, my son, repeat what you have just said. No harm will be done."

Ustoff repeated the story of Roger Sillanpaa. One detail in particular goaded the priest. "He took the note and stuffed it into Roger's pocket."

Suddenly the good Father had to mop his brow. His collar prickled his neck. Reaching for the heater knob, his hand shook. Dear Lord, I have sinned. He let the cowl fall to his shoulders. He cleared his throat. "Is there anything else?"

The young penitent paused. "No Father, that's all. I firmly resolve to amend my life. Amen."

Father Lucci intoned his absolution and the penance. "Give thanks to the Lord for He is good."

"For His mercy endures forever," Ustoff said.

Yes, for His mercy endures forever. The words howled in Father Lucci's ears.

"Come to communion in the morning," he said. "We'll talk afterward."

The Father waited until he heard the footsteps withdraw to the lobby and porch before he left the confessional. He picked up his fallen robes. His steps were heavy across the now- darkened nave. It seemed colder than ever. The confessor heard thunder crash over the roof of his church. Looking up, he shivered with a chill and hurried away to his study.

Later Maria tapped lightly on his door. Even though Tuesday was their dinner together, he sat ready to feign sleep if she entered. He thought of the tumbling hair in his dream and recoiled from it.

Maria didn't enter. He'd have welcomed their usual banter over dinner, but a change had come over him in the confessional.

He wanted to pray but couldn't.

Half an hour later, Maria was back. She spoke through the door. "Father, I'm leaving your supper tray here at the door. I'll come at eight to fetch it."

He didn't reply, but as her heels grew faint on the tile, hunger stabbed him. It would be Maria's succulent chicken. The peas were from the garden. His stomach rumbled and led him on. It would be good to eat. Food settles the soul.

Father Lucci brought the tray to his rocker. He ate greedily, without a stop. The peas were sweet and buttery. She had topped the peppered potatoes with light gravy. Barehanded, he picked up his favorite chicken parts, the drumsticks, gobbling the skin and meat and then sucking the juices and sticky remnants off his fingers.

As he wiped the bread across the plate, he again thought of stroking Maria's hair. He burst into tears. He choked and coughed and cried. Bent double, he surged from the chair and flung the tray on the desk. The rocker teetered back and forth behind him as he swept through the room. Still weeping furious tears, Father Lucci stumbled to his privy where he sat and sobbed. He couldn't tell if he cried for his wrongs, for Maria, or for Berta West and her forsaken grandson.

His fit lasted a good ten minutes. Father Lucci sorrowed for himself. He remembered his days as a young man in the seminary of his beloved hometown, Bari. How could he restore those early hopes? The world had been cruel to him. It was too confusing. He longed for simpler days—for days in Italy. "Oh, it was so warm." His clogged voice frightened him.

After a time, his trembling over, the good Father washed his face. He ran his wet hands over his hair. He straightened and examined himself as he dried his face. Growing old, but still handsome, he thought. He smiled feebly in the mirror, then lowered his gaze to his hands. He returned to the study.

By the time Maria came at eight, he had left the door ajar with the tray beside it. He felt her look in and bent closer over his desk, where the lamp glowed down on his papers.

"Is everything all right, Father?" she said.

Father Lucci turned in his chair and spoke in a formal tone. "Yes, Sister Maria. Everything is fine. Thank you for such a delicious dinner."

She hovered at the door. She hadn't taken up the tray.

He wrote on papers that lay under the lamp. "Father, you

are left-handed," she said as if she'd made a grave discovery.

He didn't reply but kept his face obscured behind the shade.

"Will you be up late, Father?"

His voice was weighted. "No, Sister. I need rest." He paused until she picked up the tray.

"Good night, Sister Maria. Good night."

25

Benson Block

SHAFTS OF SUNLIGHT SHOT through the crevices, bent while passing through the station wagon windows, and heated the interior. All round the car, stacks of cement blocks rose pallet by pallet to nine feet, forming a maze of concrete streets and alleys laid out over the three-acre yard. The storage yard was served at the front by a siding of the Northern Pacific Railroad. The treeless expanse held the back stock and seldom-purchased designs of the Benson Block Company's production from its plant four miles down Commerce Street, close to the Atlas Cement Plant. On the far side of the yard, opposite the front gate that was secured by impregnable padlocks, a car could reach the rear entry by a deep-rutted, gravel road. That entry lay open to the river pier behind the yard.

Through this entry, Ingstrom had driven the night before, making the block graveyard his hideaway. He lay in the bed of Daddy Fizzy's station wagon, eyes closed, thinking. The morning rays felt to him like burning slots shooting through his blanket, just as they had at home the day before, streaming between the Venetian blinds and spilling over his sheets.

Now, keeping his eyes shut tight, Ingstrom half expected his mother to barge in, as she had the day before, with interrogation written in furrows across her forehead. Yesterday he had held his index finger to his lips and shook his head wildly, as if he would rattle his wide-stretched eyes. She had instantly understood that her son heard the policeman at the door and knew all about what he wanted. Her instinct was to protect him. She quietly shut the door, called his name softly in the hall, and withdrew to the kitchen to deal with the cop.

Ingstrom had needed to explain the car in the garage and why it had to stay there for the day. With his family, truth worked best. "If you tell the truth, we'll always protect you," his parents often said, "Lie and you're on your own." But he knew the whole truth in all its complexity should not be exposed. His mother wouldn't want to hear it. No need for too much truth, he'd decided.

That was yesterday. Now, waking in the block yard, he wished for more truth—a different kind of verity. Lying in Daddy Fizzy's station wagon, he puzzled the happenings of the last three nights. His own actions and motives he did not examine, but he wondered about Tuomi.

Everyone on the hillside knew the detective, maybe because his father's story was still passed around. But the man wasn't on vice, so this wasn't about drugs.

What if Tuomi had recognized him two mornings before? Did he want to know about his morning walk by Brookside? What did he suspect? Ingstrom was sure he had cleared the gates and moved well past before the cop drove by and waved. No problem! Let him ask.

Then again, maybe Tuomi had talked to that loudmouth Skip. The cop might want to know about Roger. You've got to get away from this wagon. The sooner the better.

Of course, the cop's visit could have been about the fire. Could it? No, that had been too recent. Why, then, had Tuomi shown up at the my house?

It was as if the rays of sun sweeping his hiding place had pointed to a vision of Randy Belisle. That's it. Randy was behind that little visit. Randy had been out to get him. That much had been clear since his visit to the hotel. I was the living link between Randy and Roger's death.

Yes, Randy had set him up. Lie low at Grand Lake? Yes, very low, six feet low. He might as well have said, "Take a dirt-nap." Ingstrom smiled blindly, grimly to himself.

Randy would have tried to burn me one way or another. So Tuomi's visit was just insurance. It also threw off suspicion. Randy was thorough. He'd set his plan in motion that morning before Ingstrom met him at the hotel. The torch-man—did he see me out at the lake?—likely reported to Randy about what he saw. Belisle would have informed the cop.

His business with Belisle had been a contest from the beginning. Finally, he and Randy had played chess with the coin. Belisle wasn't foolish enough to want a tainted artifact. When Ingstrom finagled Randy to hold the coin, Randy countered, coaxing Ingstrom to touch that envelope. He'd wanted the extra money, but the hundred bucks were just frosting on his cake. Dumping the coin on Belisle came first. He'd outsmarted Randy on that one. At least so far. But where had the coin gone?

Worry was not his game. The sailor had other plans.

Ingstrom mulled over their contest. Randy should have been on his way to Mexico by that time. But greed had prevailed. Ingstrom smiled into the sunshine. His hunch about one last deal with Randy had been half right. But the deal hadn't been with Ingstrom, and it had gone bad.

Randy Belisle had been smart, but not the smarter.

The sun topped the stack of chimney blocks behind the wagon and burned through the back window. Ingstrom opened his eyes. He rose, wiped down everything he had touched, and shouldered his bag. He had a phone call to make. When he stepped in the direction of the gate, he heard an engine start at the front of the lot. That'd be the forklift.

Tommy climbed into the seat. It felt good to be at work. The day before he'd called his boss, Lloyd Benson, to get the morning off. Wendell had arrived late in the night. Though they didn't disturb him, after that he couldn't sleep. Everything Roger had suffered was churning in his brain. When the sun came up, troubles still roiled him. So he called Benson.

"No, I hadn't heard about it," Benson said.

Tommy felt buried with Roger, unheralded. He glared at the phone receiver and steadied his voice. "We were close, Mr. Benson. Playmates. Like family."

"I guess all this hoopla about poor Miss Crosley outplayed your tragedy. I'm sorry. Sure, kid. Take the morning. Take the whole day. I understand."

"I knew you would, Mr. Benson. I'll be in after lunch. Thanks."

Sleeping in his own bed in Oliver the following night had been a help, but even then Tommy felt there was too much happening in Duluth to allow him to saunter off to college in Minneapolis. He liked the physicality of his work. It linked him to the West End. The pay, too, brought him an independence he liked.

"You're a great worker, Tommy," Benson had said. "I'd put you on permanently if you didn't have other plans."

Tommy had heard Lloyd's words again in bed this morning. He felt part of something—a thing that connected him with Roger and Berta and his own grandmother. What was it that he was leaving? Was he running toward his future or away from himself? Either way, he felt he was moving too fast.

His eighteenth birthday was a milestone he wanted to pause over, reflect on, and assess. But time was sweeping him up and onward.

Paul had done the same thing at this age. Tommy knew

the story. He left his town with hopes to return triumphant. Instead, he had gone away and lost his bearings. Tommy could piece that much together from his mother's carefully constructed stories as well as her evasions.

Paul had cut ties with his high school sweetheart and, whether he knew it at the time or not, had placed a barrier as insurmountable as the Point of Rocks between himself and a son. Tommy knew that it was only when Paul had lost another son that he turned back, looked back, and found what he had lost. The boy had decided long ago that resentment and fondness could exist side by side. He couldn't forget that his father had left, but he did celebrate the man who had returned and had stayed for the last ten years. Tommy balked at the risks of another separation, this time by his own leaving. Paul had just begun to move closer to him, man to man. Both of them, he was sure, wanted that to continue.

Tommy reached down to the console to insert the ignition key. He turned it and the forklift engine caught. Tommy had to move onto his flatbed a dozen pallets of oversized basement block that he'd deliver to a house site in Hermantown. He worked the control levers, practicing the movements.

"Hey, good morning."

Tommy looked up from his study. It was a guy with a sack across his shoulder.

Tommy let the engine die and turned the key. Over his surprise, the kid spoke again.

"Hey, I know I'm intruding here, but I thought the shed up front might have a phone. I came in by the back. It was open."

Tommy climbed down. "There is one, but it's a direct line to the plant. It doesn't work for outside calls." He wanted to shoo him off the lot, but the fellow slung his sack down and continued talking.

"Yeah, then I ran into this car, a station wagon back there. No keys, though. No plates either." He pointed to the stacks on the left.

Tommy looked the way he indicated. "I might want to see that. Abandoned?"

The other nodded. "I'd say unoccupied." He left the bag on the ground and started off, Tommy catching up.

"Where did you come from?"

"I've been hitchhiking up 23 from Askov this morning. Not much traffic. But I'm almost there. I just need to make a call first."

To Tommy a block yard seemed an odd place to look for a phone, but then this new companion was certainly a bit unusual. True, the front shed had phone wires and power leading to it. Perhaps he had been let off somewhere between here and Atlas.

Tommy couldn't help but feel a bit investigative. "Let's see this wagon. So where are you headed?"

"I'm trying to catch a ship. Just don't know which one." He stopped his swagger and looked up at Tommy, who was half a head taller. "Rocky Irwin," Ingstrom said, holding out his hand. He often used the name.

They shook. "Tommy. Tommy Miscevich."

Rocky led him on to the wagon. It belonged to no one Tommy knew. He examined the car. A thunderstorm had passed the previous evening, but these windows were clear, the hood unspotted. The car had been dumped there sometime during the night. The dust that inevitably settled on everything in the yard hadn't coated the paint. A white glove test would've come out clean.

Tommy got in, set the brake, and stuck his head under the dash. In five seconds the engine started. "Jump in. I'll put it out front. I've got work to do here."

His companion demurred. "I'll just hoof it."

Tommy wasn't going to be so easy. He was on company property, official. "Hey, give me a hand with the blocks and I'll give you a lift to a phone."

Rocky hesitated.

"You just have to eyeball pallets for me," Tommy said.

Rocky looked at the sun now high over the yard. "Okay." He walked away toward his bag.

Tommy parked the station wagon near the front gate. Someone had gone to a peck of trouble to hide that car. Tommy left it on the lot side of the shed. It wouldn't be easily seen from the road. He disconnected his wires.

He puzzled on the walk back. What would PS do? Keep him near and watch him close. He looked up the hill to Smithville. Thanks, PS.

Tommy clambered up the forklift again. Rocky had been waiting. The bag was atop a stack of palates. "Hop on the step," Tommy said over the engine.

They worked together. This guy doesn't know how. He doesn't anticipate. "So, what do you do on ship?" Tommy asked.

The sailor took his time answering. "Deck hand. Oiler sometimes." He didn't offer details.

Tommy had his guest guide him, lining up the fork to the palate. After three or four maneuvers, Rocky got the idea and improved his directions. Tommy didn't need the help, but this way he'd keep the trespasser close and get him off the lot. The car he could deal with later when he returned from the building site.

They strapped down the load on the flatbed. Tommy looked around the pallets, checking the tension of the stays. "Okay, all aboard." He opened the truck cab door for Rocky and, after he had snapped the huge padlocks at the front gate, climbed up to the driver's seat. Tommy took it slow. They had a ways to go.

"You're shipping out, today?" Tommy said.

"Hopefully."

"Lakes or salt water?"

"I don't even know that. The call-boy will tell me."

"Call-boy?"

"Yeah, the guy I have to phone."

They bumped along Commerce Street to West Duluth, where Tommy pulled off at Kathy and Bill's Truck Stop. "If you find your ship, I'm going right past the Duluth harbor side. I can drop you at your dock."

"Thanks. You want anything inside?" Rocky climbed down and grabbed the sea bag. "Got the number in here." He sauntered to the front door, bag over his shoulder.

Rocky reached Max, the callboy. "Hey, it's Reese Ingstrom. You said you might have a ship for me today."

"Man, I told you to call this morning. It's nearly ten o'clock." Ingstrom talked tough. "I'm calling now. What you got?"

"*Bisnu's Dream*."

Ingstrom had to ask again.

"It's the Indian ship I told you about. It's loading coal right now. Just go down there but don't fool around. They're due to leave at noon."

Ingstrom brought two small coffees to the truck. "I thought we'd celebrate, hope you drink it black."

Rocky had his swagger back, Tommy noticed. "Black's fine. What's the celebration for?"

"I got my ship."

"Congratulations." To Tommy, Rocky looked hardly old enough to drive, let alone work as a seaman, though he was swaying with the truck as if already on the water. "What do they say? *Bon voyage?*"

Rocky scoffed. "That's for tourists and high-schoolers. This is the real thing."

Tommy played with it. "High school's not so bad."

"Don't take offense, but it's for suckers. College, too. I want adventure."

Tommy was ready for a little game. "What about the future? What about reading books and learning?"

Rocky got the jibe. "I read plenty, more than some of my pointy-head teachers did. And working for the man is not what I'm about."

"You going to be an oiler all your life?" Tommy was baiting Rocky, but he was also testing his own recent thoughts.

"Look. What you do is not who you are. What school does is prepare you for the traces, makes you a mule. You leave your options behind and do what you're told." Rocky pounded the dash. He was animated.

"What about family? Don't you owe it to them?"

Tommy might have lit a rocket under his friend "To hell with family. I won't be following in my father's footsteps. Counting beans isn't my style."

"Your father's an accountant?"

Though he regretted giving too much information, Rocky continued. "For sure. He thinks he's the man. But he just works for the man." Something about what he was saying calmed Rocky. "What about you?"

"Mine is a detective."

"No! A cop?"

Tommy bent the truth. "Private." He thought of PS. "Actually, he's my grandfather. My mother raised me alone."

"Now, that's not bad. At least he's independent. He knows up from down, I bet."

"He's mostly independent. He certainly knows up from

down, he does." Tommy paused for effect. "He could have gone to college." Tommy was thinking mostly about Paul now.

Rocky gave him a quizzical smile. "If you think for yourself, it isn't that bad, I suppose. It's just not for me." He laced an arm over the seat back. "What did you mean, 'mostly independent'?"

The sailor's casual air and implicit promise to listen loosened Tommy's tongue. "There were three reasons he didn't go to college: tuberculosis, bootlegging, and a gun."

"He suffered consumption?" Rocky gave it the old bookish name.

"His father had it. That put him on the streets, more or less."

Rocky nodded. "Ah, that led to bootlegging."

"Right." Tommy didn't know the whole story, but he didn't mind making it up as he went along. After all, he thought, I've been doing that about the male side of the family for years.

The sailor was interested. "How is the gun connected?"

Tommy reached for the connections. "He inherited the gun from his dad. It was about all that was left, some sort of World War I souvenir, a Manly or something." He searched for the name. "German, I think."

Rocky jumped on it. "A Mannlicher, I bet. Have you seen it? Is it filigreed?"

"I don't know." Tommy didn't get what Rocky meant. "I've never seen it. That's the problem. Someone stole it and used it in a bootlegging murder."

Now Reese Ingstrom knew the gun. He had seen it, he was sure, and he had heard the story—several times told by "the accountant" at his business parties, where his poker-playing cronies never tired of hearing the dirt from the West End.

"Was there something about a judge?"

Rocky hit a nerve. "Are you from Duluth?" Tommy said. Now he felt defensive.

"My bean counter dad was. I grew up in Rochester and The Cities." The sailor treaded water then swam with the current he found. "I think dear old Dad once cooked books for a judge up here who was, let's say, involved with whiskey."

The story sounded familiar. "It could be the same event," Tommy said. "Everybody knew about it, and it kept my grandfather tied to the shady side of things forever." Tommy was repeating what his mother had told him about PS. "'He's a good man, but he fell in with the wrong crowd.'"

Don't I know it, Ingstrom thought. "Hey, it happens, but only to good people. The scum seems to get off free." He patted Tommy's shoulder. "So that's why he didn't get to college."

Tommy hung his arm out the window and checked the side mirror. The air was fine, breezy, and clear. "I've been thinking of staying around rather than going right to the Main U."

Rocky appreciated the confidence. "You don't look like you're afraid. What gives?"

Maybe Rocky wasn't a good worker, but he was sympathetic, perceptive, and a quick wit. Tommy said: "I've seen people with a good head on their shoulders leave with high hopes and come back acting so bad you can't stand them. You know what I mean? Like cake-eaters."

Rocky smiled broadly. "Cake-eaters. Oh, yes. I do know what you mean. Give me the common man over any narrow-nosed society maven."

He spoke like a book. Rocky had read. "I don't want to lose myself, at least not for money," Tommy said. "But maybe for love."

"Love? Hey, that can be just as bad. But your worst enemy is the government. If you stay, you're draft-bait. At least college defers that problem."

Tommy nodded. Rocky suddenly sounded more encouraging. "It is a point." He had enough to think about. The two rode on in silence, glancing out the windows, avoiding eye contact.

After a while, Tommy said: "So, where can I drop you? I'm turning up at Garfield."

"The coal docks."

The docks weren't too far from Benson's office and truck shop. Maybe reporting the station wagon first was best. "All right. We're close."

The young sailor came round Tommy's side of the truck and lifted his hand. "Thanks for the ride and for bending my ear, Tommy. Good to meet you."

Even though Tommy knew his rider was not what he pretended to be, he felt they'd struck up a fellowship of sorts. "Likewise. Have a great adventure," he answered, and watched Rocky sway off toward the dock where a rusty old freighter was taking on coal. Yeah, good luck. To us both.

Tommy moved on to the Benson Block offices, where he reported the abandoned station wagon. He didn't mention Rocky.

"The contractor is waiting on that block. Hustle up there pronto," the foreman said, "I'll take care of the car out there."

All the day, making his delivery and then tending customers at the retail yard behind the offices, Tommy mulled over his encounter. Even though he had led the guy on, what Rocky said about schools and work played back on Tommy's ideas. In Rocky's voice the ideas sounded subversive, alien. But Tommy could see them making sense in his own life.

Wouldn't college isolate him, maybe put blinders between him and what was really important? Leaving felt to Tommy like a selfish act that would separate him from his people, from his rightful destiny. Rocky had struck truth when he described Tommy's grandfather as "independent."

"Yes. Independent," Tommy said. He liked the sound of the word and the feel of what it represented. It had been a fortunate accident, running into the sailor.

Tommy had some thinking to do.

26

Civic Center

IN BED AT THE ARROWHEAD, the night clamor of downtown prodded Paul's worries. Like a roving band of drunken sailors careening against garbage cans and uprooting sleeping cats in the narrow driveway behind the hotel, his troubles echoed large from window to wall in the bare alley-scape that bounded his vision of a future. Voices booming alarm shook his sleep. Central High's clock sounded two blocks away and two hundred feet above, slicing the hour awake with two sharp strokes. The lift-bridge horn goaded an outgoing ship's reply, and the two sounds twisted Paul's sheets, already soaked and bundled, tighter around his fitful sleep.

On his back aboard the thin hotel mattress, Paul sighed. "Thank God there's no fog tonight." The prospect of an all-night foghorn groaning into his dreams sent Paul turning to the wall and back again. His first night at the Arrowhead called out for him to make it his last.

Memma and Wendell Jr. had agreed that he should move to her house after the funeral. Tomorrow, Paul calculated. Wendell Jr. would be leaving shortly, taking two days to return to Bettendorf. Even though Paul would not occupy Roger's old apartment, the move nagged at him like an arguing couple on the streets below the screens of his hotel room.

"You're the one who wants to move back," a woman's voice sounded in his mind.

The husband's voice rumbled up the brickwork façade. "You make it sound like a crime."

"You can't relive the past."

"It was my home. I just want to get closer."

She mocked him. "'I just want to get closer.' Hell. To what? Ghosts?"

It was as if the man had answered without a voice.

"I said, 'To what?'"

Still he hesitated, as if searching for the truth. Finally he spoke. "To comfort."

She roared. "Bullshit."

Paul heard the suffering of that imaginary husband. The man sounded pathetic. Because these two contestants occupied his own mind, Paul couldn't tell what his own motives were— whether leaving Pamela was turning away from responsibility or moving closer to something precious and worth passing on. He reasoned that he owed Pamela nothing. Theirs had been misery for far too long. Still, Paul wasn't sure what he could offer Cindy. He couldn't see doing without her, but she had done well for years without him.

Paul rolled tighter in the sheets. Am I dragging her down with me? The half-hour clanged at the clock tower. He vaulted out of bed, drenched. "For God's sake, man!" He said aloud.

He skipped to the door in his briefs, padded back, tossed on a shirt and went into the hall. At Arrowhead half the floor shared one bath. The creak of the hall floor gave him pause. Though way past midnight and he'd likely meet no one in the hall, he worried. I should wear my robe. This isn't home.

Paul stood to pee. His thoughts ran to his work, his usual refuge from worry; but now work had invaded his private life. His West End connections played havoc with the job. He couldn't shake his uncertainties or premonitions, but he found no point in a worried review of his fellow officers' bungling. Better to focus on the day to come. Line up your day, Paul. He brought the toilet door to without a squeak or click and returned to his room.

Despite its good location at the corner of the hotel, his room depressed him.

"God, who's been sleeping in that bed?" he said. The bedding had tangled like intersecting wakes. It heaped itself loose where it had been tucked and rolled tightly where it should have lain flat. One of the pillows, naked of its case, draped over the edge, was held by a corner in a twisted sheet while the other was stuffed between mattress and headboard as if trying to hide itself.

"You're not getting back into that, mister." Paul stripped and remade the bed. He hung his shirt over a wooden chair post and stood at the window, cooling in the three o'clock breeze off the lake. To put his mind in order, he plotted out his next moves.

Paul relished grilling the Esterwalds. He had some dingers ready for the son-in-law, Robert. Who was with you in the house? Wasn't Miss Crosley already unresponsive when you attacked her? Paul knew, or thought he knew, the answers to the questions, which Bert Esterwald wouldn't answer anyway. Paul only wanted to see his face when he heard them. Visualization and interrogation were his notable talents; they often worked in tandem, as they would today. The bonus would be Esterwald's defense team. Paul expected both Fraisers to be there. He couldn't steal his father's thunder, but he felt the temptation to shine a light on LaPrairie.

Though he didn't think on it yet, Paul's gifts would be put to use that day on Roger's case, too. What he did think about, looking out over the lake from the Arrowhead, was the note whose handwriting Bushy was analyzing. Roger hadn't thought ahead. When he was hungry, he'd eaten. When tired, he'd slept. Roger did not plan. Had he felt desperate, he wouldn't think to write a note. Paul suspected someone else had written the good-bye. Just who, he did not know.

As soon as Paul got word of Roger's so-called suicide note, the coroner would be his first stop. Then he could visit Father Lucci to see if he could change the old man's mind.

Paul put in order his duties on the double murder. On the Brookside case, Paul didn't owe Skaansgard any courtesies; but just to keep up appearances, maybe for Cindy's sake, he'd call for a late-day appointment. The lawyer had phoned three times already, and Paul supposed the next call would be to the chief. So it'd be best to meet Skaansgard away from anyone's office. Paul hated to spend afternoon coffee-time with his father-in-law, but that was the only time he had.

Paul knew that PS would confront the Fraisers sometime that day. He wanted to get the report personally. That he looked forward to. After more than forty years, PS would relish Royal's comeuppance.

And Cindy. Of course there was Cindy.

Paul backed away from the window. Thinking of Cindy, as he stood in his briefs so exposed to the world, embarrassed him. With a thought like the puff of air through the screen, he wondered if their romance could live in the light of day— if that had been the fear that turned him to Pamela in the first place. He moved away from the view. The bed he had made was his refuge now. As he turned the sheet down and rested in the routine of the day he had ordered, Paul closed his eyes to dark alleys of misgivings and opened to daylight dreams that came now in the wee hours before dawn. He slept.

In a dream, he and PS were back at the shipping canal. Cindy stood between them. Paul had his arm round her shoulders. Tommy, a little boy far down the causeway, ran toward a ship leaving the harbor, sounding its horn to the bridge. Tommy covered his ears. Turning to look at the three adults, he pointed. Immediately an eighteen-year-old Tommy looked to Paul and PS, indicating a figure at the bow of the ship. As the tanker approached, PS said: "There's your man, Paul." Looking up to the bow of the ship now towering in its approach, Paul recognized the figure: a crowned, six-armed dancer as light as air itself, pirouetting on the rail. Beneath the golden crown, the curly blond locks and rounded, magnified eyes of a sailor beamed the broad smile of an imp. Paul started. He woke to sunrise glancing off the lake and streaming into his room. "Ingstrom," he said.

Before he could digest the dream, the ring of the phone swept it back. It was the chief.

"For Christ's sake, Tuomi, what is going on?"

Paul was groggy. He stammered.

"Skaansgard is all over my case. My lead detective is on the lam, living at the Arrowhead, and the DA is climbing the walls."

Paul left Ingstrom dancing at the rail. "Chief, give me a chance to wake up."

"Exactly! Wake up, call the son-of-a-bitch pronto and get down here for a briefing at six-thirty. Can you do that? Jesus, get your head out of the sack."

Paul tamped down a fierce response. "Yes, sir, I will."

He rubbed his cheeks and ran his fingers over his scalp. "Whew! Five forty-five. That's a record."

Paul splashed around at the corner washstand before calling Skaansgard. He put friendly in his voice. "I haven't had a minute, Leif, until now. Even to call."

"I know you're busy. How about this morning?"

"Sorry, Leif, we have a briefing, and then I'm interviewing the Esterwalds." Skaansgard would wait, Paul knew. He'd want to know what had come out of the interrogation.

"Fine, Paul. Somebody's House at three?"

Rather than shower down the hall, Paul washed at the stand. This time he shaved, too.

He thought about Leif. The guy had always been decent, maybe a bit formal, but what would you expect? Paul did like the guy despite his East End nature and the constant drive to pile up money. It was Skaansgard's dedication to his own code that Paul respected; and though he knew the lawyer bent rules and strayed from time to time, still he admired the style with which his father-in-law conducted himself and his business. Bullock was the dog, growling and barking all the time. Skaansgard was smooth. He shouldered elegance and decency.

Paul smoothed his hair. As he dressed from the suitcase, he surveyed the room. One more night and that's it. He loosely looped a necktie and donned a jacket for the briefing. Maybe a little of Skaansgard was rubbing off on him. It wouldn't hurt.

It was warming up again after the cool of the storm. Paul walked in the shadows of buildings over to the department. Coffee and rolls he'd have at the briefing.

Paul stopped at his office first. Bushy had worked late. Copies of the so-called suicide note and a school assignment from the past spring sat side by side on the desk. The writing could not have been more different. Paul didn't need an analyst to tell him that Roger, whose name was scrawled at the top of the school paper, couldn't have composed and did not write the suicide note.

Once more, the Ingstrom from the ship's railing seemed to dance across the note. Paul swore. "Shit. I should have known." He opened his wallet and unfolded the note he had filched from the Ingstroms. Though Roger's note was hurriedly scribbled, the writing resembled Ingstrom's refrigerator note much more closely than it did Roger's school paper. Paul was no expert, but he could see similarities despite what could have been intentional skewing to hide identity and, maybe, to approximate Roger's messy script. It was Ingstrom, and he was trying to hide.

Next to the papers was Bushy's notation: "Will Dunpool. Close friend of Ingstrom. Is Miss Crosley's second cousin." So, there was a connection between Crosley and Ingstrom, at least through a friend. The detective's mind whirled through three scenarios. Ingstrom, he decided, knew the grounds, knew the house, and likely knew its contents. But Paul had to have hard fact for the chief to buy it.

Paul gathered the other notes Bushy had left. Among them was a copy of Marly's picture along with the original. A report Bushy left told him the body at Grand Lake was determined to be that of a young woman. The sheriff was looking for the station wagon and Impala. Paul figured one was Ustoff's, the other LaPrairie's. Bushy would let the sheriff know. Paul had a feeling that dental records would confirm his suspicion that Marly's was the body at Grand Lake.

He had nothing yet on the coin. Paul wrote thanks and instructions for Bushy and walked downstairs to the briefing. Bushy was splendid. Paul could use three of him.

The briefing was something of an embarrassment. Maybe the chief intended it to be, to underline the message he had delivered that morning. And maybe the chief was right. Evidence against Robert Esterwald was mounting. Keys to a car stolen from Brookside were found in a trashcan at the Minneapolis Airport. The car had been parked in the lot. Late the morning of the murders, a man fitting Esterwald's description had purchased a travel bag at the same airport. The buyer had scratches on his face and a bound hand. That pointed to opportunity. At least one Esterwald could have been at the scene. Motive was debt reduction. The man and wife were in way over their heads and were spending like heirs to a fortune.

When the chief finished his litany of findings, he turned to Paul. "Well, detective, what do you have to add?"

Paul kept it professional and beat down a blush, though he felt his ears burn. "I'll know more when I interrogate Esterwald this morning." He decided to risk low-key mention of his ideas. "I'm still looking to question a passerby who may have seen something at Brookside. The missing jewelry and coins we are working on."

Everyone in the room could read the chief's glowering stare, but his boss said nothing.

Paul cleaved to the careful path. "I want to read the state lab report before I rule out anything." At the very least, he could win respect for caution.

At the briefing, Paul learned that Bushy had been active well into the night. The team handling Roger's death had already discovered the disparity between the suicide note and Roger's known handwriting. An analyst's report was expected that afternoon. The autopsy finished, Roger's body had been released to the Brown Mortuary for funeral arrangements. The cause of death was ruled sudden cardiac arrest.

Maybe to relieve some tension he felt in the room, Nick Preston, the drug task-force leader, credited Paul with providing the intelligence for a successful sweep of dope houses on the hillside earlier that morning. Six suspects were in custody. As the briefing broke up, Nick sidled up to Paul.

"Seeing as how you're in this already, would you like to sit in on the questioning?"

Paul demurred. "I'm afraid I've got a full plate."

Nick leaned in on Paul. "The thing is, one of the guys said something about Roger Sillanpaa. I thought you might want to follow up."

Paul looked to the chief. "All right, but with the boss's blessing. When?"

"Now," Nick said, and gracefully pointed to the chief. "He knows and approves."

The chief nodded at Paul. Having been roundly admonished, Paul was free to leave the woodshed.

"Okay. But when the Esterwalds arrive, I have to leave."

Paul needn't have worried. The Esterwalds waltzed in well past 10:30, more than an hour and a half late, giving Paul time to work on piecing together what had happened to Roger. Dell Durbin, in charge of investigating Roger's death, took part but urged Paul to do the questioning. "I like your style, Tuomi," Dell said.

Their first mark was tall, scrawny, and nervous as hell. Despite his coaxing, Dell jumped in. "Are you strung out? Or do you always look like that?"

"Hey. I've nothing to do with this stuff. People at a party must have left this shit behind."

Paul played the good cop. "I understand, Skip. Can I call you Skip?"

Skip lit up at what he thought fair treatment. "Yeah, sure."

Paul leaned forward and smiled. "All right, Skip. What was found at your apartment had been left by a party crowd. Tell me about the party."

Skip sensed an out but wanted assurance. "I've told part of it already, but you'll count this as cooperation, won't you?"

"You're being cooperative, yes. The officers told me you had mentioned Roger. Roger Sillanpaa." Skip looked terrified.

Paul laid the fact at Skip's itchy feet. "Isn't he dead?"

The man looked as if he'd leap out the window, heavy bars and all.

Dell put his big paws on Skip's shoulders. "Now, you stay right here."

Skip sat tight. "It was Ingstrom's fault."

Ingstrom was a very busy boy. Paul continued to smile. "Tell me about Ingstrom."

"He brought the dope. He split before Roger OD'd. They had to go get him to help bring Roger home."

Paul moved in on Skip. "So Roger Sillanpaa died in your apartment."

"I had nothing to do with it."

"Where?"

"Where what?"

Paul folded his hands. "Where did he die, exactly?"

"In the bathroom. We had to break the door to get in. Whew! What a stink."

Paul kept still. He didn't want to know the details but he didn't stop Skip, who now wanted to spill. He told about the car. About Marly driving. He mentioned Ingstrom at every chance. When Skip fell quiet, Paul let him have it.

"Did you write the note?"

Skip lost the little color he had left, and broke a clammy sweat. "What note?"

"Roger had a suicide note in his pocket."

"No. I didn't write any note."

"I suppose Ingstrom did that, too?"

Paul looked hard at Skip, then directly at Dell.

Skip almost laughed. "Suicide? It was an overdose."

Dell was ready. "And how do you know that? Who wrote that note?"

Skip clammed up. "I don't know."

Paul left him with something to think about. "So you did nothing, the drugs found weren't yours, and now you know nothing. Ingstrom did it all. Do I have that right?"

The two detectives left the room to compare notes.

Dell said it. "He's a lousy witness."

Paul was nodding. "When he gets an attorney, he won't confirm a word of it."

"Most of it is second-hand anyway. Let's see what the girlfriend says."

The interview with Janey was brief and very quiet. She hadn't said anything yet and wasn't about to start, no matter who asked the questions. She sat cross-legged in her chair, pushing her cuticles back with her fingernails. Her act was the opposite of her boyfriend's.

"Who is Ingstrom?"

She looked at her nails. "That sounds like a philosophical question."

"Do you know him?"

"Schopenhauer?"

"Ingstrom."

"I couldn't say."

"He was there the night of the party."

"Always seeking satisfaction."

"Ingstrom?"

"No, Schopenhauer. The German."

Janey was full of double-talk and evasion. Her attraction to Skip, if any, seemed inexplicable. She was the cleft rock, he the babbling brook.

"Gentlemen," she said, "I was asleep long before that party ended. That was days ago. Now, this morning, you sweep me off my morning walk. I wasn't holding, and Skip's isn't my apartment. So, won't you please let me go now?"

Dell hit his fist on the table. "It ain't up to me, girly."

She turned her gaze to him. "Could you get him in here then?"

Paul picked it up. "Let's see what we can do." The two left her alone.

Dell was pissed. "If it had been my warrant, she would've been down on the pavement in a second. A morning walk! Worthless. Totally worthless."

Paul patted his shoulder. "Look pal, at least we know what happened. For sure this time. When you resolve the handwriting thing, the family can rest."

"I'd like to prosecute someone," Dell said. "Driving dead teenagers around town isn't exactly legal."

Paul laughed. "Skip might want to do some time."

Dell picked up the joke. "So far he's our only volunteer." He let the smile drop. "You can meet the rest of the clan, but I have duties." He left Paul for the department and his office across the street.

The Esterwalds were still en route. Paul took a turn at the next interrogation.

The rooms on the first floor of the St. Louis County Jail were spare and echoey. No one, not even the jailers, liked to be in them. For the apprehended, it was worse than a locked jail cell. Paul looked in through the small window in the door. A girl, maybe twenty, hunched on the chair swaying left and right, wrapped in her own arms, newly rousted from bed and disheveled as a rag doll.

Siiri, the freckled blonde, had been crying. Her crime had been carrying a single reefer in her pocket. It might be enough to make her a good informant, but hardly a prize catch for the narcotics squad.

A uniformed officer sat by the door. Otherwise, Paul was

alone with the young woman.

He softened his voice. "You've been through the wringer, haven't you?"

She sobbed anew and nodded her head.

"Tell me your name."

"Siiri Laugen."

"Who got you into this? Your boyfriend?"

She looked puzzled, and gasped. "Matty? No, no. He's harmless."

She isn't covering. This one doesn't lie. "Then who?"

"Myself."

"I find that hard to believe. Aren't you from Two Harbors?"

"Yes. There are fools there too. It was entirely my fault, but I fell for Ingstrom's tricks."

Paul held back surprise. Again. The name arose at every turn. Paul glided into her story.

"Yes. He's full of them, isn't he?"

"The joint was a going-away present, he said."

"Where were you planning to go?"

She sniffled. "Not me. Him."

"Ingstrom? Where to?"

"He's shipping out. Soon. Maybe he's already gone."

"Do you know where?"

She shook her head and said, "I'm not sure." But her eyes told him she had an idea.

Paul coaxed her. "You seem sure to me."

"He showed me his seaman's card. He had just got it."

Paul nodded agreeably. "Go ahead. Tell me about it."

"I hadn't seen him in a while. Then he came to the lightshow."

"At Skip's."

"Yes. He flirted with me, and the next day he showed up at the hotel."

"You lost me."

"I work at the Hotel Duluth news stand. That's why Matty and I left the party early. Before all the trouble."

"You mean with Roger Sillanpaa."

"Poor Roger."

Paul wondered about the visit to the hotel. Though Randy Belisle thought he was keeping a low profile, Paul knew he held court there. "What time did you see him there?"

"Just after one. I invited him to my apartment after work. I thought he was sweet on me." She leaned into a sob but stopped herself. "I'm an idiot."

"Don't be too hard on yourself, Siiri." Paul was getting to know the kid. "Ingstrom isn't exactly easy to read."

"He got me stoned. We made love." She whimpered. "Inggy slipped out the front when Matty came home."

"Your boyfriend."

"He didn't like me being stoned and thought I was hiding something. Then Inggy came back to get his sea bag. All three of us smoked and that's when he left me the joint."

"What happened then, Siiri?"

She sobbed for a full minute. Paul waited.

"Matty and I started fighting. Inggy left. I stood at the window and watched him while Matty raged around the house. Inggy went up the block and got into Daddy Fizzy's car, the one Marly drives all the time."

"The station wagon."

"I wish I had never invited him over." She was crying again.

Paul handed her a tissue. "Who else was in the car?"

"Inggy and Fizzy got in the rider's side, front and back. I don't know, but Marly must have been driving. It's Marly he's sweet on."

It was a thing Paul rued in police work. Innocence was in trouble, while perpetrators danced away free. These were the young, but Paul knew too well that age didn't matter. The malign mark showed early and lasted, disguised in virtuous clothes, long into a life. Ingstrom and Randy Belisle were vernal; LaPrairie and Royal Fraiser were entrenched far past the fall.

"Just be honest, Siiri. I'll try to help you."

She nodded and cried.

A jailer knocked on the door. The Esterwalds had arrived at the courthouse. Paul left the jail and walked across the street to the meeting room where they waited with their lawyers, Royal and Mark Fraiser.

West Wind Ranch

I

THE WEST WIND RANCH lay along a gourd-shaped peninsula formed over centuries of spring flooding and backwash in the broad basin of the St. Louis River bed, a mile or two below the river's brutal cascades in Jay Cooke State Park. Downstream the river widened into low-lying islands and sloughs, then to the bay, harbor, and, fifteen miles away, the mighty Lake Superior.

Though flooding on this peninsula was rare after the construction of the Thompson Dam, the threat of it held the building of neighborhoods at bay and kept land prices and taxes low. The 40-acre ranch usually stayed dry during the spring runoff, even without the landscaping and improvements that Judge Royal Fraiser had applied over the fifty years he owned the spread. Waterfowl returned in April and May to nest in and populate the small bay at the handle of the gourd, while cowbirds, robins, and wrens filled the moisture-worshiping willows with a rackety, melodious song each day as the sun was fixing to rise.

The wrens built nests in the eaves of the stable, flitting between the dense shoreline trees and the corrals behind the stable building. Little black cowbirds lined the top rail of the white arena fences where Fraiser's six horses worked in a strict rotation, two per day, keeping them hale through half of the year. Each fall, he shipped them to his Arizona desert ranch for the winter.

It had been years since Royal Fraiser had ridden. Still, he started each morning with horses. He donned his riding gear, jeans, long boots, fancy shirt, and Stetson. He leaned on the corral fence to watch Cyril, his groom, exercise the horses. Usually Fraiser entered the corral to stroke a favorite animal's flanks, to dispense a few treats, and to talk with Cyril about the small stable. At times, the groom handed Royal the reins and urged him to ride.

"An old coot like me shouldn't be on horseback."

"You're still fit, sir."

"Damn near eighty-three, you crazy lout. You wouldn't be trying to kill me, would you?"

The two laughed at their stale conversation. They had said the same thing for years, advancing the numbers one by one. Cyril had been Fraiser's groom for more than thirty-five years, practically a member of the family.

Today, Fraiser was early at the corral. Mark was to fetch him at eight-thirty to meet the Esterwalds before they went in to answer detectives' questions. Cyril was working the mare Daisy; Fraiser showed the soft spot he had for her by bringing in a carrot.

"You are working her too hard, my boy."

Cyril stopped so Fraiser could feed and admire Daisy.

"I'm afraid she's getting old."

"No, sir. She ages like you. Not at all."

Fraiser stroked her as he looked her over closely, lifting a hoof and inspecting it carefully.

"She's still feisty to be sure. Thanks to you, Cyril."

"I do my best, sir."

Fraiser turned to the bunkhouse office and corral gate. There sat PS Tuomi atop the fence, hitching one leg on the white painted rail.

"Put that goddamned cigarette out," the lawyer said. "I'll not have smoking around the animals. Or around me either." The lawyer stomped around in his boots. "And it's about time you showed your face. I've got a meeting in half an hour."

PS took another drag on the fag and tossed it into the arena. Clutching a file folder, he lowered himself gingerly to the ground, holding the top rail. Once out of the corral, he scraped his shoes on the bottom rail.

"Come on in. Let's see what you've got."

PS continued scraping.

"Wear boots next time," Royal said.

PS followed the old man into his bunkhouse office. When the lawyer was seated in his judge's chair, he came to the desk and stood before him.

"What do they know?" Fraiser said. "Tell me."

PS remained silent. He turned the file in his hands and placed it carefully in front of the old judge.

Fraiser spanked the desk as if he were sending Daisy out of the arena. "Just tell me what they know."

PS stood above him. "I think you should take a gander at those docs."

Judge Fraiser tipped back the Stetson. "Always playing games, aren't you." He opened the folder. After a quick glance, he glared at PS. "What the hell is this?"

"Just some old family business." PS let him read a bit.

"What the hell are you trying to pull, Tuomi?"

"It gets better. Look at the next page."

The old man read on. "This is worthless. It wouldn't stand up in any court."

"It doesn't have to, since it'll never get that far. It's between us. All it means is, our little association is done. And it's way past time."

"You could have left anytime, Tuomi. You know that." The

judge paged through some of the other papers. "You didn't have to make such a big deal of this." He closed the file. "Sit down. Let's talk."

PS stood. "That's only the beginning of it, Royal. There's much more."

"All right. All right. If you want out, I wish you well." Fraiser extended his hand.

PS shook his head. "I don't shake hands with a gun at my back. But not even Mark would be that stupid, would he? Not twice."

He turned slowly. Mark, who had sneaked out from the lavatory opposite the door, had already lowered the pistol.

PS looked hard at Mark. "Maybe you know."

Mark sneered. "Know what?"

"I thought maybe you knew why Mr. LaPrairie walked into his own kitchen yesterday and flipped that light-switch."

The sneer loosened. Mark's face fell flaccid and pale.

"I was there. I lost a few hairs myself, but old R.L. breathed fire in a second. And he knew what he was doing. You know why, don't you?"

Mark stammered a voiceless answer. "That man was sick," Royal answered for his son—as usual. "Weren't you leaving?" he said to PS.

PS wasn't done. "I watched him march right into the house, Mark. He certainly knew what he was doing. The paper trail he left showed me just how bad a trafficker you are. Can't hold a candle to the old man, can you."

Mark looked as if he would drop the gun. He stared through PS, looking to his father.

PS pressed his show home. "Don't worry, sonny, Papa has known about your little business for quite some time. He might even know about your other partner. The one who set you up for the final deal. Likely I'm saving your ass."

"Get out, Tuomi!" Royal Fraiser roared from behind. "Go back to your miserable working-class life. I'll handle this. I suppose it's about time."

"I'm out. Yes, I am. Keep the file, Royal. I've got the originals. I've got what Roland kept on his cousin Mark here. I've got what was in the Impala's trunk. Your property, Mark? Of course the sheriff has the car itself. Evidence, you know."

"All right, son. Let the man go on his way. We have legitimate business to tend."

PS walked up to Mark. He grasped Mark's forearm with one hand and wrenched the filigreed pistol free with his other, simply saying: "I believe this is mine."

Out in the yard, wrens twittered in the hedges. Cyril was leading Daisy to the large grassy corral to feed on the sweet grass that would shortly go to seed if the weather held warm. A breeze off the lake found its way this far upriver. It swished the willow leaves, turning their sides, silver and green, and moved the few huge elm branches at their fluttering fingertips.

PS filled his lungs with the morning freshness that ruffled the water and blew over the lowland ranch. He felt better than he had in forty years.

II

Inside the bunkhouse office, Royal Fraiser rose behind his desk. He placed the file PS had left him in his center desk drawer and locked it.

"Listen, Dad, it isn't like he says at all." Royal's frown stopped him.

"You're a junkie. And worse, you're a stupid one."

Dad," Mark began, but Royal broke in.

"I don't need explanations. I'll tell you what, though."

Mark hung his head like any little boy. "What?"

"After this meeting, you are going to Tucson. I have a place for you there where you'll kick your habit and get your head on straight. I'll see you when I come in October."

"It's summer, Dad. It's hotter than hell there."

The old man stood stiffly, unmoved. "Good."

He went to his lavatory closet to change his clothes. When he emerged, he looked like the lawyer he had been for sixty years. He kept the Stetson.

"Now let's get going. We're an hour late already, and I didn't get a lick of help from Tuomi. We'll be shooting in the dark. *Vámonos.*"

III

Inside the ground-floor conference room of the St. Louis County Courthouse, Royal Fraiser rose and extended his hand to Paul as soon as he and Bushy entered the room.

Judicial, suave, and friendly as always, Royal gave no clue of upset or discord. Mark, on the other hand, nearly bolted when he saw Paul, and he had trouble composing himself when Paul introduced himself and his partner.

"I'm Detective Paul Tuomi." He emphasized his last name. "This is Officer William Buczynski, assisting me this morning. Bill, these gentlemen are Royal and Mark Fraiser."

"Yes sir, I know you by reputation." Bushy turned to Mark. "Pleased to meet you."

Mark mopped his brow and had to sit. He did not shake hands.

A uniformed policeman ushered the Esterwalds into the room. Royal Fraiser took command.

"I've asked Mr. and Mrs. Esterwald, as a matter of courtesy to this department, to cooperate fully in the police investigation of the death of Miss Martha Crosley and her housekeeper. We will answer any question we deem appropriate."

Paul took his soft-touch approach. "I offer heartfelt condolences, Mrs. Esterwald." He looked to Mark. "I've recently had a loss in my family and I understand how you feel." Then he directed his comments to Royal Fraiser. "At this point, we have no suspects and are simply getting background from all the family members. But, as a point of procedure, Officer Buczynski will read a statement of your client's rights."

The bullish, tense woman, looking very short next to her husband, ignored Bushy's reading, extending her arms to examine her fingernails, looking to the ceiling. She didn't look at her husband. The man was a mess. His clothes were oddly disheveled, as if he had dressed in a hurry. His right hand was wrapped in gauze that looked so uneven and frayed that it had to have been pushed tightly through a jacket sleeve. His face was badly scratched and was bruised below one cheek. He studied the floor for any movement he might find there.

Neither the man nor woman said a word. Royal Fraiser, looking fresh next to his rumpled son and frumpy clients, did all the talking. "We understand. Thank you, Mr. Buczynski. What is it that you'd like to know?"

Paul signaled the stenographer into the room. "We have just completed the Miranda message," he said. The stenographer sat and entered the fact into the record.

The interview began with the basics: names, addresses, relationships; next, information about living arrangements, habits, activities. Finally, Tuomi moved to whereabouts.

"Were the two of you together on the night of Miss Crosley's death?"

Mrs. Esterwald said her first word, shooting off a definite

'No!' before Royal Fraiser could even grumble.

"I'm not sure Mrs. Esterwald understood your question correctly. Perhaps the question deserves more detail. What part of that night do you mean?" He leaned into the woman's ear and spoke low.

After Fraiser's intervention, the couple's whereabouts were a muddle. The story did not make sense and seemed contradictory.

The man's bruised hand and facial scratches came, he said, with a fall from a horse. There had been no medical attention. The couple said little and only with prodding.

Paul tried another tack. "A passerby on Sunday morning may have seen the perpetrator or perpetrators on the property. Perhaps leaving in the housekeeper's car." He watched carefully for any reaction.

The husband continued to stare at the floor. His wife, though, stabbed Paul with a glance. "We were out of state. Who passed by, anyway?"

Fraiser cleared his throat and boomed. "So you have a witness?"

"We are studying the lead," Paul said. The pair had already told him what was important. When they were questioned separately, the truth would become clear.

The uniformed officer reentered. He handed a note to Bushy who, after reading it, passed it to Paul.

The coin had surfaced. The letter carrier had delivered it to Mr. Esterwald's residence hotel two hours before; and the FBI had intercepted it. Paul nodded to Bushy and addressed the couple.

"I understand the funeral is tomorrow. Again, my condolences, and thanks for coming in at such a difficult time."

IV

Paul Tuomi sat in the corner of his office, stirring cream into his coffee. He set the cup aside.

"I can't tell if you're delighted or disappointed, boss," Bushy said.

Paul didn't share his delight, though he knew by Mark Fraiser's sullen face that PS had struck home. That was good.

"Both, but I saw the case as more complicated than it seems now. What's your read on the Esterwalds?"

Bushy didn't hesitate. "She's odd. I don't see direct involvement. But she might be the brains behind it. He's guilty as sin, with the bruises to prove it. None too bright. He mailed the coin to himself."

"Maybe." Paul took up his coffee cup. "I can't get Ingstrom off my mind, maybe because all the honchos are pressing on the Esterwalds. Having met them, I can see the point."

"Did you pick up anything?" Bushy asked. "Any vibe, or whatever you call it?"

Paul sighed like a man known for a bad habit. "It's a curse, Bushy. Evidence is all that matters. But between you and me, yes. I know Bert Esterwald was there. But so was Ingstrom, and I can't prove either one just yet."

"Not with the coin?"

"Maybe he didn't send it. Somebody else could have."

"I suppose."

"Even an eye-witness might not be enough. But finding Ingstrom will resolve some other questions I have. And it might bring Mr. Esterwald to confession."

"For a youngster, he hasn't been easy to find."

"No," Paul said, "but now I have an idea where to look."

28

Third Street

BERTA HAD TAKEN TO BED. She had decided, but no one would know yet. Everything is leaving, or had already left. Still you have your senses. Yes, she did, and they were enough to keep her awake all night: smelling her old-lady skin, listening for the next strike of the Central High clock or the next riff of snoring from Wendell Jr. upstairs, watching the mix and shift of sunrise shadows and shimmers on her bedroom shade. Lilac silhouettes melded with outlines of maple boughs that inched down minute by minute to combine in new patterns on the scrim.

Was there a point to her aloneness? Wendell Jr. was there, of course, but no one, not he and not even Paul, would stay. We all must go. The words reverberated in the quarter-hour clock strike. The end of the clock's signal left the same silence, the same absence that Roger had sounded just three days before.

After the funeral tomorrow, her son would return to his job in Iowa. Paul, she knew, would soon make a new life. He would be gone. That was good. It was time for that. And for the first time in the sixteen years since his death, Wendell Sr. felt to Berta like a ghost. One by one, we go. Husband. Daughter. Grandson. Even the Church. No one to bake for. No will to do it. No hope for more.

Berta would take to her bed. Yes, even the Church. That was the hardest. She couldn't disdain it, as Wendell Jr. did after his father was killed. Without its presence, there was a

373

sense of loss, of being alone. You sense it in your chest. In the heart. She rubbed her chest with her hand and patted herself there.

The lilac shadows, falling low under the risen sun, had gone from the shade, were swallowed beneath the umbra of her tall maple tree. They barely left a scent. The figures still cast on the shade wavered pleasantly on the blind, but they did not beckon her to rise. Let Wendell Jr. get his own breakfast. I'm done with that as well.

Tomorrow, she would bury her grandson. She would bury him without the Church. No Mass. No wake at the hall. No shame. No. The Church would not shame her. Roger had been as careless and wild as his mother. His accident was no different than hers, a car wreck fueled by drink. Berta placed both hands on her chest. She sighed. The world itself was larger, bigger than the Church. Earth was the haven she had always sought and known. She understood its laws and found them less cruel, more just than those of the Church. And after? No. I've made my last confession. Berta had taken to her bed.

The whole of the town would look toward the lake that morning. It would step out on its front porch, maybe sweep aside its early morning brume, put hands to hips, and gaze out on the wonders that sunlight brought to water. The town had grown up looking sunward, facing the lake from the hills rising above in the west, and for a hundred years, had rolled its morning shades to glory and brightness arrayed like members of a theater audience inclined down toward a silvery screen, one head higher than the other, all wide-eyed, applauding the fresh breezes over the lake that broke the water into a million jewels. Then, just for a minute, perhaps, each citizen would pause on deck, porch, front walk, veranda or lawn to be stilled in wonder at the world they shared—though, truth be told, each one would believe he or she alone breathed the pure air and bathed in the sanctified light that the morning brought.

So had Paul Tuomi, thinking of Cindy before his screen at the Arrowhead Hotel. So had PS, free in the morning light of West Wind Ranch. So, maybe, had Pamela Skaansgard in her empty bungalow, as had her father from the breakfast table on his colonnaded widow's walk. So had Tommy and his mother, Cindy, from the kitchen deck beside the reedy St. Louis River. And so, too, had Reese Ingstrom, under the station-wagon roof shaded by stacked block pallets. All for an instant stood on the steps of a July morning made paradise, listening to one single beat of a collective heart before descending into the combative world to search, confront, contest, or control; before any of them had time to love, to murder, or, like Berta, to resign.

So Berta, lying in bed, thought to do—not in words, but by sensing the shadows that waved and set upon her shade.

A thump and a curse ended her reverie. Upstairs, Wendell Jr. had fallen out of bed. Berta giggled and called out. "Junior, are you all right?" She giggled again.

She followed his movements and curses from her bed. He clumped around on his heels. She imagined him standing on one leg, pulling on his pants, moving then onto the other. He visited the toilet and sent the water cascading down the pipes. Finally, fumbling with the buttons on his shirt, he opened her bedroom door. "Yes, mother, I'm fine."

Despite her glum thoughts, Berta laughed. She laughed hard. She shook the bed. "Oh, Junior, you haven't changed." She tried to stanch the laughter beneath a pillow. No use. They were belly laughs now and would have to run their course.

Wendell Jr. stood blushing and buttoning. "Very funny. I'm used to a double bed, if you want to know." He allowed himself a smile and a couple of self-deprecating laughs. "How about I make coffee and breakfast?"

Berta waved one hand weakly between broken fits of mirth. "Breakfast in bed? Remember burnt-toast on Mother's Day?"

He came to her and kissed her forehead. "You won't let me forget."

She wrapped his shoulders in her arms suddenly, drew him low. "You were so sweet to come. Thank you, Junior."

Wendell Jr. kissed her cheek, retreated to the doorway and looked back to her for any sign of sorrow. Berta only giggled and smiled.

"Bacon, eggs, and toast?" he offered.

"Make mine burnt."

Berta West lay in bed listening to Wendell Jr. making breakfast out in the kitchen. She reached over to the window, bringing up the shade enough to allow some air but not too high, keeping the sun's glare outside. The day would be hot, but the early morning air moved coolly through her bedroom. It is pleasant here. She allowed her thoughts to drift with the breeze.

Wendell Jr. rummaged in the pantry. He asked questions at every step. "Where do you keep the coffee, Mom?" "Where's the frying pan?" "Is this canister salt or sugar?"

"Taste it, son."

She answered easily; the kitchen was more familiar to her than her own heart. I should have taught him to cook.

Wendell Jr. banged the pans. "Got a tray?"

"Of course. On top of the fridge."

"Napkins?"

"Second drawer left of the sink," she said. "You're helpless, aren't you?"

He came to the door, a spatula in his hand. She laughed again. Wendell Jr. was wearing her apron. Hapless as a union steward on strike. He was having fun and returned to his work.

Listening to the bacon sizzle in the pan, Berta flowed along with her thoughts. The days before she met Wendell Sr. she saw as clearly as if they'd been last week. Berta had been Roberta then, a good Italian girl, though her father had changed his name from Landucci to Landis when he arrived at Ellis Island. "Blend in," he'd told her. When she met Wendell, Sr. she told him she was "Berta"—a better, Germanic version. It was only later that she found out his father at Ellis Island had dropped the "-rum" from "Westrum" to Anglicize their name. She had kept the Church, and her Wendell converted to please her. It didn't stick. No, Wendell Sr. was not a faithful Catholic. It hadn't been in his blood. And now the twice-Americanized Berta West was giving it up. Perhaps Roberta Landucci—a little girl in white ironed blouses and long pleated skirt—would recite her rosary; but Berta West would not.

"Breakfast is served," Wendell Jr. announced. He brought her tray in, moved a chair close to the bed, and retrieved his own cup and plate. "Toast burnt to order, ma'am."

He set his cup on the nightstand. "Oh. The jam. Let me get that." And he was up and gone again.

Berta surveyed the tray. Very nice, Junior. She held the sprig of Miss Kim lilacs to her nose. "You found some late bloomers. Sweet."

"Those were nestled at the back of the bush, reaching up toward your window." He bent forward to smell the sprig. "I haven't forgotten about you and lilacs."

They ate the food and chatted. Time and distance melted away.

They brought Wendell Sr. and Betty back to life. They talked of Roger a little. Paul was always on both their minds.

"Paul will set everything right, you'll see," Wendell Jr. said.

Berta handed over the tray, finished. She kept the small lilac bouquet. "Paul is very good. But it'll take time." She fluffed the pillows under her head and turned onto her side. She cuddled the pillows and looked up at Wendell Jr. "I've made a decision, Junior."

Wendell Jr. set the tray on his chair. "What is that, Mom?"

"I'm going with Bell Brothers. They'll bury Roger tomorrow, the third day."

"They're Protestant, Mom."

She turned her eyes up toward her son, took his hand. "It doesn't matter. Roger didn't finish his catechism and was less a Catholic that his mother."

Wendell Jr. gave her a reluctant nod.

"I won't be holding a wake. I want this to be family only. I'm not up to it, Junior."

He came to his knees at her bedside. "Whatever you want. Whatever." He kissed her, rose, and took the tray. "Maybe you can get some sleep now, Mom." He swung the door behind him.

"No, leave it open a bit. I like the breeze." She was instantly asleep.

Wendell Jr. tiptoed to the sink.

Berta was flying in her dream. She chortled and soared.

At first the family had been flying kites from her back yard out over the city, Wendell Jr., Betty, Paul, she, and Roger. Everyone tugged at a string that led out over the cliff, each to a different-colored kite trailing a contrasting knotted tail. Berta's was blue with a green tail. Then she spread her arms and took to the air herself, rising toward the kites. Once she was over the edge of the escarpment, Observation Hill dropped precipitously below her. She left the ground. She was having fun. She was not afraid.

Her apron strings were her tail. She laughed and sailed, spread her arms and flew high over the city. She swooped low over the West End. Friends on the street looked up to wave at her. At a pull of the apron strings she rose higher, straight up over Rice's Point, where she looped the loop from east to west and back again, over Wendell, Sr.'s dock and then around the bank buildings downtown.

The wind took her back to the hill, toward home, now over the churchyard. "Oh, my," she heard herself say as the wind shifted. Her string went slack, and she began to drop down. She'd fall on the church tower. She cried out for help.

Paul and Wendell Jr. pulled her tether. With a stout yank they stopped her fall and brought her upward. The wind grew slack. Furiously, they reeled in the string. But without wind she was plummeting past loops of kite string, tangling them around her outstretched arm and rolling toward the lawn and rocks of her back yard.

Through darkness, Berta heard muffled voices. Wendell Jr. was talking loudly. Have I fallen? His voice was nearer. Wendell Jr. was arguing. Is he shouting?

"I don't care if it is after noon! I tell you, she is asleep!" Wendell Jr. said.

The other voice was lower, softer, indistinct, but familiar. Isn't it someone I want to see? Berta pushed herself up from her dreams. The pillow fell to the floor, and she heard clearly the voice of Father Lucci.

"I must see her. I have good news."

"Junior," Berta called out, "is that Father Lucci? Is he here?"

Wendell Jr. appeared at the door. "We woke you. I'm sorry, Mom, he nearly pushed his way in."

"I do want to see him. Give me a moment to brush my hair."

"I can have him come back."

"No, no, I want to see him."

Wendell Jr. quietly closed the door.

Berta rose, feeling a little unsteady. She tidied the bed and sat at her dresser mirror. She combed her hair, dressed herself in a heavy robe, returned to the bed and climbed beneath the covers. She fluffed up the pillows and sat ready for her visitor.

She called to her son. "Wendell, please show Father Lucci in." Had she ever called him just Wendell before?

His face at the door told her. Whether he realized why or not, his voice took a deeper, more serious but softer tone. He was formal. Wendell instinctively attuned to his new position. "Father Lucci, Mother." He ushered the priest in and guided him to the chair. "I'll be in the kitchen."

Berta sat erect in her bed. "My goodness, Father. Are you all right? You look so tired."

The priest sat still except for his hands that he held heavy on his lap under his belly. His fingers kneaded his meaty thumbs in a nervous rhythm of which he seemed unaware.

"No. No. Well, yes, Roberta." Irritated. He corrected himself. "Berta. I didn't sleep well last night."

Like a young girl Berta drew her knees up under the covers and hugged them to her. "Did I hear you say you had good news?"

Father Lucci looked to his hands as if he had to command them to stop their incessant movement. "Yes. At least I hope it is good."

"Well, I have news as well, Father, but I want to hear yours first."

Berta smiled kindly at the man. For the first time since meeting this priest, after Father Arrivido died, she felt his equal.

"Of course. It is why I've come."

She waited. It seemed he had something else to say, something beside his news, but, when he finally placed his hands solidly on his knees to stop their thrumming beat, he looked as if he had changed his mind. He twice started to speak, then stopped. Berta began to think that Father Lucci had come to confession; she the confessor, he the penitent.

Finally, Father Lucci seemed to find the words he wanted. "I've thought carefully about your grandson's . . . death."

He paused so long Berta had to say something. "Of course, Father, I have too."

Her words seemed to coax him into continuing. "I'm not sure that I have drawn the right conclusion."

Again he lapsed into a brooding silence. Berta's patience outlasted her irritation with the man. She drew kindness into her voice. "Have you changed your mind, Father?"

Father Lucci was slow to speak. Though he had barged in and insisted on seeing her, now, facing her, he grew uncertain. "No, perhaps not, but I wonder if more evidence is needed before I speak finally."

Now it was Berta who searched for words. She let go her knees and placed her hands in her lap.

"Father, you may need more time and more evidence. I don't fault you for that. But I know my grandson. I love my grandson. No matter what, I'll give him a decent burial."

"Why, yes, that is why . . ."

She didn't let him finish. "That is why I've made other arrangements. We'll bury him tomorrow."

Father Lucci looked at Berta West in horror, as if unshriven he stood before St. Peter. "If you could only wait. A day or two."

Berta interlaced her fingers and folded her hands. "I've decided, Father. No one else can say."

"Just a day."

A warm afternoon breath blew in through the window, billowed the shade and let it fall.

"No, Father. We will not wait."

Father Lucci did not move. Despite the July weather, he was frozen to his chair.

Berta called to her son. "Wendell, please see Father Lucci to the door."

Wendell had been listening at the door and entered immediately. He had to urge the priest from the room, speaking low, kindly words to him. "This way, Father. Don't forget your hat. Will you be all right to drive?"

Berta listened to the voices recede. They left.

She got up, chose her lightest flowered smock, and dressed. She went to the vanity mirror, dabbed her face, added some color, teased her hair with her hands.

This is no time to lie about!

Berta shook off her slippers and stepped into shoes. She raised the bedroom shade and went to the kitchen.

29

The Triangle

WHEN PAUL TUOMI'S BUICK leveled out from the steep rise up Third Street, he saw over the dashboard that his boyhood friend was guiding Father Lucci by the elbow up the front walk of the house. He pulled into the driveway and sprang out of the car.

"Everything all right here, Junior?"

"Father Lucci has had a little shock, is all. Help me get him to his car."

The two friends each took an elbow and led the priest to the curb. "Step down, Father," Wendell said. They moved slowly.

Paul left him braced between the car and Wendell Jr. He opened the door.

Father Lucci held on to the sedan top and the door, and plopped down into the driver's seat with a sigh. He dragged his feet inside; his voice quavered.

"Thank you, boys."

Paul held the door firm. "Are you okay to drive, Father?"

The good Father stared up at Paul, his gaze unfocused— like a sheep, Paul thought. "Aren't you the policeman?" Father Lucci said.

"Yes, Father. Detective Paul Tuomi."

Lucci fumbled with his keys and finally found the ignition slot. "I was wrong. Very wrong," he muttered, and started the car.

When the priest had closed the door, Paul stepped back.

"What happened?"

Father Lucci had pulled from the curb and was heading down the street. The two stood watching the car recede then turn off toward the church, which was just six blocks away.

Only then did he answer, using Paul's name for his mother.

"Memma took the good Father to the woodshed."

"What?"

"I think he came to confess. But he couldn't do it. He knows he was wrong about Roger, but Memma wasn't having it."

"What did she say?"

"Something about loyalty. She must have said to him what she told me earlier. Memma wants a mortuary funeral. Just family. No wake."

"That is a shock."

"She's changed, Paul. She seemed depressed. Then she slept all morning, and, when that excuse for a priest came, she perked right up. Gave him the back of her hand. Finally. She called me 'Wendell.'"

Paul put his arm around Wendell's shoulders and hugged him sideways.

"Let's get some things from my car before we go in," Paul said—then added, "Wendell." They swung around as a unit. Wendell grabbed Paul round the waist.

Berta was bustling in the kitchen. "Oh. The two musketeers. I didn't know you were here, Paul."

They hugged. "You look good, Memma."

"No, I don't." Then, in a voice the two men recognized from years before she said, "Wendell, you and Paul sit down. I've got some lunch for you."

While Berta busied herself with sandwiches, Paul showed Wendell the handwriting samples. "The analyst says what any fool can tell. These are two different people."

Paul looked over his shoulder at Berta. "Roger didn't write that note."

Berta thrust the toaster lever down with a sharp snap. "Of course not. I knew that."

Wendell smiled at Paul. "Do you know who did?"

"Yes, but I'm waiting for confirmation."

"Enough police talk." Berta brought the coffee pot over. "Sugar and cream are on the window sill. Help yourselves."

Paul and Wendell laughed at once. "What do they say about the past?"

Wendell knew. "It isn't even past."

Berta cut even that cord. "Maybe not, boys, but coffee does get cold."

She set down a plate with sandwich halves cut diagonally. "This bacon isn't burnt. Now eat!" She pulled a chair over from the big table and sat with them. "Let me do the talking."

She waited until their mouths were full of BLT and started with a warning. "Now, no back talk until I'm finished."

The two men chewed and nodded.

"I'm sure Wendell has told you the funeral is tomorrow. Bell Brothers. We can call those we want to come." Berta thought a moment. "Everyone can come here afterward. I have time to prepare, and Elma will help." Her mind was already in the pantry, taking stock; but she stopped herself, cupped her hands and straightened in her chair. As if they'd been fooling around instead of paying mind, she spoke firmly.

"Listen. I've decided."

Wendell checked his chewing. Paul halted his sandwich in mid-air, mouth open, ready to bite.

"Wendell, I'll be going back with you."

Through a mouthful, Wendell said, "Move to Bettendorf?"

"Yes. I could have done it years ago, but now is the time."

She looked at her hands in her lap and raised her eyes to Paul. "I want you to stay in the house. Stay until you get settled again. When you and Cindy decide what to do, we can see."

She looked to her son. "We can sell it later, Wendell, if that's all right with you. Until then Mr. Carnegie will pay my way, God bless 'im."

"You don't have to pay your way, Mom."

"I'll pay you rent, Memma."

Berta clapped both hands on the table. "I think I'll have a coffee."

When Paul left Memma and Wendell standing together on the front walk, waving their goodbyes as he drove down the hill, he felt as unsettled as the old priest had looked. Out of sight of the house, he pounded the steering wheel. "Shit. I make a move and everything changes again."

It was as if his dreams of the previous night had washed through his new troubles. Again he heard the woman in the alley. Yes. Bullshit. He had pulled out of the East End, hoping to right himself by moving west. The stable mooring Memma represented was now cut, loosed, and floating on the lake. She's right, though. Wendell is her son. I'm only like a son.

Paul winced at his own pathetic whining. You're a fool, Tuomi. Morose thoughts and memories seeped in, flooding his mind, returning him to a midnight walk he had made twenty years before through Dinkytown, the village adjacent to his college campus. That night he'd walked for hours, past dark and silent houses, pausing over viaducts spanning railroad corridors below. He walked along the Mississippi, across bridges spanning the river as it bent through and defined the campus. His wandering had lasted well past three in the morning. He was dog-tired but would not sleep. The night had turned frosty, and he had to keep walking to stay warm. It was that night he decided to go to Chicago to spend Thanksgiving with Pamela and her grandparents. He did not remember making the choice. He recalled only the chill, his aching feet, and the emptiness of the streets.

It had been as if the vacant paths through campus had shown him the way to go, away from Cindy and toward Pamela. His unrest that night sent him out of his room, but he had resolved nothing and had postponed everything. Somehow, the grueling walk decided for him. Now, leaving Observation Hill, leaving Wendell and Memma, having split with Pamela but not yet firmly taking Cindy's hand, Paul found himself in that same place. The streets of the West End looked empty. Blocks of windows, peering out from the whitewashed shops, reflected his Buick's passing. Paul felt a midday, sleepless fatigue.

At the blare of a truck's horn, Paul screeched to a stop. I nearly ran a red light! Get a hold on yourself, Tuomi. The Buick stood well into the intersection; Paul, trying to remember where he was headed, watched the traffic pass. Drivers were shaking their heads and peering at him. He got the green, lurched straight ahead, and pulled to the far curb. His feet ached. A squad car had pulled up behind him.

Paul lowered the window. "Hello, Loren."

The officer coming up to his window stopped short. "Oh! Detective Tuomi."

"Sorry about that. I wasn't paying attention, obviously."

Loren Talbert laughed. "I'll have to let you off with a warning this time."

Paul now knew where he was headed. "Thanks. I'll be more careful."

He pulled from the curb and drove straight down to the Seamen's Hall. Ingstrom had yanked him out of his pitiful reverie, back to the light of the day. In a few minutes, with any luck, he'd have a fix on the kid.

The hall was empty. As he entered, a tall Swede came out of the office and strode to the counter. He knew the man.

"Hello, Max."

"If it isn't chief inspector Tuomi himself! How is your father?"

Max was not being friendly, but Paul ignored it. "He's better than ever, really."

His tone softened Max slightly. "How can we help the department today?"

Max was Denfeld, just like Paul but fifteen years older. It was less the age difference than Paul's college degree and his East Duluth address that separated them. That Paul was of the policemen's union wouldn't bridge the divide. Max kept the edge on. "I assume this ain't a social visit."

Paul knew that Max had sailed during the war. There had been lots of trouble. The seamen's union had pressed for better wages. The steel trust fought back with patriotism— patriotism and the police. This wouldn't be easy.

"You're right, Max. I'm looking for someone."

"Does this someone have a name?"

"He does. This is off the record, though. I don't have a warrant."

Max had the upper hand, and used it.

"Since when do you guys need one of those? What's his name? Maybe I don't like the guy."

Paul knew not to back down. He also knew not to play tough.

"Since when don't you like your guys?"

Max forced a smile.

"Look, Max, I'm not coming back with a warrant. It's off the record."

Now Max relaxed a bit. "Working one of your hunches?"

"At this point, yes."

Max stood tall, hands on the counter, waiting.

"You like a guy named Ingstrom?"

Max was still. Paul added: "Reese Ingstrom. A kid, really."

Max leaned closer to Paul on his heavy hands. "Your dad still working for that slimeball Fraiser?"

PS had chummed with Max's older brother, Chet. Had it not been for that, Paul wouldn't have bothered to come. This was now in West End parlance a personal matter.

"You know, I think that little thing is all over." Paul didn't' try to hide his pleasure being able to say it. "We had a bit of good luck come our way."

"Good. Those two devils aren't worth spit." The Fraisers were West Duluth, but hardly friends of Labor.

Now it was Paul who laid his hands on the counter, waiting.

"I can't tell you anything about your Mr. Ingstrom. The log is closed to the public. You know, though, the slowest boat to China left the harbor two hours ago. It's called *Bisnu's Dream.*"

Everything, evidence, hunches and dreams, all of it fit together. Paul patted the counter and held the ruse between them.

"Sorry you couldn't help me, Max. But thanks just the same."

"By the way, they're loading freight in Port Arthur tonight."

"It's been good to see you, Max. Tell Chet hello."

Max rapped his knuckles on the wood top. "Say hi to your dad."

Now he needed to complete the final leg of his triangle: up to Somebody's House for his appointment with Skaansgard. He was running late. Let the SOB wait.

Skaansgard did wait, for nearly half an hour. Though Paul saw him in the window as he passed up the walk, he took his time, strolling between the planter boxes that sprouted some of the summer-fresh produce Somebody's was known for. He tasted some mint and broke a leaf of basil. His father-in-law met him at the door.

"Sorry I'm late, Leif," Paul said.

The lawyer extended his hand. "Coffee?"

He's pissed but he'll never show it, Paul thought. Genteel as always. Paul had sized up his father-in-law long ago. He was all business. "I'm going to order a pastry."

"We're over here." Skaansgard indicated the lone table by the walk-window. "Bullock had to leave. It's for the best. Give us a chance to chat." His left eye twitched slightly, as if he were about to wink.

Thank God he held back, Paul thought, keeping a straight face.

They sat at the private table, off by itself overlooking the planters Paul had grazed. The lawyer stirred his coffee, giving Paul a chance to order. Time was less important to Skaansgard than appearances and results. Of those two, you could never be sure which took priority. Paul had always guessed it was appearance.

The lawyer cleared his throat. "You and Pamela are quarreling?"

Paul had readied himself for this part of the conversation. "We are separating." He said it as a matter of fact and left it to his father-in-law to carry the subject further.

"Paul, I understand. Believe me, I do." He dressed his next words in a confidential tone. "There have been times I've wanted to throw in the towel. Women can be so difficult."

"It's final this time. Pam and I both know that."

The lawyer nodded. "You have been through tremendous loss. We all feel it, even after so many years. It's tough."

Paul turned on his own *entre nous*. "Leif, I think we are over Alex's death. He left a void, that is sure, but we have other problems. Serious ones."

Paul's coffee came, and he ordered a Danish.

"I'll let you two work things out. Just know this, Paul. Whatever you two decide won't change a thing between us. She's my daughter, sure, but I think you and I have had a meeting of the minds."

Paul didn't believe a word of it, but he had learned to play Skaansgard's game. "Thank you, Leif. It means a lot to me."

The preliminaries were over. The intimate tone dissipated like the steam from Paul's coffee, and the lawyer with vested interests came to the fore. "You interrogated Robert Esterwald today."

"'Interview' would be a better description."

"What do you think?"

Paul would make him drag it out of him. "We've got a long way to go."

"Obviously. Wasn't the guy all scratched up? As if he had been in a tussle?" Skaansgard mentioned the bandaged hand.

"You clearly don't need me to tell you. But, yes."

"So, what do you think?" Skaansgard was not going to let him off.

"What do you want me to say? That I think Robert Esterwald is guilty of murder? That he sustained his injuries battling the women he killed? Hell, Leif, we're in the middle of an investigation."

Appearances were fraying. "Just keep it down, Paul." His father-in-law leaned over the table. "Paul, don't blow this opportunity. The whole damn country is watching this case. It can mean big things for you."

Sure, Paul thought, the "big things" that so many have lauded over the years: college, a helpful marriage, promotions, powerful 'friends,' and the status of making detective. What does it add up to but a big trap? Though he knew he saw it right, he also knew better than push them away like an empty dessert plate.

"Yes, I know. It is high profile."

Skaansgard thrust his face even closer. He was holding down fury, or pretending to contain a rage. "Listen, I twisted some mighty strong arms to get you this, Paul. Don't forget that."

Paul laughed. He couldn't help it. "I don't think anyone else would take it."

The lawyer held his breath. He looked ready to explode; but then came the only person who would've dared interrupt. She held a plated Danish in hand.

"Fresh from the oven." It was Thea, the owner. "*Hyvää ruokahalua*, Paul."

"Oh. *Kiitos paljon*, Thea." He translated for Skaansgard. "It's bon appétit in Finnish."

"This has been Skaansgard-Tuomi week in here," Thea said. "I'm honored."

The men looked mystified.

"Your wives were here together just yesterday. No. Day before. I was making *pulla*."

Skaansgard let his rage recede and smiled for Thea. "I'll have to keep better tabs on those girls. Who were they entertaining this time?"

Thea laughed. "Actually, they were chatting with Reese Ingstrom when I came from the kitchen. He brought a couple rough characters in with him."

Paul and Skaansgard locked eyes. It was clear that the lawyer knew about Paul's probes into Ingstrom's doings. Paul covered as best he could. "Oh! My bad penny turns up again."

"He's pleasant enough. From good people," Thea said.

Paul could pursue it later, but he wanted to know sooner. "He was here with a long-haired hippie who constantly flips his hair aside and with a young, young girl. No?"

Thea paid him a compliment. "You're psychic after all. Sounds like them."

"And they ordered Café Borgia."

"How did you know?"

Paul preferred this to wrangling with Pamela's father. He laughed agreeably. "Thea, everyone orders it."

"You're a fortune-telling rascal." She looked to Skaansgard. "More coffee, Leif?" She brushed her hand lightly on Paul's shoulder as she turned to leave. "*Naadan.*"

He answered in English. "Yes, I'll see you, Thea."

The interlude eased the tension and put Paul in a softer mood. He'd give something now. "Leif, I have to confess. If I had to decide today, Bert Esterwald would be the prime suspect, followed closely, I suppose, by his wife."

"You know about the coin."

"I do. But we have a lot of work ahead. A suspicion of convenient persons does not mean we can build a case. As you know, they're not the only suspicious people who might be involved."

His father-in-law again raised his voice toward anger. "So you do think the Ingstrom boy is involved."

"I didn't say that. I saw him outside the Brookside gates the morning of the murders. He's mixed up in a whole lot of mayhem in town."

Skaansgard slammed his fist on the table. "For God's sake, Paul, his father is the trust accountant. Did you know that?"

"I know his family is willing to cover for him," Paul offered.

The war between appearances and results seemed to play

across the lawyer's face. "Cover for what? A little harmless fun?"

The phrase offended Paul. "Harmless fun? He's implicated in an unlawful death. He might have peddled stolen property and most certainly he peddled deadly drugs. The sheriff wants to question him in connection with an arson case. And it's likely he has skipped town. Does that sound harmless?"

The lawyer clutched the tablecloth. "Where in the hell are you getting all this? From that wonderful imagination?"

The snide accusation stabbed at Paul. He rose, his knuckles on the table. "I've got five people implicating him. Three are solid identifications. At the very least, he needs to be brought in for questioning."

The lawyer stood up and looked Paul in the eye. "Listen, Tuomi, forget about pinning any of the Brookside mess on a kid. You've got your suspect. Now get the goods on him and throw him in jail."

Paul did not think of PS at that moment, but he might as well have been his dad standing in front of another lawyer. One sure thing was for sure: he wouldn't be tied to conniving shysters, no matter what. PS had shown him the way.

"I'm not working for you, Leif. I work for the people of Duluth."

At first Paul thought the lawyer would laugh. Like a caricature in a political cartoon, the man grew an oversized head and pushed it across the table at him, hanging it off a spindly neck and a tiny body.

"Fuck your people of Duluth and all their whimpering and suffering." Skaansgard had clenched and bared his teeth; he spoke, a hissing whisper. "You know something, Tuomi? If Pamela were to find out about your little high school sweetheart and her little lean-to love nest out there in Oliver, what do you think she'd want me to do?" The lawyer flung out his hand, as if tossing an underhand knife. "Ha?" His eyes were wide as a mad cow's.

The threat came at Paul like an angry wasp. He shot his fist across the table and made contact. Skaansgard sat down hard, shocked. He brought his napkin to nose. When he saw the blood on it, he paled, covered it, and hurried to the men's room.

Before his father-in-law could return, Paul had paid the bill and gone.

30

City Hall

Paul was on the phone again.

He had come straight to his office to call Cindy. He found she had left work early and wouldn't be in until Monday. That took some pressure off. He had visualized Skaansgard standing over her in a bloodied shirt, directing her to clean her desk and leave. That wouldn't happen, at least now. Still, he had to tell her about the mess he'd got into with her boss.

Next he dialed his father, but still with his mind on Cindy and Skaansgard. I cause her more trouble than I'm worth. He was listening to PS's phone ring. Six, seven . . .

"Hello?" PS was out of breath.

"Dad! Are you all right?"

"Yeah. Yeah. I was out in the yard. I guess I was snoozing on the chaise. Listening to the birds."

"Listening to the birds? Are you sure you're all right?"

"I shouldn't listen to the birds?"

It was not in the older man's résumé.

"I guess it's fine. I just never thought you were a bird lover. I . . ."

His father laughed. It was glee. "Maybe a lot of things are going to change."

Paul caught the mood; the obverse of the younger Fraiser's looks that morning. "Oh, yeah. Judging by Mark Fraiser's ghost this morning, I can understand your exuberance."

"Pure joy, my son. Pure joy." PS smiled through the phone line.

399

"Congratulations, Dad."

"It feels like a new lease on life. Thanks for calling."

Paul had not called to congratulate his father. He was thinking about the ship they'd watched come into the harbor the evening before—about Ingstrom. "Actually, I called because I need something, Dad."

"Hey, why else call?" PS would not be parted from his happiness. "What do you need?"

Paul ran through the sequence he had put together on Ingstrom. He thought he had it figured: the drugs and Randy; an accident at Skip's; stealing to build up travel money; farewell flings with his girls; the arson attack he escaped; the shipping news from Max. "I saw it in a dream, Dad."

PS took it seriously. "And you didn't pay it any mind?"

Paul told him about the dream, about Tommy pointing at a dancing Ingstrom. "It was the ship we saw, *Bisnu's Dream.*"

"Where is it now?"

It was on the lake, making for a tiny island beyond the U.S. border where the Duluth police had no reach. "It should dock in Port Arthur the other side of midnight."

PS waited for more, but Paul wanted him to connect the dots himself.

"So, you need me to intercept the ship."

Paul explained his reasons. He had reliable information, but it was all circumstance. None of it proved infraction or offense, much less crime. Some information couldn't be publicly revealed. Randy Belisle was a shadow. Max wouldn't stand by anything he had said. Siiri and Skip were under arrest. "Dreams are not the stuff arrests are made of, Dad."

"Okay, smarty pants, I'll go up there. I guess I've enough time to get back for the funeral, don't I?"

"Wendell called?"

"Funeral is at one. He phoned just before the birds sang

to me."

"Ha, ha, Dad."

Paul laid it all out for his father. He wanted to confront Ingstrom on Brookside, Roger, Marly, and Randy Belisle—why Belisle would be passing his name to the police.

His father soaked it up. "The Olds is full of gas. I should be able to beat them to port and stop for a good dinner to boot."

"This isn't a freebie, Dad."

"It isn't just business, either. When are you going to tell me about you and Pam?"

Paul was always amazed at how much information his father gleaned from just sitting in his car or doodling on a scratch pad. He let things come to him.

"You talked to Cindy."

"She was looking for you an hour ago. Before the twittering started."

"Yeah. While I was punching her boss in the nose up at Somebody's House."

His father was never surprised. "It's about time on both counts. Pamela's and her father's."

Paul appreciated the support, even though he didn't feel great about either predicament.

"It could be worse, I suppose. I could have punched her and left him." No one was laughing.

"Things have a way of settling, Paul."

"I hope to influence the results."

"I should get on the road. Take it easy, Paul."

"Thanks, I will." He held on to the conversation. They'd covered a lot of territory in the last few minutes. "Hey, Dad?" Paul said.

"What?

"We're good together, don't you think?"

Paul read through the notes and papers Bushy had left for

him; some good, some sad. Walt McConnichie, the coroner, had been true to his word and hadn't had to wait long to file Roger's death certificate. The handwriting sample tipped the balance of opinion. It would lift everyone's spirits at a funeral. They could lay the boy to rest without despair hanging over his casket.

Bushy had kept up on the arson fire as well. His cooperation with the sheriff had led to a positive identification of the body from dental records. Without a doubt, it was Marly.

Paul swung around in his chair and put his feet up on the radiator under the window behind his desk. It was his thinking position. The information brought him a step closer to being able to stop Ingstrom. He'd need a warrant to get him off that ship. Paul mulled over the possibility. There was still too much circumstance and too little time for an official arrest; especially since the ship had sailed into Canadian waters. Either Ingstrom was very lucky or he was the smartest college sophomore that Paul had never met.

He concluded his deliberations. "No, it's still too early," He said out loud.

"Too early for what, boss? Dinner?" It was Bushy, with fried chicken in a box.

Paul swung around. "How did it go?"

That afternoon, when the radio call from Brookside came in as he was driving to Somebody's House, he had dispatched Bushy with the two detectives assigned to search the Esterwalds' hotel room. The Esterwalds were walking the grounds at Brookside and trying their darnedest to enter the house. At City Hall, Bushy was just two blocks from the hotel. He delivered the warrant and secured the site before the Brookside team arrived.

Paul directed the team at the mansion to "keep the Esterwalds waiting on an answer from 'downtown' to allow enough time to do a thorough search. Don't let them enter that house. Stop them if they try."

It was a fortunate break. Rather than wait for the funeral to search the hotel room, moving now gave Paul an earlier look at the couple. Bushy might tell him that hunch turned lucky.

Bushy put the chicken on the corner of the desk and said, "We've got them."

Paul clasped his hands behind his neck and leaned back. "How's that?"

"We found some of the jewelry missing from Miss Crosley's room stuffed into a hosiery box in the hotel room. A suitcase taken from Crosley's closet was there, too."

"Go ahead and eat, Bushy," Paul said, and moved to consider the evidence.

Everything led to Esterwald: the mailed coin, the stolen car at Minneapolis Airport and car keys in the trash, the identification at the airport of a man fitting Robert Esterwald's physique complete with scratched face and bandaged hand, and now the jewelry and suitcase. Paul also felt certain of Esterwald's presence at the mansion.

What bothered him, though, was Ingstrom. I'd feel better if I knew how he fit in, he thought. Maybe he'd get a break when PS caught up with the kid. In the meantime, he'd pursue the obvious.

"Let's get us an arrest warrant."

Bushy finished licking a finger. "It's being typed, boss."

"Cut the 'boss', will you?"

Smiling widely, Bushy lifted a drumstick toward Paul. When Paul demurred, Bushy moved in on it but, mouth open, he stopped and held up the leg like a light bulb that had just flashed on. "Wait. There's another thing."

"What? More? Let me guess. You're after my job."

"Not at all! Well, maybe." The two could banter without offense. "They found the car. Ustoff's station wagon."

Paul was still recounting the Esterwald evidence. "Good. Where?"

"It was out at Benson Block. Tommy Miscevich reported it."

Paul came forward on the chair. "Tommy?"

Bushy broke protocol and secrecy at the same time. "Looks like detecting runs in the family." He smiled, unabashed.

Paul was so surprised at Tommy's involvement that he ignored Bushy's allusion to Tommy as family. "I have to make a call. Excuse me."

Bushy rose hurriedly. "Sure. I'll go over and pick up the warrant. I'd like to come for the arrest."

Paul, already dialing, nodded.

Cindy's hello sounded distressed. I got her fired, Paul thought immediately.

"Thank God it's you, Paul. I've been trying to find you. We've got to talk. Can you come over?"

"Did he tell you?"

"Yes. You know already?"

"No. But I suspected it."

"Did you two talk?"

"Yes. Up at Somebody's House."

Cindy sounded more confused than distressed. "Up there?"

"That's where it happened."

"Where what happened, Paul?"

"Where I punched Skaansgard in the nose."

She laughed.

"What's so funny, Cindy? Did he fire you?"

"Paul, what are you talking about? I'm talking about

Tommy."

Paul plunged on. "He found the station wagon."

"He found what?"

"Daddy Fizzy's station wagon."

"Have you been drinking, Paul? You're not making sense."

"Didn't he tell you?"

Cindy fell silent and gave over to him. "Let's stop. You called. You go first."

He told her about his meeting with Skaansgard and about the threats. Paul left out the derision her boss had employed.

"He doesn't mean it, Paul. He was scaring you. That's the way he works." She was matter-of-fact. "You really punched him?"

"Gave him a bloody nose."

"I wish I had been there. I might have hit him myself."

"He wasn't being kind, that's for sure."

Cindy coaxed him onto his other subject. "Now, what about this station wagon Tommy found? I heard nothing about that."

Paul told her what he knew and included Bushy's comment about Tommy being family.

"You sound proud, Paul."

"I guess I am. And he didn't say a word?"

"He told me he gave a ride to a young sailor who helped him load blocks, but nothing about a wagon."

Paul choked out a few words. "Ingstrom? Reese Ingstrom?"

"No. Something like Rocky. Anyway, he's got some ideas in his head that I don't like."

"This sailor?"

"No, Tommy. That's why I wanted to find you."

Paul listened carefully now. Her thoughts about Tommy were always important.

She had left early, as he knew, and taken the bus to the

West End Bakery. Tommy picked her up there at about 4:30.

"The first thing he said after he kissed me was, 'Mom, I'm not sure I want to go right to college.' It floored me."

Paul was angry. "Where did he get that idea?"

"He's been thinking about it, he said, for a couple of months. Benson offered him a permanent job. Of course, they like him there."

"That's ridiculous. It's a summer job. He'd be laid off in November."

"Paul, believe me, I've told him all that. I want you to talk with him. He said he'd be willing to listen."

"I just don't get it. One day he's talking about college, the next day he wants to move cement blocks for a career." A flood of indecision and fear washed over Paul from the days just before he'd left for school in Minneapolis. He had needed more push beyond the general expectations people had of him. PS provided the impetus.

"Just give it a year, Paul. It'll do you good, even if you don't like it." Once he had expressed his angst over it, indecision had receded.

Now Tommy was having the same experience. It was normal.

Cindy waited for him as he calmed down. "Will you have a talk?"

He thought he could use his own father's words. "I will, but I'm tied up with the Brookside case tonight."

They agreed the two would meet before the funeral the following day. Paul was still bothered by Tommy's encounter. "Do you think it was that sailor who said something?"

Cindy did think so. "Sailing the high seas might have sounded more romantic than sticking your nose in a textbook, but I think it's something else."

"What do you think, Cindy?"

"Honestly, Paul, he's worried about losing his way. Duluth is all he's ever known. Part of him is afraid to leave."

The parallels were clear to them both and to Tommy, too.

Paul had to acknowledge it. "I'm the guy to talk to on that one."

She let him off easily. "Tommy will make his own decision. I'm fine with what he wants. I just want him to talk to you about it." She allowed herself to laugh. "Don't worry about Leif Skaansgard. I've been handling him for seventeen years. He won't even say a word."

In the midst of the most important case in his career, certainly the most public case in the department's history, Paul was completely detached. If this was what he had worked nearly twenty years for, he couldn't blame Tommy for balking at the path others had laid out for him. Paul, maybe for the first time in those twenty years, sensed strongly what was important to his life. If he had known it before, at least this was the first time he'd been willing to act on it. It was as if the Friendly West End had invited him in, even while he danced around its borders. Finally, he felt ready to come back home.

The chief opened Paul's office door. "I need a word with you, Paul."

He guided the door closed, made sure it was latched and stepped forward.

"I understand you met with Leif Skaansgard this afternoon."

Here it comes. A blood feud. "I did. He must have called you right after."

"He tells me you're intent on investigating the little passerby you saw Monday morning."

So the punch wasn't mentioned. Paul considered his options. "'Intent' is his word. 'Interested' is what I'd say."

The chief put authority in his voice. "Well, drop it, Paul."

"Are you sure Skaansgard isn't protecting his trust accountant? It's his son. And why not follow every lead?"

His boss took another step closer. "We've been around on this before, so try this. Until you get hard evidence on this kid, I don't want to hear his name mentioned by you, by your father-in-law, by Bushy, by the Fraisers, or by anyone else in this goddamned town. If I do hear it, you're off the Brookside case." The chief stood erect and pointed.

Paul was not going to back down, but he had risen fast through diplomacy as well as talent and hard work. He conceded some, while also standing his ground.

"You won't hear a thing, Fred, but you'll be the first to see hard evidence when I find it."

The door started to open. The chief stepped over and held it shut, placed his foot down and pointed a finger directly at Paul. "Take a word to the wise, Paul." He stepped back, opened the door, and let Bushy come in. "I was just leaving, Buczynski."

Bushy saluted the chief, then handed Paul the warrant.

Paul traded his car keys for it. "Bring the Buick out front, would you? I'd like to avoid a squad car on this call. And see what other plain clothes are around to keep it low profile. I'd like to have four of us if we can. I'll be out front in a few minutes."

Paul sat alone in the office, his feet up on the radiator. He closed his eyes. Beneath those lids ran visions of the last few days, mostly formless colors: bursts of sun, smiling faces; strikes of lightning, crooked grimaces. Smells rose through the visions: the soft verdance of summer air, sweet aromas of coffee cake, the pungency of blood, dust in dark halls, stale sweat, and steamy chop suey. Paul let himself feel the brush of fine hair across his lips, the firm warmth of a strongly clasped shoulder, the passage of night air through a screen, the quick touch of knuckles to nose. Sounds rebounded from far off: the gruff huffing of industry, the rasp of a wooden stair, deep-throated groans of the fog horn, blasts from the bridge, creaking of old ships, and words uttered in love or anger, in admiration or authority, from long sorrow or from sweet inexperience, in lies or in hope. Sensations melded with thoughts: suspicions, ambitions, fears, and promises, halting avoidance, friendly duty, the waiting amongst expectant pulses, festive breath, languorous dreams, and the shock of death.

He sat. The flood of days, like the St. Louis River in spring—filled with gravel, tree limbs, a cast-off pair of pants, the remnants of a wooden boat, steel cable, swept together, bouncing, twisting, and careening through granite outcrops—was populated by all the human drayage of acts, those past and those to be, full of thinking, deliberate and casual; by feeling; and by promise; all shredded and stirred in the pitch of the city itself, passing under the stars and the clouds. It could not be stopped. It could not be channeled. It could not be navigated or controlled. One could wait for summer lulls, for fall dryness, or for the freeze of winter, but in flood the torrent could only be followed, staying alert for treachery, ready for the next turn.

Paul took the air dropping through the window deeply into his lungs. He exhaled a long breath and opened his eyes. Bushy soon would come with the Buick. He rose and took the next step.

Down the hallway outside Paul's office, a woman stood against the wall next to a figure seated in the only chair along the corridor. The man beside her who bent forward, draping long hair over his hands that cupped his cheeks, was Robert Ustoff, Daddy Fizzy. He and his mother had come to see the sheriff's deputy in charge of the Grand Lake arson case and to reclaim the station wagon if they could.

Paul stopped before the woman. "I'm so sorry to hear of your loss, Mrs. Ustoff."

She gave him a bewildered look. She would not cry.

"Mom, this is the officer who returned Marly's picture. I told you he came to the house." Daddy Fizzy extended his hand. "Thank you for caring enough to do that. No one else has been very kind."

Paul touched the woman's elbow. "Ma'am, I'm living just up the street now at Berta West's house. If you need help with anything, please let me know."

She nodded appreciatively.

"May I have a word with your son?"

Paul and Daddy Fizzy moved down the hall.

When they were out of earshot of Fizzy's mother, Paul put on his bad-cop grumble. "I tried to help you, Robert, and you lied to me."

Fizzy shook the hair off his glasses. He looked at Paul but said nothing.

"We have Siiri Laugen and Skip in custody. I know how Ingstrom moved Roger to his bed at his grandmother's house."

Paul let it sink in.

"I've already said all I'm going to say about Roger's death," Fizzy said. "I've been forgiven."

"Forgiven? By whom?"

"By Father Lucci."

The little priest's muttering that afternoon rose fresh and clear to Paul. He had said, "I was wrong. Very wrong." Whatever Ustoff had confessed was moot, unless PS brought

Ingstrom back with him. Maybe Fizzy could help that along.

He tried another tack. "You were seen with Ingstrom the next day around six o'clock at Somebody's House. You lied about that."

"I told you I had seen him."

"You had Marly at the restaurant, too. You hid that, didn't you?"

It got to Fizzy. "Look, I loved my sister. At the time, I didn't think it'd help to tell you about our draft-counseling meeting. Ingstrom wanted to help me with my draft notice is all. He asked for a ride afterward. I had to print some film, so Marly gave him a lift."

Paul wanted more. He stretched what he knew. "Ingstrom was with the car this morning when it was discovered in West Duluth."

Fizzy was not moved this time. "They had a thing. Inggy couldn't hurt her. There was something or someone else. I don't know."

Paul shot back. "What do you know?"

"I know that where I come from we don't turn on a friend, even if we know he's crossed us. Even then, we mostly take care of it between ourselves."

Paul knew better than to push beyond this point. It wasn't a matter of Ustoff's trust in him. It was deeper than that. Instead, Paul turned to a friendlier line. "How did the draft counseling go?"

Fizzy shook back his hair and looked down the hall. "Mom is learning to drive. After we bury my sister, I'm enlisting."

31

Bisnu's Dream

PAUL S. TUOMI FELT like a teenager whose parents for the first time have gone on a weekend junket, leaving him at home alone. The giddy feeling of freedom—of breaking with the Fraisers—swept him gaily out of what had been day-by-day drudgery. As he drove along the North Shore on his way to intercept *Bisnu's Dream*, the world of delectable possibility invited him to leave the coming days wide open. On the other hand, habit exhumed a craving for new tasks to fill what the old dray-horse of duty saw as a dangerous void.

PS looked in the rear-view mirror, filled with the blue of Lake Superior and the white and green of the birch trees that lined its shore. He tooted the Oldsmobile's horn to greet oncoming cars. His son's call for assistance fulfilled at once the empty feeling and the desire for a different future. PS let his struggles like the sweet summer wind ruffling his hair whisk by and fall behind him. The afternoon was too good to waste on worry.

He made good time out of town, especially measuring from his house in far west Smithville. On the northbound, lakeside lane which he traveled, the tips of the tallest pine shadows painted the pavement in an interlocking design of shady and sunlit cones. The western sun, before it set, had at least three hours to stretch ever-longer shadows that would finally paint the road dark. To his right, across the lake, Ashland and the farther-off Apostle Islands shimmered in the full light of the Wisconsin shore. I have time for a couple of stops, he thought.

At Knife River, over fifty miles from home, PS pulled into The Smoke House lot. Julie was just then reaching over the cooler to turn the open sign "closed."

PS vaulted out of the car and shook his finger at her. "Hey, what are friends for?" he said, even though he knew that she couldn't hear him through the plate-glass window. He pointed both hands inward to his chest and flipped them out as if to inquire. Julie waved him in.

When he entered, she put the counter between them. "John's out in the back. Want something?"

PS put his hand to his hips. "Same as always, I want only you."

"Go on, Tuomi. I mean fish."

"I mean business, but yes, give me three nice pieces of white fish, the same of lake trout, and half a dozen ciscoes. Could you wrap the whites and trout separately? Six packs in all. Those and two packs of ice should fill my cooler."

He watched her work, and after he paid, he lingered. "I meant what I said."

Julie walked over to lock the door and came up close to PS. Her fishy sleeves and sweaty tee shirt charmed his nostrils. "It isn't high school any more, Paul. I appreciate the attention, but I'm an old woman already, and that makes you an old man." She slapped a package of smelt on top of the other bundles he was holding. "Those are on the house. John is out back, sweetie."

PS bent toward her and kissed her cheek. "Let me out to my car." His hands were full.

Julie turned the key. "I'll grab the ice."

They went out together.

"What trouble are you making up here?"

PS placed the packets of fish between layers of ice. He

spoke while bending over, his head in the trunk. "My son is sending me to Canada."

"Whose life will you make miserable up there?"

PS stood up and stretched his back. "Not my own."

"Since when?"

"Since I got out of Fraiser and Fraiser."

Julie cocked her head and stared at him. "You've been known to fib." She took a step toward him. "Really?"

"Really." PS waited, then gave in to his instinct to share good news. "I've got the gun." He pointed to a towel-wrapped bundle in the trunk corner.

Julie smiled at him. "Good." She looked into his eyes with a steady gaze. "Are you sure you want to haul that thing over the border?"

PS considered. "No. It might mean trouble. You're right."

She put her hands out for the weapon. "I'll keep it safe until you pass by again." He handed the covered pistol to her. "Go see John now," she said.

She touched his hand in passing. "And don't eat that whole pie I see in your trunk. At least in one sitting."

She went back in the door and didn't look at him as she turned the keys.

PS didn't spend much time with John. Like most fishermen, John used few words. He worked long hours alone out on the lake and spent his shore time with his smoker. In the fall he hunted and smoked meats, in winter he ice-fished. Julie and the girls, now women, tended the shop. PS and John had maintained a cordial friendship despite Julie's history with PS, a history that had sometimes intruded into Julie's marriage. PS admired John's workingman's patience, his great faith that was fed pulling up a net that was now full, now empty. The man's virtues rose from below the chill surface of a changeable lake.

They talked of their work, of aging and getting stiff. Neither mentioned Julie.

John sat eerily still. His quiescence prodded PS to move on.

"I've got some serious driving to do yet. Have to allow time for the border crossing."

John nodded. "Got fish?"

"You know I do." They shook hands. John's hand felt delicate and unusually soft.

PS loved driving and couldn't recall when he had last driven the entire distance up the North Shore, especially during daylight. In the remaining hours of sunshine and the added hour of summer twilight, he planned to explore. He'd drive a couple hours more in darkness to reach the docks, arriving ahead of the ship. PS hummed a tune. The only company he needed was the lake itself, along with the sharp granite cliffs that at points fell below to the lake and at others rose above the road on the other side.

The rocky hills that towered over the Smithville house PS owned were as sharp and unworn as the rugged North Shore; but the land rose higher north of Duluth, in places reaching a thousand more feet above the level of the lake. The land had been lightly populated and, north of Two Harbors, was still largely vacant. It had been logged early, but appeared as unspoiled as when the Merritt Brothers tramped around nearly a century before. At that time, the giant white pine forests had spread over hills and lined river gorges, having stood for two and three centuries before they were cut and hauled to the sawmills. Those trees were converted into what people needed: carts, railroad ties, houses, boxes, and timbers. For those first to get there with their own or other peoples' cash, the forests were converted into even more sweet jingle.

PS still breathed deeply of the freshness of forests, no matter how old. The idea that these new woods covered the paths of glaciers so much more powerful than the puny fortune-hunters' companies was a comfort to him. But he could not shake loose the chimera of lumberjacks paid thirty-six pennies a day to make from two-hundred-foot-tall white pines the six-foot-wide stumps on which they were standing for photographs. PS couldn't call it rape, not of forests nor of people. But if it wasn't, it was something very much like it. A violation as sure as Mark's killing his cousin's Canadian partner. Though the wilderness would rebound—like the people—PS knew that the same villains who cropped them, woods or people, still lived among them and must be watched. PS was sure he was about to meet one of these on *Bisnu's Dream* in just a few hours.

After another long hour he told himself to get out of the car. He took two of the ciscoes and, maybe because of Julie's warning, only a small chunk of Vera's Pie Shop boysenberry pie. He placed both in a domed lunch box, a second inheritance from his father. Provisioned, he climbed the rocks along Gooseberry River. If the pie smelled of smoked fish, he didn't care. He planned to eat them together anyway.

PS climbed to the top of a house-sized cube of granite that cropped out overlooking the lower falls. It was late enough in the day that he had the rock and stretch of river to himself. Looking south through the pines which grew well this far up from the lake, he could see deep blue Superior spread to the northern azure mists that licked the horizon.

"This is a great place for fish, pie, and thinking," he said to the roar of the river as he sat on the rock. PS nibbled on one of the ciscoes. The sharpness of the smoke brought Julie and birches to mind. The fish was oily, and even using a fork he found he needed to lick his fingers. Was I five or six when I tasted these for the first time? On the smoky richness, the scene grew vivid. It was in my father's car. PS closed his eyes. No, you couldn't eat in Dad's car. I sat next to it on the roadside. Maybe at Knife River. The vision was fresh, like the cool spray rising from the tumbling waters of the fall.

Thoughts of his father rumbled through his memory like the beer-colored waters through the falls—a sepia film of a man and his son.

"I'd like to see you, again, with Paul," he said to the river. No. Paul will be a busy boy. Maybe with Tommy. "Yes, with Tommy. I'll bring him before he leaves for college." PS sealed his promise with a burst of boysenberry filling.

He continued to eat and talk to the river. "I won't leave everything behind. Just the evil times." He forked another good helping of the pie into his mouth. That's how it should taste—pie and life—deep, rich, and sweet. He swallowed. PS chuckled at himself. "And flaky, too."

He reached to his shirt pocket for his Pall Malls. He held the pack as if seeing it for the first time—as if a foreign object had dropped from a tree into his hand. Slowly and deliberately, he closed his fist around the cigarettes and tossed the crumpled mess into the empty lunch box.

Don't gloss over mistakes. You escaped the laboring life that killed your father, only to find that you'd fallen victim to a similar version of chicanery. He still didn't know how, but those missteps had guided his handling of his son. Keep him on the right side of the law. Maybe on the east side. That, too, had its troubles. It wasn't over, either. Perhaps he could still help right it.

The sun shifted. The shadows of hefty trunks glided slowly across the rock. The shafts of sun split by the trees lit the mists rising from the falls. Anchored to an abutment atop his solid granite block, PS saw stripes of a varicolored, shimmering bridge arching across the basin of the falls. As if to walk out on it, PS took a step. Pine shadows intervened. The bridge disappeared.

He reached down to latch the lunch box. Time to pack it in. PS turned to the path that led along the river to the lot where the Olds was parked. He still had some driving to do.

At Port Arthur, PS checked in with the night-shift harbormaster. In the lunch box, he brought a package of white fish. They chatted about how the Seaway was changing patterns on the lake. The man expected *Bisnu's Dream* within two hours.

"What sort of name is that for a ship?" said the harbormaster.

"Indian. East Indian. It is one of their gods, *Vishnu.*"

"Strange name for boat or a god."

PS had to agree. "It's a bucket of bolts, that's for sure. I saw it come into Duluth." PS thought: Just last night.

The man tucked his chin and squinted a question. "Why didn't you catch it there?"

"What? And have you miss this good fish?" PS pointed at the newspaper-wrapped package. "We didn't know our friend was on board until the ship had sailed."

PS left the harbormaster to his fish snack. "I'm going to catch six winks in the car. I suppose I'll hear them."

The man was rummaging in the drawer for a fork. "Oh, you'll hear them all right."

The engines of the tugs were enough to wake PS. *Bisnu's Dream* blasted its shaky thanks to the harbor pilots as the tugs brought it alongside. It was just past two in the morning.

Away from the lights and romance of the Duluth shipping canal, the moored ship looked even more haggard.

PS was first up the gangway. The harbormaster and immigration talked together below on the dock. The captain ceremoniously accepted the trout and the remaining ciscoes before he dispensed his official duties. He spoke clipped British English.

"Seaman Ingstrom just came aboard. No trouble, is there?"

"I'm here on private business. Put it this way: he doesn't get any fish."

The captain patted the packages. "We'll ask him to my quarters." He nodded at his mate. "Put these in the officers' mess."

He looked below and straightened his jacket. "Right now, though, I have dignitaries to greet." He started down the gangway.

In the captain's work quarters, PS sat to the side of the door way. There were few adornments beside the desk and side chair. He waited.

In a few minutes, the door swung open. "Seaman Ingstrom," the mate's voice sounded.

Ingstrom stepped over the threshold. Dressed in a rumpled tee shirt and bellbottom pants, he looked sleepy and took a moment to realize the man he was brought to see was not the captain. When he saw PS looking up at him, Ingstrom tugged his pants up and tee shirt down.

"Pleased to see you, Mr. Tuomi. I think I just missed your son in Duluth."

The boy was quick, PS had to admit that. "Oh, I had some deliveries to make up here. You might say I was in the neighborhood. Paul wanted me to say hello."

Ingstrom cast a grin his way. "Does it smell like fish in this room? Or is it my imagination?"

"There's another chair there. I don't think the captain will be joining us. At least for now."

Ingstrom leaned lightly against the desk. "I've been sitting for hours. Sailing equals sitting, I believe."

The kid likes to talk. That's good. PS tugged at his shirt pocket. He stopped short and fired a question instead. "You keep a journal, Reese?"

"I do, and to keep prying eyes off it, I carry it with me."

"How about a seaman's card? That off limits?"

Ingstrom brought out the card.

PS examined it thoughtfully and tapped the card edge against the knuckles of his free hand. "Now, why would anyone be so cruel as to make a shame of an innocent death?"

Ingstrom crossed his legs and his arms. He cocked his head. "Mr. Tuomi, you love to fashion riddles, don't you."

He's learned insolent nonchalance; very well I can joust, too. "Maybe I'm not alone in that." He continued to tap the card. "Is that the reason you wrote the note?"

Ingstrom splayed his legs, stood away from the desk, and swayed back and forth at its edge. "You know, I'm not surprised someone from Duluth followed me at least this far. I was expecting a visit at Sault St. Marie. Still, I'm glad it is you. Someone who can understand."

PS followed the energy. Ingstrom was taking the initiative. "What am I to understand? That playing with people's lives is like playing at puzzles?"

"Not at all. Only that breaking the mold is possible. You surely believe that. You've spent your career proving it."

PS looked on and waited. Talk kid, talk.

"You're not looking at a Skaansgard or a Fraiser or an Ingstrom here, either. Seaman Ingstrom is a workingman's man leaving the cake-eaters behind in the same way that your son, Paul, and to some extent you yourself, have immigrated west to east. Either way, Mr. Tuomi, we have made a conscious choice of it. That's what you understand."

Okay, I'll play your game, kid. PS crossed his legs and sat back comfortably. "Let me see if I have this right. You reject a life of privilege, the one given you. You hope to gain the dignity found in honest work. Is that it?"

"Close. I'm not going to be the one to suppress working people under an iron heel or a polished shoe."

"So it's an escape as well as an evasion."

"You can say that. I say it's a model to follow."

"Mighty big of you, Reese. You jettison the baggage of the past neatly. What about individual people, working or not? How do you treat them?"

Ingstrom stood firmly on widely spread feet. "Individuals? I know how to treat people."

"No need to be indignant, son. I'm sure your breeding taught you manners." PS saw his opportunity. "But really. Beyond politeness. What about Siiri Laugen? Or old lady Crosley? What about Roger? Or Daddy Fizzy's sister. What was her name? Matty?"

Ingstrom sprang off the desk. "Marly."

"You left a path of wreckage behind you, son. For all your proletarian talk, you didn't give a shit for any of those people."

Ingstrom turned and looked at the empty side chair. "I didn't do anything to them."

"You used them just like your dad uses numbers. And with the same feeling."

Ingstrom stepped close and lowed over PS. "Not true. I'm not like him. Not at all."

PS didn't move a muscle. "Tell me about it."

Ingstrom stepped back. He let his left hand trace the edge of the desk as he moved to the chair beside it. He sat.

The young sailor started where the least damage could be done. "There's a good many kids on the hillside that don't know, really, what they're doing. I try to help where I can, but they aren't my responsibility. You can only do so much."

"Like make a profit or use their bodies?"

"You know, you are much crasser than I imagined."

"*Pardon, monsieur.* I see you're used to *politesse.*"

"Cut the crap. Siiri Laugen was born with her pants around her ankles. She'd seduce her own father if he weren't such an ugly ass." Ingstrom looked at his hands. He spoke softly. "There was no harm in it."

PS had waited for Ingstrom to step in his own refuse. "Well, she's sitting in the St. Louis County Jail with the joint you gave her as evidence of harm."

Ingstrom's breath escaped in a sharp gasp. The news had jabbed him, but he said nothing.

PS took advantage. "At least she's living. Not so much like Roger. Another poor soul you helped."

Ingstrom stood again. He rifled a finger at PS. "I took care of Roger for a long time. He never knew when to stop. He couldn't get enough. He wanted to go like his mother, in a blaze of drunken glory. He waited for his chance. When he saw it, he took it."

"You know how to place the blame on the fallen. Who wrote that note?"

Ingstrom smoothed his hair. "What note?"

"It said 'Sorry, Memma. I can't take it anymore.'" PS watched Ingstrom carefully.

"Seems self-explanatory," he said.

PS stood and sprung his trap. "It's a ringer for a note you left on your refrigerator: 'Sorry, Mom, I can't make the time.' The wording and the writing are twins. You wrote both notes."

"Looks to me whoever did write it was trying to comfort

more than cover. Roger did himself. No one forced him."

"Some kind of comfort. Where did he get the stuff?"

"There's only one place anyone can get that kind of dope, and you know the source."

"Belisle?"

"I don't know." Ingstrom cast a sharp look at PS. "I'm not in the crime business."

"Moving a body is a crime."

"Shooting a man at point-blank range is murder. That's a crime."

When PS didn't take the bait, Ingstrom withdrew as if the argument had fallen dead to the floor. He changed direction. "If you had evidence on me, your son, not you would be here with the RCMP." He sat back in the chair and crossed his legs.

Roger's story might be a dead end, but PS had plenty more ways to get at Ingstrom. "You were seen outside Brookside the morning of the murders. What were you doing there?"

Ingstrom folded his hands behind his head. "I was walking home."

This kid is too cool. "You had been inside."

"In Crosley's? Years before. Not that morning."

PS used Paul's sensations. Unhinge this creep. "I'll tell you: You took your shoes off at the subway. You followed someone in, heard the stair creak. You went up through the kitchen, up the servant's stairway to Miss Crosley's room. You hid there. She recognized you. Then . . ."

Ingstrom broke in. "Why would I do that? I was dog tired and wanted nothing but sleep. I don't dig old ladies."

"Then you pushed the pillow over her head. You heard the ruckus on the stair, and when that ended, you fled."

Ingstrom sounded desperate but had answers. "You don't know all that. You can't know any of it. Besides, you're wrong. I was passing by on my way home. Detective Tuomi saw me.

He waved. I went to bed. Your son has his suspect, and it's not me."

"Like I said, you left a path of destruction behind you. After incinerating your second conquest of the day out at Grand Lake, you drove her car back to Duluth like nothing had occurred. I bet the St. Louis County Sheriff would like to know how that happened."

"I haven't seen Marly in days."

PS pounced again. "Oh, not at Somebody's House?"

The kid brought his hands down, shifted in the chair.

"You're lying. You've been lying all along."

"I was counseling her brother on the draft. She came along."

Once he had Ingstrom off balance, PS pressed harder. "And I suppose she just handed you the keys and said, 'I'm off to a bonfire.' is that it?"

"I never drove that car."

"Bullshit. You drove it out of the Holiday station in Kenwood. You parked it at Benson Block's West Duluth lot a day later. Probably kept it in Mommy's garage during the day."

"No. Not me."

"I can tell you all about the helpful 'going-to-college' conversation you had with the kid at the block lot that morning. Did you burn Marly because she didn't give in to you?"

That did it. PS had hit the right nerve. Ingstrom sprang out of the chair. He flew at the old man's throat and screamed: "I loved her!"

PS batted him to the floor with a sweep of an arm. He rose and stepped away.

"Some love, kid. You don't know what it is. You're just a cauldron of lies and selfishness."

Ingstrom did not get up. PS watched him.

"Why don't you come back to Duluth with me? Let's clear this up."

Ingstrom sat up on the floor, his hands behind him supporting his slim torso. "I've a better idea. Why don't I tell you the real who-and-why and continue on my way. You'll see; it'll be an even trade. Anyway, I'm not going back."

PS couldn't bring him back by force. There would be time for that later, but he might get something good by playing this game. "All right, we have a deal."

Ingstrom rose from the floor and leaned back against the desk. PS sat, ready to listen. He dug in his shirt pocket for the pack that wasn't there. "Okay, let's hear the who and the why."

Finally, the kid was going to spill.

32

Skunk Hollow

A T ROGER'S FUNERAL, Cindy sat removed from the family, stone-faced, though inside she wrestled as if she were teetering on the cusp of the Point of Rocks high above the chapel where she sat; half of her clinging to the hard glacier-smoothed stone, half calling to her to pitch off the precipice.

Everything split: Tommy would be going off to college; Roger was stiff in his coffin. Love for Paul should swell, now that he had broken from Pamela; but abandonment, much of it twenty years old, formed rigid bands tight around her ribs.

They all had acknowledged Paul as Tommy's father, and life was opening once more— spreading outward like the giant lake off to the northeastern horizon. She, however, felt lost without direction or mooring.

Seated near the back of the dark chapel, Cindy watched her world tip in a geologic uplift. What once had seemed in perspective now tilted and flattened like a transparent ribbon of sediment compressed between granite layers. The earth was flat. All that she knew of life, from her parents' time immigrating to the West End, from her own span there as child and adult, and from what she imagined would be for her and beyond for Tommy—like that broad, thin vein of iron ore that her uncles mined, that her father hauled, that Wendell's dad loaded and shipped—was now confined in one dimension, bedded and covered on a plane of history by more life, by more death, by years like leaves pressed on the ground under autumn rains and winter snows.

Cindy was smothering. Optimism was pressed out like Betty's breath beneath her overturned car. Cindy could barely comprehend how the people around her in the chapel moved about freely, approached and embraced Berta, filed past the coffin or spoke in low tones, sorrowful and kind. Their three-dimensional world was at that moment impossible for her.

It was not Paul but Tommy who unearthed her.

He lightly brushed her cheek. "Mom, this is Bob, a friend of Roger's."

Cindy sat mute. She stared as the world reinflated and moved slowly toward spaciousness.

The young man at Tommy's side made an odd movement, tossing his head as if to flick hair away from his eyes—though his hair was cropped short.

Cindy's tongue felt huge inside a flattened mouth, but she managed a greeting. "Happy to see you here."

Tommy offered help. "Bob is joining the army soon."

Bob squirmed in the tight-fitting belted jacket he wore over his bellbottom jeans and nodded.

Cindy realized the haircut was new. "Good luck." She was suddenly afraid that Tommy might trade college for the military.

Tommy hitched his hand over his friend's shoulder. "I told Bob we could give him a ride to the wake."

The young man lifted his dark, full brows and widened his large eyes behind circles of wire-rimmed glasses. "I'm only staying a little while." He sounded apologetic. "I can walk home, just to the West End." He shook away the shorn locks of hair.

Cindy looked away. She scanned the room. Tommy and Bob were the only boys of Roger's age at the service. No one else had come. Compassion for boys inspired Cindy's world again. Suddenly, gently, almost in a caress she grasped the young man's arms, thin beneath the jacket, and fixed his eyes in hers. "You're welcome to come with us. Of course."

Cindy fumbled through her purse and handed the keys to Tommy. "I'll ride with you." She saw that Wendell and Paul still hovered over Berta and decided to pay her respects at the house. Paul would drive them there.

The two young men chatted quietly as Tommy drove up the hill to Berta's house. Cindy sat quietly in the back, looking to the harbor and lake as they rose into view below them. She looked to the Allouez docks, ten miles away, standing tall over the shimmer of the Wisconsin shore.

As sun and the water spoke to each other in flickers and reflections, Cindy quelled her newest fear—that Tommy would scrap his college plans to follow Bob into the war that was so strange, dangerous, and far away. Paul had already talked with Tommy for an hour that morning. Earlier on the long ride from Oliver, Tommy had recounted the conversation to her. She had no need to ask. He was enthusiastic, ecstatic:

"I can call him Dad now."

"He told you?" Cindy had said.

"I knew anyway, but it means more now that he's said it."

Cindy reached over to touch her son's cheek. "I wanted him to be the one to say it."

"I get it, Mom. I wish it had been different. For you and for me, but this was the right time. We can talk more man to man."

The news pleased her, more so that it had been between the two men without her between. She waited to hear the other part, the issue she wanted resolved: college.

Tommy watched her carefully. She would not ask.

He shifted his body in her direction and extended his arm

along the back of the bench seat toward her. With a deep inhalation, he said: "It must have been hard for you back then. He told me about it. He was confused. Believe me, I can understand. I'm about as confused as I can be right now: moving, growing up, leaving everything I've known and loved. Still it's exciting, a real adventure. I can't wait, but it's crazy. I felt like I wanted to run. Paul, no, Dad felt the same thing."

She took her eyes from the road a minute as if to ask, "So?"

"We made a deal." Tommy let some tension build. "I know you want to hear it."

Cindy smiled and blushed. "Mothers, you know."

"He was open about it. I always thought he loved police work, but this case, the Crosley murders and Roger's accident seem to have gotten to him. He said he wouldn't quit in the middle, though. He was going to see it through, no matter what."

Cindy could hear Paul telling it. She could see where he was leading his son. She tried to wait for Tommy's telling. "So he asked you to do the same?"

Tommy was annoyed. "Do you want to hear?"

Cindy zipped her lips.

"He told me that we do things we don't want to do. We, people from the West End. Like shovel coal. Load iron ore. Lay track. Forge steel. Finish what we've started. Even go to college. 'We stick to our lot,' he said. He told me that sometimes we even have to bend our principles, might have to tell a lie to stick with our people, but that's what we do. We stick to our lot."

Tommy cast an approving look. "He told me, though, it is toughest when it looks like we are leaving our folk behind. 'It only looks that way, but it makes it hard. Truth is, we can't leave. We are fused together. We are it.' Mom, he made a lot of sense."

Then Tommy struck a thinking pose and drew it out. "In a way, you're right. We made a pact. I'd give college a year, and if Dad's case was still in trial, another year. Then I'd do whatever I thought right."

Tommy looked straight at her. "Mom, I think he's going to leave the police force. Maybe go into business with PS. PS Tuomi and Son. In business with Grandpa." He smiled at the new name, "Grandpa."

"PS would be pleased to hear it."

"I didn't say anything to Dad, but when I finish, if I finish school, maybe we could make it Tuomi, Miscevich and Tuomi." He gave Cindy a shy look. "Don't say anything."

She touched his cheek. He blushed and looked away at the road. "Hey, Mom, you should speed up. You're going twenty miles an hour."

No, she didn't have to worry about the army or about college. Paul's confusion might reflect on Tommy's, but his mistakes were not his son's. He had made that clear. They all ran in the same vein, a rich flow through the West End, but at the same time could spread out in new directions, each intent on living life, each committed to the wealth of the trace. Tommy's report had unearthed worry and angst, but Cindy rode them out.

From Berta's hill, the sparkling waters of Allouez dimmed under high clouds. Cindy looked at the two boys in the front seat, laughing and talking in language she didn't understand. "Hey, Tommy," his mother said, "you should slow down. You're going forty miles an hour."

Tommy pulled over and parked a block past Berta's. The wake was already that crowded.

Coffee cake and buttery goodness was going round. Berta's cinnamon loaf filled the room with spice. She allowed Cindy's mother, Elma, to bring cookies and banana bread. Elma made the best of both. Everyone knew that.

The odor of baking and the click of fork on plate enlivened Berta. She toured the living and dining rooms with plates of baked goods, chattering to each knot of people she served.

"They called it 'skunk hollow' in the old days," she said. "My family lived above a hardware store down a wooden staircase from here. The funeral home wasn't started just yet."

"Skunk Hollow?" Wendell said. "What sort of name is that?"

His mother thought for a moment, finger to her lips. "I suppose it didn't smell all that good. The outhouse pits had to be shallow because of the rocks. Even when I lived there, we collected and burned our trash out back. Phew. It did smell sometimes." She laughed and smiled, her good-hearted manner a cologne cutting through sharp, rancid memories.

When she and the boys entered the house, Cindy found Berta directly. She removed the platter of cinnamon buns from her hands, setting it on the table. She held the old woman a long time. "I'm going to miss you, Memma."

Berta would hear none of it. "Oh, you'll come visit. It'll all be fine." She kissed Cindy's forehead as she would a child's.

She returned to reminiscing, telling stories of the old days on Observation Hill, remembering her husband, Wendell, pointing her guests to the photos hung around the dining room. The pictures held her family history.

Berta led the sole representative of Saint Erasmo's church by the elbow.

"These are my stations, Sister Maria," she said.

The nun nodded and smiled thinly at her sacrilege. "We all have our crosses to bear, Berta."

"I'm afraid I won't see you again, Sister."

Sister Maria patted Berta's hand. "The Church will miss you, Berta."

"I suppose so, but Wendell has his own ways down there in Iowa, and I'll be staying with him." She looked to the little knot of people surrounding Wendell and Paul. Without another word to the nun, she plated some of Elma's banana bread and moved toward her son's group.

Cindy had said her goodbye. Tommy and Bob were buttering more cinnamon buns at the table, and she allowed Paul the room he seemed to need to part from his second family. The craving for tobacco moved her outside. Being alone felt more comfortable.

She stepped out the back door. The weather had changed. A stiff wind was up, stirring white caps on the lake. Cindy pulled her jacket around her and went down the stairs to the yard. At the landing below, she crumpled a stray strand of police tape that fluttered from a post. She walked up the slate steppingstones to the trash stored next to the shed. Pinching a cigarette from her pack, she rounded the shed to Paul and Wendell's bench. Around the corner, out of sight of the house, sat PS.

"Oh, my! PS, what are you doing out here? Are you all right?"

PS looked worn. "I'm resting. And thinking. Mostly resting."

Cindy sat. She offered him the pack of cigarettes. "Smoke?"

PS held up his hand. "If it's one thing I get out of all this mess, it's giving up cigarettes."

"You quit?"

He nodded. "For good."

"What mess are you talking about? Is that why you missed the funeral?"

PS bent forward, put his elbows on his knees, and thrust his chin over folded hands. He stared out over St. Louis Bay, maybe as far as Allouez, perhaps farther to Solon Springs or even farther, back through time as well as space. From this bench, one could see far.

He watched a long time. Cindy lit her cigarette and tossed the match.

PS straightened up. "I have to talk about it." He put an arm on the bench back and crossed a leg. He shifted toward Cindy. "I'm not going to tell this to Paul. It would complicate things for him. It'll be between you and me."

Cindy wrinkled her nose. "I suppose I'm not one to scorn family secrets, am I."

PS stared out over the expanse of the western part city to the ore docks and river. "Paul sent me up to Port Arthur to catch that kid."

"The one Tommy met at the block yard?"

"The one he suspects had something doing out at Brookside. Yes."

"Did you catch him?"

PS turned his gaze on Cindy. "I did. But I can't tell Paul."

Cindy knew he'd tell her. She knew he would make her wait.

"Sometimes you have to lie outright to save your principles. Sounds wrong, but it's right. This is one of those times."

"What happened?"

PS looked over the city and shook his head. "The same thing that has always been wrong. I'm a damned fool. I trust what I see. I don't look beyond."

She grabbed his arm. "You're one of the smartest men I know."

"I keep up the front, that's all. On the way up, I stopped by Julie's. To see her, of course, but to pick up some fish." He looked back toward the street that was hidden from them both. "I have some trout for you and Paul. In the trunk."

"Thanks." Cindy waited.

"I don't think Paul has told you, but I repossessed the gun."

"That one? From the Thompson shooting?"

"I thought it was finally going to save me." He pointed to the docks. "Come to find out that it's dirtier than that coal piled up down there." PS creased his face into a thin smile. "The kid knew all about it. Shit. If I were as smart as that little punk, I'd never be in a mess."

"Dirty how?"

"It was dirty, and it was hot."

"Was?"

"Let me back up."

Cindy took a long drag on her cigarette.

"The kid went to off this dealer. Must have been the night before Tommy met him. The dealer was Paul's informant. Belisle was his name. The kid figured it was Belisle who had burned his girlfriend out at Grand Lake."

"That propane fire?"

PS nodded. "He was right, too. But someone else got there first. The guy confronted him with a pistol. The kid knew the gun—his father collects them—but he didn't know the man. I figure it was Mark Fraiser."

"Jesus. He gets around."

"What I recouped from Mark early the next morning was a very used weapon. He let it go too easily." PS took both hands to his face and massaged his forehead with his fingers. "If Julie hadn't said something, they'd have found it at the border when they ripped my car apart."

"Where is it now?"

PS looked out at the lake. He looked back to Cindy. "I made a trade with the kid. If the information he had was good enough, I'd let him slip out."

"Did he know you had the gun?"

"I don't see how. But he certainly knew its history and could figure I'd be looking for it."

"And where is it?"

"After delay at the border I would've missed the funeral anyway, so I went fishing out of Knife River with John. We didn't catch much, but we had a good talk."

"You lose something out there?"

"The kid delivered the goods. I had to let him go."

"And Paul?"

"He needs to bow to City Hall even if he's right. He knows it."

"Paul is pretty stubborn."

"They don't want the kid. They have their suspect. This will save Paul a bunch of trouble. As far as he'll know, Ingstrom wasn't on the ship."

PS pushed off his seat, stood, and smiled a bit weakly. "Can I escort you back in?"

Cindy took his arm. "It'll end all right. We'll stick together."

They turned to the house. Paul and Wendell were coming across the lawn from the front. PS moved ahead to meet them. Wendell left father and son and came to Cindy's side.

"This is one of the saddest days of my life," he said.

Cindy nodded as she watched PS and Paul talking. as if in Earthlight

"It's also one of the happiest. Mom should have come with me years ago."

Paul was slapping his head and looking to the sky. PS had wasted no time telling him.

Cindy looked at Wendell. "You could use some looking after down there."

"And you and Paul could do a few things here at the house.

It needs some younger blood."

Up the driveway, Paul had put his hand on his father's shoulder. Cindy started toward them when she saw him slip an arm around PS in a hug.

"Come on, Wendell. Let's get out of the wind." They moved up the drive past the late-blooming lilac toward the front walk where people were grouped shaking hands, taking leave, walking off down the hill.

Just as they started toward the house, Tommy broke from the crowd and flew down the gravel drive, shouthing, "Hey, Grandpa! Where have you been?"

CPSIA information can be obtained at www.ICGtesting.com
Printed in the USA
LVOW11s0231180915

454718LV00001B/54/P